PEEPHOLE

The man stared through the tiny hole in the wall and watched the nude woman step into the shower.

If she only knew, he thought. *God!*

She turned beneath the cool spray, gliding the bar of soap over the trim belly and hips, the milk-white thighs, the sleek, gorgeous legs. Her lean body teemed in the water.

The man's heart raced. He peered harder into the peephole.

Now she was stepping out. Her flesh shined in the raw light—robust, radiant, beautiful. Beads of water clung like jewels between the high, swollen breasts . . .

Then the man's gaze roved up to her face—

Oh . . . my . . . God . . .

The face was not human. Slitlike eyes blinked beneath the runneled forehead from which a pair of tiny nubs jutted, like horns. The black mouth, full of stalactitical fangs, stretched to a heinous grin.

"Hello," she croaked into the man's frozen stare. "Do you like what you see?"

"GROSS? *SURE* HE'S GROSS. BUT EDWARD LEE HAS A *HEART* AS WELL . . . HE KEEPS IT IN A JAR ON HIS DESK."—REX MILLER, author of *Slob* and *Stone Shadow*

Diamond Books by Edward Lee

COVEN
INCUBI
SUCCUBI

SUCCUBI

EDWARD LEE

DIAMOND BOOKS, NEW YORK

SUCCUBI

A Diamond Book / published by arrangement with
the author

PRINTING HISTORY
Diamond edition / March 1992

ISBN: 1-55773-676-6

Diamond Books are published by The Berkley Publishing Group,
200 Madison Avenue, New York, New York 10016.
The name "DIAMOND" and its logo are trademarks
belonging to Charter Communications, Inc.

PRINTED IN THE UNITED STATES OF AMERICA

10 9 8 7 6 5 4 3 2 1

For Betsey Steffen
and the verity of pine needles

The past is as silent
as the present is ancient
tirelessly evil
weary and patient

—HOWARD DEVOTO,
"Luxuria"

SUCCUBI

PROLOGUE

Succubus, the dreamer thought.

The women hurried to strip, touching themselves in the prelude. Breasts were cosseted by intent, soft hands. Nipples were plucked, pubes were stroked. The ring of naked flesh glistened slickly in the heat of the midnight chancel.

Moans merged with the sacred litany. Before the great stone dolmen, the orgy ensued—random sweating bodies conjoined to form an entity of its own. Bare breasts jutted. Legs were splayed and buttocks were parted. Sweat-sheened abdomens sucked tensely in and out as genitals were bared to descending mouths. Arms and legs were wrapped around backs; bare hips fidgeted in a desperate plea to deepen penetration. The firelight raged as the festival drew on, time proceeding not in seconds or minutes but in rolling eyes, in gasps, and in the pulses of orgasm. Men's bleak faces were sat upon as dominant women grinned in macabre glee . . .

Succubus, the dreamer thought.

But was it really a thought? Thoughts were not corporeal, they did not exist in substance, but this thought seemed different. It seemed fraught, embodied. It seemed *real.* Yes—real as liquid beads of wax running down the shaft of a taper made of human fat. Real as lust. Real as blood . . .

Succubus . . .

The dreamer writhed.

Were these really dreams?

They were painting him with blood. *Brygorwreccan!* The dreamer couldn't breathe. *Peow! You belong to us!* Their monstrous grins held him down as surely as iron cuffs. They took

1

turns with him, they always did—he was a new steed to be ridden, to be tried out by all. Slick hands prodded his genitals. Sharpened nails drew scratches up and down his chest as teeth bit into his nipples. One plopped her bushy sex right down onto his face as others took turns impaling themselves on his erection. Their laughter, their sheer delight at his terror, felt thick as blood in his ears.

If you come too soon, we'll cut it off.
We might cut it off anyway, peow!
Little peow, little bug . . .
You belong to us forever . . .

No, these were not dreams, not really. They were vestiges summoned to the future from a heinous past. They were revenants. They were ghosts.

And the ghosts continued to beckon . . .

The helots were cooking heads.

Crusted rods stoked the great flames of the fire pits. Sheets of human skin were pinned up to dry. Hatchets rose and fell, adroit blades sloughed scalps off screaming skulls. Long bones were expertly cut out of satchels of muscle as organs were tossed whole into roaring cauldrons of blood . . .

The orison drew on:

"Ardat-Lil, o Modor . . ."

"O sweoster . . ."

"Us macain wīhan, o Modor. Us fulluht with ēower blud."

Fat hissed in the fire. Their slaves travailed toward the nave, bearing baskets of smoking meat.

And deeper, deeper into the past, the vision lurched . . .

The dreamer saw peasants fleeing in horror at the thunder of hoofs, shadows descending, swords held high. He saw the innocent butchered in place, torsos shorn and limbs severed in the wake of horses and dust. Great blades glimmered, sinking into random flesh as simple dwellings were set ablaze. The beautiful women dismounted amid the terror, their bodies limber in battledress. Dismembered corpses twitched in the dirt as heads were cut off shoulders. Blood gushed. Screams wheeled into the air. The conquerors directed blank-faced slaves to eviscerate the dying and the dead. Still more such slaves held torches as screaming figures were systematically sacrificed on blood-slicked slabs of shale. The women, cloaked and hooded, chanted praise as they joined in the demented feast. Later, as always, they shed their cloaks, to slake themselves of the groin as well as of the belly. Their lust shimmered through their grins, through their wanton eyes and open, wet mouths, and they descended upon the helots, tearing off their sackcloth clothes and dragging them down into the dirt.

The dreamer then smothered in the dream. He felt buried in their heady musk. Breasts bobbed before his eyes. Anxious hips straddled his groin, and legs wrapped around his head. When they were finished, he watched exhausted as they knelt naked before the altar of their most hideous god . . .

"Dother fo Dother . . ."

"Ardat-Lil . . ."

"Us macain wīhan!"

He roused from the dream as if crawling out from under a corpse pile that had moldered for weeks. His heart chugged; his breath revived him in snatches. He felt so sick he wished he could die. Shapes seemed to dissipate in the dark, black points of revolting outlines falling apart. They would always be there, he knew, eager to drag him back into their evil bowels. All he could do was stare up in the aftermath. The bed sheets beneath him lay damp with sweat, and with the repeated nocturnal releases of his semen.

"Succubi," he whispered to the dark.

The moon shone in the tiny window.

It's almost time, it seemed to answer back.

CHAPTER ONE

Up ahead, shadows merged behind flashing red and blue lights. Her headlights illumined the great orange sign: "State Police field sobriety checkpoint. Prepare to stop."

Oh, goodie, she thought. By now, after all the hubbub at the office, then Dr. Harold's diagnostic inexplicabilities, Ann needed something to liven her up.

I am going to kick some ass.

Naturally, the police would pick the least convenient place to conduct this infamous unconstitutionality: the city's main drag during homeward rush hour. Ann stopped her Mustang GT before one state trooper's opened palm. Two more troopers, faceless before the stroboscopic backlighting, approached the driver's window.

"Good evening, ma'am," one said.

"It was," Ann replied.

"Pardon me?"

"I mean to say it *was* a good evening until you saw fit to burdening me with this unwarranted and unreasonable deprivation of my civilian right to vehicular transit."

"That's not a very good attitude, is it, ma'am?"

"Is it the prerogative of the state police to enforce *attitudes*, Officer?"

The trooper paused. "Can I see your driver's license and registration, please?"

"I don't know if you can, Officer. I'm not an eye doctor. Therefore, I'm in no credible position to determine what you can see. *May* you see my driver's license and registration? Well, I suppose so." Ann handed them over.

"Have you been drinking, Ms. Slavik?"

"Yes," she replied.

"How much?"

"I'm not quite sure. I didn't know it was a requirement of law for citizens to inventory their daily intake of fluids. Is it?"

"How much have you had to drink today, Ms. Slavik?"

She considered this. "Probably half a dozen cups of coffee. One diet Coke for lunch. And one bottle of Yoo-Hoo for the ride home." She held the Yoo-Hoo bottle up for him to see.

The trooper paused. "Have you been drinking any *alcohol* today, Ms. Slavik?"

"Alcohol? You mean the volatile and highly flammable hydroxyl compound commonly used in industrial solvents and cleaners, a deadly poison? No, Officer, I have not been drinking alcohol today. If you mean have I been drinking any *alcoholic beverages*, the answer is no."

Again, the trooper paused. "Ms. Slavik, I'd like for you to get out of your car."

"Why?" she asked. "To make me touch my nose against my will? To make me walk on a line against my will? To make me blow into a 1.0-mean Smith & Wesson Breathalyzer?"

"We call it a sobriety field test, Ms. Slavik."

"Is that what you call it? I call it police harassment. It's not against the law to be uncoordinated, Officer, nor are you professionally qualified to determine my state of physical coordination. Nor can you guarantee the judge beyond a doubt the accurate function and calibration of a breathalization device. Now, listen to me, Officer. I'm thirty-seven years old. I stand five feet and four inches, and I weigh 109 pounds. You're what? Early twenties, six foot two, 200 pounds at least, am I right, and your friend there, he's even larger. In other words you two constables are big, strong, young men who can easily remove me from my vehicle against my will on a city thoroughfare. And, yes, I suppose, you could also force me to perform your ridiculous sobriety field test. I would be helpless to stop you, considering the state of fear I would be in. In fact, I suppose any woman would be helpless in such an instance against two big, strong, young men with deadly weapons on their hips. What I'm saying, Officer, is that if you want to forcibly remove me from my vehicle on a city street and force me to perform your embarrassing and grossly unconstitutional test, then go right ahead. If you do, however, I will sue your department for lost wages, future harm, and mental anguish, since such an instance would surely distress me to the point that I would miss work, that my employment status would be compromised, and that I would suffer mentally as a result. If, on the other hand, you choose to arrest me, I will sue your department for all of the above, plus false arrest."

The two troopers seemed to waver in silence. "You a lawyer, Ms. Slavik?" the second one asked.

"Is it within the power of the police to forcibly extract the employment status of random citizens? I think I will reserve the right to remain silent from this point on, Officer, unless of course the United States Constitution has somehow been rescinded since the last time I looked. Now . . . let me pass."

The two troopers stepped back and waved her on.

Much better, Ann Slavik thought, and continued down West Street. She knew they were only doing their job, but she needed to play with them to get her mind off things. *All right, so I'm an asshole. I can't help it. I'm a lawyer.*

The day had been the most unusual of her life, a great triumph and a great confusion. She'd been waiting for this day for seven years, she should be happy. But all she could think about now was what Dr. Harold had said.

About the dream. About the nightmare.

She could hear Martin typing when she let herself in. Why didn't he get himself a word processor? At least they didn't make as much noise. She'd offered to pay for it, but he'd assured her that he didn't want one. "I will not allow my muse to be tainted by floppy disks and blips on a TV screen," he'd said. Ann knew the real reason: he couldn't afford one on his "slave wages" from the college. And his male pride would not allow her to buy him one.

She came into the slate foyer and closed the door with her butt. Then she groaned relief, setting down her litigation bag, which weighed more than a suitcase. The lit bag was any attorney's bane; you carried your life around in it, and a lawyer's life weighed a lot. A professional studio portrait of her with Melanie and Martin smiled at her when she hung up her Burberry raincoat. *My family,* she abstracted. But was it really? Or was it just her own weak compromise at normality? Often the portrait depressed her—it reminded her of what her indecision must be doing to Martin. She feared that as each month passed,

Martin grew more disgruntled with her reluctance to marry him. She knew that he blamed himself, that he lived each day in some inner dread wondering what it was about him that wasn't good enough, and this only made her feel shittier because it had nothing to do with his inadequacies at all. It was something in herself that she didn't know how to express. *What's holding me back?* her mind dimly asked the portrait. She knew it would never answer.

She wandered to the living room and switched on the TV out of habit. She expected the same dismal disclosures: deficits, bank failures, murder. Instead, a newscaster with too much makeup on was saying: ". . . the recently repaired Hubble telescope. Last week astronomers at NASA reported the approach of what is known as a full tangental lunar apogee, a full moon that will occur at the same moment as this year's vernal equinox. 'It doesn't sound like much of a big deal to the average person,' John Tuby of MIT told reporters this morning, 'but to astronomers it's significant news. The moon will appear pink at times, due to a straticulate refraction. It's the first phenomenon of its kind in a thousand years.' So get out your telescopes, stargazers, and get ready," the silly newscaster went on. "Up next, poodles on skis!"

Poodles on skis. Ann turned off the set. At least it beat the usual news. She'd been hearing about the equinox thing for several days, like it was a paramount event. She didn't care what color the moon was, nor why. All she cared about now was relaxing.

She turned to the hall. "I'm home," she announced.

Home was a luxury three-bedroom condo just off the Circle. It was perfect, but for $240,000 it should be; that's what condos went for on the water. Ann liked it. Melanie had the second bedroom, and the third Ann used for an office. Martin had the little den for his writing. It was a corner unit. The balcony off the master faced the water, and the den faced State Circle, which was beautiful to look at at night. Ann would miss the place. When you made partner, you didn't live in a condo.

Martin was out of the den in moments, with his worrywart eyes. Writers were weird, but Martin's weirdnesses were different. At least once a week he threatened to quit writing in order to strengthen their relationship, and she grimly believed him. He felt guilty about his money situation, which was ridiculous.

He taught literature part-time at the college and wrote the rest of the time. Ann paid more federal tax than Martin grossed per year. He was a poet, critically acclaimed. "Critically acclaimed means you get great reviews and don't make any money," he'd once told her. His poetry collections, four so far, and by a major publisher, had been written up very positively in the *Post*'s *BookWorld*, the *New York Times*, *Newsweek*, and every major literary magazine in the country. Last year his agent had sold three of his short stories to *Atlantic Monthly*, *The New Yorker*, and *Esquire*, and he'd made more money from those than the total royalties from his last book of poetry. "Write more short stories," she'd suggested. "No, no," he'd lamented. "Prose is defectible. Verse is the only truth in the written word as an art form." *Whatever,* she'd thought.

"What did Dr. Harold say?" he asked now, and put his arms around her.

"The same. Sometimes I think I'm wasting my time."

"Christ, Ann, you've only had three appointments so far. Give it a chance."

A chance, she thought. The nightmare had started two months ago. She had it every night. Sometimes the details differed, but its bulk always remained the same. It bothered her now to the extent that she was fatigued at work; she felt off track. Martin had been the one to suggest seeing a psychiatrist. "It's probably some subconscious worry about Melanie," Martin had proposed. "A good shrink can isolate the cause and then find a way for you to deal with it." She supposed that made sense. It wasn't the $200 per hour that bothered her (Ann's firm routinely billed that much per hour for an average client), it was that if she didn't get to the bottom of it fast, her career might suffer, and if her career suffered, so would Melanie's future, not to mention her relationship with Martin.

An abstract print on the wall showed the blotched back of a person's head viewing a pointillistic twilight. *Dream of the Dreamer*, it was called, by a local expressionist. She and Martin had bought it at the Sarnath Gallery. Now, though, the warped shape of its subject reminded her of the pregnant belly of her dream.

She turned and kissed Martin. "Melanie here?"

"She's with her friends."

Oh, God. Melanie's "friends" worried Ann more than any

other aspect of her life. "The Main Street Punks," the papers had dubbed them. Leather jackets, torn jeans held together with safety pins, and hairstyles that might compel Vidal Sassoon to hang himself. Ann realized it was a prejudice on her own part; these "punks" were to her what the hippies were to Ann's parents' generation. Martin had met some of them and assured her that they were okay. They looked wild was all, they looked different. The protective mother in Ann didn't want Melanie to be different, even though the term was not relative. She knew she was being narrow-minded but somehow that didn't matter when it was your own daughter. Other people's daughters, fine. *But not mine.* She loved Martin more truly than she'd ever loved in her life; however, all too often, his liberalism ate at her. They'd argued about it many times. "It's a sensibility, Ann. When you were her age you were wearing peace signs and beads and listening to Hendrix. This is the same thing. It's a trend that she relates to. Maybe if you tried to understand her more, she wouldn't be so unsure of herself." "Oh, I see," Ann had countered. "Blame me. I must be a bad mother because I don't want my only child hanging around with a bunch of people who look like Sex Pistols rejects! Jesus Christ, Martin, have you seen some of them? One of them has a purple Mohawk!" "They look different, so they must be negative influences? Is that what you're saying, Ann? Have you ever heard of self-expression? Maybe if they all wore loafers with no socks and had names like Biff and Muffy, then they'd meet with your approval." "Eat shit, Martin." "They're just innocent kids with a different view of the world, Ann. You can't *pick* Melanie's friends for her. That's up to her, and you should respect that."

Goddamn him sometimes. So what if he was right? Dr. Harold had proposed that her objection to Melanie's friends was a defense mechanism. Ann felt so guilty about being away from Melanie so often that she sought out another, easier avenue of blame. "You work very hard," the doctor had said. "You've made a tremendous success of yourself, but you use that fact to attack the ones you love. Subconsciously, you feel that you've been a neglectful mother, and you feel that that's the cause of your daughter's lack of confidence. But rather than admit that, and act upon it, you have chosen not to face it at all."

Goddamn him too. "I'm paying two bills an hour to be insulted?"

Dr. Harold had laughed. "To see into yourself more clearly is no insult. If you want your daughter to be happy you have to support the way she feels about things. Every time you take a heated exception to her views, that's an insult to *her*. Things like that can hurt a young mind."

"She's not a baby anymore, Ann," Martin told her. "She's a bright, creative seventeen-year-old now. Don't worry about it."

Ann sputtered. The day had been just too confusing, and Martin could see that. He glanced at his watch. "Ah, it's beer o'clock." He poured her a Sapphire and tonic and got himself one of his snob beers. Politely changing a bad subject was his way of not rubbing her misgivings in her face.

"You get much writing done today?" she asked. The first sip of her gin began to unwind her at once.

"All kinds. Would've gotten more, though, if it weren't for the interruptions. Some guy kept calling for you. I'll bet he called five, six times."

"Some *guy*?"

"I kept telling him you wouldn't be in till early evening. Asked if I could take a message, and he kept saying no."

"Some guy?" she queried again.

"It must be your other lover," Martin said.

"Yeah, but which one? I have dozens, you know."

"Sure, but why bother with them when you've got a charming, intelligent, and very considerate man such as myself? Not to mention one of exceptional bedroom prowess."

"I hate to burst your balloon, honey, but the only reason I keep you around is because you're a good cook."

"Ah, so that's it."

All jokes aside, this caller made her wonder. Perhaps it was someone from the office calling to congratulate her.

"The guy had a real funny voice, like someone with emphysema or something, or strep throat."

Ann frowned it off. Whoever it was, they'd probably call back.

"I haven't started dinner yet," Martin admitted, and lit a cigarette. "I could thaw some—"

Ann's state of distraction finally occurred to her. She hadn't even told him yet, had she? "Don't thaw anything," she said. "We're going out. I already made reservations at the Emerald Room."

Suddenly, Martin looked grim. "That's the most expensive restaurant in town."

"It's also the best."

"Sure, but, uh, can we afford that?"

She wanted to laugh. Ann was rich by just about anyone's standards, and much richer as of today. Martin's financial pride always emerged at times like this. Ann essentially supported him, and they both knew that. By saying *can we afford that?* he was actually saying, *I'm broke as usual, so you'll have to pay for dinner. As usual.*

"We're celebrating, Martin."

He tapped an ash suspiciously. "Celebrating what?"

"I made partner today."

This news seemed to numb him for a moment. He just stood there, looking at her. "You're kidding?"

"Nope. They took me by complete surprise. Yesterday I worked for Collims, Lemco, and Lipnick. Today I work for Collims, Lemco, Lipnick, and *Slavik.*"

"That's *great!*" Martin finally rejoiced, and hugged her tight. But Ann had to masquerade her own joy. She'd waited seven years for this day, any lawyer's greatest triumph, and all she could think about was the nightmare.

Martin had proposed to her twice. Ann had said no both times, and even now she wasn't quite sure why. *Backwash,* she thought. Her first husband had left over ten years ago. Those had been hard times, and Mark hadn't made them any easier. Ann was going to law school during the day, working at night, and raising Melanie as best she could in between. Mark's failures hadn't been all his fault. Her parents hadn't liked him at all. Mom thought he looked "shifty," and Dad assured her he was a "layabout." Construction work paid well in this area so long as you were employed by a reliable contractor. Mark had been through several contractors who weren't. He always felt inferior to Ann. At least all his time not working had saved Ann a lot of day-care and baby-sitter fees. A week after she'd graduated from law school, Mark disappeared. *I'm sorry but I can't hack it anymore,* the note read. *Find someone more worthy of you. Mark.*

Her parents were actually happy about it, something for which she'd never really forgiven them. She'd never seen Mark again. Melanie had been about five at the time; she barely even remembered who her father was.

Ann's first years with the firm had been so harried she'd had no social life at all. The few dates here and there were never allowed to amount to anything, not as a lawyer and a single mother. One day it dawned on her that three years had gone by without her having sex once. She couldn't expect many men to want to assume the role of husband to a woman who worked ten to twelve hours a day six days a week and had a pensive teenage daughter by another man.

But Martin had been different. She'd met him at the college; the firm had purchased a computer system, and Ann had been required to take a three-day word-processing course. Martin had been sitting in the cafeteria, smoking over a pile of student essays about the thematics of Randall Jarrell. He'd merely looked up, made some small talk, and asked her out for a drink. They'd had a nice, polite, and innocuous time at the Undercroft, and that had been that. A week later they were dating regular. What helped was that his writing schedule conformed to her work schedule. There was never any tension there, and she never had to force herself to go out when she was too tired. Before he'd moved in with her and Melanie, he'd laid it all right out. "I'm a poet, this is my only occupational aspiration. I write six to eight hours a day, every day, and I teach part-time at the college. I could teach full-time and take extra classes for more money, but if I did that, my writing would suffer. I will never do that. I'll probably never make more than twenty thousand a year. Before we go any further with this, I want you to know that. I want it all on the table so there won't be any misunderstandings later. A poor poet is all I will ever be." Were all men so money-conscious? Ann had never doubted her love for him; she didn't care how much money he made as long as he loved her. And she never doubted that either.

Martin was a good househusband. He taught two classes on Tuesday and Thursday mornings. The other days he wrote from morning to dinnertime. He liked routines; "psychical and creative order," he called it. He'd take Melanie to school every morning, then he'd go home and write or go to school and teach, then he'd write some more and pick Melanie up. He cooked all their meals (all writers were good cooks) and even washed the dishes! He split the laundry and cleaning chores with Melanie. Many nights Ann wasn't home for dinner, but that had never been a problem either. Melanie had taken to him instantly. He encouraged her and counseled her better than Ann could ever expect to, and since they were both flaming liberals, they both agreed on everything. Martin even liked Melanie's wild, discordant music. At least once a month he would drive her and some of her friends to one of the New Wave clubs in D.C. to see bands like the Butthole Surfers, Blind Idiot God, and Nixon's Head. "Nixon's *Head*!" Ann had once tiraded. "You took her to see a band called *Nixon's Head*?" "Creative alternativism, my dear," Martin had quietly responded. "Without it we'd be another Russia." Maybe Ann was stupid but she didn't understand how a group called Nixon's Head could be proof of democracy. Nevertheless, without Martin, Melanie would have no father figure at all, and would probably have run away for good by now. Martin was tolerant of things most men could never be: stable, kind in the face of her job stress, never jealous, and someone who wouldn't rant and rave every time she had to work late on depositions or had to take clients out to restaurants where dinner for two cost more than Martin made in a week. He didn't feel subservient at all; he even jokingly referred to himself as her "wife." He insisted on contributing the little he could toward the mortgage, and refused to let her replace his ten-year-old Ford Pinto with a Corvette. "People will think I'm your gigolo," he'd objected. "Any poet who doesn't drive a ten-year-old car with at least 150,000 miles on it is a complete fake."

His first proposal had been made in good humor. "If you don't marry me soon, the neighbors'll think all I'm good for is sex." "That's not true, Martin. You're also a very good cook. Let's talk about it later." The second time had turned ugly. "I'm not comfortable with the idea of marriage right now," she'd said, now twice turning down the ring which he must've saved years for. "Why?" he asked. "Because I was married once before and it didn't work out," she said. "It's not my fault you married an asshole!" he yelled back. She'd felt terrible about it for days because his point was legitimate. Part of it was she didn't want to be married until she knew she was occupationally secure.

But was that really the problem?

What's wrong with me? she thought.

• • •

Getting Melanie to dress appropriately had been like pulling teeth. "Yes, you're going," Ann had ordered. "And, no, you can't wear leather pants and that Siouxsie and the Banshees T-shirt." It had been Martin, of course, who'd convinced her. "Conforming to conformity is a statement too, isn't it?" he'd asked. Melanie had then actually put on a dress without another word. "I feel like a yuppie," she'd said, grinning as the hostess had seated them by the window. The Emerald Room was indeed the best restaurant in town. The state legislature had their power lunches here every day while in session, and brought plenty of lobbyists for dinner. The governor appeared weekly, and the county executive often came in late. Any celebrity who happened to pass through town always wound up here via the recommendations of other celebrities. Stallone was once overheard remarking to a producer: "Preeminent grub."

"What exactly does being a partner mean, Mom?" Melanie asked.

"It means I share in all the firm's profits."

It also meant sharing in all the responsibilities, but Ann wasn't worried about that. She'd snagged their biggest client, Air National, herself, and had managed to hold on to them twice as long as any other firm. It was a sleazy acknowledgment, but the best thing about representing an irresponsible airline was that they paid any amount to get out of hot water. What partner meant most of all, though, was more delegation, and that meant more time she could spend with Martin and Melanie. From now on it would be the associates who scrambled over interrogatories till 3 A.M. Maybe now things would evolve into the domestic solvency she knew she needed. Maybe now they could be a family.

The maître d' expertly reeled off the day's specials and left them to peruse leather-bound menus.

"How're things going at school?" Ann asked.

"Okay," Melanie meekly replied. Okay meant no D's on the horizon. She was a smart girl but just couldn't adjust. Before Martin, she'd been cutting class, failing all her subjects. But then she beamed: "I'm gonna get an A in my art class."

Art, Jesus, Ann thought. "Melanie, art isn't going to get you very far in this world."

"Rembrandt would probably disagree with that statement," Martin said, and discreetly scowled at her.

"What I mean, honey, is that art doesn't usually make a good living. Art never sells till after the artist is dead."

Martin was still scowling. "Your mother's right, Melanie. Peter Max only makes $500,000 a week. Last year de Kooning sold a twelve-inch canvas for seventeen million. A person could starve on that kind of money."

There I go again, Ann thought. Martin's jovial sarcasm was his way of objecting to Ann's negativity. What Melanie needed was maternal support, not criticism. More and more she feared Martin was totally right, that Melanie's maladjustment stemmed from a *lack* of such support. Ann's own parents had been infuriated by her decision to attend law school. "Lawyers are sharks, liars," her mother had said. "It's not a job for a woman." "You'll never cut it as an attorney, Ann. It's too tough out there," her father had assured her. Ann doubted that she'd ever been hurt so badly in her life, and now she felt worse. How many times had she hurt Melanie with similar ridicule?

"I'm sorry, honey," she said, but it sounded terribly fake.

Martin quickly changed the subject with more comedy. "What kind of dump is this? No chili dogs on the menu."

"Don't worry, dear," Ann said. "I'm sure they'll put your beef Wellington on a hot-dog roll if you ask them."

"They damn well better unless they want me to start tipping tables over. And they better bring me catsup for my fries too."

Melanie loved it when Martin poked fun at the establishment, or at least where the establishment ate. But Martin turned serious when they deliberated over appetizers. "Jesus." He leaned forward and whispered. "The poached salmon costs seven bucks. That's a lot of dough for an appetizer."

"Don't worry about it, Martin," Ann assured. "This is my celebration dinner, remember? Cost no object."

"I don't want an appetizer," Melanie said. "I'd rather have a beer."

"You're too young to drink beer," Ann reminded her.

Then Martin: "I'll have the oysters Chesapeake. That's two bucks cheaper than the salmon."

Ann didn't know whether to laugh or scream. *Would you get the fucking salmon and shut up?* she felt like saying. *I just got a forty-thousand-dollar raise today. I think I can handle a seven-*

dollar appetizer! "I'll order for everyone," she said instead. "It'll save trouble."

A beautiful redhead took their orders, as robotic attendants brought bread and filled their water glasses. Martin and Melanie chatted about local art shows, during which three different opposition attorneys appeared to congratulate Ann on her partnership. This surprised—even startled—her, the enemy camps acknowledging her success without so much as a hint of jealousy. "You seem to be quite the talk of the local legal world," Martin suggested when Melanie excused herself to the ladies' room.

"It's a strange feeling."

"I'm very happy for you," he said.

He was, she could tell. So why wasn't she? Ann felt skewed; making partner still felt numbly distant. Why? "I'll be home more now," she said. "I'll be able to get Melanie off your back a little."

"Ann, she's a great kid, she's no trouble at all. I think she's really starting to come out of her shell now."

"No help from me."

"Would you stop. Everything's working out great, isn't it?"

Actually it was. Ann just didn't understand why she didn't feel that way herself. Everything *was* working out.

"Are you all right?"

"What?" she said.

"You look pale all of a sudden."

Ann tried to shake it off. She *felt* pale too. "I don't know what's wrong. I'll snap out of it."

"You've been working too hard," Martin suggested. "It's no wonder. And then this nightmare business . . ."

The nightmare, she thought. The hands on her.

"That'll work out too—you watch," Martin said, and sipped his Wild Goose lager. "It's all stress-related. All the hours you put in, plus worrying about Melanie, it gangs up on you. Harold's a great doctor. I know a bunch of profs at the college who see him. The guy works wonders."

But was that really the answer to her problem? Ann wasn't even sure what her problems were. Beyond the great window, the city extended in glittery darkness. The moon suspended above the old post office; it seemed pink. Ann was staring at it. Its gibbous shape fixated her, and its bizarre pinkness.

"Mom, are you okay?" came Melanie's voice.

Now they were both giving her long looks. "Maybe we should go," Martin said. "You need to get some rest."

"I'm fine, really," she feebled. "Once I eat something, I'll be fine."

Ann had to force herself to act normal, but everything distracted her. *Subconscious ideas of reference,* Dr. Harold had called it. *Image symbolization.* Even irrelevancies reminded her of the nightmare. The glass candle orb on the table. The pretty hands of the waitress as she set out their appetizers. The fleshy pinkness of Martin's poached salmon, like the pink flesh of the dream which seemed the same eerie pink of the bulbous moon beyond the window. The moon looked bloated, pregnant.

She was pregnant in the dream. Her belly was stretched huge and *pink.* Then she saw the faces . . .

The faceless faces.

"Some guy called you a bunch of times yesterday," Melanie said. "I asked what he wanted but he wouldn't say."

Martin looked up. "Did his voice sound—"

"It sounded creepy, like he had a chest cold maybe."

The same person Martin had mentioned. "It's probably somebody selling magazine subscriptions," Ann attempted. But now her curiosity was festering. She didn't like the idea of someone calling her and not knowing who or even why.

"Whoever he is, I'm sure he'll call back," Martin remarked. "I'm a little curious myself now."

Ann felt a little better when she got something in her stomach. Her glazed Muscovy duck appetizer had been prepared to perfection, and Martin devoured his poached salmon. But Ann realized that her sudden weird behavior had dampened the entire evening. Melanie and Martin were good sports but it showed. They knew something was wrong. Again, Ann struggled to make conversation, to normalize. "I'll be able to drive Melanie to school most mornings," she said, but the fact assailed her. Melanie had been in high school two years now, and Ann didn't even know what the place looked like. She didn't even know where it was. Martin had registered Melanie.

"Next week I figure I'll take her to some of the museums in the District," Martin said. "Too bad you can't get off."

Ann didn't know what he was talking about. "Museums?"

"Sure, and some of the galleries."

"I've always wanted to go to the National Gallery," Melanie said.

This observation made Ann feel worse; it was just another thing she'd been promising Melanie for years but had never made good on. Still, though, she didn't understand. "Martin, how can you take her downtown? She has school."

Martin tried not to frown at her neglect. "It's spring break, Ann. I've been reminding you for weeks."

Had he been? *God*, she thought. She remembered now. It had slipped her mind completely.

"Melanie's off for the whole week, and so am I," Martin said.

A vacation, it dawned on her. It would be perfect. "I'm sorry, I forgot all about it. We'll go someplace, the three of us."

Martin looked at her funny. She hadn't had a vacation in years, and in the past, whenever he brought it up, an argument usually resulted. "You serious? They'll give you a week off just like that?"

"Martin, I'm one of them now. I can take off whenever I want provided everything's in order."

Martin looked incredulous, poised over his salmon. "This I don't believe," Melanie scoffed. "Mom's going to take *time off*? That's a change."

"A lot of things are going to change now, honey," Ann assured her.

Melanie was ecstatic. "I don't believe it. I'm finally going to get to see the National Gallery and the Corcoran."

"Since your mother's talking mighty big now," Martin added, "maybe she can do you one better. Maybe Giverny. Maybe the Louvre."

They think I'm bullshitting? Ann couldn't help but smile. Finally, she could do something for them that involved her. "It's settled, then," she stated. "This weekend we leave for Paris."

Melanie squealed.

"You better check with your bosses first," Martin suggested. "We don't want to get our hopes up for nothing."

"Don't you understand, Martin? I *am* one of the bosses now. This'll be great. Paris. The three of us together. The timing couldn't be better."

That much was true. The timing couldn't have been better. But what Ann Slavik didn't realize just then was that the circumstances couldn't have been worse.

CHAPTER TWO

They never came to him here. They could, he knew, if they wanted to, but there was no reason. He could still see them in his mind and in his dreams; he was always dreaming of them: their swollen, perfect breasts, their beautiful bodies glazed in sweat and moonlight, their unearthly faces. They were like the drugs he used to take, euphoric, potent without mercy. In his dreams he remembered how he'd cowered before them in the promise of flesh. Five years ago they hadn't been dreams at all.

The phone rang and rang. *No one home,* he thought, and hung up. He retrieved his quarter and waited.

"Hurry it up," Duke complained. "I'm missin' Ping-Pong."

"Just a few more minutes," Erik grated. "Please."

Duke shrugged. "It'll cost ya, fairy."

Yeah, he thought. "All right. Five minutes?"

Duke grinned.

Erik Tharp didn't even care anymore. He was doing what he had to do. "The Rubber Ramada," the staff called this place. It was the state mental hospital. He'd been locked away, forgotten, but that was good, wasn't it? The world had forgotten about him now, after five years. But so had *they.*

They'd never been able to control him as well as the others. They had no use for people they couldn't control. The kid thing had been a frame; Erik hadn't done any of it. He'd dug for them, sure, and he'd snatched some people. But he hadn't murdered those kids.

Duke was another story; he *was* crazy. Not like the schizo-affectives of the delusional psychotics. He was just plain, don't-give-a-shit, mean-ass crazy. Ganser syndrome, it was called. He belonged in prison, not here. He'd made up a story in court about how aliens from the Orion complex communicated through a transmitter that had been implanted in one of his fillings. "The dentist was in on it," he'd told the judge. "They forced me to do it." He raped a sixteen-year-old girl and cut off her arms. "They said they needed the arms," Duke had informed the jury. "Never said what for, though. Just bring us the arms." He'd been found not guilty by reason of clinical insanity. In a state like this, Duke would never walk the street again.

But neither would Erik. They'd seen to that.

Erik knew what they were doing. He'd been one of their ilk once. *Brygorwreccan. Digger.*

I've got to get through, he thought.

"You don't hurry it up, you'll have to do it twice," Duke informed him.

There were four classes of patients here. Precaution, Class I, Class II, and Class III. Precautions were restricted to the observation dorm. Mostly autistics and suicidals. Two techs were in the room at all times, and most of the pats remained restrained, either in Posey bed nets or Bard-Parker straitjackets. Class I's couldn't leave A Building, the main wing; their world was a dorm and a dayroom. But Class II's got to live in B Building and were allowed to eat in the cafeteria. II's also enjoyed the luxury of supervised field trips, outside volleyball, and full roam of Buildings B through E. They could go to the rec unit—which had a library, a music room, and an automat—provided they signed out with a tech or a Class III patient.

Last week Erik had passed his board review for Class II status. And Duke had been Class III for almost a year.

The two of them made a deal.

Another luxury of the higher-class status was that you got to use the pay phone in the rec unit anytime between 9 A.M. and 10 P.M. Duke's deal was this: he'd use his Class III escort privilege to take Erik to the pay phone, and he'd also give him quarters to make calls. Duke had an uncle who sent him money and cigarettes every month. In the automat II's and III's could buy anything they wanted from the machines: microwave sandwiches, candy bars, Cokes. The Diebold magnetometer at the B entrance would prevent any sharp metal objects like bottle caps and pop tops from being brought back into the dorm. "So here's the deal," Duke had proposed. "One trip to the phone and one quarter per nut."

The first few times had been awful, but Erik forced himself to get used to it. He had money on the outside, but there was no one to bring it to him. How else could he earn money here? Several times Duke refused to pay. "Not till you get it right, fairy. Keep your lips over the teeth." Eventually, Erik learned to "get it right."

"Just 'cause I let you do it," Duke had once verified, "I don't want you thinking I'm some kind of faggot. I think about all the chicks I reamed while you're gettin' down on it."

Duke was what the doctors called a "stage sociopath with unipolar hypererotic tendencies." He bragged about the sex crimes of his past. He'd raped dozens of girls, mostly "bar rednecks and druggers," he called them.

"Killed a lot of them too."

"Why?" Erik had queried with his shredded voice.

"Aw, shit, fairy. Killing them's the best part. Ain't no kick if ya don't kill 'em." He'd cackled laughter. "One time I picked up this skinny blond bitch. I got her in the back of my van, see, and I'm cornholing the shit out of her. Man, she was so fucked up on drugs she didn't know which way was up; I coulda stuck a leg of lamb up her ass. Anyway, just as I'm gettin' ready to come, I blow the back of her head off with my Ruger Redhawk."

"That's disgusting, man," Erik replied. "You're a fuckin' monster."

"Look who's talking," Duke came back. "You snuff a bunch of babies and you call *me* a monster. The fact is, bitch, we're all monsters on the inside."

It was almost funny the way he'd said that. Erik knew some people who were monsters on the outside as well.

Please be home, he prayed. The quarter fell into the slot. He held his breath as he dialed.

"Got a big nut for my bitch tonight," Duke said, and laughed.

The phone was ringing—

Please be home.

—and ringing—

Jesus, please.

Twenty rings later, he hung up. He retrieved the quarter.

"Who you callin' anyway?"

Destiny, he thought. "Just someone."

Duke chuckled. "Don't matter none to me."

"Listen, Duke, there's something I need to talk to you about."

"Fuck talking, fairy. You're out of time. Ping-Pong's startin' and you got something to take care of first."

"It's important, man. It's about the lawn contractors."

"The fuckin' *what*?"

"The people who cut the grass. They come out every day with their mowers and do the hospital grounds. They park right out—"

"Quit stallin', faggot." Duke shoved him toward the hall. "You're just tryin' to get out of the suck."

They left the rec unit and crossed to B Building via the promenade. It was dark now. Above the trees, Erik could see the moon.

Almost spring, he realized.

The moon was pink.

They signed back in on the ward after walking through the metal detector and passing their change through in a plastic bucket. "No Ping-Pong tonight, Duke?" one of the techs asked. Duke was the champ. "I'll be in. Gotta hang a piss first." But Erik was already walking down the hall.

"How's your eye?" Jeff asked. Jeff was a delusional narcomaniac.

"My eye?" Erik grated back.

"Yeah, I saw it hanging out of its socket yesterday. I was concerned that your brain might get infected."

You had to go along with these people. "Oh, right. It's fine now. I just popped it right back in."

"Good, good," Jeff said, and shuffled away.

Nurse Walsh was tapping up a needle full of chlorpromazine in the med station while a bunch of burly techs four-pointed Christofer the hydrophobe. "Four-pointing" was just more psych-ward rhetoric. "We'll four-point you if you don't cooperate" was a polite way of saying, "These goons will pin you to the fucking floor if you don't stop acting like an asshole." "Tech-assisted med administration" was executed when a patient "physically resisted chemical therapy."

In the dayroom several pats were vegged out on the couch. Ten years of antipsychotics will take the zing out of anyone. All they made Erik take were mild tricyclics, none of the heavy stuff like Stelazine or Prolixin. "Zombie pills," the pats called them. Many of the heavily drugged patients had to take large doses of Cogentin in conjunction with their psych meds, to off-set the accompanying dyskinesia.

He went into the john, into the stall. You could always tell a psych ward bathroom from a normal one: there were never any locks on the stall doors, and the graffiti took diverse turns. "Do the Thorazine shuffle," someone had written. "God stole my brain but he can have it," and, "Ect, what a rush!"

Erik sat down and waited. He tried to concentrate on his plan, the lawn contractors, the supervisor, but the ideas kept slipping away. Sometimes he couldn't think right.

But he could always remember.

Them.

Their sleek bodies, their breasts and legs—all flawless. The things they did to him, and the things they made him do. *Blud. Mete. You are the meat of our spirit, Erik. Feed us.* They'd con-sumed him, hadn't they? With their kisses and their sex?

"Them," he whispered.

He could still see them clearly as if they were standing before him.

But it was none of them that stood before him now. This was no midnight grove on the holy solstice—this was a psych ward toilet stall. There was none of that; the heralds were gone.

It was Duke who stood before him now. Grinning. Fat. The rasp of the zipper, however familiar, made Erik wince.

"Do it good, fairy, and maybe I'll give you two quarters."

Later, Erik sat in his dorm. They were really cells, but they called them dorms. They called the ward a "unit," and they called drugs "meds." They called escape "elopement." They had names for everything. Manacles were "restraints." Jerking off was "autoerotic manipulation," and shooting the bull was "vocalization."

The steel mesh over his window was a "safety barrier." In the window he could see the moon, and the moon was pink.

The ruckus of Ping-Pong could be heard from the dayroom. Someone was playing piano. The television blared inanities.

Erik doodled in his pad. They didn't call it doodling, of course. They called it "occupational therapy." He drew fairly well, he was left-handed. He'd read that left-handed people were three times more likely to be creative. They were also three times more likely to be mentally ill. Something about inverted brain hemispheres, and a bigger corpus callosum, whatever that was. He drew the moon, and figures looking up to it. He drew their bodies to scrupulous detail. What he could never bring himself to sketch, though, were their faces.

It wasn't that he *didn't* remember their faces, it was that he *did*.

Around the sketch he scribed the glyph. *The night mirror,* he thought. How many times had he looked into it and seen the most unspeakable things?

My God, he thought, but behind the thought he was sure he heard their warm, viscid laughter, like beating wings, like screams in a canyon.

He looked at the moon. The moon was pink.

Beneath the sketches, and with no conscious thought at all, he scribbled one word:

liloc

CHAPTER THREE

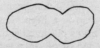

The dream was vivid, hot—it always was.

"Dooer, dooer."

It was always the same: the back arching up and waves of moans. The tense legs spread ever wide, the swollen belly stretched pinprick tight and pushing . . . pushing . . . pushing forth . . .

Then the image of the cup, like a chalice, and the emblem on its bowl like a squashed double circle:

She sensed flame behind her, a fireplace perhaps. She sensed warmth. Firelight flickered on the pocked brick walls as shadows hovered. A larger version of the emblem seemed suspended in the background, much larger. And again she heard the bizarre words:

"Dooer, dooer."

She was dreaming of her daughter's birth, she knew. Birth was painful, yet she felt no pain. All she felt was the wonder of creation, for it *was* a wonder, wasn't it? Her own warm belly displacing life into the world? It was a joyous thing.

Joyous, yes. So why did the dream always revert to nightmare?

The figures surrounded her; they seemed cloaked or enshadowed. Soft hands stroked the tense sweating skin. For a time they were all her eyes could focus on. The hands. They caressed her not just in comfort but also—somehow—in adoration. Here was where the dream lost its wonder. Soon the hands grew too ardent. They were *fondling* her. They stroked the enflamed breasts, the quivering belly. They ran up and down the parted, shining thighs. The belly continued to quiver and push. No faces could be seen, only the hands, but soon heads lowered. Tongues began to lap up the hot sweat which ran in rivulets. Soft lips kissed her eyes, her forehead, her throat. Tongues churned over her clitoris. Voracious mouths sucked milk from her breasts.

The images wrenched her; they were revolting, obscene. *Wake up! Wake up!* she commanded herself. She could not move. She could not speak.

Her orgasm was obvious, a lewd and clenching irony in time with the very contractions of birth. Behind her she sensed frenzied motion. She heard grunts, moans—

—then screams.

Screams?

But they weren't her screams, were they?

She glimpsed dim figures tossing bundles onto a crackling fire. Still more figures seemed to wield knives or hatchets. The figures seemed palsied, numb. She heard chopping sounds.

The dream's eye rose to a high vantage point; the circle moved away. Naked backs clustered about the childbirth table. Now only a lone, hooded shape stood between the spread legs. It looked down, as if in reverence, at the wet, bloated belly. The belly was pink.

Moans rose up, and excited squeals. The firelight danced. The chopping sounds thunked on and on, on and on . . .

"Dooer, dooer," spake the hooded shape.

The belly shivered, collapsing.

A baby began to cry.

Ann wakened suddenly, lost of breath. *The dream,* she thought. *The nightmare.* She reached blindly for Martin, but he wasn't there. The digital clock read 4:12 A.M.

Did she always have the dream at the same time, or did she imagine that? Months now, and nearly every night. Beneath her felt sodden, and her mind swam. The dream sickened her, not just the glaring, pornographic imagery, but what it must say about some part of her subconscious. She didn't like to think like that—she was a lawyer. She didn't like to contemplate a part of herself that she couldn't break down, assimilate, and recognize structurally.

She knew the dream was about Melanie's birth. The abstractions—the bizarre words, the emblem on the chalice and the wall, the firelight, etc.—were what Dr. Harold termed "subconscious detritus." "Dreams are always outwardly symbolic, Ms. Slavik, subjectivities surrounding a concrete point. The birth of your daughter, in other words, surrounded by encryptions. You're here to find a means to expose those encryptions, and to identify them, after which we can determine how they relate to the *central* notion of the dream."

Ann couldn't imagine such a notion, but she suspected, quite grimly, that much of this "detritus" was sexual. She'd told Dr. Harold everything he asked about her, except one detail. She was having orgasms in her sleep. The wetness, as well as the acute vaginal sensitivity upon waking, left no doubt. Worse was that these "dream orgasms" had proved her only orgasmic release for some time. Martin was by far the best lover of her life, yet she hadn't had an orgasm with him for as long as she'd been having the nightmare. This worried her very much.

Everything did.

Yuck, she thought, and got up in the darkness. Her nightgown stuck to her, she felt doused in slime, and the coldness of her sweat shriveled her nipples.

She padded down the hall and peeked into her daughter's room. Melanie lay asleep amid a turmoil of sheets. The sheets were black and so were the walls. "Killing Joke," one big poster read. Her favorite group. Martin had taken her to see them last year. Ann vowed one day to go to one of these wild concerts with her, but the more she determined to get involved with her daughter's joys, the more impossible it seemed to achieve. *Not trying hard enough,* she lamented. She knew this neglect was part of Melanie's seclusion. Growing up without a father was tough for a kid, and with a mother submerged at work six, sometimes seven days a week made it even tougher. Dr. Harold informed her that Melanie's "alternative" tastes reflected a "self-developed" identity. Most seventeen-year-olds read *Tiger Beat* and watched sitcoms. Melanie read Poe and watched Polanski.

Sleepy eyes fluttered open. "Mom?"

"Hi, honey."

"Is something wrong?"

"Shh. Go back to sleep."

Melanie shifted under the covers. "I love you, Mom."

"I love you too. Go back to sleep."

Ann closed the door.

She worried too much, she knew that. Melanie was coming of age, and Ann often had a hard time reckoning with that. It had caused some awful arguments in the past—Melanie had run away several times, all of which were Ann's own doing. She lost herself too often. The last time, it had taken Martin two days to find her, while Ann had been in the office working on counterlitigation for Air National. Ann's success as an attorney haunted her with her failure as a mother.

Tonight she'd promised things would change, but would this prove another failure? To think so would crush her. The trip to Paris would bring them together; it would start the relationship that should've started properly seventeen years ago. *Too late's better than nothing,* she considered.

Through the living room now, and soft darkness. She stepped into Martin's moonlit den. The drapes billowed around the open French doors. Indeed, Martin stood on the terrace. Often she'd find him here, in wee hours when he couldn't sleep, looking down into the city, the water, the docks. Always looking for something. Tonight, though, he stood straight in his robe, staring up at the sky.

"Martin?"

No reply. Staring. He looked sad or confused.

He turned, startled. His cigarette fell. "What's wrong?"

"I—" she said.

He hugged her at once. "I know. The dream again. You were—"

"I'm sorry I woke you."

"You didn't," he lied. "I just couldn't sleep. Too much caffeine."

Suddenly, she was crying. She hated that. His arms encircled her more tightly then. "You can cry," he whispered. "It's all right."

Oh, God, I can't stand this. She felt out of control, which was her greatest fear. "What's wrong with me?"

"Nothing. You'll feel better tomorrow."

He closed the door, sealing out the night, then led her back to the bedroom. Martin hugged her once more at the foot of the bed, and then she was hugging him back, clinging to him as if to a ledge. He was a ledge perhaps. He was the only thing that kept her from dropping into blackness.

"I love you," he said. "Everything will be all right."

My whole life is falling apart, she thought.

His robe fell to the floor. He crawled into bed with her and covered her up, then draped an arm about her. That vital contact, his warm body against hers, was all that made her feel safe from herself.

"I love you," he said.

But the safety was false. In a moment she fell back to sleep, and back into the bowels of the dream.

"I was sick. The doctor said I almost died."

"Interesting," Dr. Harold observed. He chuckled. "I mean, it's not interesting that you almost died. The parallel, I mean."

"Parallel?" Ann asked.

Dr. Herman Harold's office looked more like a rich man's study. It was darkly appointed in fine paneling, oak and cherry furniture, plush dark carpet. High bookcases consumed one entire wall, their shelves curiously lacking psychiatric texts. Instead, tomes of classic literature filled the cases. Only a single copy of *The American Journal of Psychiatry* gave any clue that this was a headshrinker's office. No proverbial couch could be found.

"I've told you, dreams mix symbols with our outward, objective concerns. Here, the symbol is obvious."

Was it? "I'm a lawyer," Ann iterated. "Lawyers think concretely."

Dr. Harold's eyes always appeared bemused. He had a pleasant face with snow-white hair, and big bushy white eyebrows and a bushier white mustache. He spoke slowly, contemplatively, placing words like bricks in a wall. "The symbolic duality," he said. "Life and death. The notion that you almost died while creating life. The proximity of utter extremes."

Life and death, she thought. "It was borderline pneumonia or something like that. Thank God Melanie was okay. I was barely conscious for about two weeks after the birth."

"What do you remember of the birth?"

"Nothing."

"It's pretty clear, then, that the dream is dredging up *aspects* of Melanie's birth that were infused into your *subconscious* mind. Think of it as a spillover, from the subconscious into the conscious. We call it 'composite imagery.' Your mind is trying to form a real picture of Melanie's birth with unacknowledged memory fragments."

"Why?" Ann asked.

"Why isn't nearly as important as why *now*. Why is this occurring at this precise point in your life? Let me ask you, was Melanie a planned pregnancy?"

"Yes and no. We wanted a child, that is."

"You had no reservations, in other words?"

"No, I didn't. I think my husband did. He didn't think we could afford to have a child, and I'll admit, things were pretty tight. He never made much money, I was young, nineteen, I was pregnant in my first year of college, and I was determined to go to law school afterward. I think maybe one reason I wanted a child was because I thought it would make our marriage stronger."

"You considered your marriage weak?"

"Yeah. I honestly wanted it to work, but now that I think of it, I guess I wanted it to work for the wrong reasons."

Dr. Harold raised a bushy white brow.

"I don't like failure," Ann said. "Mark and I probably never should have gotten married. My parents couldn't stand him, they were convinced the marriage would fail, and I suppose that fueled my own determination to see that it didn't. They were also convinced that I'd never make it through law school. Their discouragement was probably my greatest motivating factor. I graduated third in my class. I waited tables at night, went to school during the day. I missed a semester of college to have Melanie, but I made up for it and then some by taking a heavier credit load afterward. In fact, I graduated a year early even with the missed semester."

"Impressive," Dr. Harold remarked. "But I'm more interested in your parents. You've never mentioned them before."

"They're a bit of a sore subject," Ann admitted. "They're very old-fashioned. They wanted me to assume a traditional female role in life, clean the house, raise the kids, cook, while hubby brought home the bacon. That's not for me. They never supported my desires and my views, and that hurt a lot."

"Do you see them often?"

"Once every couple of years. I take Melanie up, they love Melanie. She's really the only bond at all that exists between me and my parents."

"Are you on good terms with them now?"

"Not good, not bad. Things are much better between me and Dad than me and Mom. She's a very overbearing woman. I think a lot of the time, Dad was all for my endeavors but he was afraid to express that because of her."

Dr. Harold leaned back behind the plush veneered desk. "Another parallel, a *parental* one."

Ann didn't see what he meant.

"There's a lot of guilt in you, Ann. You feel guilty that you've put your job before your daughter because you feel that in doing the opposite, you'd satisfy your parents' convictions of occupational failure. More important, you feel guilty about neglecting to support Melanie's social views. Your own mother neglected to support *your* social views. You're afraid of becoming your mother."

Ann wasn't sure if she could buy that. Nevertheless, she felt stupid for not considering the possibility.

"Since the day you left home, you've been torn between opposites. You want to be right in the traditional sense, and you want to be right for yourself. You want both ends of the spectrum."

Was that it?

"You're very unhappy," Dr. Harold said.

I know, she thought. It depressed her that he could read her so easily. "I need a solution," she said. "The nightmare is ruining me. I'm not getting enough sleep, my work is slipping, I'm in a bad mood when I get home. Don't you guys have some wonder drug I could take that would make the nightmare stop?"

"Yes," Dr. Harold said. "But that wouldn't solve any of your problems; it would only cover them up. You're having the nightmare for a reason. We must identify that reason."

Dr. Harold was right. There was no quick fix.

"How is Martin taking all of this?"

"Better than most guys would. I know it's hard on him. He's not getting any sleep either, because I'm always waking him up during the dream. He's pretending that it's no big deal, but it's starting to show."

"More fear."

"What?"

"More fear of failure. You're afraid of failing with Melanie, and you're afraid of failing with him. You're afraid at the end of your life all you'll have to show for your existence is selfishness."

"Thanks."

"I'm merely being objective. You love Martin, don't you?"

"Yes," she said with no hesitation. "I'd do anything for him."

"Anything except marry him. Still more fear."

Jesus Christ! she thought.

Dr. Harold smiled, as if he'd read the thought. "You're afraid that Martin thinks you're holding your first marriage against him."

"He's suggested that himself. Is it true?"

"It seems to be quite true."

This was depressing. Coming here didn't make her feel better, it made her feel worse. "What am I going to do?"

"The first thing you must do is be patient. You're a very complex person. Understanding your problems will be a complex affair."

Tell me something I don't know, Doc.

"The images and ideas expressed in dreams function in two fundamental modes," Dr. Harold went on. "One, the *manifest mode*, which relates to the content as it occurs to the dreamer, and, two, the *latent mode*, the dream's hidden or symbolic qualities. The dream is about you giving birth to Melanie. There's a strange emblem in the dream, there're dark, hooded figures and cryptic words like incantations. The dream sounds almost satanic. Dreams of devils often signify a rebellion to Christianity. Are you a Christian?"

"No," Ann said.

Dr. Harold smiled. "Are you a satanist?"

"Of course not. I'm not anything, really."

"You're saying you were raised with no religious beliefs at all?"

"None."

"Don't you find that strange, especially with the traditional sentiments of your parents?"

"It is strange," she agreed. "I was born and raised in Lockwood, a small town up in the northern edge of the county, up in the hills. Only about five hundred people in the entire town. There was a big church, everyone attended every Sunday. Except my parents. It was almost like they deliberately shielded me from religion. They kept me blind to it. I really don't know much about religion."

"What about your daughter?"

"The same. I try not to influence her that way. I wouldn't know how to even raise the subject."

Dr. Harold contemplated this. He remained silent for some time, looking up with his eyes closed. "The dream is definitely about an array of subconscious guilt. How can you feel guilty about a religious void when you've had virtually no religious upbringing?"

"I don't," Ann stated.

"And you don't feel that a religious belief might help Melanie become better rounded in life?"

"I don't think so. I don't see how it could. She's never been a problem that way."

"Is she a virgin?"

The question stunned her. "Yes," she said.

"You're sure?"

"As sure as I can be, I suppose."

"Do you find that unusual?"

"Why should I?"

"The average first sexual experience for white females in this country occurs at the age of seventeen. Did you know that?"

"No, I didn't." *Ann, see if you can guess the next question.*

"How old were you when you had your first sexual experience?"

"Seventeen," Ann replied, though *None of your fucking business* would've been a better reply. "What's that got to do with it?"

"Isn't it possible that you possess some subconscious concern regarding your daughter's virginity?"

Ann's frown cut lines in her face. She didn't like all this Freudian stuff. Innuendos were hard to defend against, especially sexual innuendos. "I can't see why."

"Of course you can't," Dr. Harold said, still smiling. What did he mean by that? Then he asked, a bit too abruptly for Ann's liking, "Have you ever had a *lesbian* experience?"

"Of course not."

"Have you ever wanted to?"

"No." *I'm getting pissed,* she thought. *Really pissed, Doc.*

"You're sure?"

Ann blushed. "Yes, I'm sure," she nearly snapped.

"The dream is rife with overt sexual overtones, that's the only reason I ask such questions. What is the word you keep hearing in the dream?"

"Dooer," she said, pronouncing *doo-er*. "What's it mean?"

"I don't know. It's your dream, isn't it?"

"Yeah, and what might it, or any of the dream, have to do with lesbianism?" Now the lawyer in her was making an interrogatory that she knew he couldn't answer.

But he did answer it, by making her answer it. "The voice that spoke the word—*dooer*—was it male or female?"

"Female. I already told you."

"And the figures around the birth table, the figures touching you, caressing you, were—"

"All right, yes, they were female." *That's what I get for trying to play games with a shrink,* she thought.

His next observations disturbed her most of all. "It's interesting that you take such aversion to questions pertaining to lesbianism, or potential lesbianism. It's interesting, too, that you are now exhibiting a guilt complex about that."

"I'm not a lesbian," she said.

"I'm quite sure that you're not, but you're afraid that I might *think* you are."

"How do you know?"

"I know a lot of things, Ann. I know a lot of things just by looking at you, by assessing the way you structure your replies, by your facial inflections, your body language, and so forth."

"I think you're grabbing for shit, Doc."

"Perhaps, and it certainly wouldn't be the first time a psychiatrist has been accused as such. What I mean is that no mode of rapport between a doctor and a patient is more important than openness."

"You think I'm not being completely open with you?"

"No, Ann, I don't."

How about if I gave that big mustache of yours a good hard yank? Would that be sufficient proof of openness?

"You're outwardly rebellious and defensive, which is a sure

sign of a deep sensitivity. You haven't been fully open to me about the dream, have you?"

Of course she hadn't. But what was she supposed to say?

"Are there any men in the dream, Ann?"

"I think so. At least, there seem to be men in the background, chopping things, chopping wood, I think. They seem to be throwing wood on a fire."

"Wood. On a fire. But you say the men are in the *background*?"

"Yes," she said.

"And the figures in the foreground are women?"

"Yes."

"And who is the center of attention to these women?"

"Me."

"You. Naked. Pregnant. On the birth table."

"Yes."

"Don't you find it interesting that the active participants of the dream are women, while men remain in the background, clearly symbolizing a *subordinate* role?"

"I plead the Fifth," Ann said. Dr. Harold was boxing her in now, cornering her. It made her feel on guard. Moreover, it made her feel stupid, because she didn't know what he was driving at. "A minute ago you said you didn't think I'd been completely open with you about the dream. How so?"

"My conclusions will make you mad."

"Hey, Doc, I'm already mad. Go ahead. Lawyers don't like to be accused of withholding information."

"But they do, don't they? Isn't that part of the trade? Withholding facts from the opposition?"

"I'm leaving," Ann said.

"Don't leave yet," Dr. Harold said, lightly laughing. "We're just beginning to get somewhere."

Ann stalled. Her head felt like it was ticking.

"First, I'm not the opposition," Dr. Harold asserted. "Second, I make references that trouble you because being troubled is a demonstration of the very subconscious underpinnings that have recently made you feel unfocused and confused."

Ann didn't care about any of that now. She wanted to know what he was going to say. "What? What conclusions? What is it you feel I haven't told you?"

"You already know."

Ann's eyes bore into him. But, again, he was right, wasn't he? She did already know.

"Tell me," she said.

"What you haven't admitted to me is that the dream aroused you. Outwardly, you were repelled, but inwardly, you were stimulated. You were stimulated sexually. Am I right or wrong?"

Stonily, she answered, "You're right."

"You were aroused and you had an orgasm. Right or wrong?"

Her throat felt dry. "Right."

She'd told him neither of these facts, yet he knew them. Somehow she suspected he knew them on her first visit three weeks ago. The man was a walking lie detector.

"Are you experiencing an orgasmic dysfunction at home, with Martin?"

Now Ann laughed, bitterly. What difference would it make? "Yeah," she said. "Sex has never been a problem for me. I've always been ... orgasmic. Until now. Since I've been having this nightmare, I haven't had an orgasm with Martin."

"But you do have an orgasm in the dream?"

"Yes, every time."

"You're afraid that an aspect of your past will ruin your future."

The words seemed echoed, hovering about her head. Is that what the dream meant? And if so, *what* aspect of her past?

Dr. Harold went on, "Do you—"

"I don't want to talk anymore," Ann said. "I really don't."

"Why?"

"I'm upset."

"There are times when being upset is good."

"I don't feel very good right now."

"You have a lot of fixations, the most paramount of which is a fear of seeming weak to others. You associate being upset with being weak. It's not, though. In being upset, you're releasing a part of yourself that you've kept hidden. That's an essential element of effective therapy. The exposure of our fears, the release of what we keep hidden. It helps us see ourselves in such a way that we can understand ourselves. When we don't understand ourselves, we don't understand the world, the people around us, what we want and what we have to do—we don't understand anything."

I understand that I need a drink, she thought.

"I think that it's important for you to continue coming here," he said.

She nodded.

"One more question, then I'll let you go for today." Dr. Harold unconsciously stroked his mustache. "What makes you certain that you're giving birth to *Melanie* in the dream? You said that you were very ill, and that you remained barely conscious for several weeks after the birth. What makes you—"

"The setting," she said. "All I see of myself in the dream is my body. It's almost like a movie, going from cut to cut. I never even really see myself, but I feel things and I see things around me. The cinder-block walls and earthen floor—it's the fruit cellar at my parents' house."

"Melanie was born in a fruit cellar?"

"Yes. There's no hospital in Lockwood, just a resident doctor. I went into labor early, and there was a bad storm, a hurricane warning or something, so they took me down into the fruit cellar where it would be safer."

"And this strange emblem, the one on the chalice and the larger one on the wall, was there anything in the fruit cellar that reminded you of that?"

"No," she said. "It's just a normal fruit cellar. My mother cans and jars her own fruits and vegetables."

Dr. Harold pushed a pad and pencil across his big desk. "Draw the emblem for me if you will."

She felt sapped, and the last thing she wanted to do was draw. Quickly, she outlined the emblem, the warped double circle on the pad.

Dr. Harold didn't look at it when he took the pad back. "So you're off—where is it? To Paris?"

Ann smiled genuinely for the first time. "We're leaving tomorrow. I've just got a few things to wrap up at the office this afternoon, then I'm picking up the tickets. Melanie's an art enthusiast, she's always wanted to see the Louvre. It'll be the first time the three of us have been away together in years."

"I think it's important for you to be with Martin and Melanie on a leisure basis. It'll give you a chance to get reacquainted with yourself."

"Maybe the dream will go away for a while," she said, almost wistfully.

"Perhaps, but even if it doesn't, don't dwell on it. And we'll talk about how you feel when you get back."

"Okay," she said.

"I hope you have a wonderful time. Feel free to call me if you have any problems or concerns."

"Sure. Bye."

Ann left the office.

Dr. Harold sat in silence. He closed his eyes, thinking. He thought about her. Type A, occupationally obsessive, sexually dysfunctional. *Dream methodizing,* he thought. The emblem she'd drawn on the pad looked scrambled, dashed. Kinesthetically, it was obvious: she'd drawn it hurriedly because it scared her. He knew that a lot of things scared Ann Slavik.

An awful lot of things.

CHAPTER FOUR

"So what happened?" Duke asked. "You never said."

Erik finished his Macke cheese dog. He always ladled them with onions—the kind that came in the little tubes—to get the taste out of his mouth. Not the taste of the cheese dog, the taste of Duke.

"What happened what?" Erik asked.

"You know, your voice. How come your voice is so fucked up?"

Suddenly, he tasted memory, salt and copper. Blood. He'd tried to break away from them several times. They hadn't liked it.

We offer you everything, Erik. And still you rebel.

That had been weeks before the police had caught him. *Holy Mother of God,* Chief Bard had said, staring into the pit. They all called him "Chief Lard"; he had a belly like a medicine ball. Rumor was he'd been chief of some town in Maryland; a state sting operation had caught him laundering mob money through the town bingo games at the fire hall. They'd told him he could be prosecuted or he could move on quietly. It had been Bard and Byron who'd caught Erik that night. *Whatchoo doin' with that shovel, boy?* Byron had demanded. *Holy Mother of God,* Bard had said.

Erik knew he had been set up. They no longer trusted him.

We love you, Erik, one of them had whispered.

We want you to be good, whispered the other.

So we're going to give you a little reminder.

So that whenever you talk, you'll think of us.

They'd tied him down. The one had been blowing him while the other went to work on his throat. The doctor at the emergency room had said that he only had one vocal cord left. He was lucky to have lived.

"A scratch awl," Erik finally answered Duke. "They stuck a scratch awl in my throat."

"Christ," Duke muttered. "Who's *they*?"

"Muggers," Erik lied. That's what he'd told the people at the hospital and the police. That muggers had done it.

Duke picked his nose. "Bummer."

The girl named Dawn walked in, approached the candy machine without looking at them. She'd recently made Class III status too. Duke chuckled under his breath. They'd heard Dr. Greene talking to one of the techs about her. "Katasexual," he'd said. "Sexual obsession with a dead person." Erik had heard that before they got her on the right medication, she would masturbate ten times a day. There were a lot of winners on the ward. The three-hundred-pound schizophrenic who claimed she was pregnant by her collie. "I'm going to give Dr. Greene the pick of the litter!" she'd rejoiced. One night the city police had brought in a raving PCP overdose. "I can fly anything that God can make!" he'd informed them as he strapped him into a jacket. Lots of the pats had religious fixations. Many were hypersexual yet devoutly religious, like the prostitute who was "tricking for Jesus," or the unipolar serial killer they'd brought in from Tylersville who forced women to accept Christ as their savior and then killed them before they could change their minds. "Lotta people in heaven who wouldn't be if it weren't for me," he'd bragged.

"God loves you," Dawn turned with a Snickers and said to Duke.

"If he does, tell him to let me the fuck out of this dump, you floppy-tit psycho bitch. How about sucking my balls?"

Dawn hmmffed and left.

"Fizzlehead!"

Erik tried the phone again. No answer. *Where are they?* he wondered. "See, that's how I know I ain't queer," Duke was analyzing himself when Erik returned. "That fizzlehead there? I could have her right on this table. Boy, I could *tear her up*."

Erik didn't need to be convinced. He was thinking. Duke was a fat, disgusting sociopathic slob with bad teeth and hair like a mop. *But he's strong,* Erik thought. Three times a week the techs took all Class II's and III's to the gym in the other building. Erik had seen Duke bench-press 250 ten times. *Yeah, real strong,* he mused.

"I been thinking, Duke," Erik's ruined voice grated.

"About what, faggot?"

"You and me, we'll never get out of here. Greene's review board wouldn't okay us for the street in a hundred years."

"I know that."

Erik leaned over the table. "I got something I gotta take care of, on the outside."

"What, kill more babies?"

"I never killed any babies. It was a setup—"

"Sure, faggot. That's what they all say, ain't it? Just like I never chopped the arms off that bimbo."

"Would you listen to me, goddamn it. I think I know a way we can get out."

Suddenly, Duke was listening.

Erik took Duke to the window, pointed out the "safety barrier." A high fence surrounded the hospital grounds, yet beyond was a parking lot where the staff and contractors parked their cars. "See that white van?" Erik asked. "And the pickup trucks beside it?"

Letters on the van read "Lawn King." "Big deal," Duke remarked.

"They're groundskeepers. I've been watching them. They get here every morning at seven-thirty and start cutting the grass. The hospital grounds are huge, these guys are all over the place. They don't have to come in and out the front gate 'cause the trailers they haul their lawn mowers on are too big. There's a service gate, right over there behind those trees. If we can get past that gate, we can drive out the main entrance."

"In what? Chitty-Chitty Bang-Bang?"

"In one of their trucks. See all those pickups parked next to the van? They belong to the crew."

"Awright. Keep talking."

"At eleven-thirty they start breaking for lunch. They break for lunch in four shifts, three at a time. They get to the parking lot through the service gate. The supervisor has to let them out. He's the only one authorized to have the key to the service gate. See that guy there? He's the supervisor."

Duke peered through the wire window. Several workers were fueling tractors which hauled the cutting platforms. A man in overalls stood in attendance. He was tall. Broad shoulders and back. Knurly.

"Big fucker," Duke commented.

"Yeah, but so are you."

Duke continued to peer out the window.

"I've been watching him regular," Erik grated on. It hurt just to talk. "He's got a routine. They start breaking for lunch at eleven-thirty, like I said. But at eleven he eats his own lunch. He doesn't leave like the others—he brings his own in a bag. That's what he does every day at eleven. He sits down by those trees all by himself and eats his lunch."

Very slowly, Duke nodded.

"No one else is around. All the workers are still out on the grounds cutting the grass. And this guy, like I said, I been watching him. He's the boss, so he's the first guy out here every morning at seven-thirty. He drives that blue and white Ford pickup right there. We wouldn't have to waste time looking for which truck is his 'cause we already know."

"But the gate, the service gate. I don't even see it."

"That's why this'll work," Erik came back. "You can't see the service gate from the grounds because it's behind those trees, the same trees where that big guy sits and eats his lunch every day at eleven o'clock."

"Eleven o'clock," Duke murmured.

"That's an hour from now. And you know what we're doing an hour from now?"

"What?"

"The techs are taking our whole wing outside for volleyball."

Duke had his duties down pat. II's and III's achieved their privileged status by demonstrating good behavior for protracted periods. Nothing ever happened because no one ever expected it to. Three techs supervised the volleyball games: Nurse Dallion, who was so thin she looked like she might blow away, and Charlie and Mike. They would have to take all three of them out before someone could get back inside and hit the security button. Mike would be tough—most of the male techs were hired for physical size, and Mike was young and strong—but not stronger than Duke. And Charlie, the black guy, was huge. Erik figured they had maybe two minutes after the fight broke out to overpower the lawn supervisor, get his keys, unlock the service gate, and take off in the pickup. Duke's job was to take out Mike quickly, then get over to the trees, while Erik took out Nurse Dallion and Charlie. Though Charlie was big, he was also hopelessly myopic. Without his soda-bottle-lens glasses, he couldn't see past his face.

It was sunny out and warm. Spring was just days away.

"Great day for volleyball," Erik grated to Charlie.

"Sure is. Glad to see you're playing for a change, Erik. Do ya good to get out with the others."

Yeah, he thought. He glanced behind him as they chose up sides. At four minutes past eleven, the lawn supervisor was walking down the hills, toward the trees.

"Chad's a faggot," Duke barked. "I don't want him on my side."

"Enough of that, Duke," Mike warned. "We're all here to have fun."

"Fuck fun, I wanna win."

"I'm no faggot," Chad complained.

"Come on, folks," Charlie said. "Let's get playing."

What a clusterfuck, Erik thought once they started going. Many of the pats were extrapyramidal, a neurological side effect of long-term phenothiazine therapy. Slow. Uncoordinated. Twitchy. One of the girls served and the ball didn't make it over the net.

"My turn, thank God," Duke said, and batted the ball across. It went back and forth maybe twice before Harry the nyctophobic knocked it into the net.

"Jesus to Pete," Duke complained. "Can't any of you faggots play?"

"I'm telling you, Duke. Any more comments like that and you're back inside," Mike told him, standing aside.

"Your turn to serve, Erik," Nurse Dallion pointed out. They rotated. Erik took the ball.

"Come on, Erik, let's see a good one," Charlie said, and clapped.

"Aw, Erik can't serve for dick," Duke yelled. "He's a faggot too, just like all of ya. Just like Chad."

"I'm no fag!" Chad yelled, fists clenched at his sides.

"Shit, you suck your daddy's dick. He told me so last time he came to visit."

"He did not!"

Dawn started crying. "I can't play!" she screamed. "Not while Duke's here!"

"You go down on your mother, fizzlehead," Duke guffawed, and rubbed his crotch. "Why don't you just shut up and suck my knob, huh?"

"That's it, Duke." Mike gave him a shove. "Inside."

Erik, still holding the ball, nodded.

"I fucked your girlfriend," Duke reported to Mike. "I ever tell you that?"

Nurse Dallion commanded, "Get him inside, Mike. He's ruining this for everyone."

"She wasn't nearly as good as Nurse Dallion, though." Duke busted out a laugh. "Yeah, Nurse Dallion, she can suck a good one. Suck your balls right out your dickhole."

Dawn sat down on the grass, bawling. Several other pats began to wander. Mike grabbed Duke by the collar and began escorting him off the field. "You just lost your Class III, Duke."

"Shag my balls, queer. Your girlfriend licks my crack."

"Now!" Erik yelled.

Duke lunged, then rammed his elbow back into Mike's throat. Simultaneously, Erik rocketed the volleyball into Charlie's face. Nurse Dallion was running up: "Erik, what are you—"

"Sorry," he said. He really was, because Nurse Dallion was nice. He slugged the heel of his palm right into her forehead. Suddenly, the pats were running all over the place. Erik glimpsed figures dashing. Duke was stomping Mike's face, then breaking. "Motherfuckers!" Charlie yelled. Erik had time to palm-heel Nurse Dallion in the head again, and that was it for her. Charlie grabbed him, lifted him up, and Erik spun. He raked Charlie's glasses off, kicked him in the groin, then stomped on the glasses. They crunched.

Charlie's teeth were gritted in pain. One hand held his groin, the other reached out. "I'm sorry," Erik grated, and kicked him in the head.

Erik broke for the trees.

Two minutes, he told himself. *If we're lucky.*

Mike, Charlie, and Nurse Dallion were all out cold. The pats fled every which way. "Fly, Fleance! Fly!" Harry the nyctophobe quoted Shakespeare. Dawn was still blubbering in the grass, while Chad shouted to the sky, "I'm no fag!" as he urinated on the net post.

Erik disappeared behind the stand of trees.

"I took care of this big fucker sure as shit," Duke was gloating. The lawn super lay limp. Duke pulled two clumps of keys out of the guy's overalls, and his wallet.

"Jesus Christ!" Erik yelled. "You killed the guy!"

Duke looked up, disinterested. The supervisor's neck was broken. Erik grabbed the keys and gratingly shouted, "Come on!"

The lock on the service gate was a big Rollings Mark IV with a tubular keyway. Erik fished out the only tubular key on the ring; the big lock snapped open instantly.

This is too easy, he considered. "Walk," he whispered to Duke. "Walk normal. We're just two lawn guys walking to our truck."

Duke loped along beside him, whistling "Hail to the Redskins." The Ford keys had black plastic shrouds; Erik isolated them at once. Ten seconds later they were pulling the big pickup out of the lot.

"Shit yeah!" Duke exclaimed. "The faggot was right! We're out of this shithole!"

"We're not out yet," Erik reminded him. "We still have the main entrance to get by, and the security guards."

"Those creamcakes? I'll bust all their heads."

"You shouldn't have killed that guy."

"Fuck him. Killed Mike too, the faggot. Heard his windpipe crunch." Duke laughed. "Sounded like steppin' on walnuts."

Jesus, Erik thought. "Get ready to talk," he grated. "I can't talk, so you're going to have to."

This was what would make or break them; Erik doubted Duke's expertise at method acting. Quickly, Erik opened the super's wallet. "Phillip Alan Richards," read the name on the driver's license. In the back of the pickup were several five-gallon gas cans. "Tell them we're making a fuel run for Mr. Richards," he said.

"Fuel run, sure."

The guard at the entrance stopped them. The gate was down. *Shit,* Erik thought. He might have to drive through. He might have to kill the guard, and he didn't want to do that.

"We're makin' a fuel run for Mr. Richards," Duke said. "Lawn King."

The guard nodded. He handed Erik a clipboard through the window. *A sign-out log,* Erik thought. He scribbled a name, wrote the time in the Out column, then paused. Tag Number, the next column requested. His eyes scanned up the sheet, found the name Richards signed in at 7:23 A.M., put the following tag number in his column, then passed the clipboard back to the guard. The guard glanced into the pickup bed. Then he glanced in the cab again.

"Later, guys." He raised the gate and waved them on.

Erik pulled through. *Slow,* he thought. *Normal.* A moment later he heard the phone ringing in the guard booth. Erik turned the pickup truck off the court and onto the main road.

Ten seconds later the elopement alarm began to blare at the hospital.

Erik pressed the accelerator to the floor.

CHAPTER FIVE

The old man saw horror in his mind. He saw *them*.

He saw them naked, praying before their blasphemous slab. He saw their open faces, their soft hands reaching out, for— something. What? The sound of their incantations made him sick, but not nearly as sick as the things they'd made him do. *Scieror*, they'd dubbed him—a cutter. *Bring us ælmesse. Wīhan to this pig.*

He couldn't resist them, none of them could. He'd been good with the cnif, a master; the sensation defied description. To flense a woman, to fillet a man. Once they'd made him cut off a girl's head and bleed her into the chettle. *Broo for the cuppe!* and they'd laughed, drinking. Then they'd made him watch as several wreccans had fornicated with the corpse.

Give lof! they'd cry. *Give lof!*

Others stoked the fire, for smaller and more potent lof.

He'd even eaten with them.

"Don't worry, dear," came the wifmunuc's soft voice now. "This will make you feel better."

"No, please." *They're killing me,* he thought.

Several figures surrounded him. He lay paralyzed on the bed. They'd been doing this to him for weeks now—he felt more dead every day. Several of the younger ones looked on from behind, their faces bright in wonder, their naked bodies glowing in youth. But he was wizened now, shriveled like a dried fruit.

"You're sure this is safe?"

A man's voice replied, "Quite sure. It merely retards the heart rate for a time and restricts the cerebral blood vessels. The brain damage will be minor but significant enough to produce the desired effects."

"Good. Just don't kill him."

A needle jabbed his arm. A cold rush.

From her black mentel, the wifmunuc extended her hand. "Come, girls. You may come and touch."

They approached timidly at first, then scampered forward. Their small breasts bobbed as they leaned over. When the syringe was retracted, one licked the blood off the puncture. Soon the hands roved his old skin. They giggled.

"It's providence," whispered the wifmunuc. "What a wondrous thing, yes? To lay our hands upon the flesh of providence."

The girls seemed awed. They were finicking with him, like an animal at a petting zoo. *I'm a showpiece,* he thought as his vision darkened. The room felt warm, his blood turned to sludge. He shuddered as a soft hand gently squeezed his genitals.

"No, honey, you mustn't do that. He's a very *special* hüsl."

The hand slipped away.

Just let me die, the old man thought. But they wouldn't do that. They'd kill him, instead, day to day, a piece at a time. Now he could scarcely see at all.

Worse were the things he saw in his mind.

Just let me die and go to hell.

"Enough," came the wifmunuc's maternal voice. "We mustn't get him too excited."

"Such lovely girls," commented the male voice.

"Yes, aren't they?"

The hands drifted away. The young figures stepped back.

"The doefolmon comes soon," elated the wifmunuc. "You can play tonight, if you like."

"Oh, yes!" exclaimed one.

"We'd like that!" exclaimed another.

"But you must eat first, for sustenance. Let us go and eat now."

The wifmunuc took the group of girls out of the room.

"Why are you doing this to me?" the old man managed to rasp.

The male figure turned. "Oh, come on, don't be like that. Like she said, it's providence, and you're part of it. We all are. It's a privilege."

He closed the bag he'd brought his needles and poisons in.

"Good night, old friend," he said.

The old man began to convulse.

Erik watched the rearview. "First off, we dump the truck."

"Huh?" Duke asked.

"They know what we're driving," Erik's voice grated. "You can bet they got an APB out on this truck. If we don't get rid of it right now, we're dead meat."

Duke didn't seem interested; he was rummaging through the lawn super's wallet. "Shit," he spat. "All the motherfucker had on him was six bucks. We need money, man."

"We can get money later. I got a stash."

Duke glanced over. "Whadaya mean?"

Erik had abducted a lot of people for them, for their hideous hūslfeks. Most were runaways and drifters, but every now and then he'd run into someone with some money. Erik always took the money. For the years he'd served them, he'd socked away at least a thousand dollars. He kept it in the church basement with his things.

"Just don't worry about it. I got all the money we need hidden back where I used to live."

"That where we're headed?"

"Yeah. Little town called Lockwood, half hour's drive."

Suddenly, Duke beamed; in the glove box he found a big sheath knife. "A Gerber. Sort of like the one I used to have."

This was not good. An escaped erotomanic sociopath with a knife probably did not add up to anything cheery. Erik knew he'd have to be very careful. "Listen, Duke, you can't be pulling any crazy shit right now. You start up any of that and we've had it. We'll be four-pointed in the precaution unit for the next decade."

Duke didn't like to be told what to do. "No, you listen to me, fairy. I don't take orders from no one, 'specially a baby-killer faggot like you. We wouldn't even be outa that shithole if it wasn't that I had the balls to bust up those two cocksuckers. I haven't seen the street since fucking Carter was President. I'm gonna have me some fun, and no one's gonna stop me, and if you don't like it, just say so." Duke was fingering the knife, glaring.

Careful, careful. "I hear you, Duke. Relax. All I'm saying is we gotta be real careful from here on. You can have your fun, just careful like, okay?"

"Yeah. Careful like."

"And since I know these parts better than you, it's probably a better idea we do things the way I see them. I know all the back roads, all the towns. Okay?"

"Sure. You're the brains, I'm the balls. That's fine by me. Just so long as we got an understanding."

Thank God, Erik thought.

Another thing in their favor was that Class II's and III's got to wear regular clothes, not hospital linens. But they still had faces.

"Another thing we gotta change is the way we look. Cut our hair, dye it, stuff like that. And it's probably a good idea for you to lose those sideburns."

Duke forlornly stroked said muttonchops. "Yeah, guess you're right. Cocksuckers'll have our pictures all over the papers tomorrow."

"And probably TV by tonight. But like I said, first thing we gotta get a new set of wheels."

"Convenience store," Duke offered his wisdom. "I used to snatch cars at convenience stores all the time. Most people figure they'll be in and out real fast, so lots of 'em leave the keys in the ignition."

Good idea, but it had too many flaws. "We can't just take a car, Duke. If all we do is take a car, the owner will know right off and call the police. The cops'll know what kind of car to be on the lookout for, which is the same problem we got right now."

Duke's sharp smile showed his understanding of the situation.

Erik went on, "So that means we gotta take the owner too. And we gotta do it so no one else sees. If there are no witnesses, there'll be no one to tell the cops what kind of car we took."

"And would ya looky there!" Duke exclaimed.

Just ahead the sign loomed: Qwik-Stop.

Erik pulled the pickup around back by the dumpster where it couldn't be seen from the main road. Two cars had been parked out front, a muddy Dodge Colt and an old beige Plymouth station wagon.

"Two cars out front," Erik observed. "That means one cus-

tomer in the store. The second car belongs to whoever's working the register. Here's what we do. We walk in like we're looking for something, wait for the customer to leave. Then you take
out the person working the register. We'll get his keys, take him
with us, and take off."

"Sure," Duke said. He put the knife under his shirt.

A cowbell clanged when they entered. An old bald man behind the counter looked up. Erik had been correct in his predic-
tion: there was only one customer, a ruddy-looking blonde in
cutoffs and an orange halter. She stood on skinny, knobby-
kneed legs before the rear reach-in, furiously tapping a sandaled
foot. "Jaysus Chrast, pops," she complained in a bent twang.
"Dollah saxty a half-gallon? Whut kand of prass is that?"

"I don't make the prices," replied the old man, scowling.

Erik and Duke perused the magazine rack up front. "Baby
Born with Elvis Tattoo," boasted the *Enquirer*. "Careful of
guns," Erik whispered. "Lots of shopkeepers around here keep
guns under the counter."

"Ain't afraid of no guns." Duke was leering at the blonde.

Oh, no, Erik suddenly thought.

"Ah ain't payin' no dallah saxty fer a dag half-gallon of
milk."

"Fine. Pay a dollar seventy down the road." The old man
shrugged.

"Shee-it!" The blonde opened the reach-in and bent over.

"When the girl leaves," Erik whispered, "we take down the
old guy."

But Duke was eyeing the blonde as she bent over. "Change of
plans, partner," he whispered back. "We're taking the girl."

Erik should've known something like this might happen.
"Damn it, Duke," he whispered more fiercely. "If we do that,
the old guy'll see! He'll tell the cops what kind of car we took!"

"Shadap," Duke replied. "We're taking the girl."

"No way, Duke! We agreed to do this my—"

"Shadap."

"This ain't no library, fellas," said the old man. "You all can
buy one of those magazines or you can leave."

Erik felt sick. The blonde was sputtering. "Dollah goddamn
saxty, Ah say Ah cain't *bull-leave* it!"

"We don't want no magazine, pops." Duke lumbered up to
the counter.

"Whatcha want, then?"

The blonde was coming down the aisle.

Aw, no no no no, was all Erik could think.

"Could use a pack of Kools, though," Duke said, showing his grin.

No no no no no . . .

When the old man turned to get the cigarettes, Duke sank the knife into his lower back.

The old man screamed.

The blonde dropped her milk and screamed.

Erik shouted, "Goddamn it, Duke!"

"There, pops." Duke chuckled. "How's that?"

The blonde, still screaming, made for the back. Erik tackled her, but it was like wrestling with a greased snake.

Duke continued to chuckle, emptying the register. The old guy was flip-flopping facedown on the floor. Dark blood pumped out of the hole just above his right kidney.

The blonde slapped, punched, and clawed for all she was worth. For a moment, she was on top of Erik, fury in her eyes, teeth snapping. Erik had to hold her back to keep her from biting his face.

"Damn if you weren't right, fairy!" Duke celebrated. "Looky!" Under the counter he found a big old Webley revolver. He held it up like a prize.

When Erik finally got the blonde up, she screamed and kicked him squarely between the legs. "Feisty little cooze, ain't she?" Duke guffawed.

Erik went down.

Duke gestured. "Hey, darlin'. It ain't polite to like leave without even sayin' hello, now, is it?" The blonde was running for the door. Duke grinned behind the Webley's sights and fired. The giant bullet struck the blonde in the left buttock, shattering her hip, and knocked her to the floor.

"Fuckin' fairy." Duke chuckled. "Ya let a woman kick your ass."

The old guy was still churning in his own blood. "Looky there," Duke observed. "Old fucker shat himself . . . Lights out, pops." He fired a second shot into the old man's head, which promptly exploded like a melon dropped from a great height. "I don't think we have to worry about him tellin' the cops nothin' now, huh? You think so?"

Erik dragged himself up. "Fucking crazy psychopath!" he yelled, rasping. "We haven't even been off the ward fifteen minutes and you've already killed three people!"

"It's a kick, ain't it?" Duke laughed back.

The blonde's face ballooned red from pain and screaming. Her leg stuck out funny from her hip as she tried to drag herself out before a smear of blood.

Duke stuffed the money along with a box of shells into a plastic bag which read "Qwik-Stop, the Happy Place to Shop."

"Come on, fairy. Help me with the bimbo."

The blonde blubbered, shivering, as they carried her out. The station wagon had keys in the ignition. Erik started it up while Duke pulled the blonde in the back.

"Glad this ain't my car." Duke chuckled. "This bimbo's bleedin' all over the place. Looks like she's got some nice little titties, though."

Erik spun wheels out of the lot. The girl shrieked steadily. "We can't just let her die," Erik yelled. "We're gonna have to drop her off at a hospital or something."

Duke's grin flared in the rearview. "Oh, we'll drop her off, all right. But not at no hospital. And not till I'm done."

What have I let loose? Erik thought.

The girl screamed and screamed as Duke hauled off her shorts. He gave her leg a twist, snorting laughter, and she passed out. "Ain't heard a woman scream like that in years. Makes my dog *haaaaaaaaaard*." Erik could hear the shattered hip bones grinding. "Yes, sir, there's some nice little titties," Duke approved, and pulled the orange halter over her head. "Big cooze on her, though. Like you could drive a truck through it."

Erik felt numb as he drove. *This is all my fault,* he thought. He should never have brought Duke with him. He should've found a way to get out himself.

"Hey, fairy, take a look. Show ya how a *real man* treats a woman."

Duke's mad, pumpkin-grinning face descended. He gnawed, grunting, bit off a nipple, and spat it out the window.

Erik kept his eyes on the road. His heart was still racing. Duke had the knife and gun—Erik was helpless. *All my fault,* he thought over and over. He shivered when he heard Duke unbuckling his pants.

All my fault . . .

"Later, baby," Duke said when he was done. He popped open the back door. "Happy landings. And give Saint Pete a great big kiss from Duke."

He shoved her out the door. The wind rushed. The naked body tumbled off the road into high grass.

Duke leaned forward, grinning. He put his arm around Erik. "You know somethin', I ain't had me this much fun since high school."

Erik just drove.

Up ahead, the green road sign read "Lockwood 15 miles."

CHAPTER SIX

Ann fingered the plane tickets wistfully. "I want you to get those Delany 'rogs out tonight; give the assholes enough time to stew but not enough time to do the work, and also get the responses out to Winters' document requests. Tonight."

"Tonight?" asked the associate. He was young and lean, he had the hunger in his eyes. "That'll be tough."

"You're the one who wanted to be a litigation lawyer. Get the stuff out tonight."

The associate nodded, attempted a smile.

"I've looked through the documents you marked as privileged," she went on, yet her fingers did not come away from the tickets. "I think we're probably right, but I'm uneasy about those six internal memoranda on the maintenance procedures. If the bolts cracked while the plane was in flight, that's fine. We just got to make damn sure the bolts were maintained according to SOP. So we need to get with these guys and track down a solid basis on anything Jolly Roger might be preparing in anticipation of litigation." Jolly Roger was what they called the opposition firm. They were well named. Ann's firm was better named: the Snake Pit.

"Well," replied the associate, "it wasn't addressed to inside counsel, so we may be a little weak there."

"I know, but these in-house guys might've made a call to the addressees and asked for the junk on the memo. I'll leave it to you and Karl to make the final decision." *God, I can't wait to get out of here,* she thought.

"Gotcha," said the associate.

"And remember, when I come back we'll only have a week to get the preliminary jury instructions out for the JAX Avionics trial. You'll have to hump on that too."

"Right," said the associate.

"I'm out of here," Ann said. "Good luck. I'll leave my number with the paralegals in case you need me."

"Okay, Ann. Hope you have a good time." He paused, smiled. "You flying Air National?"

"Hell, no. The Atlantic Ocean's a bit too cold for my tastes."

The associate laughed and left.

Ann felt strangely at ease with the idea of being away from the firm for a week. Usually, she couldn't let go of things. Today, though, she couldn't wait to. She was a partner now—the associates served *her*. Eventually, they'd have a nickname for her, something nasty like "She-Devil" or "Ann of a Thousand Teeth." Partners considered derogatory nicknames a secret compliment.

She turned off her office light and closed the door.

Suddenly, she shivered. It wasn't cold. *A squirrel just ran over your grave,* her mother would tell her as a child.

What was it?

For a second, she felt as though she were leaving the firm for good.

Martin and Melanie were packing when she got home. Their excitement was clear—they were hustling about with big smiles on their faces, Melanie's stereo pounding away.

This is going to be great, she thought, and shed her coat.

"I'm home," she said. She held up the tickets.

"Hi, Mom!" Melanie greeted.

Martin came and kissed her. He looked longingly at the tickets. "This is going to be great," he said.

"I was recently thinking along those same lines."

"Everything tied up at work?"

"Yep. For the next nine days, I'm not a lawyer."

"And I'm not a teacher."

"And I'm not a student!" Melanie added.

For once, we get to be a family, Ann thought.

"The itinerary's all planned," she said at dinner. Martin had cooked one of his favorite culinary inventions, which he called "Poet's Seafood and Pasta in a Bowl." It was simple but quite good: pasta twists in olive oil, a little garlic, and powdered red pepper, heaped with steamed shrimp and cherrystone clams.

"When do we go to the Louvre?" Melanie asked, and speared a shrimp.

"Days two through four. It's a big place, honey. It takes days to see it all."

"We can have lunch in the café where Sartre met deBeauvoir. What an inspiration," Martin said. "Maybe I should bring a typewriter."

"Bring a pad and a pencil, Martin," Ann suggested. "Sartre wrote *No Exit* with a pencil."

"Good point."

"Can we go to the Métal Urbain?" Melanie asked. "It's a famous New Wave club in Pigalle. All the great bands play there."

"Uh," Ann faltered.

Martin gave her a look.

"Of course, honey." *Bring earplugs,* she reminded herself. "And we'll eat at Taillevent; it's one of the best restaurants in the world—no offense to your cooking, dear."

"None taken, so long as you pay," he joked. But it was no joke. The last time she'd been to Taillevent, with a client from Dassault, the check for two had been about $700.

"We'll also be going to the Orsay Museum of Modern Art, where they have all the expressionistic stuff, and the Centre-Pompidou."

"This is gonna be neat as shit!" Melanie exclaimed.

Martin laughed. "It'll probably even be neater than that."

But Ann felt disheartened. She'd seen all those places when they'd had Dassault as an auxiliary client, and she'd never really cared. Yet Melanie, her own daughter, longed to see these museums, and Ann had never even considered it.

She plucked her last clam out of the shell when the phone rang.

"I'll get it," Martin said.

"It's probably that guy with the creepy voice," Melanie ventured.

"No, let me get it," Ann insisted. This was one thing she wanted to get to the bottom of.

"Hello?"

The line seemed to drift. She thought of wastelands. She heard a distant rushing like trucks on the freeway.

The ruined voice sounded wet, exerted. "Ann Slavik?"

"Who is this? Why have you been calling me?"

Martin got up.

"Listen," the voice creaked. It stalled again, as if each word demanded a pointed effort. "Don't come," it said.

"What? Who is this!" Ann demanded.

"You don't know me."

"Who the hell is this!"

"Just . . . don't come."

"Give me that," Martin said.

She held him off. "Don't come where?" she asked of the caller.

The voice sounded shredded. "Take your daughter . . . Go far away."

"If you don't tell me who you are—"

The voice grated on, but Martin snatched the phone away. "Listen, fucker," he said. "Don't call here anymore or I'll have the phone traced. I'll have the police on your sick ass, you hear me?"

Martin looked at the phone, mouth pursed. "He hung up," he said.

"Who was it, Mom?" Melanie asked.

"No one, honey."

"Some nut, that's all," Martin contributed. "What did he say?"

Don't come, she thought. *Take your daughter . . . Go far away.*

What could he have meant?

What bothered her most, though, was what the voice had said as Martin had been taking the phone.

The moon, Ann. Do you remember? asked the abraded voice. *Look at the moon tonight.*

Down the hill, trucks roared past along Route 154.

Erik hung up the pay phone.

"You make your precious phone call?" Duke asked when he came back to the station wagon. He was eating Twinkies.

"Yeah," Erik grated, and closed the door.

Duke grinned, showing cream between his teeth. "You busted out of a psych ward just for that, huh? Just to make a call?"

"Not quite."

"Who was it?"

"The past," he said.

Duke chuckled.

Erik drove the station wagon out of the truck stop. Duke had bagged over a hundred dollars at the Qwik-Stop. Since then, they had purchased a Norelco electric razor, some food, some different clothes, and hair dye.

She'll come, Erik thought.

He hoped a cryptic warning might work, but somehow, now he knew it wouldn't. *Providence,* they'd called it.

"Where to now, fairy?"

"Duke, please don't call me that."

Duke slapped Erik's back. "I'm just joshin', man. We're buddies, right?"

"Yeah. Buddies."

"Where to, *buddy?*"

Home, he thought. *She's going to come, and she's going to bring her daughter.*

"We'll find some out-of-the-way motel for tonight. We gotta change how we look and get some rest."

"What then?"

"Tomorrow we'll go to Lockwood."

Duke guffawed. "Sounds good to me, fa—I mean, buddy. I got nothin' on my agender." He crammed another Twinkie in his mouth.

Home, Erik thought. *Providence.*

He drove the car down the route. He did not look at the moon.

CHAPTER SEVEN

That night, Martin made love to her. Lately, he hadn't been, sensing her skewed moods. Tonight, though, it had been Ann's advance. She'd felt her juices flowing all day; she was geared up for Paris—they all were—and Ann supposed that she wanted to see how this prospect of change would affect her responses. She hadn't had a normal orgasm in two months. She thought sure that tonight, given her different feelings, she could . . .

But, of course, she didn't.

She knew just minutes after they started. Martin was very vigorous in his passion; he wanted to do anything she liked, anything that made her feel good. When foreplay failed to moisten her, he went down on her, yet the harder she tried to get into it, the more remote she felt. After an hour they were engaged in positions they'd never attempted. Poor Martin, he was trying so hard, and so was she. *But how can he know?* she thought, turned upside down over the edge of the bed. Thank God for the dark. What would Martin think if he could see her face squeezed closed in anguish? It was like pushing a refrigerator up a steep incline, the effort she exerted to keep the images of the dream out of her mind's eye.

His penis felt cold in her. She didn't even feel like herself. *It's more like watching Martin fuck someone else,* she thought, despairing. Each thrust into her flesh jerked the nightmare's face closer. She was starting to get sore. She put on her act, which she'd gotten quite good at recently, and then it was over. He spent himself in her and collapsed.

Fear and guilt. But of what? Dr. Harold's implications were hard to put into decipherable terms. Everything was a matrix of symbols. The symbols were sexual. Having real sex with Martin—the man she loved—reminded her of sex as it should be. The fear and guilt in her psyche prolapsed that reminder, filling her subconscious with ideas of sex as it shouldn't be. She was afraid of the nightmare because the nightmare attracted her in some way, aroused her, and being aroused by an aberration caused a negative response. Hence, no orgasm under normal circumstances. Her consciousness battled with her subconsciousness. A vicious cycle.

She felt guilty about the dream because the dream came from her. The dream disgusted her, yet it also fulfilled her. More guilt, more fear. The dream was destroying them all.

Yes. *Thank God it's dark.*

She pushed her face in the pillows to dry her tears.

Eventually, Martin fell asleep. His semen trickled in her; it felt cold. *None of this is his fault, yet even he's becoming a victim.*

Does he know? she dared to ask herself. It was a question she'd kept buried. Did he know that she faked her orgasms? Martin was very perceptive, often uncannily so. How long could their relationship last like that?

Then another dread drifted up: Melanie. *Do I really doubt that she's a virgin?* Dr. Harold seemed to think so. The dream was of Melanie's birth, and it was sexual. What was her subconscious trying to suggest in that? Ann had always left sexual issues to the board of education, which only highlighted her failures as a mother. Mothers were supposed to talk about such things with their daughters, weren't they? Ann's mother hadn't, though, and again Dr. Harold came to mind. *You're afraid of becoming your mother,* he'd said. A few times Martin had talked to Melanie about sex, considering the AIDS crisis and the world's growing list of STDs. But never Ann. Ann was always "working." Ann was "too busy." It was fear, she knew, fear of acknowledging something that she didn't want to acknowledge. She absolutely could not imagine her daughter in a sexual situation. The image distressed her, and the punky-looking leather-and-New-Wave-button-clad creeps Melanie hung around with amplified the image to one of utter terror. It all made her mind feel jammed. *Too much to deal with,* she thought, and whined. Just like Harold's other inferences. Lesbianism. Religious voids. Did Dr. Harold really think she had lesbian tendencies because the nightmare involved women touching her?

God, she thought.

The bedroom's darkness seemed particulate, grainy. It distilled her discomfort. Martin's breathing sounded strangely loud, and her own heartbeat could've been someone kicking a wall. The room's only light oozed similarly through the window, from the moon.

The moon, Ann, clicked the riven voice in her mind. *Do you remember?*

Remember what?

Look at the moon tonight.

Carefully, she got up. She walked naked to the blinds and peeked out. Boats rocked gently along endless docks. Moonlight rippled on the water. It seemed pink.

Her gaze rose. The moon hung low on the horizon. *An egg moon,* her mother would say—it was lopsided, not quite full.

Look at the moon tonight.

All right, I'm looking. It did look funny, its inordinate size and the queer pinkish hue. She'd been hearing about it on the news the last few days, some rare astronomical occurrence. The first day of spring was just days away; apparently, the moon's position in conjunction with this caused an atmospheric anomaly that pinkened its light at certain times.

Big deal, she thought.

But the more steadily she stared . . .

It's pink, she thought. *It's bloated.*

Like her belly in the dream. Pink. Bloated.

But that was stupid. She was letting too much get to her. Everything reminded her of the dream. Her own belly felt bloated as she backed away from the window and padded to the bathroom.

She closed the door and turned on the lights. The mirror's brightness shocked her, and the sharp clarity of her nakedness. She still looked good for thirty-seven. Her skin was tight, bereft of stretch marks. *Could use some sun, though,* she realized. When was the last time she'd actually lain out in the sun? Years. Her skin was very white, creamy, which contrasted intensely with her very dark brown eyes and ashen-brown hair. Her nipples, too, were more brownish than pink, and large. She'd had little to compare herself to. There'd been occasions in college—phys ed electives—when she'd showered with other girls. Her body had always seemed more robust, her nipples larger and darker, her skin tighter and white. It pleased her to see how little her body had changed. At the firm there was a junior partner named Louise who was the same age as Ann. Once they'd shared a hotel room in Detroit during prelim litigation for an air wreck, and they'd changed together. Louise's thighs looked like bags of cottage cheese. Her breasts depended, and her belly sagged. "I'll loan you my best dress if you loan me your body," she'd said with a sullen laugh.

Ann pinched her thighs. No signs of dreaded cellulite. She pinched her tummy and came up with almost nothing in the way of excess. Maybe it was her hair that made her look younger too. It hung thick and plainly straight to her shoulders, the way she'd always worn it. The full plot of pubic hair, the same color as her hair, seemed to shine.

But suddenly, she felt adrift before the bright mirror. *Mirror,* she thought. The sensation of portent returned for no reason. Her nakedness. Her brown nipples and white skin. She closed her eyes and saw the spraddled, sweating body, the spread legs, the tight bloated belly pushing . . .

She thought of the emblem, the bizarre double circle engraved upon the dream's chalice and suspended upon the wall.

When the phone rang in the bedroom, she nearly shrieked. For a moment she could only stand there staring at the vivid image of herself in the mirror, as the phone shrilled on. *Not him again,* she pleaded. *Not the caller.*

Martin was answering it just as she opened the door. The bright bathroom light threw a block into the bedroom.

"It's . . . it's for you," Martin said. Sleep roughened his voice. "It's your mother."

Ann sat down on the bed's edge and took the phone.

"Mom?"

Her mother's voice sounded curt, businesslike. It sounded . . . stoic. "Ann, there's been a . . ."

"What, Mom?"

"Your father," the voice hesitated.

Oh, no. Please, no, Ann's thoughts dripped.

"Your father's had a stroke. It's bad. Dr. Heyd says he might not last the week."

As the words sank in, Ann could only stare. Through the minute slats in the window blinds, she could see the pinkened, pregnant moon.

● ● ●

In another place, two girls sat side by side in the grove. They were young. They were naked and holding hands. Wistfully, they peered up into crystal black sky.

"Heofan," one whispered.

"Give lof," whispered the other.

They had. They could taste it in their mouths, salty sweet blood.

"The wifmunuc will be happy."

"I'm happy too!"

The old pickup truck sat in darkness down the grove. So stupid the helots were. Like animals. The girls had only had to hang around the parking lot for a few minutes before they'd been approached. "Whatchoo two purdy thangs doin' standin' 'round here all by yerselfs?" the fat one had asked. "Our boyfriends left us," one of the dohtors had replied. "Can you guys give us a ride home?" "Why, shore!" offered the tall one. "Cain't have two purdy thangs like yawl hitchhikin' these dark roads all by yerselfs."

The two girls had grinned.

All four squeezed into the big bench seat. The tall one drove. He was nice-looking, long black hair, nice boots, nice smile. He cranked up Led Zeppelin. The fat one looked . . . fat. Long hair too, sideburns, flannel shirt. He looked like a redneck Meat Loaf. "We alls from Crick City," he said. "Where yawl from?"

"Lockwood," answered the young dohtor.

"This here's Gary, I'm Lee," the fat one said.

Then Gary said, "Still a bit early, though. And Lee an' me was fixin' on partyin' a little more."

Lee's chubby face grinned. "Yawl like ta join us awhile?"

"Sure," said the younger.

"The night is young," said the older.

They both grinned again in the darkness.

"We know a place we can go. Nice and quiet."

"Just lead me the way, sweetheart," Gary enthused, and cranked the Led Zep up a little more, "Houses of the Holy." Lee cracked open beers for all of them, Iron City. "Best brew ya can buy, an' only a buck ninety-nine a six!"

It had been a glorious fulluht; the girls had learned well. The younger had reveled in the look on Lee's face in the moonlight. She'd had to push his tremendous beer belly up to get on him right, though. It hadn't been easy.

"We give lof," said the younger.

"Through hūsl," finished the older.

The younger drooled, straining over the fat one's thrusting hips. The older was moaning, riding the tall one in the dirt. They were powerless now; the dohtors had taken them quick. They'd seeped into the peows' gasts like balm. The tall one hadn't even screamed when the elder dohtor sank the æsc into his heart. The younger one had plunged her own æsc delightfully in and out of the fat one's belly in time with his fervid spurts. Blood flew, painting her. She shrieked in bliss as the big, dumb body twitched between her legs.

Sated, they rose and went to work. The blood on their young flesh looked black in the beautiful moonlight. They worked hard and happily.

The older dragged their bodies back into the truck as the younger siphoned gasoline into a paegel, which she then splashed into the cab.

They sat for a time first, they always did. They liked to stretch naked beneath the moon and dream of red heofan, of the godspellere, and the coming blissful nihtloc.

Later, they dressed and collected their things. The older carried the laden bags. "See ya 'round, Gary," she said, laughing.

"Nice partyin' with ya, Lee," called the younger. She lit a pack of matches and tossed it into the cab.

The cab burst into beautiful flames, like a fek oven. Within the fire, the meat hissed and sizzled.

CHAPTER EIGHT

"I'm sorry," she said.

"Ann, it's not your fault." Martin poured coffee for her in the kitchen. He drew the curtains and let the morning sun beam in.

"I want you two to go. I'll go home by myself."

"That's ridiculous," he said. "This is an emergency, and we're a family. We'll go together."

"Melanie will be crushed," Ann said.

"Ann, Melanie will *understand*. This is your father we're talking about, and her grandfather."

Sometimes Martin was *too* understanding. Ann knew he would do everything he could to help her, to make things work, in spite of the fact that her parents never really approved of him. "A poet?" her mother had objected. "Poets don't make any money, Ann. Why do you insist on getting involved with these deadbeats?" Yes, Martin knew all about that, and still he would do everything he could to smooth things out.

"We'll go to Paris next time," he said.

Next time. When would that be? A year? Two?

Suddenly, she was crying.

Martin put his arm around her, stroked her hair.

"Every time something good happens, something bad happens," she sobbed.

"It'll be all right. There was nothing you could do."

"He's *dying*."

"Ann, just because he had a stroke doesn't mean he's dying."

"But the doctor said—"

"Come on, Ann, that old guy? He doesn't know a stethoscope from a periscope. The best thing we could do is get your father out of that town and into a real hospital."

It would never happen, Ann knew. Her parents believed in fate, not CAT scanners and ICUs.

"We better start getting ready," Martin said.

As Ann rose, Melanie traipsed into the kitchen. "What time are we—" She stopped, looked at them, hesitated. "What's wrong?"

Ann and Martin hesitated in return. Ann looked up at Martin in panic. The look said, *Please tell her, Martin. I can't. I just can't.*

Martin understood at once. "Melanie, we're not going to be able to go to Paris this time," he began. "Something bad happened yesterday . . ."

"Tharp's escaped. Erik Tharp—remember him?"

Sergeant Tom Byron just stood there, mouth open.

Chief Bard sipped coffee from a spider-cracked NRA mug. "Fucker busted out of the Rubber Ramada yesterday. Can you believe it?"

"Erik Tharp," Byron said. "Escaped."

"That's right, boy. State's saturated the whole area with their units, and they want all municipal departments on watch. He busted out with a rapist, killed four people already, two hospital people, old Farley from the Qwik-Stop out on 154, and some redneck broad from Luntville. Raped the stuffing out of the broad before they killed her. And they got a piece. State M.E. says he pulled a .455 out of the girl's ass, Farley's Webley."

"Erik . . . Tharp," Byron repeated. The name put him in a daze. He remembered, all right. The pit full of tiny charred skeletons, and Tharp himself poised in moonlight with the shovel.

Bard had no lap when he sat down. He sipped more coffee and winced. "They're driving old Farley's Plymouth—the station wagon—you've seen it."

At last Sergeant Byron regained his ability to speak polysyllabically. "You figure he's comin' back here, Chief?"

"State says there's no way in hell. Probably headed north, they said."

"Tharp ain't got a set brass enough to come back here."

Bard frowned. What could he say to Byron? He was pretty much just a kid.

"I should've killed him five years ago," Byron muttered.

Yeah, you should have, Bard thought. Instead, he said, "Don't wanna hear no talk like that, boy. We're professionals.

With that, Bard scratched his belly and spat in the waste can.

"Lemme go lookin', Chief. I'll drive my own car. Just lemme—"

"Forget it. You mind your manners unless you wanna take old Farley's place for five bucks an hour at the Qwik-Stop, ya hear?"

Byron, reluctantly, nodded.

"LW-One,"squawked the base station. "Citizen report of signal 5F two miles south of junction 154 and Old Dunwich. M.E. en route. Check for possible relation to state signal fifty-five slash twelve in progress."

"LW-One, ten-four," Bard groaned into the mike.

Byron stared.

"Get on it, boy," Bard said, and stood up exertedly. "Maybe Tharp's closer than the state thinks."

We look like idiots, Erik thought, glaring at the mirror.

"Jesus," Duke murmured, standing aside.

They'd cut their hair short, in efforts to get with the times. Instead, they looked like they'd stuck their heads in blenders. The hair bleach hadn't worked very well either. Erik had followed the instructions, or at least he thought he had. It turned their hair almost snow white.

Duke slapped the back of Erik's head. "Ya a-hole, look whatcha done."

"It's not that bad," Erik tried to commiserate.

"Not that bad? Man, we can't walk the street like this. We look like a couple of rejects from some California homo farm." Duke glared at Erik, then stomped out of the bathroom.

At least we don't look like our file pictures, Erik thought. That much was correct. The hospital updated their ward-residence photos every year. The police probably wouldn't be looking for two guys with *white* hair.

Duke slouched on the bed. He was watching the Three Stooges: Shemp was pumping Larry up with a fireplace bellows stuck in his mouth. Erik changed the channel.

"Hey, man! Whataya think you're doin? It's a Shemp!"

Shemp, Erik thought. *We're two killers trying to outrun the entire state, and all he cares about is Shemp.* "We have to monitor the news as much as we can," his voice creaked. He flipped through late-morning cartoons, then—

—froze. Suddenly, he was looking at *himself* on the TV screen, and a newscaster was saying, ". . . have killed four in less than twenty-four hours. Erik Tharp and Richard 'Duke' Belluxi escaped the state mental facility near Luntville yesterday morning at eleven-thirty, overpowering two employees and murdering two more. They fled the grounds in a lawn contractor's vehicle which was later found abandoned at a nearby convenience store, where they murdered a clerk and abducted a twenty-year-old Luntville woman only minutes after their escape. The woman, whose name is being withheld, was found dead later that afternoon in a ditch off State Route 154. She'd been shot, beaten, and raped, police say."

Duke chortled laughter, pointing. "Looky! It's us!"

Indeed it was. Both their faces filled the screen. Duke was grinning in his picture. Erik stared.

"Yeah, my mama, I'll bet she's proud!" Duke laughed. "Can tell all her friends her son's a TV star!"

"Come on!" Erik shouted. "We gotta get out of—"

"What are you shittin' a brick about?"

"They found the girl's body, Duke. That means they know what kind of car we're driving!"

The station wagon was parked right out in front of the motel, in full view from the main road. The first cop car that drove by would see it and then . . .

"Get our stuff together," Erik commanded. "I'm gonna move the car around back so no one can see it from the road. We'll have to leave on foot, get a new car somewhere else."

"Right," Duke said.

Erik slipped out the front door and got in the station wagon. How long had the police known what they were driving? It was incredible that the car hadn't been seen yet.

Too incredible.

Something clicked behind his ear.

"Right there, fella," a voice whispered.

Erik's whole body seized.

The female cop had sneaked up alongside the car. She leaned over, pressing the barrel of a Ruger .357 to his temple. "You blink and your brains go out the other side of your head. Understand?"

"Uh, yes," Erik croaked. His eyes darted right. A police cruiser was parked on the side of the last room. "Luntville Police Department," a seal read.

The woman had dark red hair tied in a bun behind her hat. She wore mirrored sunglasses in which Erik could see twins of his own face. "You and me," she whispered, "we're gonna walk over to that squad car nice and quiet, right?"

"Uh, yes," Erik croaked.

"You get out real slow and keep your hands up."

The woman opened the station wagon door. She kept her gun trained on him. It was a big gun, but then Erik thought of Duke's, which was even bigger. Right now, Duke was doing one of two things. He'd either crawled out the bathroom window and was heading for the hills, or he was standing behind that tacky louvered motel room door and lining up the sights of the gun he'd taken off the old man at the Qwik-Stop.

Erik stood straight, his hands in the air. He whispered, "Lady, the other guy's in the room right in front of us and he's got a—"

It was a strange collision of sounds and sights crammed into a single second. The woman's police hat shot up in the air, and suddenly she was standing before Erik with no head. It simply . . . disappeared. Only then did Erik hear the loud *bang*! The woman, headless now, seemed to stand for a moment, her pistol still thrust out. Then the body collapsed.

Erik's expression collapsed as well. He lowered his arms. *More blood on my hands,* he thought.

"Ooooo-eee!" Duke celebrated. He'd fired through the louvers. "Perfect head shot, man, fifteen, maybe twenty feet!"

Duke loped out, the Webley still smoking. He picked up the policewoman's hat and put it on, laughing.

My God, Erik thought.

"Get the stuff," he said, "and move the cop's body into the room. I'm moving the car."

Duke whistled gaily, dragging the body toward the room. "S'shame, though, you know? Wasted a perfectly good set of tits. Could've had me a good ol' time with this girlfuzz."

Erik parked the station wagon behind the motel. Then he jogged back around to see what was keeping Duke.

Duke was sitting in the passenger side of the woman's patrol car. He adjusted the hat on his head and looked up, grinning.

"Come on, buddy. We might as well ride in style, right? I'll ride shotgun."

By now Erik had resigned to Duke's sociopathy. He had no choice. He started the car and tromped the accelerator. Duke wailed.

Luntville was just north. Erik sped south. The cop had probably radioed in her location when she'd spotted the station wagon. When she didn't answer up, her friends would come looking.

Duke looked like a kid in a candy shop, surveying the car's interior. Erik's mind raced. "We've probably got five minutes before they're onto us. When they find the cop you killed, there'll be a hundred cars after us." Erik turned off the main road, fishtailing. The further off the main roads they got, the more time they'd have to change cars. He remembered the area well. The back roads were a maze. "We have to ditch this car and get a new one real fast."

"Why? I like this car," Duke complained. He tore open a pack of Twinkies. "How come we gotta change cars all the time?"

"Don't you understand anything? As long as they know what we're driving, we don't stand a chance. We need a car that nobody knows we're in."

And that prospect worried him. Taking a car meant taking (or killing) the owner. Erik didn't want any more people dead, but he knew Duke had other ideas in that regard. *How can I control an uncontrollable person?* he grimly asked himself.

The mobile radio, a plug-in Motorola, began jabbering. Then, much more clearly, a woman's voice broke: "Two-zero-eight?"

Erik stuck his head out the window. The front fender bore the stencil: 208. "That's us," he croaked.

"Two-zero-eight, do you copy?"

Duke gaped at him, cheeks stuffed.

"Two-zero-eight, acknowledge."

"Give it a shot," Erik advised. "We've got nothing to lose except our lives, and we'll probably lose those anyway."

"Think positive, buddy." Duke pointed to his own head. "Positive, that's the way. How do you work this thing?"

"Just pick it up and push the button when you want to talk."

Duke keyed the mike. "This is two-zero-eight. Go ahead."

"Two-zero-eight, what's your status?"

"A-okay. Everything's just fine."

Erik was shaking his head.

The radio fizzed through a pause. "Two-zero-eight, are you ten-eight?"

"That's a roger. I'm the big ten-eight." He released the button and chuckled. "What the fuck's ten-eight?"

"I don't know," Erik said. "What do I look like? Adam 12?"

Duke laughed.

"Two-zero-eight, do you want a disregard on that possible fifty-five?"

"Yeah, sure, gimme a disregard. Why not?"

Another fizzy pause. Then: "Two-zero-eight, state your ID number."

Duke looked at Erik. They both shrugged.

"Two-zero-eight, identify yourself by name and ID."

"This is bad boy Duke Belluxi, baby!" Duke wailed into the mike. "'I am your friendly neighborhood walkin' and talkin' schizo-affective paranoid schizophrenic. And sittin' right by my side is Captain Erik Tharp of the Starship *Psychopath*. We boldly go where no escaped mental patients have gone before, oooooo-doggie!"

"Jesus," the dispatcher muttered. "Two-zero-eight, please put the unit's officer on the line."

"Oh, you mean that pretty redheaded girlfuzz? Well, she can't talk right now on account of she seems to have misplaced her mouth. Oh, and do me a favor, okay? Shag my balls."

Suddenly, a wave of voices panicked over the transmission. "Thirteen, thirteen! Officer down at Gein's Motel!" Others shouted in the background. "She's dead! The motherfuckers killed her!" "Check the back!" "Harley, get the gas gun!" "Holy fucking—" "The car, the motherfuckers took her car!" "Jesus Christ, they blew off her—"

"Head," Duke finished into the mike.

"This is two-one-two to dispatch. Officer is shot and killed. No sign of unit two-zero-eight. Repeat, unit two-zero-eight is *missing*."

Duke made pig noises in the microphone. Then he stuck the mike between his legs and farted. "How about all you pigs out there go fuck each other, and lick my crack too, while you're at it, just like all your mamas do to me every night. Catch me if you can, piggies! Oink oink oink!"

The dispatcher was yelling over the air: "Ten-three! All units ten-three! Ten-three, ten-three, ten-three!"

A crystal-clear silence filled the void, which seemed antici-patory and vivid. Then: "Duke Belluxi, Erik Tharp, this is Chief Lawrence Mulligan of the Luntville Police Department." The slight drawl sounded easy, almost chummy. "I want you boys to come to your senses. Give it up. Give us your location."

"We're at your mama's house, Chief. Where'd you think?" Duke said, then made some more pig noises. "Looks like we're going to have to wait, though. See, there's a big line going all the way around the house, starting at the bedroom. Course, good poon like your mama's is always worth waitin' for, don't ya think?"

"I want you fellas to know that every available state and local police car in this county is heading your way from every direc-tion. You got a world of hurt bearin' down on your asses, boys."

Duke bubbled laughter. "Say, Chief, your wife's the one with the really big titties who blows every guy in town for free, ain't she? Think maybe she'd tongue my balls if I asked her nice?"

All this time during Duke's profane fun, Erik had been fish-tailing deeper and deeper into the back roads.

"You're askin' for serious trouble, boys," Mulligan was say-ing. "You don't want my men to catch ya on the run. Now be reasonable."

"Shag my balls, Chief," Duke answered. "How's that for rea-sonable? Say, I heard your daughters do the football team. That true?"

"Listen to me, son. It's goddamn impossible for you all to get away. Pull that car over right now, give us your location, and give yourselves up. You all have my personal guarantee that you won't be harmed."

"I got a better idea, Chief." Duke chuckled. "You give me your *mama's* location, and I'll give you *my* personal guarantee that I'll diddle her poon like your daddy never dreamed."

Duke then repeated his rendition of pig noises into the micro-phone.

Erik turned off the radio.

"Say, buddy, you're whippin' this car around these turns like a regular Mariano Mandetti." Duke dug into some more Twinkies, and burped. "And how do you like that no-dick chief? Thinks we're just gonna give up, just like that. Fuckers would kill us in less time than it takes me to shake the piss off my pecker."

Duke had that right, however uneloquently. Most cops down here thought the U.S. Constitution was a ship from the War of 1812. They'd shoot first and ask questions next month.

The network of back roads would hide them for a while but not forever. Unless they got an inconspicuous car, it was only a matter of time before somebody spotted them.

"We need a new car," he said. "Now."

"Way out here in the sticks, there ain't nothing," Duke observed. "We need a shopping center, grocery store, something like that."

"I don't think there are any this far in."

Abruptly, Duke peered forward. "Well, looky there."

Erik saw it.

"Tell me God ain't on our side," Duke said.

The road wound down through the woods. Up ahead was a one-lane truss bridge which crossed a deep creek.

Parked off the side was a white van.

It was one of those custom jobs, cursive pinstriping, multiple coats of lacquer, Keystone mags. And lower, a guy and a girl sat at the creekside with fishing rods.

"We're taking them with us, Duke, right? You're not going to kill them, right?"

"No sweat, buddy. I swear on my daddy's grave. From here on I don't kill nobody."

Erik pulled over. The two kids looked up the crest. Duke fiddled with some switches until the flashing red and blues popped on. "This is the police," he barked out the window. "You two get on up here."

The girl looked questioningly to her boyfriend. She wore white shorts, flip-flops, and a maroon bikini top. The guy wore overalls. They both looked in their late teens.

"Come on, come on, I ain't got all day."

They rose and began to move forward. Duke fiddled with the LECCO on the console, which secured a Remington 870P. The lock was designed to prevent unauthorized removal of the weapon when the officer was out of the car and the keys weren't in the ignition. Unfortunately, now the keys *were* in the ignition, and all it took was the press of a little button to remove the shotgun. Duke promptly racked a round of 12-gauge into the chamber.

"Duke—"

"Don't worry, buddy. I ain't gonna kill 'em. But we sure as shit ain't gonna get their van by pointing our fingers at 'em."

The two kids loped up the hill, approached the passenger side.

"Whuh-what seems to be th-the problem, sir?" the guy asked.

"The problem is this, son," Duke explained. "We're not really cops, we're escaped mental patients. And we need a new set of wheels real bad." He stuck the shotgun out the window, aiming at the kid's head. "Now, that van there, it looks mighty nice."

The girl's face paled instantly. A light yellow wet spot appeared at the crotch of her pretty white shorts.

"Please don't kill us," the boy pleaded.

"Relax, kid. Just throw me the keys."

"The keys are in it, sir."

"Why, that's just *daaaaaandy*, son," Duke falsettoed, then squeezed the Remington's trigger.

The boy's head blew to pulpy bits. A plop of brains splashed in the creek.

"God*damn* it, Duke!" Erik shouted, and pounded the dash. "You promised you wouldn't!"

Duke grinned. "That's right, buddy. I swore on my daddy's grave. Thing is, my daddy ain't dead."

The girl had fainted right away. The boy lay splayed on his back, his arms extended. He looked like a headless referee signaling a touchdown.

"Get them both in the van," Erik said, now weary with disgust.

Duke stuffed the last Twinkie in his face and got out. He threw their things in the van as Erik pulled the patrol car as deeply into the woods as he could. Then he checked the trunk. A box contained shotgun and pistol cartridges, a Second Chance bulletproof vest, several flashlights, and some flares. Erik took the whole box and put it in the van.

"Hurry up!" he shouted.

Duke scratched his head over the fallen boy, whose own head was gone from the jaw up. A few cerebral arteries hung like scraps from what was left of the ruptured cranial vault. "Can't

we leave the dude?" Duke asked. "Seems silly to drive around
with a dead fella."

Erik jumped in the van and started it up. "Duke, how many
times do I have to tell you? When we leave bodies, we leave
clues. If the cops find a body, they'll ID it, run the name through
MVA, and then they'll know what we're driving. Drag 'em both
in here and let's get going!"

Duke complied, hauling the kid to the van by overall straps.
He paused to chuckle. "That's the third head I blowed off since
we been out. Think that's some sort of record? Three blowed-
off heads in a day?"

"Come on!"

Duke dumped the boy in back, then dragged over the unconscious girl and did the same. He slammed the rear doors closed.

Erik backed the van up, shifted, and took off down the road.
He headed south.

Eleven minutes later, two Luntville units and a state police
pursuit car, heading south on Governor Bridge road, slammed
on their brakes in succession, just past the old truss bridge by
the fishing dell. They'd all seen it at once, the rear end of a patrol car sticking out of the woods. The car bore the stencil along
the back fender: 208.

At first it looked like it might've crashed. This prospect
pleased one of the officers very much. His name was Lawrence
Mulligan, chief of the Luntville Police Department. Yes, it
looked like they'd been driving too fast over the bridge, lost
control, and plowed into the woods. *Aw, please, God, let it be
so. Let 'em be sittin' in front with their heads busted open.*

But God, today, would not be so obliging to Chief Lawrence
Mulligan.

The three cops approached the still vehicle with their weapons drawn. The state had an AR-15A2, which he kept trained on
unit 208's back window. A Luntville PFC edged in toward the
passenger side, while Chief Mulligan squeezed through trees
toward the driver's side.

"Careful, Chief," warned the PFC. "They might still be in
there."

Please still be in there, Chief Mulligan fairly prayed. It was a
misguided prayer to begin with. One does not generally pray
with a 10mm Colt automatic in one's hand. Nevertheless, Chief

Mulligan prayed again, aloud this time: "Aw, please, please still be in there."

The eloped mental patients were not in there.

All that remained to reward Chief Mulligan for his efforts was a quick note scribbled on the back of a standard traffic complaint and citation form.

The note read: *Shag my balls, Chief.*

CHAPTER NINE

The vast forest belt rose toward the county's northern line. They cruised down long, straight two-lane hardtops, passing endless tracts of newly tilled soil. The air was filled with fecund scents, which seemed alien to Ann. She was used to smog. The hour-and-a-half drive seemed to transpose worlds. Ann had almost forgotten what the country was like.

Some vacation, she thought.

Melanie sat quietly in the back, reading Kafka. Martin drove. Ann could imagine his reservations. It was never easy for him. He would always be a city person to her parents, a cosmopolite. *Strangers in a strange land,* she mused. But wasn't the same true of her? She'd been born and raised out here, a product of the same sensibilities, but she'd turned her back on those sensibilities without thinking twice. It *was* a transposition of worlds, one of which she felt no part.

"Is Grandpa going to die?" Melanie asked.

Ann couldn't fathom a response. Melanie was old enough now that she needed to be leveled with. It had been easy when she was younger; the innocence of children could be taken advantage of when life turned grim. *Where's Daddy?* she'd asked when Mark had left. *He had to go away for a while,* was all Ann needed to say. *He'll be back sometime.* As Melanie grew older, she put the pieces together herself. But this?

"He had a stroke," Martin said. "Sometimes strokes can be very serious, and sometimes they're not. We'll have to wait and see."

Martin always had answers for the unanswerable.

The last neck of the drive took them down State Route 154, the county's only main line to the web of tiny townships which rimmed the northern belt. Oddly, there seemed to be a lot of police out today, when ordinarily she wouldn't see any. She saw cars from Luntville, Crick City, Tylersville, Waynesville. She couldn't figure what all these cars would be doing so far out of their jurisdictions. Lockwood had its own department too, one of the smallest. They only had two full-time cops, Chief Bard and some kid named Byron, and one car, which was another oddity. Lockwood's small population did not generate much in the way of municipal funds, yet the town council insisted on a police department, and no one objected. It was Ann's mother who headed the town council, an elected post. No one had ever run against her, and that, too, seemed strange. "Lockwood is crime free," Ann had once observed. "That's why we must have a police department," her mother had replied. "To keep it that way. You'll find out all about crime once you get to the big city."

Everything her mother said seemed to possess some level of insult. Ann couldn't remember her ever being different.

"What's this?" Martin queried, slowing down.

"Prepare to stop," read signs propped up on the shoulder. Stubs of road flares had burned down. *Roadblock,* Ann instinctively thought. But it wasn't a drunk-trap. State police pursuit cars sat facing each way at the point, their motors running. Cops of various townships stood alertly along the shoulder and examined each vehicle which slowed before the point. Many had the thumb snaps of their holsters open, others openly grasped shotguns.

Melanie leaned between them as Martin pulled up to the point. The vehicle ahead of them was being searched.

"This doesn't look right," Martin said, and lit a cigarette.

Police to either side stared into their car as they waited. One's gun hand hovered over his holster.

"Today must be National Terrorize Citizens Day," Ann said. "I hope they don't think they're going to search *our* car."

"Don't start a fuss," Martin advised. "We'll just cooperate and be on our way that much sooner."

Cooperate, my ass, Ann thought. *This isn't Iran.*

They waved the pickup through. Martin pulled up.

"Is there a problem?" he asked.

A short, portly cop leaned over their window, his hand on the butt of his service pistol. "Sorry about the inconvenience. We need to look things over real quick."

"What you need to look at first," Ann suggested, "is the state annotated code. Check Chapter VII, paragraph 7:1, 'Predispositions Pursuant to Unlawful Vehicular Search.' You also might want to take a look at the Fourth Amendment of the United States Constitution. Ever heard of it?"

The cop squinted. He was bald, with a short mustache that looked like a brush in a gun-cleaning kit. "I know you, don't I?" he questioned. "Yeah, you're Josh Slavik's daughter, right? The lawyer?"

Great, she thought. She recognized him now—Chief Bard. *What the hell is Bard doing running roadblocks ten miles out of Lockwood?* "Hello, Chief Bard," she said.

"Well, I'll be," he replied, smiling.

"We've just come up from the city," Martin offered.

"Oh, yeah, I guess on account of Josh," Bard realized.

"Have you seen him?" Ann asked.

"Well, no, but your mom told me it was a stroke, they think. Happened real sudden. I see your mom quite a bit."

Of course he did; she ran the town council, which ran the police. "What's with the roadblock?" she asked next.

Bard's frown seemed to shrivel his face. "Couple of crazies escaped the state hospital yesterday. Bastards moved so fast they got through our net. We're checking everybody coming in and out just to be on the safe side. One of them's from Lockwood, but you probably don't remember him; he came along several years after you moved. Erik Tharp."

Erik. Tharp. It was a name she slightly recalled. She remembered her mother telling her about it years ago. A drifter, a substance-abuser. Something about him burying bodies off the town limits. Several of the bodies had been children, babies.

"Trouble is, like I said," Bard went on, "they moved real quick and changed cars a couple of times before we could get a fix on them. We just missed nailing them earlier today. Damn shame too. They killed a cop."

Christ, Ann thought. *No wonder every cop in the area is out.*

"Well, you all go on now," Bard bid. "Give your mom my regards. I'll be stopping by later to see how Josh is doing."

"Thanks, Chief." Ann waved.

Martin pulled through the point. "How do you know him?" he asked.

"I don't, really. My mom hired him when the old chief died.

That was years after I moved out of Lockwood. I talked to him a few times in the past when I'd come home to visit my parents. He keeps a low profile. Not much use for a police department in Lockwood."

"Until today," Melanie suggested. "Escaped lunatics!"

Ann thought of a lot of things when they entered town. None of them were good. Lockwood was a splotch, a bad meld of memory: her frustrated childhood, social isolation, her mother's dominance and her father's passivity. Her past felt like a shadow she was about to reenter. She felt suddenly sullen.

The town looked equally sullen. It looked deserted. Martin idled the Mustang down Pickman Avenue, Lockwood's main drag. Almost everything here had been built a hundred years ago, refurbished since. A little brick fire station, the police station alongside. A general store, a diner called Joe's. Most of the economy here was agricultural; the men either worked the vast corn and soybean fields to the south, marketed farm supplies, or serviced tractors. Lockwood had always seemed to do better than the surrounding townships. There was no poverty and, hence, no drugs and no crime. It was almost idyllic.

Almost, Ann thought. Lockwood was isolated, remote. At times it seemed untouched by the modern world, and that's the way everyone wanted it. There was a curfew for minors, and town ordinances against package liquor sales. The only place a person could get a drink in this town was a dusty little tavern called the Crossroads. Kids had a dress code for school. More ordinances prohibited late-night convenience stores, bowling alleys, arcades, and the like. "As a community, we must strive to resist debilitating attractions for our youth," her mother had proposed before the town council years and years ago. Motels were prohibited too. Outsiders were not encouraged to visit.

"What's the matter?" Martin asked.

Ann's thoughts had been adrift. "Just . . . thinking," she answered. Did she blame her parents for her constrained childhood, or the town itself? Lockwood seemed to emanate repression. Here it was, early afternoon, and the town looked dead. Kids should be out playing, housewives should be out shopping. There should be traffic, activity, etc., typical things of any small town. But there was none of that here.

"Where is everybody?" Melanie asked. "Aren't the kids here on spring break too?"

"In Lockwood?" Martin chuckled. "Who knows? They probably have a town ordinance now against children."

"It's not that bad," Ann said. "Just . . . different."

"Yeah, different. I'm surprised we haven't passed a horse and buggy."

The end of Pickman Avenue formed the large town square. Here was the old, steepled white church that Ann had never attended, and the town hall. Beyond that all that could be seen was the vast rise of the forest belt, which kept the town dark till midafternoon.

"Oh, yeah, and there's probably an ordinance against sunlight too," Martin said. "This place has always been creepy, but never like this."

Martin was right. They hadn't seen a single person yet.

He turned left onto Lockhaven Road. The residential section extended from here past the old middle school. The town possessed fewer than five hundred people; dark, narrow streets led past modest homes, mostly one floor, which all seemed to be white with dark trim, and big trees in the yards. More trees lined the streets, adding to the queer darkness. The entire town seemed to brood.

"Which one is it?" Martin asked.

"Turn here," she instructed. It had been so long even Ann wasn't sure. The narrow road seemed to rise. "Ah, here," Martin said. He turned onto Blake Court and stopped.

"Jesus."

The long cul-de-sac was filled with cars.

"Looks like half the town's here," Melanie said.

They're all at the house, Ann thought without knowing why. But what would bring so many people here?

A long drive led to the Slavik house. It was the largest house in town, large and gabled on a big lot full of trees. Very little of the house's original brick could be seen, covered by sheets of crawling ivy.

Martin pulled up next to her parents' old Fleetwood and parked. He sat a minute, peering out, and stubbed his cigarette in the ashtray.

"This is bizarre," he said.

Melanie leaned forward. "Mom, how come—"

"I don't know, honey," she said, but she was thinking, *Maybe Dad's already died.* What else could explain the crowd of vehicles?

The cast of Martin's face indicated he had similar thoughts. Instead, he just said, "Let's go."

Walking up, Ann thought the rest of the town must be jealous. The house was old but well kept. The spacious yard and topiary were meticulously maintained. Ann knew her father had never made lots of money working farmland, and her mother accepted no pay for running the town council. The town had incorporated itself years ago; the farmland to the south was not privately but collectively owned, which was common in these parts. The profits were shared, yet Ann couldn't imagine that they were significant. How did this town maintain itself? Moreover, how did her parents? All towns had their share of poor and wealthy. Everybody here seemed to be the same, save for the Slaviks.

The silence weighed her down. They approached the house, saying nothing, and ludicrously paused at the porticoed front door. Nothing could be heard within, yet she saw subtle movements past the narrow windows. Like people standing around.

Like a funeral reception, she had to think.

Her hand locked in midair. That door knocker always rasped her eye—a small oval of dull, old brass in the shape of a face. But the face was bereft of features, save for two, wide empty eyes. There was no mouth, no nose, no jawline really—just the eyes.

That's what bothered her—it always had. The eyes, though ominous, seemed somehow to welcome her.

"I'm sure you've all heard about it by now," Dr. Greene supposed. He sat at his big ugly gray metal desk, eating a Chunky. He had very short blond hair and was built like a fireplug, which never quite helped him look the part. He was chief of Psychiatric Services at the state mental hospital. A welter of psychiatric paraphernalia filled his office: Smith, Klein, and French calenders, Stelazine paperweights, a desk set advertising Lily pharmaceuticals. He drank juice out of a Haldol coffee cup and wrote with a pen that read "Xanax (alprazolam) 0.5mg tabs. Use it first!" He got all the stuff free from drug reps. These guys were like car salesmen, hyping themselves over the competition. Large orders often promised paid vacations. Dr. Greene didn't want vacations in return for providing drugs that frequently turned human beings into docile dayroom potatoes. But he did like the pens and coffee cups. "Serious elopement yesterday," he said.

Dr. Harold sat down. "How many?"

"Two."

"Not bad."

"Not good," Greene countered. "They killed two people before they even got off the grounds. Today they killed a municipal cop."

"What are their profiles?"

Dr. Harold, though a successful private practitioner, did free consulting and in-patient profile evaluation on the side. Many private doctors did this as a gesture of professional goodwill. The state hospitals were overcrowded and understaffed, some to the breaking point. Dr. Harold offered his services a few hours per week to allow state staff to tend to more essential duties.

Greene took another bite of his Chunky. "First we got Richard 'Duke' Belluxi. Thirty-five years old, I.Q. 113. Stage sociopath. They got him on a rapo fifteen years ago, but we know he did a lot more. We Amytaled the son of a bitch and figure he killed at least half a dozen people in his late teens, all sexually motivated. LH levels out the roof, this guy would fuck a brick wall if there was a hole in it. He did about ten years here before we gave him a roam status."

"Why isn't he in prison?"

Greene laughed without smiling. "He Gansered his way in. Made up a detailed delusion and stuck to it, then started doing the word salad for the court. You know how the judges are in this state. The guy raped a sixteen-year-old girl and cut off her arms for kicks, and the judge makes Belluxi look like the victim. Tell that to the girl—she lived. Anyway, we were stuck with him. A decade went by and he never caused much trouble, just mouthing off, a few confrontations with some techs. ACLU lawyer said he was going to sue the hospital if we didn't give Belluxi some GB status. Said we were violating the guy's rights. The way I see it his rights went out the window when he chopped off that girl's arms, but you know how that is. Bet those grapeheads would sing a different tune if it was *their* daughters that Belluxi was cutting up."

"Like Kojak says: 'The system stinks, baby, but there ain't a better one.' "

"Sure."

"Who's the second elopement?"

"Tharp, Erik, twenty-nine, I.Q. 137, but he doesn't do much on the diagnostics. A drug burnout. Never a problem. Been in almost five years. We gave him Class II last week. We figure he's calling the shots, and Belluxi's the muscle."

"What did he do?"

Greene put his feet up on the desk, sighed. "We're not sure. He got caught burying bodies, but there was never any evidence that he killed anyone. He's no killer, you can see that. But there was a big to-do because a lot of the bodies were kids and babies. So they sent him to us."

"Diagnosis?"

"Unipolar depression. We put him on Elavil and he evened out. He was delusional and probably hallucinotic when we first got him. Read his story, it's wild." Dr. Greene pointed to a big leather bag on the floor. "It's all there."

"What can I do to help?" Dr. Harold inquired.

"Update the evaluations, augment them. Look for anything we might've missed; it would help if we could figure out where these guys are going. After twenty-four hours the stats for reapprehension go into the ground. Try to have something for me soon; I need something to show the state mental hygiene board, and right now I'm too busy with the cops and the press."

Dr. Harold nodded and rose.

This should be some very interesting reading, he thought.

The bag was very heavy.

"Why . . . is it—Ann?" asked the astonished face at the door.

"Hello, Mrs. Gargan," Ann greeted.

"Come in, come in," the woman hurried. "I almost didn't recognize you at first. It's been so long."

"Yes, it has."

Ann, Martin, and Melanie entered the dark half-paneled foyer. At once, familiarity struck home, and memory. This was the house she grew up in. It never changed. The same old paintings were on the walls, the same carpets on the floor. The same

grandfather clock she remembered tolling in the wee hours as a
child. The moment seemed surreal. She was not merely stepping into her parents' house, she was stepping back into her
past. Ann felt instantly morose.

"Melanie! How are you, child?" Mrs. Gargan leaned over
and gave Melanie a big kiss. "Look how big you've gotten, and
how beautiful!"

"Melanie, you remember Mrs. Gargan."

"Hi," Melanie said, a bit stunned by the sudden gush of affec-
tion.

"And this is Martin White," Ann introduced.

Mrs. Gargan had been a close friend of the family's for as
long as Ann could remember. She was in her fifties but didn't
look it; she beamed good health and didn't have a single gray
hair. Her husband, Sam, ran the farm supply store on Pickman,
which served the entire town. They were nice people, if not a bit
weird—Sam, like a lot of the men in town, seemed withdrawn
against his wife's popularity and outgoing demeanor.

Just like my father, Ann thought.

Though Mrs. Gargan tried not to show it, her enthusiasm
hitched down a bit upon introduction to Martin. "Oh, yes, you
must be the poet," she said. "We've heard lots about you."

"Very nice to meet you," Martin said.

Ann lowered her voice. "How's Dad?" she asked.

But Mrs. Gargan turned. Had she ignored the question deliberately? "Everybody, Ann Slavik and her daughter are here."

Dim lights glowed in the large colonial dining room. Cold
cuts, cheese, and the like had been spread out on the table,
around which at least a dozen people stood quietly conversing.
The room went dead silent when she entered. Suddenly, she saw
them all as they looked when she was younger. Mrs. Heyd, the
town doctor's wife. The Crolls and the Trotters. Mrs. Virasak,
whose husband had been Lockwood's police chief until he'd
died several years back. In fact, there were many widows here,
whose now-dead husbands Ann ghostily remembered. These
were staunch, robust women, conservative, and polite with an
edge, and who looked good for their ages. Several younger
women—Ann's age, she guessed—stood in the background,
with what seemed attendant daughters. Ann had indeed lost
touch; the more she looked around, the more she took note of

people she didn't know at all. No, she didn't know many of them. So why did she have the gut feeling that they knew her?

They went through the round of grueling introductions. The elders constantly fussed over her and Melanie, yet all but ignored Martin. All the while Ann felt like wilting. These people. This place. Her father sick upstairs. Perhaps he had already died—that would explain this bizarre scene, but certainly someone would've told her by now.

"Your mother's upstairs, dear, with Josh," Mrs. Croll said.

"She'll be down presently," added Mrs. Virasak.

This was frustrating, cryptic. Ann still didn't quite know what was going on. She took Mrs. Gargan aside. "How's my father? How bad is it?"

The woman stalled but maintained her cordial smile. "He's resting," she said. "He's—"

"Is he even conscious?"

"Well, sometimes. We'll go up when you're ready."

But that was it: Ann didn't know if she was ready. She felt threatened by *images*. The image of her father as she'd always known him, and the image of what he must look like now: bedridden, sallow.

Abruptly, then, Mrs. Gargan hugged her. "Oh, Ann, it's so good to see you. I'm just so sorry it has to be under these circumstances."

Ann stiffened in the embrace. For her whole life she'd felt distanced by the townspeople, and now it seemed like a homecoming. More images crashed.

Again, the room fell silent. Ann turned.

A figure stood in the entry. A solid figure, unflinching like a chess piece. She was sixty but looked forty-five, well bosomed, shining dark hair pinned in a bun. Fine lines embellished rather than depreciated her face. That face, like this house, the town—like everything here—hadn't seemed to have changed at all. Stoic touched with kindness. Hard and compassionate at the same time.

The figure stepped into the dining room.

"Hello, Mother," Ann said.

CHAPTER TEN

💧

"Women sure are noisy sons of guns, ain't they?" Duke chuckled.

Erik remained numb in the driver's seat. They'd parked on an old abandoned logging road, figuring they'd wait out the heat; the police probably didn't even know this road existed. This, however, left them with time on their hands, and Duke Belluxi was never one to waste time.

The girl screamed and screamed.

She'd fainted after Duke had blown her boyfriend's head off, but she'd come to real fast when Duke had pried off one of her long, shiny-painted fingernails with a pair of Craftsman pliers he found in the toolbox. She'd lurched awake, screaming. "Sleep tight?" Duke asked, and began tearing off her scant clothes. Little as she was, though, she put up a formidable objection to Duke's plans, clawing, slapping, trying to bite, so Duke clunked her in the head a couple of times with an empty Corona bottle to take some of the zing out of her. By now Erik knew the futility of trying to intervene—the guns were all in back with Duke. Now all the girl could do was moan and churn a little. Duke spraddled her out right on top of her dead boyfriend and began raping her at once. "Some bed, huh, honey?" he said, chuckling. Erik had no desire to watch this, yet every so often something—guilt perhaps—forced him to take a glance. "Oh yeah, oh yeah," Duke was going. When the missionary position lost its thrill, he flipped her over and began to sodomize her. She jerked into full consciousness again and vomited. "Aw, shit, girl!" Duke objected, thrusting. "Look what you done! Puked all over our nice van!" Soon the girl started screaming again, in gusts, so Duke gave her another clunk with the Corona. "Simmer down, sweetheart," he advised, then laughed.

He pushed her face down into her dead boyfriend's crotch. "Give your honey a nice big kiss from Duke!" Then he yanked her head back by her hair, stepping up his thrusts. Erik stared blankly out the windshield.

This cannot go on, the thought hammered in his mind. Once Duke got going, he was beyond reason, beyond control. He was on a killing spree, and it was Erik's fault. He had to do . . . something.

He glanced in back again. The Remington and the Webley lay beside the real wheel hump. *No way I can get to them,* Erik realized. The box of stuff they'd taken out of the Luntville car was reachable but useless. All it contained were a few boxes of shotgun shells, some road flares, and the bulletproof vest— nothing he could use to fight Duke. *I'm going to have to kill him,* he reasoned. *But I've got to get to those guns.*

"Aw, come on, Duke!" he yelled when he saw what his associate was doing.

Duke chortled like a farm hog, grunting. His orgasm was obvious, spurting into the air and onto the girl's back as he slowly strangled her with a battery cable. Duke wiped himself off with her panties, laughing. "Thanks, baby. Hope it was as good for you as it was for me."

Erik just stared—at this monster he'd helped escape.

Again, he thought: *Yeah, I'm going to have to kill him.*

"Hey, partner, we got any more of them Twinkies?" Duke asked.

The Lockwood police station was a small brick extension of the fire station on Pickman Avenue. It had two holding cells, an office for Chief Bard, whose only window offered a resplendent view of the garbage dumpster in back, and an anteroom where they kept their files and supplies.

Sergeant Tom Byron trudged into the office. He was a young big brawny kid, and a good cop. Now, though, he looked pale, disgusted.

"Where the hell have you been?" Bard asked. "I could've used some help out on the state roadblock."

"I was on that 5F, remember?" Byron sat down, sighed. "You sent me on it."

"That was hours ago."

"Took the damn M.E. that long to get out there. I had to se-

cure the scene and wait. Unless you want me to leave two
cooked bodies sittin' in a pickup truck."

Bard set down his coffee. "What do you mean . . . cooked?"

"They was burned up, Chief. Somebody iced these two
fellas, doused 'em with gas, and lit 'em up. Right on the town
line, past Croll's fields."

"Lockwood residents?"

"Naw, two guys from the other side of the line. Gary
Lexington and Lee More, both twenty-five. No rap sheets, no
trouble."

"How were they killed?"

"M.E. don't know yet. It was hard to tell anything by lookin'
at 'em, burned as they were. They was naked, though, clothes
throwed in after. Ready for the best part?"

Bard gazed at him.

"M.E. said some of their organs were gone. Someone gutted
these fellas, then torched 'em. Ready for more?"

Bard nodded, though he thought he already had a good idea.

"Fellas' heads were busted open. Brains were gone."

Bard opened his proverbial small-town police chief desk
drawer. He removed two glasses and a bottle of Maker's Mark.
He poured them each a shot.

"I know you're thinkin' what I'm thinkin', Chief. Heads
busted open. Brains gone. Shee-it."

Bard tossed back his shot, smirked, and nodded. But what
could he say? What could he tell him?

"Just like some of the bodies we caught Tharp buryin' five
years ago," Byron finished. He threw back his Maker's and put
his glass back up for another.

"How have you been, Mom?" Ann asked.

She followed her mother up the heavily banistered staircase.
On the landing wall hung a mirror which had always scared her
as a child—at night she'd come up the stairs to find herself
waiting for her.

"Thoughtful of you to ask," her mother replied.

Here we go, Ann thought.

"It's absolutely disgraceful that you've seen fit to completely
ig—"

"Mom, please. I didn't come here to fight."

"I'm surprised you came at all. We haven't heard from you in six months—we thought you'd written us off altogether."

"Damn it, Mom. Just stop it, would you?"

The headache was already flaring. This happened every time; they'd tear at each other until there was nothing left. Almost twenty years now, and the only bind that remained constant between them was bitterness, scorn.

"I came here to see Dad, not to argue with you."

"Fine," her mother said. "Fine."

Down the hall, another lane of memory.

"I suppose you'll stick your head in, look at him, and then be off again, back to your ever-important job in the city."

Ann felt her nails dig into her palm. "I'm off all next week."

"Oh, a week, a whole entire week. I suppose we should feel privileged here in lowly Lockwood, that the prodigal daughter has graced us with a full week of her cherished time in order to spend it with her family, one member of whom is dying."

Ann's teeth ground together. Her jaw clenched. *No,* she thought. *I will not fight with her. I . . . will . . . not.*

They'd set up a convalescent bed in the end spare room. The shades were drawn; pale yellow lamplight cut wedges in the room. From a corner chair, a stout man rose in a baggy suit. He was bald on top, with tufts of salt-and-pepper hair jutting from the sides like wings, and a bushy goatee. This was the man who'd delivered Melanie on that stormy night, and the same man who'd brought Ann into the world through her mother's womb. Dr. Ashby Heyd.

He smiled warmly and offered his hand. "Ann. I'm so glad you could come."

"Hello, Dr. Heyd." But Ann's attention was already being pricked at, dragged toward the high bed. Antiseptic scents blended with the musk of the old house. The room seemed stiflingly warm. Inverted bottles on a stand depended IV lines to the still form on the bed.

Ann looked down at her father.

It scarcely looked like him. The vision crushed her, as expected. Joshua Slavik's face had thinned, leaving his mouth open to a slit. His eyes were closed, and one forearm had been secured to a board, needles taped into blue veins large as earthworms.

"He's borderline comatose, I'm afraid. A massive cerebral hemorrhage."

Ann felt desolate looking down. Her father barely seemed to be breathing; Ann had to fight back tears. Even in her worst moment, or during her mother's worst tirades, Joshua Slavik had always had a smile for her, a simple encouragement, the slightest note of hope to help her feel better. He'd given her his love, but what had she given him in return?

Abandonment, she answered.

"He looks so peaceful," her mother remarked.

Ann snapped. "Jesus Christ, Mom! You're talking like he's already dead! He's not *dead*! You've even got this whole goddamn house full of people like it's some kind of goddamn funeral home!"

Dr. Heyd took a step back. Her mother's face went dark.

"We've got to get him to a hospital," Ann went on. "He should be in an ICU, not lying in this stuffy crypt. What kind of care can he get here?"

"Dr. Heyd is perfectly capable of—"

Ann rolled her eyes. "Dr. Heyd's just a small-town general practitioner. He delivers babies and treats sore throats, for God's sake. We need a neurologist, we need a CAT scan and an intensive-care facility. We're taking him to a hospital right now."

"I forbid it," her mother said.

Dr. Heyd stepped in, "Ann, what you don't understand is—"

"All I understand is my father's dying and nobody's doing shit about it!" Ann yelled at both of them. "And if you think you can forbid me from taking my own father to a proper hospital facility, then you better think again. You may run this ridiculous little backward town but you're not the law. I'll go straight to the state probate judge and file a petition for guardianship. The court will appoint me guardian ad litem, and there'll be nothing you can do about it. I might even—"

"Why not sue me while you're at it, Ann?" her mother suggested. "Sue me for mental anguish. That's what lawyers do, isn't it? Sue people? And you'd do it too, I know you would, Ann. You'd sue your own mother."

Ann caught herself. Her mother and Dr. Heyd exchanged silent glances. Ann stared, more at herself than them. *What am I saying?* she thought.

Her father groaned once, lurched and twitched a few times.

"Are you happy now?" her mother asked. "Look what you've done, you've upset him. Haven't you upset him enough in your life? You'll even upset him on his deathbed."

Ann wished she could melt into the wall. For that moment she'd felt completely out of control of herself.

"This is a disgrace," her mother said, and left the room.

Dr. Heyd followed her. He quietly closed the door behind him.

Ann sat down. Her outburst left her limp, jointless. Her gaze returned to her father. She seemed to be looking at him from miles away, or through a fish-eye lens.

"I'm sorry, Dad," she muttered.

He lay still. The flesh on his thin face seemed translucent, sagging into the crags of his skull. Then he moved.

Ann leaned forward, held her breath.

Very slowly, her father's right arm lifted. His hand turned, and his index finger extended feebly.

Shakily, and only for a second, the finger pointed directly at her.

The house was emptying when she came back down. Visitors smiled curtly, bid subtle goodbyes, and left. A few teenage girls were picking up the dining room, putting things away. Martin stood alone in the corner, his arms crossed.

"We could hear you yelling all the way down here," he said.

Ann sulked.

"I know it's not easy for you, Ann. But it's not easy for your mother either. It's not exactly sincere to threaten your own mother with legal action when her husband's dying in the same room. You're going to have to get a grip on yourself."

"I know," she said. "I'm sorry."

"Don't tell me." Martin lit a cigarette and frowned at his cup of punch. "She went out back with Melanie. Dr. Heyd's in the kitchen, I think."

Ann nodded. She shuffled into the kitchen. Dr. Heyd was hanging up the phone.

"Dr. Heyd . . . I'm very sorry about the things I said to you. I don't know what came over me. I didn't mean—"

"No apology necessary, Ann," he said. "This is a difficult time for everyone; I know what you must be going through. But you must realize the facts. The symptoms are undeniable. Your father suffered a massive orbital hemorrhage. Regrettably, no medical technology in the world can help him. There's little anyone can do except try to make him as comfortable as possible. Your mother thinks it best that he stay here, closest to the ones he loves, in familiar surroundings."

Dr. Heyd's politeness, and his reason, made Ann feel even worse. *What a shitheel I am,* she thought. "How much time does he have? Do you think he'll linger on like that for very long?"

"Highly unlikely. A stroke of this magnitude generally produces the same result. It's a large hemorrhage. The hemorrhage will systematically clot, dispersing particles of coagulation into the major cerebral blood vessels. I'd say a week at the very most, though he could go at any time."

Ann looked down at the floor. "Is there anything I can do?"

"Simply being here is the best thing you can do for him. And for your mother."

Ann sighed quietly. *Shitheel, shitheel, shitheel.*

"He'll be under constant supervision. I'll be checking on him several times a day, and there'll be a nurse 'round the clock. Do you remember Millicent Godwin? She's several years younger than you, I believe."

The name seemed familiar. *High school,* she thought.

"She's a registered nurse now," Dr. Heyd explained. "She'll be staying at the house, to look after Josh when I'm not here. You needn't worry. She's quite qualified."

"I can't thank you enough for all you've done, Dr. Heyd. And, again, I'm very sorry about—"

"Think nothing of it, Ann." He smiled and grabbed his bag. "I've got a house call to make right now, but I'll see you soon."

The doctor left. Ann craved a drink after all this, but then she remembered liquor was not kept in the house. She looked out the kitchen window. Large, gnarled trees kept the spacious backyard in shadow. Beyond the kiosk, Melanie could be seen walking through the grass with Ann's mother.

CHAPTER ELEVEN

The top line read: THARP, ERIK.

The second line read: ADMITTANCE STATUS: NGRI.

And the third line: DIAGNOSIS: Acute Schizo-affective Schizophrenia.

The standard form, Statement of Clinical Status, was dated five years ago.

PHYSICAL STATUS: The admittee is a 25-year-old white male. Build within ectomorphic range, 69 inches, 121 pounds.

BOARD EVALUATION, INITIAL: The patient was oriented, alert, and coherent. His motor behavior was unremarkable, his speech deliberate and monotone. His facial expression showed sadness, and he described his mood as ". . . tired, but I'm relieved to finally be away from them." His thought processes seemed clear though there were clear paranoid ideations. Somatic complaints included difficulty in getting to sleep and morbid dreams. The patient appeared to have a high I.Q., though his recent, past, and immediate recall was clearly impaired.

NARRATIVE SYNOPSIS: Admittee is subject to bizarre delusions highly sexual and subservient in nature. Admits to extensive CDS use during late teens and early twenties, though denies any such use within the past two years. Board concludes likelihood of PCP-related receptor damage, which could explain delusion-fixe and hallucinotic inferences. MMPI results indicate overly concrete abstract association and reduced multimodal creative assembly. No paranoic or delusional tendencies, however, via MMPI results, which is curious. Patient demonstrated above average scores on Muller-Urban diagnostic, which is puzzling given the nature and detail of delusions. TAT recommended prior to med therapy. Narcosynthesis is advised.

For the next hour, Dr. Harold read the narrative summation of
Erik Tharp's madness. The hospital board had evaluated him
yearly. The last three narratives were fairly dull; Tharp denied
the delusion outright, claimed to no longer be bothered by his
nightmares, and dismissed all that had happened to him as
"Craziness, I must have been crazy," he told Dr. Greene. "I
can't believe that I believed those things, if you know what I
mean." *Lying,* Greene had written in the comments section of
the evaluation form. *Still believes delusion, just not admitting it
anymore.* But why would Tharp do that?

To qualify for roam status? Dr. Harold thought.

Of course, and to eventually—

"Escape," he muttered.

It was obvious. Tharp had been planning his escape for some
time.

Dr. Harold ruminated. Five years ago Erik Tharp had believed a disturbing delusion. So thereafter he lied, hoping
Greene would think he was no longer possessed by the delusion
and hence give him roam status.

His premeditation, even though it hadn't fooled Greene,
proved something very clear. Tharp had a preconceived motive
for his elopement. He wasn't escaping just to escape. He wanted
to escape in order to do something specific. But what?

Why had Erik Tharp denied his own delusion after one year?
The problem was, delusional people weren't able to do that unless they weren't delusional in the first place.

*There's something on the outside that he feels he needs to do.
Whatever it is, it involves the original delusion, and the original
delusion involves the place of his original crime.*

At once, he dialed Dr. Greene. "I have some impressions for
you," he said. "I don't think Tharp and Belluxi have fled the
state, nor do I believe they plan to. I think they're heading for
the immediate area surrounding Tharp's crime scene."

"Because Tharp's not cured of the demon thing even though
he pretended to be?" Greene postulated.

"Yes."

"You think the delusion is still important to him?"

"Very important. It's the sole motive for the elopement."

"Okay, I'll go along with that. What else?"

"Tharp will abandon Belluxi as soon as possible."

"Because he doesn't need Belluxi anymore, right?"

"Right. Tharp only needed Belluxi to get off the ward, and he's probably regretting it right now. Tharp isn't homicidal—my guess is Belluxi's the one doing all the killing, and Tharp doesn't want any part of that. Tharp's MMPIs indicate a high order of morality."

"We're talking about a guy who buried babies. Morality?"

"Sure. Tharp didn't kill anyone, he just buried the bodies. But he may kill Belluxi in order to prevent more murders. That's my guess anyway. However crude, Tharp's TATs reveal highly focused guilt assemblies and even ethics. Plus, now Belluxi is baggage to Tharp. For every minute that Belluxi is with him, Tharp's goals are jeopardized."

"What do you think his goals are?" Dr. Greene asked.

"That's anybody's guess. Tharp believes in demons, so who knows? But you know what bothers me more than anything else?"

Dr. Greene laughed. "Tharp's pathologically obsessed with a delusion but he's not pathological."

"Exactly. And that makes me wonder."

Dr. Greene maintained his laughter. "Let me guess. You consider the existence of demons as a possible reality?"

"No, but maybe the *base* of Tharp's belief is real."

"The cult, you mean?"

"Why not? I just read in *Time* that there are over a hundred fifty *incorporated* devil-worship cults in the United States. I for one don't believe in the devil, but I can't deny the reality that there are cults that worship him."

"That's an interesting point," Greene remarked. "Maybe Tharp really did belong to some crackpot cult."

"And if that's the case, you just answered your own question. Tharp is motivated by a delusion. The delusion is motivated by a cult. Therefore—"

"That's what he's returning to," Greene considered. "A cult. There was never an investigation because the state NGRI'd him almost immediately. The state attorney's office was satisfied that Tharp perpetrated the murders."

"At least it's something for the police to go on," Dr. Harold pointed out.

"I'm going to give them a call right now. Maybe you're right, and even if you're not, so what?"

"That's the fun of clinical psychiatry, isn't it?"

"Actually, I'm only in it for the free pens and coffee cups . . . Yeah, I think I'll tell the cops to keep a real close eye on Tharp's hometown."

"Where is Tharp from, by the way?"

"A little town about twenty miles north of the hospital. Lockwood."

Lockwood, Dr. Harold pondered. What a coincidence. Hadn't Ann Slavik said she was from a town called Lockwood?

"I don't know," Ann said. "It's just that your grandmother and I don't always get along. We don't always see things the same way."

"Like you and me?" Melanie responded.

What a comeback, Ann thought. But it was proof of her innocence—the simple way in which she perceived the truth and how she associated it to herself. "Everybody has disagreements, honey. We'll work it out, we always do."

How honest a reply was that? In a sense, she knew she had never worked anything out with her mother. Adversity was their only common denominator. Ann Slavik had become everything in life that her mother opposed.

You're afraid of becoming your mother, Dr. Harold's voice haunted her again. Had she really been repressing Melanie's perceptions all these years, by condemning her alternativism, by objecting to her friends? It was times like this that Ann wondered if she had any business being a mother at all. She would have to try harder, she knew, much harder, to give her daughter the conceptual freedom that she herself had never been allowed to have.

Melanie would be staying in the last bedroom on the east wing. It had been Ann's room as a child. When she'd left home after high school, her mother had changed it as much as she could, "To turn it into a guest room," she'd said, but Ann knew better. Back then her mother had felt so betrayed she'd gone out of her way to remove all reminders of Ann—a subconscious punishment. She'd gotten rid of all the furniture, and all of her things she'd left behind. She'd even changed the carpet and the wallpaper.

Ann looked out the same window she'd ruminated through so many times as a child. The backyard dimmed in early dusk. How many times had she peered through this same glass in complete misery, contemplating a future that did not include this place at all?

"Can I see Grandpa now?" Melanie asked.

"Let's wait. He's not conscious very often, and he's probably very tired." The truth was Ann was afraid. She didn't know how to prepare Melanie for the still figure in the room at the other end of the house. Sometimes the facts of life included the facts of death. "Tomorrow, maybe," she said.

Melanie seemed sullen. She loved her grandparents. She didn't understand, but maybe that was the problem. Ann had never taken the time to explain the real world to her daughter. Melanie had been left to interpret it herself.

"I'm going for a walk," Melanie said. When Ann turned, her daughter was stripped down to her underwear and was pulling on jeans.

"I don't know, Melanie. It's getting late."

"This isn't exactly New York, Mom," Melanie observed. "I doubt if there are any drug dealers or rapists around. You think?"

Ann frowned. She couldn't very well blame Melanie for her sarcasm. *She's had a great teacher,* she thought. "Just don't stay out too late, all right?"

"I'm only going for a walk, Mom. I'm not going to join the circus." Melanie pulled on a T-shirt that read "Cherry Red Records," then she grabbed her Walkman. "Why don't you come with me?"

Ann hesitated. "No, you go, honey. I'm going to straighten up our room."

"Okay. Bye."

Ann went down the hall to the room she and Martin had. It was on the other side of the house, across from her father's room. Again, it was little things that bothered her, insignificant things. She didn't want Melanie out by herself. She didn't want Melanie to see her father in his present condition. She didn't even like the idea of Melanie's room being so far from her and Martin's.

Now she felt isolated. Martin had gone out earlier. "I need some air," he'd said. "I'm going for a drive." Now Ann wished he and Melanie had gone to Paris without her; this scene was a dice of strained proximities and discomfort. It was a family matter surrounding a family that had never accepted Martin and had never been sufficiently exposed to Melanie by Ann's own devices.

There was no sign of her mother at all. Where could she be at this hour? Perhaps Ann and her father were the only ones in the house. Down the carpeted hall, a slice of light glimmered. Dr. Heyd said that her father would have a nurse. But no one could be found when Ann stuck her head into the cramped, warmly lit room.

Only her father lay there, swaddled in covers.

He shouldn't be here alone, she thought, but then she heard something downstairs.

In the kitchen, a figure leaned over the refrigerator, a plainly attractive woman about Ann's height and build dressed in traditional nurse's garb, a trim starchy white dress, white stockings, white shoes. Light brown hair had been cut short, and she looked up with very dark brown eyes.

"Hello, Ann," she said. She removed a little bottle from the refrigerator. "You probably don't remember me, but we went to high school together."

"Milly Godwin," Ann said. "Of course I remember."

"You're sort of a legend around here. You know, Local Girl Makes Good. Dr. Heyd probably told you, I'm the only RN in town. I'll be looking after your dad. Your mother put me up in the room next to his."

"I can't thank you enough for that," Ann said. "Just let me know your rates and I'll write you a check."

Milly Godwin looked slighted. She closed the refrigerator. "That won't be necessary," she said.

The offer probably offended her, Ann realized. She'd have to remember that this wasn't the city; here time was not redefined in terms of money.

"We thought it best that I stay at the house, and if there are any complications I can't handle, Dr. Heyd can be here in minutes. He has a beeper."

"Well, again, we're very grateful for your time."

"I could never even begin to repay your parents for all they've done for me. They're the most wonderful people, the whole town's in debt to them. I would never have been able to go to nursing school without their help."

What did that mean? Had her mother helped her financially? Ann thought it best not to ask.

"We're feeding him intravenously," Milly Godwin said, shaking the little bottle. "Most of the meds have to be refrigerated."

Ann followed the nurse back upstairs. In the room she proficiently injected the bottle's contents into one of the IV connections. When she looked down at Joshua Slavik, her expression remained flat.

Ann deliberately averted her eyes. It was hard for her, too, to see her father this way. *Hopeless,* she thought now.

"He comes to every now and then," Milly enthusiastically remarked. "You should try to be around as much as you can."

Ann knew what the woman was saying. The next time he comes to may be his last.

Milly could see Ann's restrained despair. "Let's let him rest now," she said, and went out. "Even though he's comatose, he shouldn't be disturbed at night. The brain continues the normal sleep cycles. Unnecessary noise and movement can disturb him."

"Is that what this is considered? A coma?"

"I realize it's a scary word, but, yes, unfortunately. I'm sure Dr. Heyd has explained . . ." The rest fell off. Ann didn't need to be retold that her father was dying.

They went back downstairs. Milly poured two iced teas and took Ann out back. Potted plants hung off the enclosure over the slate patio. Peepers thrilled gaily from the woods beyond. "This is the most beautiful house in town," Milly remarked, "and such a lovely yard. Your mother does a terrific job keeping it up."

"Where is she, by the way?"

"Board meeting. They have several per week. The town wouldn't run without your mother. It'd be like any other town."

Would that be so bad? Ann wondered. "Where do you live, Milly?"

"I have a house two blocks up from the town square. It's small but very nice."

Ann couldn't imagine that Milly made much money, not as an RN in Lockwood. How could she afford her own house? "What are mortgages like around here?" she strategically asked.

Milly looked at her as if shocked. "There are no mortgages. Lockwood is a collective incorporate. Didn't you know that?

Anyone who lives in the town contributes to the town. The town gave me the house, and my car too. For as long as I live here."

Ann winced. *Whatever happened to private enterprise?*

"Plus, the town pays me. Fifteen thousand a year." Milly Godwin beamed.

Ann's firm paid more than that in overtime for their three paralegals. "Couldn't you do a lot better somewhere else, like at a hospital. RNs start at thirty-five where I live."

"Yeah, and they also pay rent, car payments, auto insurance, health insurance, and thirty percent in taxes. Lockwood pays all that for me. It's part of the community employment plan. Besides, I wouldn't dream of leaving Lockwood."

"Why?"

"No crime, no drugs, no corruption and sleazy politics. No gangs and no half-assed education. I'd never want my daughter growing up in all that."

"Oh, you have a daughter?"

"Her name's Rena, she's fifteen."

"I have a seventeen-year-old myself," Ann said.

"I know. Melanie. She's lovely. Oh, and I didn't mean to imply that you're wrong to raise her in the city. I only meant—"

"I know," Ann said.

"We're happy here, and that's the important thing."

"Sure."

They sat down on a stone bench past the slate. "What's your husband do?" Ann asked, sipping her iced tea.

Milly Godwin laughed abruptly. "He ran out years ago."

"I hear that," Ann said. "Same thing happened to me."

"I'm not even sorry he left. Rena and I are much better off without him. The bastard left when I was eight months pregnant. This was when your mother started the community assistance program. The town took care of me, then sent me to nursing school. I don't know what I would've done if I was on my own."

Again, her mother's shadow reared. This town ran itself among itself. It breeded what it needed to exist. It perpetuated from within.

"Lockwood's New Mothers Program is really good too. If a woman gets pregnant, she doesn't work for two years but she retains her pay. After that there's free day care. There's also a retirement program, an accident program, and an education program. Lockwood takes care of it all. The town has a multimillion-dollar investment fund. Jake and Ellie Wynn are trained brokers. Lockwood's been in the black for decades."

But how could that be? How could Lockwood, with a population of five hundred, generate such a level of prosperity? The vast farmland to the south was valuable, but it must have taken some risky investments with produce profits to make all this work. Maybe Ann's mother was smarter than she thought. Nobody was really rich, yet nobody seemed to want for anything.

"I saw your man earlier," Milly said. "He seems very nice."

Your man, the words echoed. What an antiquated way to put it, yet it sounded nice. *My man,* she thought. "He's a teacher, and a published author."

"Not bad-looking either." Milly grinned. "But don't worry, I won't go gunning for him."

You fucking better not, Ann thought. "You date anyone regular?"

"Oh, no. Pretty slim pickings in Lockwood as far as single men are concerned. All the good ones get taken right away, and what's left just hang around, drink beer at the Crossroads. Your mother figured she'd let them have a watering hole at least. Every animal needs a trough."

Ann nearly spat out her iced tea. "And I thought I was a cynical feminist."

"It's not feminism," Milly said, and sat back. "I see it more as realism. What's the one thing that all the world's problems have in common? Men. Not good for much of anything except filling potholes and fixing cars when they break."

Ann couldn't help but laugh.

"Why get involved with something that's going to turn rotten anyway? After they have you, they take you for granted. Pretty soon you find out that you're married to a couch that drinks beer, watches football, and farts."

Now Ann was really laughing.

"I can live quite nicely without that," Milly went on. "And I don't need a man in my life to feel complete . . . Oh, but I didn't mean to imply that your man—"

"I know, Milly, you're just generalizing, right?"

"Right. And when I need to get laid, I get laid."

The promptitude of this comment almost stunned her.

"I mean, why mince words, you know?" Milly stood up and

traipsed into the dark yard. "It's like fruit on a tree; it's out there when you want it. Doesn't mean you have to marry the tree every time you want an apple."

Ann laughed again. "That's some metaphor."

But Millicent Godwin drifted into a sudden, sentient silence, facing the woods. Suddenly, she seemed reflective.

What was it?

Crickets and peepers echoed back their chorus.

"It's a beautiful night, isn't it?" Milly whispered.

"Yes, it is," Ann replied. She looked up into the dark. The moon seemed idled over the horizon, tiny in its ascent, and pinkish.

Milly turned slowly, surreally. In the moonlight her face looked wanton, her eyes large and clear. "Beautiful things are born on nights like these," she whispered.

Ann stared at her.

"Yes, the most lovely things."

CHAPTER TWELVE

"I ain't burying 'em. You're the expert on that, ain't you?" Duke chuckled. "How many babies did you bury anyway?"

I've got to get rid of this guy, Erik thought. His throat hurt, and he was hungry. Duke laxed back in the van's seat, chugging the last beer. "Dead man's beer sure tastes better than regular," he commented. "Something neat about it, you know."

Erik winced at the two bodies. They'd start stinking soon. There was nothing he could use for a shovel, so he dragged each of them out of the back and into the woods. Their flesh felt clammy, cool. He covered them best he could with leaves. *Rest in peace,* he thought.

"Say, buddy, I'm like really hungry, you know, like I could eat a horse," Duke despaired. "How much longer are we gonna sit here anyway? Let's go get some food, huh?"

Erik went to close the van doors. Duke had the Webley on him, and the shotgun was too far up to reach.

They'd been here all day; they'd have to move sometime. The van would only remain inconspicuous for so long— eventually, the guy and his girlfriend would be reported missing, and the police would put two and two together.

"We're moving now," Erik said, his ragged throat throbbing with each word. "I want you to ride in back so you can't be seen through the windshield."

Duke looked offended. "What's the matter? How come I can't ride up front with you?"

"Because one guy with ridiculous white hair is less conspicuous than two guys with ridiculous white hair. The cops are looking for two guys. Come on, we'll stop along the way and pick up some food."

Duke perked up. "Yeah, man! Food! Twinkies!"

Erik shook his head and started the van up. Duke climbed in back. They drove several miles without seeing a single car. Getting into Lockwood would be tough; Pickman Avenue was the only access, and it would take them straight past the police station. Either Bard or Byron—one of them—would probably be on the road. Erik would have to bypass the town and take one of the dirt roads through the woods. Then he could go in on foot.

"Here we go," Duke said. "Open twenty-four hours. Ain't that somethin'?"

The big sign glowed eerily in the night. *Great,* Erik thought. *Another Qwik-Stop.* But they were in luck; the parking lot was empty.

Erik pulled in. He wondered if Duke would take his bait. "Wait here, I'll be right back."

"Bullshit, partner. I'm going too."

"Only one of us can go, Duke. Someone's got to wait in the van in case we have to get out fast."

"You wait in the fuckin' van. I'll go. What if the guy at the counter asks you something? You can't talk with that fucked-up voice of yours."

"You're right, Duke," Erik went along. "You go. Make it quick, this isn't a shopping spree. Pick up some food and some batteries for the flashlight, D size. Get the stuff, pay for it, and leave. Don't talk to anyone, and don't start any trouble, okay?"

"Gotcha, buddy."

"I'm serious, Duke. No trouble. We can't risk it."

"Don't worry, man."

"And don't kill anybody, right?"

"Right."

"Come on, Duke. Say it. Say 'I won't kill anybody.' "

Duke's big teeth showed through his grin. "I won't kill anybody, man."

"Good. Now make it quick."

Duke got out and loped into the store. *That was easy,* Erik considered. He'd gotten Duke out of the van without so much as a hint. There was only one option. Simply driving off and abandoning Duke wouldn't be any good. For one thing, Duke would call the police immediately and notify them of Erik's destination. For another, he'd rape and kill at least a dozen more people before the police caught him. *No more innocents,* Erik promised himself. He'd never killed anyone in his life, but killing Duke would be the same as killing a rabid dog. You *have* to kill it, before it gets into the playground.

As predicted, Duke had left the shotgun in back. Erik picked it up and racked a round.

Aw, no, he suddenly thought. Headlights plowed across the lot. A big old Chevy pickup pulled in. Rebel flag in the back window. ZZ Top pumping out. Two guys in jeans and T-shirts got out, whooping it up and chewing tobacco. And they were *big* guys, really big. One's shirt emblazoned a Confederate flag and read "Try burning this flag, fucker." The other's shirt showed a Smurf giving the world the finger. Next, a skinny, pock-faced blonde slid out—cutoff jeans, flip-flops, tattoos. The three of them were rucking it up real loud, heading for the store. *Drunk rednecks,* Erik fretted. *The only thing worse than rednecks are loud, rowdy, drunk rednecks. Like them.*

And Duke didn't like rednecks.

Duke loped out just as they were about to enter the store.

"Nice hair," Smurf-shirt snickered, though he'd pronounced the word *nice* as *nass.*

Buddy, you just made the biggest mistake of your life, Erik thought.

"What was that, pal?" Duke demanded.

The three rednecks laughed. Duke stared. Erik had to admit, though, Duke *did* look ludicrous: an overweight chronic sociopath with cropped white hair and mismatched bargain-rack clothes standing in a Qwik-Stop parking lot with one arm around a grocery bag full of Twinkies and Hostess Ho-Ho's.

"Whatchoo starin' at, fat boy?" inquired Flag-shirt.

"Two redneck faggots and a titless chick with a face that looks like it got run over by an aerator. That's what I'm staring at," Duke answered.

The three rednecks could not believe this response. It was purely social common sense: talking back to big, drunk, uncultured rednecks was bad enough, but implying that they were of an alternative sexual orientation was exponentially worse.

Finally the stasis broke. Flag-shirt spat a stream of tobacco juice onto Duke's shoe.

"Doesn't bother me," Duke replied to the gesture. "It's not even my shoe. It's your daddy's. I took it out of his closet last night when I was fucking your ma. And what's that you got in your mouth? Dogshit?" Then, to the blonde: "Grow some tits, craterface."

"You cain't talk to me like that!" the blonde wailed.

"Shit, honey, I've seen sheets of plywood with more chest than you," Duke then ingratiated her. "And that face—ooo-eee! Got more nooks and crannies than a Thomas' English muffin."

"Fuck you, you fad pud! Eat shit and die!"

"Your daddy eats shit every night. When he goes down on you." Duke blurted a coarse laugh. "Know what he told me? He told me you got the biggest pussy this side of the Mississippi. Says you blow farm animals too. That true?"

"Jory! Jim-Bob!" the blonde wailed louder. "You gonna let him talk to me like that?"

Ory-eyed, Smurf-shirt stepped forward. Duke said: "Know what your mama told me last night, I mean, last night when she was shagging my balls? She says you two fellas fuck each other. That true?"

Then Flag-shirt stepped up, clenching his fist, which was about the size of a croquet ball, and probably as hard.

Duke grinned. "Is it true you blow your dad? That's what I hear. When your no-tit Swiss-cheese-for-a-face girlfriend's not blowing him, that is."

By now all Erik could do was shake his head.

Duke railed on. "You fudge-packing flower-sniffing redneck queers just gonna stand there, or are you gonna do something?"

"That's it, fat boy," said Flag-shirt.

"We'se kickin' yore fat ass," promised Smurf-shirt.

"Bust his fuckin' haid!" the blonde screamed.

Duke laughed out loud. "These two pansies? They couldn't fight their way out of kindergarten class. During naptime."

Flag-shirt rushed.

Duke was pretty good with his technique—it was almost magic. In a split second the bag of Twinkies and Ho-Ho's fell, and Duke's hand was filled with the big Webley revolver.

The three rednecks froze.

"Wah-wah-we don't want no trouble, man," Smurf-shirt stammered.

"Yeah, man," offered Flag-shirt. "We was just funnin'."

No no no no no, Erik thought.

"Funnin'," Duke iterated. "Well, I'm just funnin' too. How's this for some fun?"

Duke shot Flag-shirt square in the head, which instantaneously burst. The report concussed like a cannon shot. Brain pulp slopped on the Qwik-Stop window, besmirching a sign: "Briardale Cola! Six for $1.69!"

The girl broke. She'd managed to flee all of about a yard and a half when the second round went off. The Webley's rudely large .455 slug caught her at the base of the spine, picked her up, and dropped her. Without the support of intact vertebrae, she lay on the pavement, folded in half.

Duke seemed pleased by the effect. "Poor sweet thang," he mocked in southern drawl. "Looks lak she done blowed her last egg-suck dog, shore 'nough, huh, Jim-Bob buddy ol' boy?"

Smurf-shirt shivered, splaying his hands. "Look, man, I got money an' all. Nice truck there too. Take it. Just don't kill me."

"Well, that's mighty generous of you," Duke responded. "Answer me a question first, okay?"

"Sure, man."

"Do you have balls?"

Smurf-shirt looked cruxed. "Huh?"

"Do-you-have-*balls*?" Duke repeated more slowly.

"Well, yeah . . . shore."

Duke fired the Webley into the guy's crotch. "Not anymore!" he celebrated. Smurf collapsed, bellowing and clutching his groin, which now gushed blood quite liberally. Duke laughed all the way back into the store. The clerk was picking up the phone. "Shag my balls!" came the familiar prefix. Another round went off. The clerk's head exploded.

"Damn if I ain't good!" he railed when he came back outside. "You see that shot!" he said to Erik. But Erik lowered his head to the wheel, lamenting. Duke fired another round into Smurf-shirt's head, to finish him off. Then he did the moon walk, guffawing, over to the blonde, who still twitched folded in half. He shot her in the face.

"Goddamn it, Duke!" Erik yelled out the window. "You said you wouldn't kill anybody this time!"

"I didn't," Duke defended himself. "I didn't kill anybody. I killed *everybody*!" Then he threw back his head and laughed.

Erik's hands felt clammy on the shotgun. It felt hot in his lap. Duke took his time extracting the wallets from the pockets of jeans which now clothed dead men. Then he picked up the bag and came back to the van.

"Relax," he said. "No one left to tell the tale." But then he opened the passenger door. His gaze locked down on the shotgun, which Erik raised to chest level.

"Why, you cocksucking fairy faggot turncoat motherf—"

Ba-BAM! Erik replied.

The 12-gauge spray socked into Duke's chest. The massive muzzle flash lit the van like lightning. Duke flew back and landed flat on his back. Erik racked another round and fired again into Duke's torso. Then again, and again.

"Sorry, Duke," he muttered.

Then he drove off and headed down the dark road.

Erik was a fairly intelligent person. He was also more observant than most. Tonight, though, his vigilance slipped. Earlier he'd noted that the box they'd taken from the Luntville police car contained road flares, ammunition, and sundry supplies. It had also contained a Second Chance brand bulletproof vest.

Erik didn't notice that the vest was now missing.

CHAPTER THIRTEEN

❦❦❦

The sign blazed tackily in blue neon: Crossroads. The writer in Martin mused over the name's allegorical possibilities. Dust eddied up from the wood floor's seams; the door creaked closed behind him. Yes, here was a real "slice of life" sort of bar: a dump. Its frowziness—its rough wood-slat walls, old linoleum floor, and wear-worn pool table—its overall *vacuus spiritum*—piqued him. This was not exactly the bar at the Hyatt-Regency.

But a beer would go good now, as long as it was a decent beer.

Martin walked up. Only three other patrons graced these eloquent confines, roughened working-class types, dusty from a day in the fields. No women could be found. An ancient black-and-white TV sported a ball game with the sound low. Martin was glad to see that the Yankees were showing the Orioles it was a long way back to Baltimore.

He waited at the bar. No one seemed to notice him. An inveterate beer snob, he doubted that the Crossroads stocked anything more refined than Carling. The giant barkeep was ignoring him, sipping a mug of draft as he watched the game.

"Excuse me," Martin interjected.

The keep frowned, and without taking his eyes off the game, said, "You want somethin'?"

An odd reply. "Well, yeah. I'd like a beer."

"No beer tonight," the keep replied. "Just blew the last keg."

Talk about the bum's rush, Martin thought. "What's that you and those guys are drinking? Kickapoo Joy Juice?"

"Yeah, home. That's what it is."

"Fine. I'll take one."

"Sorry. Just ran out of that too."

Just leave, Martin thought. That would be the wise thing to

111

do. But when he wanted a beer, he *wanted* a beer. Why were these guys giving him the business? "What is this? I gotta dress black-tie to get served in this pit?"

Now the keep looked at him. He set down his beer and came over.

The three other guys at the bar stood up.

"Listen, home, and listen good. You want trouble, you'll get more 'n you can handle."

"I don't want trouble," Martin groaned. *"I just want a beer."*

"We don't serve to outsiders here. If ya don't live in Lockwood, ya don't drink at the 'Roads."

"This has been one pleasant visit," Martin said. "You guys want to kick my ass because I walk into a bar and order a beer. If I want to fill my car at the gas station, they gonna kick my ass too?"

The keep gave him a high look. "You're visiting Lockwood, huh? And just who might you be visiting?"

"The Slaviks," Martin began, but then he thought, *To hell with it.* He got up to leave.

"Hold up there, buddy," one of the guys at the bar said.

And the keep: "You're that writer fella. Gonna marry Ann, Josh and Kath Slavik's girl."

"That's right," Martin told him. "How the hell do you know—"

"Come on back, home," the keep invited. "Just that we've had some trouble with outsiders. This here's Wally Bitner, Bill Eberhart, and Dave Kromer."

Martin didn't quite know how to gauge this sudden change of attitude. *What the hell's going on?* "I'm Martin—"

"Martin White, that right?" Dave Kromer said.

"You're some kind of writer, huh?" Bill Whateverhis-namewas added.

First they're practically booting me out the door, now they know my name, Martin pondered.

"Yeah, we've heard about ya," the keep said. "From Kath and Josh. You kind of help Ann out with Melanie, on account of Ann's lawyer job, right?"

"Uh, yeah," Martin said. He wondered what else Ann's mother had said about him. Probably nothing good. "We came up from the city today, to see Ann's dad."

They all nodded glumly. "Damn shame, it is," Wally Whoever bid. "Josh is a great guy."

"And Doc Heyd," added the keep, "he says there's not much
hope. Poor guy. We'll all sure miss the hell out of him."

This was not cheerful talk. Before Martin could shift subjects, they did it for him. "Name's Andre, by the way. Any
friend of the Slaviks' is a friend of ours. You drinking beer or
hard stuff?"

"Uh, beer," Martin faltered. Now came the dreaded question
of any beer snob in a place like this. "Do you have any imports?"

"Nope. No imports. No domestics either."

What else is there? Martin thought.

"We got LL," the keep said.

"That's one even I've never heard of."

"Lockwood Lager. Can't get any fresher—I make it right
here, right in back."

A local microbrew, Martin thought. This was unique. In a
place like this he'd have expected the cheapest, and worst.
"Pour me one," he said.

"No bullshit here either," Andre said. "I grow my own hops
and barley. Age each keg about sixty days. And I won't sell to
the other towns—let 'em have their piss. I make our own vodka,
scotch, and gin too."

Andre set the mug down. Martin reached for his wallet, but
Andre put his big hand up. "No way, friend. That there's a tin
roof."

"A tin roof?"

"Yeah, man. It's on the house."

Andre and his three locals broke out laughing.

Martin took a sniff and a sip. A full, robust taste, very malty
without being sweet or overpowering. "My compliments to the
brewmaster. This is great. You ought to bottle it, you'd make a
killing."

"Not my speed," Andre said. "Ann's mom, Kath, you probably know she's kinda like the mayor here, and none too keen on
alcohol. That's why there's no package store in town. I been
brewin' fifteen kegs a month for the last fifteen years. That does
us just fine."

This beer really was good; Martin was amazed. A brewmaster of Andre's skill could become a millionaire in today's U.S.

microbrew market. In the back, Martin noticed wooden, not aluminum, kegs, and an ice line instead of a keg cooler. When it came to authenticity, Andre didn't fool around.

"Yeah, Ann, she's a great gal," Andre went on. "I knowed her kind of when she was growing up. Real smart."

Wally Whatever offered, "She's a real legend around here. Most Lockwood gals, they stick home. We're all rootin' for Ann out there in the big city."

"Hope things work out for yawl," added Bill Whateverhis-fuckingnamewas.

"Thanks," Martin said. He continued to survey the bar as he drank. There was no falseness here: this was a place where the working class came to drink when they were done in the fields. There were no Bud Light clocks, no Beefeater coasters, and none of the phony bar eclecticism found in the city. The Crossroads was . . . *real*. Just a roof, some stools, and a bar. Martin didn't even notice a cash register in the place.

Andre looked about fifty but in good shape; in fact, all of them did—physicalities and demeanors honed by lifetimes of hard, honest work. Andre wore jeans, a black T-shirt, and a buck on his belt. He had wiry hair and a big friendly face, but a *hardness* about him too, like you could sock a 20-sledge right into his barrel chest, and all it would do was piss him off. Martin set aside his first impression. He liked this place, and he liked these people.

"You guys all from around here?" he asked.

"Aw, no," Andre answered. "We all just kind of found our ways here, and Kath, she gave us a break. Me, I had a little trouble down South"—he chuckled—"so Kath, bless her, she gives me the job right off, and a place to live to boot. Same story for all of us pretty much. Bill here, he does engine work, and Wally runs a thresher."

This was odd, though. Martin couldn't figure it. If they'd been local, that would be different—localities were adhesive. But why would men like this, with serviceable skills, *come* to a town like Lockwood? The farmland was small, and Martin doubted that Bill Whateverhisnamewas was fixing more tractors here than he could in a big farm belt.

"I work for Micah Crimm," the guy named Dave said. He laughed. "He's the fire chief, and I'm the fire department. Hang around awhile, the rest of the boys'll be in shortly. We've all been wantin' to meet ya."

"I will," Martin accepted. He finished his LL, and Andre poured him another. "I haven't even been here a day, and already I'm starting to really like this town of yours."

Melanie strolled the outer residential streets. This was so different from the city. Quiet, peaceful. The woods ran opposite Hastings Street; she could hear crickets, a sound like waves. Small, neat houses stood off the road; a few even sat up in the woods. There was no traffic, no commotion, just tranquil twilight.

Melanie couldn't picture herself ever living here; it was too far away from things. But she liked visiting, she liked the change. Melanie never really understood why her mother didn't like to bring her here. Lockwood was almost like a different world.

"Hi. You're Melanie, right?"

Melanie stopped. At first she didn't even see who'd said it. What were they doing there, standing in the dark?

"Yeah. How did you know?"

"We've heard all about you," came another, younger voice. "You're the Slaviks' granddaughter."

The darkness at the edge of the woods seemed misty. The two girls looked like slowly forming ghosts. "My name's Wendlyn," one of the shapes said. "And this is Rena."

Melanie squinted.

Rena looked younger. She was willowy, slim, and nearly breastless, while Wendlyn had a bosom that made Melanie slightly jealous. They wore plain pastelish sundresses and sandals. Both had hair the same light brown as Melanie's, but Wendlyn's was short, and Rena's hung perfectly straight down past her waist.

"Your mom's a lawyer, right?"

"Yeah, she just made partner," Melanie responded, though she still didn't quite understand that. It sounded to her that partners made more money but did less work.

"Rena's mom's a nurse. She's staying at your house to look after your grandpop," Wendlyn informed. "My mom runs the general store on Pickman Avenue."

"What do your dads do?" Melanie asked.

"Mine died," Wendlyn said.

"Mine ran off," Rena said.

"So did mine, but my mom's going to marry—"

"Martin," Wendlyn cut in. "He's a novelist or something, isn't he?"

"Poet," Melanie replied. But who were these girls? She'd never met them before, yet they knew all about her. They seemed nice, though. In the city, people never went out of their way to be nice.

They began walking down the street. "What grades are you in?" Melanie inquired.

"I'm in eleventh, like you. Rena's in ninth. There aren't many girls our age in Lockwood."

"What about boys?" Melanie asked.

Both girls laughed.

"What's so funny?"

"Come on," Wendlyn cut in. She took Melanie by the hand and led her into an opening in the trees. Melanie was too startled to object. The darkness cloaked her yet somehow she could see the path's outline quite well in the starlight. Soon they led her into a cramped, moonlit grove.

"This is our place," Rena said.

"No one knows about it," Wendlyn added.

Melanie still didn't know what was going on. The two girls sat down on a log.

"Sit down. We don't bite."

Again, both girls laughed.

Melanie sat down on a log opposite them. "How come you laughed when I asked about guys?"

"There really aren't any," Wendlyn said. Rena bent over, digging at something. "Most of the men are old, married, or they just work their jobs. No one our age."

"Except Zack," Rena said.

For the third time, both girls, inexplicably, laughed.

"Come on, what's so funny?"

"Zack's nineteen. He's the janitor for the church."

"He lives there," Rena added.

What was she digging at?

"He *lives* at the church?" Melanie questioned. "What about his parents?"

"He doesn't have any. He's an orphan or something. Your

grandmother sort of adopted him, took him in. She's done that with a lot of the guys in Lockwood. Likes to help people in need."

"You'll meet Zack." Rena giggled. "You'll like him. He's hung like a horse."

"Rena!" Wendyln objected.

Melanie blushed slightly. *If she knows that, she must've . . .* She couldn't help but put two and two together. She felt odd. She'd only just met these girls, yet for some reason she did not feel too inhibited to ask the next question. "Have you ever done it with him?"

"Bunch of times," Rena admitted. "We both have. Zack's our toy."

Toy? Melanie thought.

Rena had lifted up a big flat rock. There was a hole underneath, and from the hole she had extracted a cigar box. Next, her face glowed orange for a moment—she was lighting a cigarette, or a joint.

Wendlyn passed it over. "Try some. It's leahroot."

Melanie'd never heard of it. "What, is it like pot or something?"

"No, it's an herb. It gives you a good buzz, but it doesn't make you stupid like pot. My mom grows it behind the store."

It looked like pot to Melanie, which she'd only done twice, and didn't like. Pot gave her tunnel vision and made her eat like a pig. But when the smoke wafted over, it smelled nice. It smelled sort of like cinnamon.

She took a light drag. In a moment she felt woozy, relaxed.

"See?" Wendlyn said.

"Have you ever done it?" Rena asked.

"What, this stuff? I've never even heard of it."

"No, I mean have you ever gotten laid?"

"Rena! That's none of your business," Wendlyn scolded.

"I say she hasn't."

"Rena, shut up!"

"That's all right," Melanie said, and it was. She felt good now, and she liked Wendlyn and Rena. "And to answer your question, no, I haven't."

"That's good," Rena said. "You shouldn't."

"Why?"

" 'Cause you're special," Wendlyn said.

Special? Melanie thought. What did that mean? Their comments were so odd, but just as odd, Melanie didn't care. "I could have a couple times, but I was afraid. You know, AIDS and herpes and all that."

"We don't worry about stuff like that here," Wendlyn said.

What a crazy thing to say. Were these girls stupid? She must mean they use condoms.

Melanie took another drag. Now she felt really good. The buzz titillated her. What had they called the stuff? A pleasant heat seemed to caress her chest.

"Feel it?" Rena asked.

"Yeah," Melanie said.

The moon felt cool on her face. She could not account for the beat of thoughts that next filled her mind, nor the feelings. She looked at the two girls sitting across from her. They were looking back, grinning at her in the moonlight.

"I have to go," Melanie said.

"We know," Wendlyn replied.

"My mom'll get pissed if I'm late."

"See you tomorrow, okay?"

"Sure." Melanie rushed off. She could not define her feelings. As she wended down the path, she could hear Wendlyn and Rena laughing.

CHAPTER FOURTEEN

"Dooer, dooer," croaked the voice.

Wet lips sipped from the cup. The cup looked full of blood.

Shadows hovered. Firelight flickered on the earthen walls, and she sensed a great heat.

"Dooer," she heard, and then distant, soft singing.

Women . . . singing.

The emblem, same as that upon the cup, seemed huge behind the shadows, as if suspended in the air:

The flurry of hands roved over sweating skin, stroking the tight, distended belly. Hot mouths licked off rivulets of perspiration; she felt milk being sucked from the painfully swollen breasts. Then voracious tongues trailed up her legs, up her thighs, to the radiating, wet inlet to her womb.

Her orgasm jolted her, followed by a string of smaller yet longer ones. It felt as though every inch of exposed flesh was either being caressed, licked, kneaded, or sucked. Beyond she noticed other shadows, which seemed to be men. Men, watching before a stoked fire. Forms of other figures seemed to squirm on the dirt floor, naked, coupling legs wrapped around backs, faces buried between legs.

"Dooer, dooer," she heard again as her own orgasms pulsed down and the contractions began to throb.

"Join us."

Two hands formed a basket between her legs. Squeals rose, in joy, in awe. The great, gravid belly shuddered, pulsed, shuddered, then collapsed very quickly. She felt something leaving, pushed from the womb into open air. Wet and stirring, the baby was held aloft. It began to cry at once.

The hands and mouths came away. Dozens of eyes looked up at the newborn.

The eyes were wide, glittering.

Staring up as if in reverence.

Ann churned awake. The bedroom's dark felt like a crushing weight, a blanket of hot, wet cement. She lurched up.

The clock read 4:12 A.M.

The nightmare, she thought. *Again.*

Martin snored faintly beside her. He'd come home late, enthusing about his excursion to Lockwood's only bar. "What a great bunch of guys," he's said. "You'll never meet people like that in the city. *Real* people, you know? They have their lives and they live them in their own honest way."

He rambled on happily, not drunk, just feeling good. It pleased Ann to see him so happy. It was hard for him here, she knew, in a place so different from the world he was used to, especially with the shadow of her mother's cynicism constantly over his head. "It's strange," he'd gone on. "I've been here a few times in the past, but for some reason it's different now. I wouldn't even mind living here, to be honest. I feel at peace here."

He'd made love to her when they'd gone to bed. She'd straddled him, touching herself between their hips. She'd wanted so badly to come with him, but as usual it hadn't happened. She'd had to pretend again. Thank God he didn't know.

The nightmare haunted her now. Its crisp images and vivid heat seemed to linger in the dark. When she got up, her sex tingled—the giveaway that she'd come in her sleep. How could she know so little about herself? She felt desperate without Dr. Harold. The dream's scenario always roved like a camera lens, escalating to perversion. Why? What had Melanie's birth proposed to Ann's subconscious? Rampant lesbianism. Orgies beneath the birth table. Occult undertones, and that cryptic warped double circle.

She crept out of the room and closed the door. A faint beeping unbalanced the dead silence of the house. She peeked in on her father. Milly Godwin, the nurse, had dozed off in a chair with a book in her lap. A Lifepak heart monitor blipped green, rather slowly. Her father lay still beneath the sheets.

Next, she peeked into Melanie's room at the other end of the house. Melanie's bed was empty, but a quick glance up showed her daughter standing before the high, narrow window, gazing out.

"Melanie? Are you okay?"

At first her daughter didn't respond.

"Melanie?"

She turned very slowly. Like Ann, her nightgown stuck to her from sweat. Her eyes looked glazed.

"Mother," she said.

"What, honey?"

"The moon is pink."

What had she been dreaming?

She'd been smoking that stuff with Wendlyn and Rena. Yeah, they'd been smoking that stuff—what had they called it? Leahroot?—and they'd been looking at her, and there was something about that, wasn't there? Something about the looks on their faces. Something . . . *knowing*.

Melanie knew too, but she didn't admit it to herself. How could she imagine such a thing? So she'd left abruptly, hadn't she? Yes, she left Wendlyn and Rena in their little hidden moonlit grove, and she'd gone home. She'd gone home and gone to bed.

And in bed she dreamed.

She dreamed of the little grove again. In the dream she was still there, with Wendlyn and Rena, smoking that stuff. But it hadn't been like before.

"Yeah, Zack's cock is almost ten inches," Rena was saying.

"We made him measure it once," Wendlyn came in.

Rena giggled. "Yeah, we made him play with himself till it got hard and told him to measure it. You should've seen him, Melanie, Zack standing there with his pants down, jerking himself and then holding a ruler to it. We laughed our asses off."

"Zack does anything we say," Wendlyn added. "He's such a weak idiot."

"All guys are."

"One time we came back here and there was this old droopy dog snuffling around—"

Rena was slapping her knee, laughing. "And we told Zack to do it to the dog—"

"And he did!" Wendlyn finished.

And in the dream Melanie just looked back at them. She felt neutral, observant. She was just sitting there watching them, listening to them, and riding the buzz of the stuff they smoked.

Rena was grinning. "Hot out, isn't it?"

"Yeah, it's hot," Wendlyn agreed. She was grinning too.

Melanie knew. She was not the least bit shocked when both girls skimmed their pale sundresses off. They leaned on one another and, without qualm, began touching themselves. Melanie watched them, equally without qualm. Their skin looked pure white, like a summer cloud. They both had dark brown nipples, like Melanie's. Rena's stuck out more on her tiny breasts. Wendlyn's breasts looked much bigger, and firm.

"It feels better when someone else does it," Rena said, then both girls switched hands, touching each other.

"Yeah, it feels a lot better," Wendlyn agreed. "We do it to each other a lot."

Melanie continued to watch. She felt hot herself.

Rena's long slim legs began to tense, her heels digging in the dirt, while Wendlyn sat poised with her legs spread. Moonlight bathed Rena's face. She was looking up with her eyes closed, squirming. She began to moan, and soon the moans were so loud Melanie feared the sound might carry out of the woods to the street.

When they were done, they lay back in each other's arms. Their grins subsided to soft, sated smiles.

Melanie noticed now that her own hand had found its way to her crotch. Rubbing against the tight denim. Her mouth felt dry, her heart was thrumming. She did not resist the impulse; she stood up and took off her clothes.

The moonlight was pink in her eyes. She felt out of breath, desperate for something. Now Wendlyn and Rena were sitting on either side of her. Rena grabbed Melanie's hand and placed it between her own legs. Wendlyn was kissing her nipples. They were giggling softly, stroking her, running their smooth white hands over her entire body. Between glances, Melanie noticed that they wore pendants of some kind, not chain necklaces, but thin white cords each with a thing like a little stone on the end. Rena's pendant lay flat against her little breasts. Wendlyn's swayed as she leaned over further and began to suck Melanie's large dark nipples. All the while Melanie's breath thinned as her fingers massaged the wet button of her sex.

"It feels better when someone else does it," Rena said.

"Yeah," Wendlyn said.

Rena's hand pushed Melanie's away. It did feel better, it felt a lot better. Melanie had masturbated a few times before, but it never felt like this. Rena's fingers began to rub harder, faster. Wendlyn was kneading her breasts and slipping her tongue in her mouth. It didn't take long; Rena's fingers seemed to know exactly the best way to touch her. Melanie gasped against Wendlyn's lips, and she came quite abruptly, a throbbing gust from her loins.

She lay back, slaked. "You're very special," Wendlyn whispered, her pendant swaying. All Melanie could see now was the strange pink light of the moon.

"Melanie? Are you okay?"

The dream was over.

"Melanie?" Her mother's voice.

Had she actually been standing in her sleep? When she came awake, she was standing at the window, looking out. The dream lapsed, yet the pink phosphorescence remained. She was awake now. In her room. Staring at the moon.

"Mother, the moon is pink," she said groggily.

"I know, honey," her mother was saying, urging her over to the bed. "It's a special equinox or something. It's nothing."

Melanie sat down on the bed. "God, I feel—"

"You're soaked!" her mother exclaimed.

She was. Sweat dampened her nightgown to the skin.

"Are you sure you're all right? You're not sick?"

"I'm . . . fine. It was just a nightmare."

Ann sat down next to her, pushed her damp hair off her brow. "Join the club. I had a nightmare too, as usual," she said. "Why don't you tell me about yours. Sometimes when you tell someone else your nightmare, it's not scary anymore."

God! Melanie thought. *Sure, Mom, I dreamed I made out with two girls. And I liked it.* "It was stupid," she dismissed.

"You look pale. Do you want me to get you something?"

"No thanks. I'm fine, Mom, really."

"Okay." Ann kissed her on the cheek. "Get some sleep."

"Good night, Mom."

"Good night."

Her mother left.

Melanie lay atop the covers, still perplexed by the dream. The pink moon beamed in on her. *A special equinox or something*. That's right, it was almost spring. The moonlight looked pretty, but she shivered. It reminded her of the dream. That shimmering, faint pinkness. *You're very special,* Wendlyn had said in the dream. They'd said that, too, for real, hadn't they? That she was *special*? The more she tried to forget the dream, the more vividly she remembered it. It seemed enticingly forbidden, not repulsive. She closed her eyes and saw it more lewdly. They were pretty girls, with pretty faces. She saw their breasts again, from the dream, and those odd pendants. Then she gasped.

She lay still for a moment, until she realized what must've happened. It was that stuff they'd smoked, that was it. It clouded her memory, mixed some of the dream with reality. The pendants—the little gray stones on white strings. Her hand lay between her breasts. She was awake now—the dream was over.

Yet an identical pendant hung about her own neck this very moment.

CHAPTER FIFTEEN

Sergeant Tom Byron loaded his left cheek with Skoal, then spat into a paper cup.

Chief Bard, fat behind his desk, wasn't sure about how to make the revelation. "Tharp and Belluxi shot up another Qwik-Stop last night. Killed the clerk and three stoners."

"Where?" Byron asked.

"North of Waynesville."

Byron's lips puckered. "But that's—"

"I know, it's thirty miles away from us. And those two guys burned up in their pickup were found right on our town line."

Sergeant Byron was no mental giant, but he didn't need to be told of this particular inexplicability. "That don't make no sense, Chief. The bodies we caught Tharp buryin' were burned up just like the two Crick City guys yesterday."

"Yeah, yeah, I know, and their brains were missing, and some of their organs, just like five years ago. So why would Tharp risk driving all the way back here just to go thirty miles *backward* last night to do the Qwik-Stop?"

Byron chewed and spat again. "Maybe Tharp didn't do the Qwik-Stop. Maybe it was a fluke, someone else done it."

"No way. The state just called me with the ballistics. They pulled Webley .455 slugs out of those kids last night. And that's what they ripped off of old Farley at the first Qwik-Stop."

"Ain't never heard of a Webley."

"It's a big piece, a big old British thing. Used 'em in the Boer War or some fucked-up war like that. Got more stopping power than a .44 Mag, .45, 10mm, you name it. Slug's so big, you hit a guy in the face with one, his whole head'll explode."

"And they also got the 870 from the Luntville car."

"Yeah. Ain't that grand?"

Byron sucked his wad of Skoal reflectively. "Maybe this means they're headin' away now."

No, Bard thought. *They're coming back here. That's what Tharp wants. He's just driving back and forth to keep us off his tail.* "Maybe," was all he said. "And worst thing is we got no idea what they're driving. They kill everyone who sees 'em, cops included."

Byron continued to venture. "Maybe Tharp didn't do the two guys in the pickup. Sounds crazy, shore, but maybe it was someone else."

"Don't be a moron," Bard said. "Who else would do something like that? Burn up two kids, take their *brains?*"

But that's not what Bard was thinking at all. As preposterous as the suggestion sounded, he knew too well that Byron was right.

"Any change?" Ann asked.

She stood in the kitchen, morning sunlight pouring in. It shined like glare off Dr. Heyd's bald head. "No, he's still the same. He hasn't gotten any better, but at least he hasn't gotten any worse."

That was about as hopeful a prognosis as she could ask. Milly was putting little IV bottles into the refrigerator, medication and intravenous sustenance. "He didn't stir at all last night."

"Sometimes he convulses," Dr. Heyd added.

"Why?" Ann asked.

"Really, Ann, the details would only upset you."

"Tell me," she said.

Dr. Heyd sighed. "A massive stroke causes a massive blockage, a clot. Every so often his blood pressure will break up some of the clot and he'll revive for a short time."

"But that's good, isn't it?"

"No, I'm afraid not. All it does is disperse more particles of the clot deeper into the brain, which will cause further clots and microscopic arterial ruptures. I have to be honest with you, Ann. The stroke has occluded the blood supply to a large portion of his brain. Therefore, when he is conscious, he's completely insensible."

"But he came to for a moment yesterday when I was in the room," Ann said. "He seemed to recognize me."

"Perhaps, but probably not."

Wishful thinking, she concluded.

Milly put her arm around her. "It's best not to think about the details, Ann."

"I know. I'm just worried about Melanie. I haven't taken her in to see him yet. I don't know how much of this she'll understand."

"She's almost an adult now. You'd be surprised."

"I guess I should do it soon," Ann said more softly.

"Yes," Dr. Heyd agreed. "I think that's a good idea."

Ann thanked them and left the room. It was awkward, thanking people for attending a loved one's death. Upstairs, she found Melanie's bedroom empty. She mustn't have slept well at all, and Ann could easily sympathize. *Maybe nightmares are hereditary,* she tried to joke to herself. She'd had her own nightmare again too. She knew what it was like to not be able to sleep because of a dream.

Back down the other end of the house, she heard voices. She walked up to her father's door and stopped.

". . . sometimes things seem bad to us, but they're not really bad," a voice was saying. The voice was unmistakably her mother's.

"You mean, like God?" queried Melanie's voice.

"You can think of it that way, dear. But it's more than that. Somewhere, yes, there is an overseer, that watches over us and our lives. But everything is part of something else. We are all pieces of a great plan, Melanie."

"What kind of plan?"

"It's not an easy thing to define. It's in the heart. It overrides what we are, or what we may think we are, as individuals, because there really are no individuals. We're all *part* of something that is greater than what we can ever be by ourselves. Do you understand, honey?"

"I think so."

"Everything happens for a reason."

"Is that the same as saying that God works in strange ways?"

"It's more than that, much more. It's the same as saying we're all here for a reason that's so complex, we can't possibly see it all at once. And everything that happens, happens as *part* of that reason."

Ann stood outside the door, infuriated. She did not make herself known, she only listened.

Melanie's silence reflected her confusion.

"Let me put it this way, dear," Ann's mother continued. "It's like what we were talking about yesterday. We think of death as bad. Your grandfather is dying, and we see that as bad because we love him. But it's not really bad, we only think it is because we're not capable of understanding the plan completely." Her mother's voice lowered. "People die for a reason. It's more than just a part of nature. Death isn't the end, it's a stepping-stone to a better place."

"Heaven, you mean."

"Yes, Melanie, heaven."

Ann stepped back into another room so as not to be seen. She was seething. Her anger pulsed like a headache.

"I hear you've met some new friends." Now they were out in the hall. "You go and see them now. We'll talk later."

"Okay, Grandma."

Melanie went down the stairs.

"What the *hell* are you doing?" Ann demanded when she stepped out of the room.

"Oh, good morning, Ann," her mother said. "I'm glad to see you're in your usual cheery mood."

"Where do you get off saying things like that to my daughter?"

"The poor thing is confused. Someone has to talk to her about reality, about death."

"I'm her mother," Ann reminded. "That's my job."

"Indeed it is, and just one of countless aspects of motherhood that you've conveniently neglected. Were you ever going to take her in to see him?"

"I wanted to give her some time, for God's sake!"

"Time, yes." Her mother chuckled. "You've given her seventeen years to wallow in confusion. Isn't it time you started explaining some things to her?"

"What? About *plans*? About *heaven*? Since when are you religious? You have no right to influence her spiritually."

"I have more right than you. What do you know about spirituality? You're a lawyer, remember? You're more concerned about litigation and lawsuits than your own daughter's upbringing."

Ann stormed off. She fled down the stairs and out into the backyard. She wanted to scream. She wanted to run away.

Yes, it would be nice to run, to run away from everything.

It took her hours to cool off. How could her mother have said such things?

But when the anger wore away, a grayness set in. It always did after a deliberation. Here, or in court—it didn't matter where. At the end of the confrontation, she was always left to wonder if the opposition was right.

"You'll always be at odds with her, Ann," Martin said. "I don't know why, that's between you and her. The best way to deal with it is to try to understand the reason."

"She's a contemptuous bitch! That's the reason!" Ann yelled.

"Listen to yourself," Martin said. "You're going to have to be more reasonable about this than that. You have to come to terms with your mother's bitterness, and your own—"

"My own!" she objected.

"Ann, you just referred to your mother as a contemptuous bitch. That sounds pretty bitter to me. I don't understand how you can be so cool and objective about everything, but the minute your mother's involved, you fly off the handle."

Ann seethed in the car seat.

"All I mean is that the way you and your mother deal with each other isn't working. It never has, and never will. You'll have to find another way to deal with each other."

"Yeah, how about *not* dealing with each other? That sounds good to me."

"I think that's been the problem all along, Ann."

"I can't believe you're siding with her."

"I'm not *siding* with her, Ann. She's not exactly my favorite person, you know. But it happens every time. You two can't even be in the same room without going at it like a couple of pit bulls. It's tearing you up, and it's not a good thing for Melanie to be exposed to. Someday you're going to have to resolve this, and the resolution isn't going to come from her, Ann. It's going to have to come from you. Your mother's obstinate and stubborn. She'll never change the way she perceives you. You're going to have to adapt to that."

Good Christ, she thought. How could she *adapt* to her mother's contempt? Was everyone against her?

"Just forget it for now," he suggested. "Let's go for a walk."

Ann frowned as he parked the Mustang in front of the town hall. It was a pretty day, warm but not humid. At the end of the great court, the white church loomed.

It made her think of what her mother had been telling Melanie. Why should a woman so incognizant of religion put the topic of death in such terms? And that question made her think of Dr. Harold, who'd suggested that the occult trimmings of Ann's nightmare reflected a subconscious guilt from raising Melanie in a neutral religious atmosphere.

Martin put his arm around her. "Let's get an ice cream cone."

"There's no ice cream parlor in Lockwood."

"Ah, well, it's bad for us anyway. What's that?"

Nale's, the big sign read. "It's the general store," Ann told him.

"They sell generals there?"

"Funny, Martin. Stop trying to cheer me up with bad jokes."

"Okay, how about a worse joke? How do you sneak up on celery?"

"How, Martin?"

"Stalk."

"You're right, that is worse."

The scent of spices and ginger greeted them when they entered. Nale's was more like a country gift shop than a general store. Lots of knickknacks, dolls, homemade preserves, and the like. From a long rod hung hand-dipped candles. Evidently, everything here was handmade: quilts, pot holders, utensils, even some chairs and tables. Ann remembered Mr. Nale, the nice old man who ran the store. He made his own licorice and would give all the kids a piece on their way to school.

"Would you like some ice cream?"

Ann and Martin turned. A rather short woman smiled at them from behind the counter. She was roughly pretty, sort of rustic-looking, and had thick straight brown hair to her shoulders. "I'm Maedeen," she said.

Martin laughed. "You must be psychic. We were just wondering where we could get an ice cream cone."

Maedeen opened a cooler and gave them each a vanilla scoop on sugar cones. "I make it myself," she said.

"Thank you," Ann said. "I'm—"

"Ann, and you must be Martin," Maedeen told them. "And, no, I'm not psychic. Your mother told me you'd be in town."

"Does Mr. Nale still work here?"

"No, he died several years ago. I run the store now."

Martin looked the place over. "Quaint," he remarked. "They sure don't have stores like this in the city."

"Everything in the shop is made by yours truly," Maedeen informed him. "Ann's mother said you're a writer?"

"Yeah, or at least I try to be. I have four books out. Out, as in *out of print*."

"It must be exciting, to be able to perpetuate yourself so creatively. I've always wanted to write but could never seem to get anything down."

"Don't let that stop you." Martin laughed. "It hasn't stopped me. But you're right, it is exciting to actually have something you've written published and put out into the world."

Ann felt faintly jealous of this short and rather spacy woman, but then Maedeen addressed Ann directly. "Melanie and my daughter, Wendlyn, seem to be hitting it off very well."

This took Ann by surprise. "Oh, I didn't even know—"

"They met yesterday, she and Rena—that's Milly's daughter." Maedeen smiled. "I hope they all get to be good friends."

"She seems nice," Martin said when they drove back to the house.

"She seems *weird*," Ann elaborated.

"Why do you say that?"

Ann finished her ice cream cone. "I don't know. It's just weird how she knew about us."

"You're right about that. It was the same way last night at the bar. I'd never met any of those guys before, but they all knew about me, and you. It's like your mother announced our coming to the whole town."

Ann nodded. "And it's strange that Melanie didn't mention anything to me about meeting Maedeen's and Milly's daughters."

"Well, at least it's good that she's found some kids her own age."

"And I didn't particularly care for the way she was looking at you."

"Who? Maedeen?"

"Yeah, Maedeen."

Martin let out a laugh. "It's not easy being God's gift to women, Ann. Women can't resist me, which is understandable, considering my vast intellect, undisputable charm, and obvious good looks."

"Martin, you're so full of shit you need a toilet brush to clean your ears."

"Hey, look." Martin pointed. "Is that Melanie?"

"It better not be," Ann said when she looked across. Three girls and a boy were going into a house. The boy wore jeans, combat boots, and a leather jacket with buttons on it. His black hair was very short on the back and sides but so long in front that some strands hung past his nose. And one of the girls looked like Melanie.

The four went into the house and closed the door.

"Jesus Christ," Ann commented. "Is there no end to it?"

"Here we go—"

"Did you see that guy, Martin? I thought Sid Vicious was dead. Just once I'd like to see her hang out with someone *normal*."

"Normal by *your* standards, you mean."

"Don't you start that shit again, Martin. I'm going to get her."

"You'll do no such thing," Martin told her.

"Well, pardon me. Need I remind you that she's *my* daughter?"

"And need I remind you that she's capable of choosing her friends herself—"

"That guy looks like a nut!"

"Why? Because he's not wearing Brooks Brothers? Get with it, Ann. All her friends back in the city dress like that."

"Yeah, and they're all nuts too!"

"How do you know? You've never even made the effort to meet any of her friends. And did you stop to think that maybe the reason Melanie feels so alienated is because *you* alienate her?"

Ann sputtered. *He's starting to sound like my mother.* Could she help if it she didn't want her only child hanging around with a guy who looked like he just stepped off the drug train? At least the girls looked normal.

"Trust her, Ann," Martin went on. "Just because the guy

looks different doesn't mean they're going in there to smoke dope."

Zack removed the joint from his jacket pocket. He passed it and a lighter to Wendlyn.

"So how long are you in town?" he asked Melanie.

"Just for the week, I think," she said, but she felt so distracted she barely heard her own words. Zack was a dream. Cool blue eyes, great haircut, great body. Under the black leather jacket he wore a "Minor Threat" T-shirt which was tight enough to show off his washboard abdominals. Zack was the last kind of person she'd ever expect to find in a town like Lockwood.

"Rena and Wendlyn said you live at the church."

"Yeah, I take care of the place. They give me a room in the basement. It's not a bad deal."

Wendlyn and Rena huddled together on the couch. They passed the joint back and forth a few times. Then Rena passed it to Melanie.

"You sure this stuff isn't pot?"

"We told you, it's leahroot," Wendlyn said.

"Go ahead," Rena said.

Melanie looked at the tiny joint. She remembered how it had affected her last night. *What the hell,* she thought.

One hit, and Melanie felt weightless, giddy. She lazily looked around. Rena's house was cramped and old but it was neat. It felt lived in, more like a real home than Melanie's antiseptic apartment.

"I had a dream about you last night," Rena said.

Melanie looked at her. *I had a dream about you too,* she was tempted to reply but didn't dare.

Wendlyn, oddly, seemed to be grinning.

"We'll let you two get better acquainted," Rena feigned in a floozy accent. Then she and Wendlyn went toward the back of the house.

Melanie wondered why she didn't feel nervous. Ordinarily, she would be, suddenly sitting here with a near-perfect stranger. But there was something about Zack, though he hadn't said much, that put her at ease.

"Where are you from?" she asked.

"Kind of all over," Zack said. "I was on my own for a while, when I was younger. Your grandmother sort of took me in. I owe her a lot."

She wanted to ask him something commonplace, like about school, but then it occurred to her that he probably hadn't had much education. Some people were more fortunate than others.

His jacket sported several New Wave buttons. One of them read "Killing Joke."

"Killing Joke?" she enthused. "That's my favorite group."

"Yeah? I saw 'em a few years ago when I was passing through D.C. I met 'em after the show—pretty cool bunch of guys."

This astonished Melanie. "You *met* Killing Joke?"

"Yeah, backstage after the show. They autographed one of my CD covers. I'll show it to you sometime."

Melanie didn't know if she believed this. To her, meeting Killing Joke was the equivalent of a priest meeting the Apostles.

"Only bad thing about Lockwood is not many people are into good music," he said. "Come on, I'll show you my record collection."

Melanie was taken aback. Should she go? She'd like to. But where to exactly? "Where did Wendlyn and Rena go?"

Zack shrugged. "Who cares? We'll run into them later. Come on."

"Okay," she said. Zack stubbed out the joint and pocketed it. *Mom would love this,* she thought, amused. He led her outside across some yards. More houses like Rena's could be seen, small but picturesque. Melanie walked along, still high from the joint. Zack walked close behind her; he took off his jacket and slung it over his shoulder. *God,* she thought. The tight T-shirt clung to a well-developed back and shoulders. He was lean but well built. His biceps bulged.

"You're probably bored here already," he suggested.

"Why do you say that?"

"I mean, a girl like you—in Lockwood."

"What do you mean, a girl like me?"

"You know. Classy. Educated."

Melanie felt flattered. "I like Lockwood. It's different."

Zack seemed to snort a laugh. "You're right about that."

She wasn't quite sure what he meant. *Great ass too,* she thought, taking a glance. "Did you really meet Killing Joke?"

"You don't believe me?"

"Oh, I believe you, I just—"

"You'll see," he said.

She found his aloofness as attractive as his body. His slow casual gait somehow propelled him so quickly that Melanie nearly had to jog to keep up. She didn't feel comfortable cutting between houses—someone might call the police; at least, in the city they would. In one window she saw several women sitting around a table; they seemed huddled. Then she saw the same thing in a window of the next house. Another room showed a man sitting alone. He was staring at the wall.

"That was quick," she said.

The shortcut brought them to the town square in minutes. The sun was going down just over the peaked roof of the church.

That's where he was taking her: the church.

What a strange place to live, she thought.

"Down here."

In back, steps descended into a brick-walled enclosure in the ground, and a door. A hinge keened.

"Home, sweet home," Zack remarked. Light from a bare bulb lit a long cinder-block-walled room. One end was cramped with a small bed, a dresser, and a chair. But then she saw what most of the room was devoted to: rows of shelves which contained hundreds, if not thousands, of records and compact discs.

"Jesus," she whispered.

"It ain't Buckingham Palace, but it's all I need."

"No, I meant . . . your collection."

"Yeah, and check out my gear."

Arranged at the back of the basement was a stereo system the likes of which Melanie could never imagine. Steel racks on floor points housed dual amplifiers the size of televisions, a Nakamichi DAT recorder, an ARCAM CD player, and a line conditioner. Another stand on points supported a turntable with a linear air-bearing tone arm. A subwoofer separated two giant electrostatic speakers the size of doors.

"It's my pride and joy," Zack said. "Gotta leave the equipment on all the time or else it sounds edgy. A high-end turntable blows CD away; most people don't realize that. Of course, most people don't spend twenty-five grand on a stereo system."

"Twenty . . . five . . . grand?" Melanie whispered.

"Sure. Music's my only pleasure. I don't cut corners."

"They must pay you pretty well to clean up the church."

Zack laughed faintly. "They don't pay me nothing, 'cept they give me the room for free."

"Then how can you afford . . . all this?"

"Odd jobs," Zack replied. He walked over to one of the shelves and removed something. "Check this out."

Melanie held it as if it were an icon. The CD version of Killing Joke's *Nighttime*. It had been autographed by all members of the band, and inside was a Polaroid of Zack standing next to the lead singer.

"Believe me now?"

Melanie nodded. All she could say was: "Wow."

"You can have it," he said.

Melanie was shocked. "Oh, no, I could never take—"

"If you want it, take it." Abruptly, he turned away.

Melanie's sense of cordiality lapsed. She knew she shouldn't take it, but she did anyway. *An autographed Killing Joke,* she thought, awed. She would frame it, hang it in her room. "Thanks," she said.

She perused his record shelves. He had everything. Everything by Killing Joke, PiL, the Banshees, Magazine, Monochrome Set, Section 25, Strange Boutique. Melanie couldn't believe the coincidence: her and Zack's musical tastes were identical. He had everything by anyone good.

He played some records and discs for her. The huge speakers threw a soundstage that overwhelmed her. Zack seemed to enjoy playing the music as much as she enjoyed listening to it. He mustn't get much of a chance to show off his system, not in a town like Lockwood.

They listened for hours. She never got bored, but eventually she grew fidgety. She knew what it was. When her high wore off, it left something like a hot anguish in its place. She felt steamy, tingly.

She'd never done anything so overt before.

She took his hand and led him toward the bed.

"You're very special," he said, and turned off the lights.

CHAPTER SIXTEEN

Providence, Erik thought.

He had to travel in snatches, at night. Several times police had passed him—he'd thought sure that was the end. How much longer would his luck last?

He'd lay low tonight, he couldn't afford not to. He'd driven past Lockwood on Route 13, to the woodlands. An old trail he remembered took him deep into the forest belt. They'd never find him here. He covered the van with brush and mud, to mask its lacquered white paint.

He knew he still had a few days.

He felt buried in the dark woods. *Buried,* he thought. *Brygorwreccan.*

I'm a peow, he thought.

The moon shone down. Its light pinkened the dense woods.

Doefolmon, he thought.

Wiffek.

Fulluht-Loc.

In the moon's bleary light, he saw it all again. He saw *them.* Bathing in glee, in blood. He saw their mad feasts, their supple bodies, and their longing eyes and lust which stripped him of his soul.

They weren't people. They were monsters.

How many graves did I dig for them?

He'd watched their mad rituals many times. They'd held the hūsls down on the slab, slicing them open like fish and reeling out their entrails, oblivious to the mad, lurching screams. Erik knew that he would hear those screams forever. The more privileged wreccans tended to far worse matters, things which beggared description . . .

Dohtor, he thought.

Dother.

Dother fo Dother.

He'd seen it once, in the night-mirror. That had been many years ago. They'd held his head by his hair and *made* him look, had pried his eyelids open with their fingers. It had been like being drowned in blood.

Afterward, they'd nearly fucked him to death.

Martin dreamed of Maedeen.

Even within the dream, he knew it was a dream. Because he would never do such things for real. Never.

He loved Ann more than he'd ever loved anyone in his life. Cheating on her would be like cutting her. It was unthinkable.

So what did the dream mean?

He was walking in the darkness, in the woods. Tinder crunched—the moon's pink light led him through a labyrinth of trees.

He'd been assigned a task. A cramped clearing formed, bright in moonlight. At his feet lay a pile of bags. They were regular plastic garbage bags, Hefty kitchen size. They'd been tied up and neatly stacked. Martin didn't know what was in them, and he didn't care. He only knew he was supposed to do something with them.

He was supposed to bury them.

It hadn't taken long to dig the hole. Next, he was placing the bags, one at a time, into the hole. Though small, they felt heavy, weighted. He calmly filled the hole with the little bags, then covered them with earth. *Plap, plap, plap!* came the sound as the dirt landed on the plastic.

When he was done, he leaned against a tree and flinched. There was something wet and slick on the tree trunk. In the moonlight, his palm looked black.

Faint giggling bubbled out of the dark.

Martin wended back into the woods. The giggling sounded like girls, children perhaps. The moonlight was bright and pink.

He stopped, tried to focus.

A slender, naked girl was leaning over. Martin stared. He looked at her long, slender legs, the sparse cleft of fur where they joined. The fur protruded as she leaned over further, and he could see the bottoms of her beasts jiggling slightly as her arm moved in some arcane task. This sudden sight—this beautiful nude girl pristine in moonlight, her buttocks jutting—aroused Martin at once. But when she turned, he gasped.

It was Melanie.

"Hi, Martin," she said. She was grinning.

Embarrassment flooded him. Her nakedness faced him without inhibition. This was a seventeen-year-old—his lover's *daughter*. Yet she seemed to sense his unease, she seemed to delight in it.

"You want to fuck me, don't you?" she queried.

"No," Martin said, but the reply was roughened, dry.

"Don't lie to me, you pig. When I was leaning over a minute ago, you wanted to take your cock out, didn't you? You wanted to walk right up behind me and put it in me. Didn't you?"

"No," Martin croaked.

She grinned back at him. She looked just like Ann, the same breasts and nipples, the same legs—just younger. In one hand she held a pail, but it looked old, rusty. It looked like a relic. In her other hand she held a crude brush, like a paintbrush.

That's what she'd been doing. She'd been painting something on the trees.

Then two more girls emerged from the darkness. They, too, were naked. Their matching grins seemed obscene, their bodies tinted pink. They each held a brush and a pail too.

What was this? Why were they painting *trees*?

One girl seemed younger, slimmer; she scarcely had any pubic hair at all. The third girl's bosom jutted. She was more developed, more curvy and plush.

"Get that shit off," said the youngest.

"What?"

"Your clothes, shithead," said the third.

"The wifford wants you ready," Melanie added.

"The *what*?" Martin asked.

"Just shut up and get your clothes off."

Strangest of all, Martin obeyed these commands. The pink moon beat down on him, glare in his eyes. Next thing he knew he lay sprawled on the thatchy forest ground. The girls converged. Their hands ran all over him. His erection throbbed as if to burst, pulsing with his heart. All Martin could do was lie back and cringe.

No, no, he thought. This was perverse. These girls were teenagers, he was a thirty-eight-year-old man. And Melanie, for God's sake . . .

It's got to be. It's got to be a—

"That's right, asshole," Melanie said. "It's a dream."

But that knowledge did not legitimize the *wrongness* of this. Lust felt stuffed into his head; his entire body throbbed with it. Without preamble, Melanie straddled his face. "Eat it, peow," she said. "Stick your tongue in it." Martin tried, but couldn't— she was keeping it too far away. She laughed, touching herself. Her thighs clenched against his head.

And the other two girls . . . what were they doing? Martin couldn't see, but he felt rough, swirling sensations. They giggled with their work. As Melanie brought herself to orgasm, little daubs touched his penis, his testicles—though the contact was insubstantial, Martin thought he might explode.

"We're initiating you, peow," one of them said, giggling.

"We're making you ours," said the other.

He realized then what they were doing.

They were *painting* him. They were painting him with whatever they'd been painting on the trees.

This was crazy. They were just girls. Martin easily had the strength to overpower them, but even the thought of that weighed him down more. He felt as though roots had emerged, had lashed him to the pulpy ground.

"Poor little lamb must be thirsty."

"Give him a drink, Melanie."

The three girls shrieked laughter—a mad, clicking, witchlike sound. Then Melanie began to urinate into his face.

The hot stream inundated him. He gagged, eyes squeezed shut as their laughter rose. *Is she going to piss forever?* he thought.

Martin wasn't used to this kind of humiliation, even in dreams. He thought how wonderful it would be to lurch up, shrug them off. Yet his hate collided with his paralysis and broke apart, as though any thought of rebellion weakened him further.

"Bet he's not thirsty now."

"Look at his cock! Let's cut it off!"

Martin's heart raced.

The girls scurried away. Suddenly, a shape blocked out the

moonlight. Martin could only move his eyes. They roved up the figure, up sleek white legs, over a bushy pubis, over breasts and nipples. Then to the face: Maedeen's.

Yes, it was Maedeen, the shopkeeper. She was grinning, looking down at him with her hands on her hips.

She straddled him at once. "Fok, peow. You are wreccan now."

Martin shuddered. She traced his cheek with a nail that felt inches long and sharp as a pin.

"You belong to us."

She inserted him into her sex, which seemed inordinately hot. As she rode him, she looked up to the moon, whispering words he'd never heard. Her bare hips pounded him, her breasts bobbed. Despite the sensation, Martin wanted to throw up. The three girls crawled forward to watch, still giggling. The third pressed her palm over his mouth—she pressed down hard. Then Melanie, her pink face floating above him, pinched his nostrils shut.

Martin lay frozen. They were killing him, but he couldn't budge. Each time he thought his lungs would burst, Melanie released the pinch on his nostrils, gave him a second to breathe, then pinched them closed again.

"You can play, Melanie. Just don't kill him," Maedeen said.

"Let's cut him up while she's fucking him!" enthused one girl.

"Let's cut off his balls when he comes!" suggested the third.

Martin felt buried in terror. Melanie continued to pinch and release. The palm pressed harder against his lips. The youngest girl began slapping at his testicles between Maedeen's colliding strokes. Their laughter smothered him like a tarp.

But something was happening. Martin's eyes bulged in the pink light. He felt death sliding close. Melanie was giving him less air. The younger girl squeezed his testicles so hard he thought they'd split as Maedeen's sex gulped his erection. He could see them only in mad glimpses, in blurs. Their nails seemed heinously long, like talons. And their faces . . . their faces . . .

"Every night, peow. Every night we do whatever we want with you."

But the words seemed sunken now, a black rattle. Maedeen's voice barely sounded human.

And her face—

My God—

—her face didn't look human at all.

CHAPTER SEVENTEEN

I can't, the words seemed to loll in the dark. *You're special.*

Melanie awakened, frowning. A slant of sunlight lay across her eyes from the gap in the curtains.

I want to, but I can't. You're too special.

She'd slept like a bag of rocks. It only took a moment to remember last night's embarrassment. *Zack must think I'm a slut.* She couldn't believe how forward she'd been. She'd initiated everything—she'd practically dragged him to the bed. It had been great at first. Melanie had made out with a lot of guys in the past, but this had been different. It seemed they were on the bed for hours, just kissing and touching each other. *You're so beautiful,* he kept whispering. Then everything had fallen apart as quickly as it had started.

She'd never gone all the way before. She'd had plenty of chances, she'd just never really wanted to. But with Zack . . . After a while, their petting had wrung her out. She could feel her own wetness seeping, and his own arousal was plain each time she ran her hand across his crotch. The sensations that swelled in her made her feel like a tightly wound wire. A few more twists and she would break. She skimmed off his T-shirt and ran her hands over his muscles, his strong back and chest, his abdomen. She wasn't afraid, she was *ready*. She took off her own top. Her breasts felt hot. Then she unsnapped her jeans, began to slide them down, and—

Zack got up. He was putting his T-shirt back on.

"Zack, what's wrong?"

He stared at her. He looked hurt. "I can't," he said.

"Why?"

"You're special."

Melanie's embarrassment flared. He couldn't have picked a

worse moment. She was naked from the waist up and her jeans were halfway down, and now he didn't want to?

"I want to, but I can't. You're too special."

She pulled her clothes back on. "I'm sorry, Melanie," he was saying as she fled the little basement. He came up the steps after her. "You don't understand!"

I understand, all right! She'd almost been crying as she'd scurried off into the woods.

Special. You're too special.

Hadn't Wendlyn and Rena said that she was special?

Now she lay in bed, the sun in her eyes. What would she say the next time she saw Zack? And what would he say?

Special. The words kept nipping at her.

You're too special.

She fingered the tiny pendant around her neck. "What's so special about me?" she muttered to herself. A tear formed in her eye.

The hospital videotaped all preliminary admittance interviews. It was protocol. Dr. Harold pressed the Play button and sat back. Erik Tharp looked quite different back then. He looked scary. Long hair. Beard. Slim but muscular, a physique honed by hard work. Yes, of course. Digging graves was very hard work. There was an aura about him in the tape, a presence that five years of inactivity and starchy psych ward food had drained. Erik Tharp waited at the interview table. Every so often he looked up at the hidden video camera and smiled.

It was Dr. Greene who sat down across from him.

"Good morning, Erik. That's your name, right? Erik?"

"I'm called brygorwreccan," Erik Tharp replied. His voice sounded corroded, unearthly.

"Okay. Is that what you'd like me to call you?"

"You can call me Erik. They call me brygorwreccan."

"Who's they?"

Erik stared, stone-faced, through long strands of hair.

"What happened to your voice, Erik?"

"Doctor said I only got one vocal cord left." He smiled vaguely. "They always had a hard time controlling me. Said it was because I used to do drugs."

"What kind of drugs, Erik?"

"Crank, dust. Dust, mostly. Coke sometimes."

"And they couldn't control you because you used to use drugs?"

"That's what they said. The other peows, they could control them easy. Sometimes I got out of hand, though. They thought I was gonna blow the whistle on them. So they'd punish me."

"How?"

"Sometimes they'd tie me up, burn me."

"They *burned* you? How?"

"They'd lay a metal rod in the fire." Erik stood up and raised his black T-shirt. Several long scars could be seen along his abdomen. *Self-induced,* Dr. Harold concluded. He was sure Dr. Greene had made the same conclusion.

Erik sat back down. "I could handle that, though. Sometimes they made me look in the mirror. And they always made me watch the hustig."

"The what?"

"The rituals. Watching those was *worse* than torture."

"Why didn't you just leave?"

"Couldn't. The closer you are to them, the more power they have over you."

"I see," Dr. Greene said. "But let's backtrack a minute, okay? We were talking about your voice. What exactly did they do?"

"Oh, yeah. They stuck an awl in my throat."

"As punishment for insubordination?"

"Yeah."

"Erik, the night you were arrested, you told the police that *muggers* stuck an awl in your throat."

"I lied."

"Why?"

"I was scared. I didn't know what was happening. But I know now, so I can tell the truth and it won't matter."

"Why doesn't it matter?"

Erik laughed. "Because I'm in a mental hospital now. They don't care what I say because they know no one will believe me. They're the ones who got me put here."

"Erik, the police caught you burying bodies in a field off Route 154. Do you deny that?"

"No," Erik Tharp said. "That was my job. After a hūsl, I had to bury the bodies. They decided I was too hard to control, so after the last hustig, they told the cops where I'd be. The whole thing was a setup."

"Okay, Erik. Tell me more about the bodies. Some of them were children, babies. Why did you kill them? For the hūsls?"

"No, no, I didn't kill any of them, I just buried them, and, yeah, I snatched some people, sure, but I never killed anyone."

"You *snatched* people?"

"I abducted people for them, that was my job too. Hitchhikers, runaways, people like that, people who weren't local."

"What about the babies, Erik? Did you abduct the babies too?"

"No."

"Then who did?"

"No one. They weren't abductions."

"Then—"

"I don't want to talk about the babies anymore."

Dr. Greene nodded. "All right, Erik. Tell me about the—"

"I don't want to talk about anything anymore."

Erik Tharp put his head down on the table and began to cry.

Dr. Harold ejected the tape. Now he knew exactly what Dr. Greene meant. Erik Tharp displayed no signs of story-mixing, referencing, or even lying. Most clinical psychiatrists could spot lying in a matter of minutes by gauging facial inflections via question structure. Only a pathological mind-set could repress such inflections, and Erik Tharp clearly was not pathological.

Next were transcripts of a court-authorized narcoanalysis, a process in which all conscious mental barriers were dropped with hypnotic drugs. "T" was for Tharp. "G" was for Greene. A light dose of a drug called scopolamine maintained unconsciousness without dropping most brain-wave activity. It was even harder to lie under narcoanalysis.

G: How many people did you kill, Erik?
T: None.
G: Why were you burying bodies?
T: Bludcynn.
G: Erik, were you part of a satanic cult?
T: Dohtor.
G: What?
T: Dother fo Dother.
G: Erik, tell me about the cult.

T: Hūsl. Blood. Bludcynn. Dother fo Dother. I am peow. I am wreccan. We are all wreccan for the face in the mirror.

G: What do you see in the mirror, Erik?

T: Hell.

G: You see hell?

T: Her.

G: Who?

(Patient begins to convulse. A-waves erratic.)

T: They make us wreccan for her. I am wreccan. I have no soul.

G: What happened to your soul, Erik?

T: They gave it to her. They fuck.

(A-waves still jumping. Heart rate 121.)

T: They fuck us and make us wreccan. For her.

G: Erik, who is *her*?

T: Dohtor.

G: Erik, what is *dohtor*?

T: Dother fo Dother. Liiiiii . . . Liiiiii . . . Liiiii . . .

(Patient's eyes are open, lacrimation evident. Heart rate 148.)

T: I am brygorwreccan, I am digger. Scierors cut, cokkers cook. We are hūslpegns. We work for them. They eat, they fuck, they kill—for *her*.

G: Who is *her*, Erik?

T: Liiiiii . . . Liiiiii . . . Arrrrrrdaaaaa—

(Patient screams. A-waves cessate to REM levels, heart rate drops steadily. Narcoanalysis suspended as patient no longer responds.)

Two weeks later they'd attempted hypnosynthesis: hypnotic vocal commands in conjunction with fluctuating doses of sodium amobarbital, which kept the patient's subconscious accessible without inducing high autonomic responses. The idea was to solicit the patient in the first or second stage of sleep, which weren't dream stages.

T: They practiced these rituals.

G: What kind of rituals, Erik?

T: They worshipped this . . . thing.

G: Yes?

T: This . . . demon.

G: Tell me about the demon, Erik.

T: They made me watch, they made us all watch.

(Patient's voice is regulated, monotonal. Heart rate 67.)

G: What did they make you watch, Erik?

T: They cut people up alive. They hate all outsiders.

G: Why do they hate outsiders, Erik?

T: They hate anyone out of the bludcynn, especially men.

G: Because of the demon? They hate men because of the demon?

T: It lives on hate.

G: What lives on hate, Erik? The demon?

T: They like to cause pain, because it likes pain.

G: Who, Erik? The cult? The demon?

T: They like to cut cocks off of guys.

(Interviewer pauses.)

G: What?

T: They eat people after they're done torturing them. They cut off their heads and make us cook the heads. On feks they'd sacrifice kids. It was all part of the preparation.

G: Preparation for what, Erik?

T: The Fulluht-Loc.

G: What's that, Erik? I don't know what that is.

T: They love to fuck. They love to fuck and kill people, torture people. That's their power—fucking. It's in their eyes. Their eyes are like the mirror. They make you look in their eyes while they're fucking you. Lots of times they made us fuck corpses, 'cause it gets them off.

(Interviewer pauses. Patient is trembling, perspiring.)

G: Tell me about the fulluht, Erik.

T: I buried the bodies when the feks were over. That was my job. It was also my job to bring in the hūsls.

G: What's a hūsl, Erik?

T: They cooked heads.

G: What?

T: Girls they pretty much just sacrificed. They'd chain them up downstairs, save them for the important hustigs.

G: What's a hustig, Erik?

T: They did the worst shit to the guys. Guys were their fun. They hate men because it hates men.

G: Erik, I want you to tell me about the terms you're using. Tell me about fulluht, wīhan, hūsl. What do these words mean?

T: Fucking is their power. That's how they worship her.

G: The demon, you mean. What's the demon's name?

T: I got a lot of hūsls picking up hitchhikers or drunks. Girls I got mainly hitchhiking.

G: Erik, let's backtrack a little, okay?

T: I'd bring these guys down, usually at gunpoint. Sometimes I'd have to knock them out. The munucs would take it from there.

G: What's a munuc, Erik? Is a munuc someone in the cult?

T: They'd fuck these guys, and sometimes they'd kill him while they were fucking him, they really got off on that. The wifmunuc loved it, she'd do it all the time.

G: Is the wifmunuc the leader of the cult?

T: This guy, the wreccans held him down and they cut the guy's cock off just like that, and then the scierors skinned him right there on the slab, and I swear to God this poor guy was still alive when they tossed him in the fire. They did all kinds of awful shit like that, things you wouldn't believe, like sometimes the scierors'd cut a guy open while the munucs were fucking him, and a lot of times the wifford would sit on a guy's face so he couldn't see what was going on while the other munucs took turns blowing him, and then just like that they'd cut his cock off, he'd never even know it was coming, and he's shooting blood all over the place running around screaming and then they'd throw the guy right into the fire, and I'll tell you something, it takes a while for a guy to die in a fire pit, I've seen them lashing around in there screaming their heads off while they're turning black, and a lot of times they'd try to crawl out and the munucs would just laugh it up and order the cokkers to push him back in, it's a sight I'll tell you seeing some poor guy sizzling alive in the pit and screaming and screaming and the girls in the pens would be watching this and they'd be screaming too there was so much screaming man screaming and shrieking and the munucs laughing it was so bad you couldn't think it was so bad sometimes you'd just want to die . . .

G: How often did this happen, Erik?

T: Usually, a couple times a year they'd have a big hustig, but every hustig was like a preparation for the Fulluht-Loc.

G: Tell me more about the Fulluht-Loc, Erik.

T: And sometimes they'd punish us, the wreccans, I mean, if we didn't bring in enough hūsls, or they'd punish us just for kicks, 'cause they got off on that. I remember one time I was supposed to bring in a hūsl but I couldn't find any so the wifmunuc had all the wreccans fuck me, and other times they'd order us to fuck one of the corpses before they cooked it—

G: Tell me more about the demon, Erik.

T: —all kinds of awful shit, stuff like you never heard, like you could never imagine, but they've been doing it for eons, man, for *her*. That's how they worship *her*.

G: The demon, you mean? That's how they worshipped the—

T: —and I can't tell you how many times I went down there and they're cutting some guy's head off and bleeding him into a chettle, a chettle's a big pot they cook in, and a lotta times they'd be sitting on some guy hammering nails into his head or sticking knitting needles in his ears—

G: Erik, Erik—

T: Yeah man the grossest shit you could imagine and it was all a big kick to them like hauling some guy's guts out while he's still alive or hanging some girl upside down and cutting off her head and bleeding her into a chettle for a hustig and all kinds of shit yeah man, that's what the dreams were like . . .

G: Dreams, Erik? These were dreams?

T: No, no, I mean they were like dreams, they seemed like dreams but after a while you knew they weren't dreams at all. You knew they were real.

(Patient suddenly cessates. Heart rate 72. Hypnosynthesis suspended as patient no longer responds.)

Dreams, Dr. Harold reflected. *Demons.* The court would not authorize further hypnosynthesis or narcoanalysis. They were satisfied that Tharp was just a bipolar schizophrenic acting out a dream delusion. The case was closed.

But that did not erase the discrepancies. No wonder Greene was never satisfied. Erik Tharp clearly suffered from a hallucinotic delusion, yet his tarsal plate reactivity, his psych test results, and his visual assessment scores did not indicate delusional behavior. These weren't things a person could fake.

He put the transcripts up and dug back into the bag, ex-

tracting the notebooks. Tharp's only real recreation on the ward
was drawing. Immediately, Dr. Harold noticed a rudimentary
yet detailed artistic skill. The drawings were fascinating; there
were hundreds of them. Many of the strange words from
Tharp's monologues had been written between the scenes. *Hūsl.
Peow. Wreccan.* A sketch of a queue of naked women cutting up
a man had been underscored with: *Wīhan.* More women looked
up to a full moon with arms outstretched: *doefolmon.* Many of
the sketches depicted orgies, nude women drawn to great detail
on top of blank-faced men. *Sexespelle,* they read, and many had
subordinate figures standing aside, similarly blank-faced. Yet
one face in each was obviously Tharp's artistic rendition of
himself: pallid, wide-eyed, staring. And here was a full-page
sketch: he'd drawn himself holding a shovel in some dense forest dell. *Byrgorwreccan,* it read. Patients, particularly schizophrenics and hallucinotics, frequently created their own
vocabularies for their personal dementias. The word *Fulluht-
Loc* appeared frequently, and even more frequently: *liloc.*

It was all sexual. Tharp's madness must have been a by-
product of gross sexual fears. He didn't hate women, like
temporal mysogynists, he *feared* them. The male figures in the
sketches had been assigned crude facial identities. But the
women were different. Their bodies had been drawn to pain-
staking erotic detail, yet there was one thing they all lacked.

Faces.

None of the women had faces, and that was another clear sign
of a delusional sexual phobia. *He can't,* Dr. Harold realized. *He
can't draw their faces because he's afraid to.*

Dr. Harold turned a random page. He paused.

Here was a face.

God, he thought. Its clarity stunned him. He was looking at a
full-page drawing of a woman. The moon shone through brambles and streaks of trees; the woman was standing in a dell. Dr.
Harold actually shivered. The sketch was more than a
sketch—it was a dichotomy, a wedding of extremes. Revulsion
clashed with erotic beauty. The perverse clashed with the rever-
ent. *What was going on in Tharp's mind when he penned this?*
Dr. Harold had seen quite a bit of patient artwork in his time.
Art was a catharsis, and a demented person's catharsis logically
reflected demented art. But this . . .

Dr. Harold had never seen anything like it. It was atrocious

. . . and lovely. Eloquent, and harrowing. He'd never looked at a work of art so beautiful and yet so obscene.

The woman stood beseechingly. Her hands were out, as if to invite embrace, yet the fingers were exceedingly long, and nails protracted like sleek, fine talons. Long legs rose to form a perfect hourglass figure. The breasts had been drawn so scrupulously they seemed three-dimensional upon the page. They were high, large, with large dark circles for nipples. The pubis had been drawn similarly: a shining, downy thatch against pure white skin. The woman's hair was a great dark mane. Twin diminutive nubs seemed to protrude from the forehead, almost like—

Like horns, Dr. Harold realized.

And the face . . .

The face was nothing more than two slitlike eyes above a black opened maw full of needle teeth.

CHAPTER EIGHTEEN

Something bothered Martin all day. The dream, of course. The naked girls queerly painting trees in the middle of the night. The parcels he'd buried, and then Melanie . . . and Maedeen . . .

He tried all day to forget about it. Even Ann, with her own dream traumas, had noticed he wasn't himself. They'd had lunch and taken a drive. He'd hoped a nice scenic drive would get his thoughts away, but anywhere he looked he saw the woods, and when he saw the woods he saw the dream. They'd driven by the general store and he'd seen Maedeen outside sweeping the walk. She'd turned and waved as if she'd sensed them driving by. Martin subtly shuddered. The momentary glimpse gave him an erection.

All right, I'm attracted to her, he realized. *So what? That's why God made women good-looking, isn't it?*

But it was more than that. He knew it was.

That morning, he and Ann had made love. Lately, it seemed something wasn't right between them, that she wasn't enjoying it. *Male paranoia,* he'd always concluded. Was he rationalizing? It was a fact he didn't want to face: this time, when they'd made love, he hadn't been thinking of Ann at all. He had been thinking of Maedeen.

Suddenly, Ann shivered.

"What's wrong?"

She looked distractedly past the windshield, just as Martin pulled the Mustang around the town square, past the church. "I don't know," she said. "I just feel fidgety." But it seemed that she'd shivered just as they'd passed the church.

"You didn't sleep well last night. You had the nightmare again, didn't you?"

153

Ann nodded. "It keeps getting worse, and there's more to it now, more details. And lately . . ." Her words trailed off.

"What?"

"I don't know," she said. She seemed confused. "Lately, I've been having some kind of vertigo. Like just now. I'll be wide awake, and all of a sudden I'll see something."

Martin slowed through the crossing lights. "What did you see?"

Ann shivered again. "Nothing."

Martin knew when to lay off. "You're not getting enough sleep," he ventured. "This nightmare's turning you inside out. Maybe you should call Dr. Harold, see what he thinks."

"No, that would be silly. I will not let my whole life shake apart because of a stupid nightmare."

"Don't feel bad," Martin said. "I had a nightmare last night too."

Ann looked at him abruptly. "Melanie's also having nightmares."

"It must run in the family," Martin attempted to laugh it off. "Relax, will you? You worry way too much about her."

"Martin, let's not get into that again."

"Okay, okay." He headed back to the house. But he knew he was right. Ann's difficulties were compounding. Her father dying, her mother's adversity, the canceled vacation. Now she had this "vertigo" in conjunction with the nightmare. Too many things were building up at once, weighing her down.

Martin wondered how close she was to breaking.

Ann didn't know what to tell him. *Sooner or later he's going to think I'm going nuts.* Yes, her nightmare just kept getting worse, and now this *vertigo*. She couldn't think of any other way to describe it. Was it part of the dream she wasn't remembering? It was like a gory daydream. Wide awake she'd suddenly shiver—

—and see red.

She'd see hands plunging a knife into someone, a wide silver blade sinking repeatedly into naked flesh. The dead-silent backdrop made it even worse; in this vision all she could hear was the steady *slup-slup-slup* of the knife. And all she could see: blood flying everywhere, breasts and belly quivering as the blade continued to rise and fall, rise and fall . . .

Slup-slup-slup . . . slup-slup-slup . . .

The face of the victim couldn't be seen, but somehow she felt convinced that the person being butchered was herself.

Martin parked the Mustang on the street; several cars filled the driveway. In the foyer, Ann noticed her mother entertaining several guests in the dining room. Mrs. Gargan was there, and Constance, Dr. Heyd's wife, plus the widowed Mrs. Virasak, and a few of Lockwood's other elderwomen. They chatted softly, drinking tea. But when Ann's mother noticed her, she got up quickly from the table and drew closed the dining room doors.

"She knows how to make a person feel welcome," Martin joked. "What are they doing in there?"

"Who knows?" Ann said. "Who cares?"

"I'm going to sit out back, try to get some writing done."

"Okay," Ann said. Several times now she'd seen him grab his pad and disappear into the spacious backyard. He seemed to find peace here, every poet's quest, which made Ann slightly jealous. Martin liked it here. At least if he hated it, she wouldn't feel so alone.

Upstairs she looked around for Melanie. Her room was empty, but she heard water running—the shower. Ann peered out the window and saw Martin sitting in a lawn chair at the edge of the woods. His pad lay in his lap, his hand poised. He seemed to be looking up at the sky with his eyes closed.

"Hi, Mom," Melanie greeted. She came in wearing her dark robe and had a towel around her head. "Where have you been?"

"Martin and I went for a drive. We were thinking of going to the inn for dinner. Want to come?"

"I won't be able to make it. I'm meeting some friends."

Ann sat down on the bed, perturbed. "You haven't mentioned much about these new friends of yours."

"Oh, Wendlyn, Rena? They're pretty cool."

Pretty cool. Ann smirked. "I saw you with a boy yesterday."

Melanie smiled. "That's Zack. He's cool too."

"He looks like your friends back home, leather jacket and—"

"Come on, Mom," Melanie dismissed, drying her light brown hair with the towel. "He's really nice, and we have a lot in common."

"Like what?"

"Music. He listens to all the groups I like, even Killing Joke. And you should see his stereo, it's *huge*."

"Melanie"—Ann leaned forward as if concentrating—"are you telling me you were in this boy's house? Alone?"

"He doesn't live in a house. He lives in the church basement."

This didn't sound right. "He lives in the *church*? What about his parents?"

"He doesn't have any; he's an orphan. Grandma gave him a job as a custodian or something."

Grandma, Ann thought sourly. It was one obstruction after the next. Ann's mother was regarded as the town's matriarch, loved by all. Melanie was making friends here. Martin wrote better here. Where did all this leave Ann?

On the outside, she answered herself. "I just don't think I approve of your hanging around with some boy you just met—"

"I'm not a little kid anymore, Mom. I'm an adult."

"Is that so?"

"Let's not argue." Very abruptly, Melanie took off her robe. She sat down naked at the antique vanity to comb her hair.

Ann swallowed her shock. Melanie had never disrobed in front of her, at least not down to the skin. But she did so now as if it were natural. Ann felt she should comment on this immodesty, but what could she say? Certainly, there was nothing unnatural about a mother seeing her daughter unclothed.

"Mom, what's wrong?" Melanie could see Ann's face in the vanity's big framed mirror. "You act like you've never seen me naked."

"Well, I haven't really. Not in years." But she thought: *She is an adult.* Melanie's body had indeed blossomed. She'd been skinny as an adolescent, boyish. Now her breasts had filled out, and the straight lines of her early teens had given over to a nice feminine shapeliness. The firm orbs of her breasts jogged slightly as she combed her hair out in the mirror. Then she stood up, just as abruptly, and turned. Ann couldn't help but glimpse the fresh young body from head to toe.

"I'm growing up, Mom."

"I know, honey. Sometimes that's a hard thing for a mother to realize, that's all."

And it was, wasn't it? Her shock reverted to a dim despair. Melanie had bloomed into womanhood nearly without Ann's even knowing it. *Too busy,* she regretted. *Too busy trying to make partner to even notice your own daughter growing up.*

Melanie quickly slipped into a pair of black acid-washed jeans, then pulled on a dark-blue "Luxuria" T-shirt. Ann felt like an old curmudgeon sitting on the bed.

Melanie kissed her on the cheek. "I'll be home early."

"Bye."

But Ann had wanted to stop her, to ask her something that had been bothering her of late. *Are you a virgin?* she'd wanted to ask. But how could she ask something like that without sounding even more curmudgeonish?

Melanie left.

Ann felt old, depressed, naive—all at once. A glance out the window showed Martin wandering off into the looming woods, seeking his muse. How much more distanced could Ann feel from the people in her life? She and her mother were constantly at odds. She didn't understand Martin's creative joys at all. And her daughter had grown up right under her nose.

She sat back down on the bed. *And my father's dying, and I hardly ever even knew him.*

A tear threatened to form in her eye.

Then she shivered . . .

Slup-slup-slup, she heard . . . *slup-slup-slup* . . .

The vertigo returned. The glaring red vision streamed again through her mind: a fisted hand plunging the knife down. Blood spewing. Naked breasts and belly quivering each time the blade buried itself to the hilt . . .

CHAPTER NINETEEN

"Oh, hello, Ann."

Ann gave a start. The double doors to the den abruptly slid open, and standing there was Mrs. Gargan, redolent with cologne.

"How are you today, Mrs. Gargan?"

"Oh, I'm fine. What are you up to?"

But Mrs. Gargan's stiff posture and stiff, makeupped face made Ann feel sidetracked. Past her shoulder, Ann could see her mother and several friends looking through a photo album at the table. Mrs. Gargan's rigid smile and dark eyes seemed fixed on her.

"I've just been puttering around," she said after a pause. "I thought I'd go upstairs and look in on my father."

"Yes, of course. Feel free to join us later for tea."

Yeah, right. Ann's mother and friends flipped through the photo album as if in deep concentration. They commented quietly at each turn of a page. Ann couldn't hear them.

"I will," Ann balked. "See you later."

She went upstairs as Mrs. Gargan headed for the kitchen. Ann could imagine the banality of joining her mother and friends for tea, pooh-poohing over the album. Mrs. Gargan, of course, was just being polite. The stiff cordiality told Ann what she already knew: Ann was Lockwood's prodigal daughter—she would never be fully welcome here.

Upstairs, the grimly familiar beep led her to the room. Her father's cardiac monitor. Ann hated that sound. Milly was sponging off her father's chest. The chest looked waxen, pale.

"Hi, Milly."

The nurse turned, smiled. "Have you seen Dr. Heyd around?"

"No, not in a while. Is anything wrong?"

"Oh, no, no." Milly fidgeted in a medical bag, hooked up a new IV. "Everything's fine." Her smile turned coy. "I've heard Melanie has taken a liking to someone."

"Oh, yeah. Zack. Do you know him?"

Milly laughed, a strange reaction. "You don't have to worry about him. Actually, he's a very nice boy, very helpful. You might be put off a little by the way he dresses, but that's kind of silly nowadays, isn't it?"

"Yeah, I guess it is," Ann said, though reluctantly.

"But you seem bothered by it, or something."

Did she? *I'm bothered by a lot of things.* "Motherly concern, I suppose. Do things like that ever bother you?"

Milly laughed again. "My daughter's a bit too young for Zack; she's only fifteen. But as mothers we have to realize that eventually our daughters grow up. Didn't you have a crush on boys when you were a teenager?"

Ann sat down, thinking. It was a revelatory question. "I guess I did," she said. "But there never seemed to be many boys my age in Lockwood."

"Well, that's still pretty much the case, not many children at all, especially Melanie and Rena's age group. Lockwood's pretty remote, but I like it better that way. It's safer. It's more real, don't you think?"

Ann shrugged. She remembered how bored she'd been in Lockwood as a child. It must be even worse for an adult. Now that she thought of it, she didn't remember seeing many kids of any age around town, and not many established men. "What do you do for fun around here?"

"Lockwood may seem like the sticks to you, but actually, there's a lot for a single woman to do."

Ann recalled Milly's rather militant statements about her social life, about men.

"It's just that Lockwood is so different for you," Milly went on. "If you'd lived here your whole life, you'd feel different. You're talking about sex, right?"

The spontaneity of the question surprised her. But she supposed that's what she meant all along. "I was just curious, that's all. Your romantic life is none of my business."

"You can say it," Milly offered. "I'm no prude. You want to know how a woman in a town like Lockwood finds sexual satisfaction."

"Really, Milly, I didn't mean—"

"We're not *that* remote, you know. There are men in town, mostly transients, come here to work. It's out there, it's easy enough to find if you look."

This was getting embarrassing. Then Milly added, "But you don't have to worry about that yourself. You have a man."

Jesus, did everyone around here regard men as property, as prizes? Was that what love was when you got right down to it? Territorial? Nevertheless, now that they'd broken the ice, Ann couldn't resist asking: "Tell me about Maedeen."

Milly offered a huge grin. "Let me guess. You and Martin met Maedeen recently, and now you're jealous."

"I wouldn't go so far as to say jealous. She just seems—"

"A little forward? Well, don't worry. That's just the way she is. She's outgoing, friendly. She likes everybody and everybody likes her. Your mother gave her the store when the old man died. She's done a wonderful job."

Is that how I seem? Ann wondered. *A jealous city priss?*

"She and I go out sometimes. We have a wild time."

But what could Milly mean? There were no dance clubs or night spots in Lockwood. Where did they have a *wild* time around here?

"A woman's gotta do what she's gotta do." Milly pushed her hair back and laughed. But, "Oh, damn," she said next. She rummaged through the medical bag. "It's time for your father's B$_{12}$ shot. I don't have any left. Would you mind running to my house and getting me some? It's just a short walk. I don't want to leave your father alone between IVs."

"Sure," Ann said. Actually, it would be a relief. She liked Milly, but her straightforwardness sometimes got too nettling. Milly gave her instructions for what to get and where. When Ann went back downstairs, she noticed her mother and friends still chatting over the photo albums. Her mother looked up suddenly, frowned, then looked back down. She scarcely even spoke to Ann anymore. *I'm the prodigal daughter, all right,* she thought again. Ann wondered if there was anything she could ever do to win her mother's approval.

Forget it, she dismissed. Ann cut through the town square to Milly's house. The town looked idle as usual. Several old men sat on the porch of Maedeen's general store, bantering and chewing tobacco. A dog lazed in the sun. Not a single car could be seen. Ann felt obstinate; she was always too quick to criticize. Lockwood, however idle, had something the city never had. Peace. But suddenly, the thought waned. At the end of the square, she saw the church, its great front door and stained-glass windows staring at her like a looming face.

Milly lived in a little one-floor house on Bathory Street. Quaint little shrubs out front. A quaint little yard. It seemed *honest* somehow. No luxuries, just an honest little house. Milly hadn't given her the keys; there was no need. No one in Lockwood locked their doors. Inside was just as honest. Sparse but clean. Old but well-kept furniture. A bowl of potpourri filled the living room with pleasant herby scents. Milly had said the B_{12} was in the kitchen, above the refrigerator. Ann went down the short hall, but stopped. She thought she heard something . . .

It sounded like a humming noise, ever faint. But she heard something else enlaced with it. From down the hall.

Was it Rena, Milly's daughter? The noise bothered Ann. She hesitated, then advanced. The hall was dim. The carpet left her footfalls silent. To the left, a door stood half open.

Ann peeked in.

A bedroom, sparse but comfortable like the rest of the house. The decor, however—bright curtains, brightly painted furniture—couldn't possibly be an adult's. It must be Rena's room.

But what was that humming noise?

She looked in further. Sunlight slanted in, and movement caught her eye. White movement in the glare of sun. *What the—* Ann blinked, staring. The soft, faint hum persisted.

Ann gulped when she realized what she was seeing.

A figure squirmed on the little, neat bed. Bright white skin in the glare. It was Rena. Naked. Her back arching. Moans and hot breath escaped her throat. At first Ann thought the girl must be convulsing from some illness. But another moment's staring showed her that it was not discomfort which sent Rena's young body into clenching spasms. It was ecstasy.

The hum persisted, wavering. Ann noted its source.

Milly's daughter manipulated a shiny white vibrator between her legs. The vibrator was huge. Tendons strained at the apex of the girl's legs as she wielded the device with both hands. The girl's breasts were tiny on her heaving chest. Her stomach sucked in and out; her toes dug in the sheets. The giant vibrator's volume rose and fell each time it was inserted and withdrawn. The size of the thing, compared to Rena's tiny sex, made Ann visibly tremor.

Rena continued to writhe, drawing the device slowly in and out. The sensations contorted her face. Melding murmurs of words escaped her lips.

"Doefolmon, bludmon, all the dothers give lof . . ."

Each time the humming device plunged, Ann thought she could feel it herself. This disgusted her. Immediately, she felt compelled to barge into the room, to stop this.

But would that really be within her rights? This was another woman's daughter. What right did Ann have to discipline *Milly's* child? And what would she say anyway?

"Give lof, give lof, I give lof . . ."

Lof? Ann thought. What were these words she was muttering? The vibrator hummed. Rena moaned then, her eyes rolling back in her head, when she next pushed the vibrator so deeply into herself that only the end showed. Ann grew faint.

She retreated back down the hall, not making herself known. Quickly, quietly, she found the vial of O'Neal 50mcg B_{12}. As she left the house, she could still hear the vibrator's steady hum and Rena's anguished voice: "Doefolmon, doefolmon . . ."

Ann walked briskly away from the house. Was she being unrealistic? She didn't care that it was none of her business, nor did she care how sexually liberal the times had become. *Fifteen-year-olds are not supposed to be masturbating with vibrators,* she felt convinced. Did Milly know what her daughter was doing when she was out? The walk back through the town square cooled her down. True, it was none of her business, yet one point wouldn't let go. This was the same girl who had become friends with Melanie. Ann didn't want to contemplate her reaction if she ever caught Melanie doing the same thing.

And what were those bizarre words Rena had been muttering?

Ann decided to let it pass. Mentioning it to Milly might cause a misgiving, not to mention embarrassment. What could she possibly say? Hey, Milly, I saw your kid masturbating with a vibrator the size of an ear of corn. No, she couldn't say that. *Let Milly worry about her kid herself,* she settled.

Pickman Avenue remained as idle as before. The big steepled

church reflected bright white in the sun. Ann crossed at the walk, then stopped. A car was pulling away from Nale's, the general store.

Ann stood in the street, staring back.

It was a blue Mustang GT. *My car,* she realized.

Though she couldn't be sure, there appeared to be two people riding in it. The one on the left appeared to be Martin.

The one on the right appeared to be Maedeen.

The glass tube measured eight inches in length, three eighths of an inch wide. The dother liberally lubricated it with petroleum jelly. She paused, grinning. Then she began to slide the tube into the tiny hole at the end of Zack's penis.

"Do it slowly, dear," advised the wifford. "We don't want it to break . . . yet."

Terror gushed in Zack's mind. The two wreccans had tied him down to the table with thick hemp. One of the wreccans was new, the other was the brēowor. They stood aside now, behind Maedeen and Wendlyn. Zack fought against his restraints but only abraded himself for his efforts. *They're sticking a glass tube up my cock,* came the base fact in thought. *And they're going to break it.* This was his punishment.

"You were going to fuck her, weren't you?" asked Maedeen, the wifford. Her voice was as stony and cold as her face.

"No," Zack groaned. "I swear. We made out a little, that's all. I wasn't gonna do anything more."

"No?"

"I *swear!*"

"He's lying, Mom," remarked Wendlyn, the dother. She held his flaccid penis gently in one hand, and the end of the glass tube with the other. Very slowly, she slid the tube in another inch.

"Please," Zack's voice tremored.

The wifford crossed her arms, appraising him. "If you had fucked her, you would've tainted her. You would've tainted the holy fulluht, ruined it."

"But I didn't!" Zack shouted. "I didn't!"

"He would've, Mom. He's a pig. He's a peow."

"I know, dear."

Zack felt the hemp burn his wrists as he squirmed.

"Nis woh fo gast be mek a peow?" said the wifford. "Give lof, no? Be folclagu, ur godspellere, iesprece."

"We should do it, Mom," the dother persuaded.

"Wīhan thus wer, thus peow?"

"Please," Zack groaned. "I would never disgrace you in the eyes of—"

"Shut your mouth!" the wifford exploded. "Never, *never,* speak her name, you unworthy piece of shit! *Never!*"

Zack shuddered, but he better not shudder much, or else he might break the tube himself. The other two wreccans seemed to strain against an inner anguish but remained out of the way. They wouldn't help, Zack knew. They couldn't.

Now the wifford smiled. Her gaze moved from Zack's face to his genitals. The dother pushed the tube in another inch.

"Aw, Mom, let me do it."

"Well . . ."

"Mom, pleeeeeease?"

Zack's body felt coursing with high-tension current. The young dother licked her lips in steady concentration as she deftly slid the glass tube still deeper into his urethra.

"You've been a bad boy, Zack. But this will make you good."

Zack's terror made him feel stretched over a bed of nails. He fought not to shake. The tube had now been inserted over four inches into his penis.

"Zackie, Zackie," chanted the dother. She was swaying the tube back and forth and spinning it between her fingers. "Can I break it now, Mom? Can I?"

"Put it in a little deeper first, dear."

The dother did so. How much further could the tube go?

"Please, please don't," Zack murmured.

"Now, Mom?"

"All right, but let's make it suspenseful. On the count of three, break the tube."

"Okay."

"Ready?"

"Yeah, Mom."

Sweat popped out of Zack's brow. Every joint in his body felt fused.

"One," said the wifford.

Zack's teeth ground.

"Zackie, Zackie," sang the dother.

"Two."

Aw no holy Christ please . . .

"Two and a half . . ."

Zack could feel the tube embedded down the entire length of his limp penis . . .

"Three!" shouted the wifford.

Zack screamed.

Laughter raced 'round the room like mad animals. In one quick movement, the dother—

Noooooooooooooooo!

—withdrew the tube without breaking it.

Zack turned to putty. The wreccans cut his bonds and pushed him off the table. Zack, wheezing, fumbled to pull up his pants.

"Thank you thank you," he gibbered.

They were walking away, but the wifford turned at the door. "Melanie is special," she said. "Very special. Remember that, or next time we'll break that tube into so many pieces you'll be pissing glass for a year."

CHAPTER TWENTY

Ann waited up late. What would she say? And could she be sure that it was Maedeen she'd seen in the car with Martin? But she didn't worry about such reasonable considerations. Ann was mad, and she let her anger sit up with her.

Furthermore, Melanie hadn't come home yet either, which made Ann madder. The grandfather clock in the foyer ticked past 10 P.M. Where could she be at this hour? What was she doing?

That afternoon she brought the B_{12} to Milly and hadn't mentioned what she'd witnessed Rena doing on the bed, as she'd previously decided. By then she was too mad to care anyway.

She couldn't imagine Martin's fascination with Maedeen. *The little scrub.* Ann had see how Martin was looking at her the time they went to the store. Ann was well aware of her tendency to misinterpret certain things. Was she just being paranoid?

I'd still like to drag her little ass down the street.

She sat in the library off the foyer. The silence and dim lamplight made her feel watched. Earlier her mother had been seen going down to the basement with the photo albums. She'd unlocked the basement door, entered and exited, then locked the door and came back upstairs. She'd said nothing to Ann as she'd crossed the landing, which was typical. But why lock the basement door?

Again, at this moment, Ann didn't care. All she could think about was how bad she was going to grill Martin's ass when he had the nerve to come home.

She thought she'd pass time watching TV, then remembered her mother didn't approve of television. There were no TVs, in other words, in the house. She hadn't noticed one in Milly's house either. Did Lockwood consider anything modern to be a corrupt influence? She wandered about the quiet house, each journey bringing her back to the front window where she'd peek outside to see if the car was in the driveway yet. But what was she really thinking? That Martin and Maedeen had something going? Even Ann knew that was ridiculous. She just didn't like Maedeen, for her own womanly reasons, and she didn't care what Milly said. Sometimes a woman could just *tell*, could sense a woman who was trouble. *The little flirt,* she dismissed. And Martin didn't have to be so quick to assert that Maedeen was "nice." *I'll show her nice,* Ann mused. *Maybe I'll shove one of her homemade ice cream cones up her scrawny ass. See how nice she is then.*

By 11 P.M., Martin and Melanie still had not returned. Ann's mother had long since gone to bed. Bored now in her anger, Ann went upstairs to talk to Milly but instead found Dr. Heyd in her father's room.

"Ah, hello, Ann. You're up late, aren't you?"

"I'm waiting for Martin. He went out a while ago."

Dr. Heyd made some nameless adjustment to the cardiac monitor. "I think I saw him going into the Crossroads earlier. I understand he's getting along well with some of Lockwood's men."

And some of Lockwood's women too. But was that where he was? At the bar? "He mentioned some of them yesterday," she said.

"Fine fellows, all of them. If you're looking for Milly, she's asleep in the next room right now. The poor girl hasn't gotten much rest these past few days. I sent her to bed. I'll be looking after your father tonight myself."

The monitor beeped on. Her father looked pallid as a wax dummy in the bed.

"But would you watch him a few minutes?" Dr. Heyd asked. He wore baggy slacks and suspenders, his bald pate shining. "I'd like to go down and fix myself a sandwich."

"Sure," Ann said.

Dr. Heyd left her to her own unease. She didn't like to look at her father, because her mind could not associate the vision she had of him with the sunken form in the bed. She sat down and flipped through one of Milly's romance novels. A random page revealed a rather explicit sex scene. She remembered when romance fiction was innocuously tame. *Not anymore,* she thought now. *Nothing is.* She hadn't read a complete novel herself, though, in years.

Milly's purse lay opened on the floor, and inside a large woman's wallet hung similarly open. Ann noticed pictures. What was the harm? She took the wallet out and looked through it. No credit cards or the like, of course not. But there were several snapshots in the string of clear-plastic envelopes, all either of Rena at different ages, or Rena and Milly smiling together. Ann looked closely at one school portrait of Rena, probably at around age six. The picture made Ann clench. It was almost impossible to believe that the adorable little girl in this snapshot was the same girl she'd seen today masturbating with a vibrator.

Toward the end were some baby pictures, even more adorable. But the last picture caused her to stare.

A baby, days old, lying atop a quilt. But the tiny pudenda left no doubt. It was a baby *boy.*

Milly had never referred to a son. Ann immediately feared why that might be. Did the baby die?

She put the wallet back in the purse. What an awful thing. She could be wrong, of course, but why else would Milly have never mentioned a son? Or perhaps it was a relative's child.

Ann glanced up. The beeps of the heart monitor seemed to change their rhythm a moment, then increase in pitch. Ann was about to call for Dr. Heyd, but her gaze was quickly overwhelmed.

Her father's eyes opened.

His mouth was moving, and he was looking at her.

"Dad!" Ann jumped up, raced to the bed. Her father's own gaze followed her. *He's conscious,* she realized in a burst of exuberance. "Dad, it's me," she said. "It's Ann . . ."

She could see his mouth working. It opened and closed; it was obvious to her that he was trying to say her name. Ann's heart was racing.

Next, his crabbed hand took hold of her wrist. It felt cool, dry, wriggling in infirmity. The other hand faltered, rising over the bed. It moved around in some cryptic gesture.

"What, Dad? Can you try to talk?"

He clearly couldn't. It crushed Ann to see the frustration on his infirm face. The mouth moving but giving no voice, the futile concentration in efforts to communicate to the daughter he hadn't seen in over a year.

"Dad, what . . ."

His hand moved furiously, not pointing but seeming to mimic an act.

The act of writing. Thumb pressed to fingers, the withered hand made gestures of writing.

"A pen, Dad? Do you want a pen?"

He actually huffed in relief. His tired face nodded.

He couldn't talk but he wanted to write. He must be much more lucid than they'd thought. Ann took one of Dr. Heyd's notepads and sat down on the bed. She lay it against her knee. Then she placed a ballpoint pen into her father's right hand.

"Go on, Dad. Take your time."

First just scribble. The old man chewed his lip as he struggled to wield the pen. Ann felt tears in her eyes, witnessing her father's desperation at so simple a task.

He began to whimper, eyes fluttering, then closing. "Dad, Dad?" she cried. He fell unconscious again, and the monitor slowed back to its normal pitch.

"Ann, what's happened?"

Dr. Heyd came back into the room, rushing over. She excitedly explained what happened. But he only half listened as he quickened to take vital signs. Suddenly, Milly and Ann's mother were crowded into the room, both in robes and slippers. Ann repeated everything for them in desperate joy.

"He was seeing me," she went on. "I know he knew it was me."

But Dr. Heyd seemed disapproving, busying with an injection.

"What's wrong?" Ann asked, dismayed. "Isn't this good?"

"No, Ann, it's not," Dr. Heyd replied. "You should've called me at once."

"But he was writing, he was trying to talk. He recognized me. I'm sure of it."

"Ann, you're forgetting what I told you the other day. Undue excitement is the worst thing for him right now. The excitement of suddenly being conscious and of seeing you at the same time made his blood pressure and heart rate skyrocket. You should've called for me first, so I could give him something to keep his heart rate at a lower level."

"Why!" Ann objected. "He was conscious!"

"My God, Ann," her mother muttered.

"What the hell is *wrong*?" Ann continued.

"The drastic rise in blood pressure caused a physical strain against the occluded blood vessels in his brain. You shouldn't have encouraged him to write, because that only increased the strain further. It challenged him to a physical task he's no longer physically capable of."

Ann still didn't understand. All she understood was that her father had been conscious, and now everybody was acting like Ann had done something grievously wrong.

"Before inducing him to write, you should've called me so I could lower his heart rate to a safe level. All that excitement at once was too much for him. The rise in systolic pulse more than likely forced some of the clot apart, sending pieces further into the brain. He may die now."

Ann felt paralyzed in turmoil.

"My God, Ann!" her mother yelled.

"It's my fault," Dr. Heyd offered. "I should have explained more specifically before I left the room."

"It's not *your* fault, Ashby," Ann's mother hotly replied. "The problem is my fine daughter doesn't realize the fragility of anything! She has no forethought at all!"

"Mom, I—"

"I invited you home to see him, Ann, not kill him!"

Ann's mother stormed out of the room. Ann stood teary-eyed. Milly put her arm around her shoulder.

"It couldn't be helped, Ann," Dr. Heyd said, watching the monitor. "You didn't know."

I may have just killed my own father, Ann realized.

Ann watched in mute numbness as Milly and Dr. Heyd tended to her father. In a few minutes, Dr. Heyd confirmed, "He seems to be stabilizing for now. We'll know more by morning." Then he looked down at Ann's hand. "Is that what he wrote?"

Ann still held the piece of notepaper her father had scribbled on. She looked at it now, for the first time. Just scrambled letters, nothing coherent. "It doesn't make sense," she said, and gave the note to Dr. Heyd.

"To your father, though, it probably does," the doctor told her after reading the note himself. "Unfortunately, orbital strokes of this magnitude frequently obfuscate the learned-memory faculties in the brain. In other words, he was writing without a sequenced memory of the alphabet. It's quite common in these cases."

Dr. Heyd, it seemed, had a professional answer for everything. Ann felt disappointed. She would never know what her father, in what may have been his last conscious moment in life, had been trying to communicate to her.

What he'd written was this:

BLUDCYNN HŪSL— DOTHER FO DOTHER

CHAPTER TWENTY-ONE

"Secean we," bid the wifmunuc. Becloaked, she knelt before the blessed nihtmir.

"Eternal mother, bless us!" came the chorus.

Yielding to the rushes of love, of bliss and sanctity, the wifmunuc remained solemn. In silence, then, she prayed before the slab. Her holy sweosters joined her from behind, menteled in black, in the cirice.

"Modor, Druiwif, Dother fo Nisfan," the wifmunuc bid, raising her arms. "We give lof fom eard, os hūslpegns, in yur soo, we fi wuldor, lar, gliw."

"O, Blessed One, hear our prayer."

"Ure heofan yur nisfan."

"Receive our prayer."

Each wifhand then dropped their mentels, nude beneath. They bowed in the cirice, sweat shining on their backs. Several wreccans stood to the rear, blank-faced, bearing torches to give light in their conqueror's eard. Then the wifmunuc rose and stepped out of her own cæppe, which was black as the others', but sewn of the finest silk. Naked, she pressed a hand to the slab. Untold wonders bloomed on her face, the most holy visions, unspeakable, incalculable. She looked into the slab, staring.

Two more wreccans dragged in a hūsl, who had been properly gagged so as not to disrupt the wifmunuc's muse. Now the wifhands broke. A second hūsl, a female, was removed from one of the pens. Wreccans gagged her, stripped her, brought her forth.

The male hūsl was held upright. He was typical, a stray drunk picked up hitchhiking. But the wreccans had sought well—this

172

one was young, muscular, handsome. As they stripped him, the terror in his young eyes was beautiful.

Yes, the pig would make a beautiful sacrifice.

More wreccans—the cokwors—stoked the great fire in the cooking pit. Each stoke flooded the cirice in lovely, hot waves. For a time, the wifhands took turns touching the male, reveling in the sensation of flesh. They caressed the chest, buttocks, and genitals, their faces grinning in firelight. Then:

"Wīhan!" ordered the wifford.

The male was laid upon the dolmen, which was encrusted from countless feks. Wreccans tied him down. Pots of leahroot smoked fragrantly about the dolmen, charging them all with the sweet passion of their god. The wifford began to fellate the male, while others stroked his flesh with flaxbalm. They took turns, moving in a watchful circle, each taking the helot unto their mouths. Soon the leahroot and balms had seeped into his blood. Despite his terror, his genitals hardened.

The female was forced to watch. Her tainted features proved her distance from the bludcynn. Stringy white-blond hair, blue eyes, faint pink nipples on large breasts. She shook, sweating, as two wreccans held her up. Urine streamed freely down her tanned legs.

In the nave, though, the wifmunuc continued to supplicate their god, her face peering into the nihtmir. The cold stone against her fingertips filled her with coruscating heat. Her vision delved; it was being led away deep into the stygian field. Deeper, deeper . . .

Each wifhand took turns straddling the male helot, their faces turned up in bliss, while the others looked on.

. . . and down. She was in a different realm now, where madness was the only order, darkness the only light. It was beautiful . . .

The helot shuddered in his own sweat as he lay there to be taken again and again. The wreccans brought the blonde closer still, to see. When she dared to close her eyes, a white-hot stoking rod was lain across her buttocks. Two more wreccans approached the dolmen, with knives.

. . . so beautiful to be led into their god's wondrous lair. Her physical body behind her, the wifmunuc seemed to float through the shifting blackness like a feather on the wind. Soon she drifted out of the chasm and onto a strange precipice. It was another time, or, perhaps, another world . . .

"Soo, soo," hotly whispered the wifford. It began with her, and it would end with her. She pushed a sweoster off and restraddled the helot, penetrating herself upon his penis. She grunted, thrusting down.

. . . yes, a precipice backed by the strangest twilight, scarlet and flashing black stars. Two masci guarded the summit, hairless, swollen-faced things, eyes long since healed over. Blindly, they sensed the wifmunuc's presence, tilting up their heinous, misshapen heads. They let her pass, then went back to their meal of bones, black maws cracking down to expose the succulent marrow. Suddenly, the wifmunuc was reborn. She was a child, naked in twilight, standing amid the highest trees. A sound could be heard beyond the forest, a presence could be felt. The wifmunuc lost her breath . . .

"Wīhan," panted the wifford. She leaned back on her hands, to deepen the penetration as her orgasm spasmed. The helot, too, began to tremor—his semen exploding into her sex, and then—

"Wīhan, wīhan!" she shrieked.

—the wreccans sliced his belly open at the same time. The helot convulsed on the slab. The wifford chortled. Blood flew this way and that as the wreccans' hands delved into the rive to expeditiously extract the more delectable organs. The wifhands rejoiced, in awe of the scarlet spectacle. The blonde was in shock now. Very quickly, her ankles were tied, she was hung upside down against the wall on an iron hook, and her head was cut off with a machete. The body still twitched for a time, as the stump bled like a spigot into a small chettle. The helot's head, too, was cut off, and both were tossed into the fire, to cook. The blonde was gutted similarly, then all of the organs were thrown into the chettle. Seasonings were added, and the chettle was set on the fire.

The wifmunuc's eyes widened in wonder, in love. The lambent figure approached, beautiful in its grace and perfection. Tall, lean, naked, dark hair flowing behind it like an endless mane. The wifmunuc, still a child now, began to sob in this vision of holiness. Moonlight dappled the dell through high branches. The moonlight was pink . . .

While the festival meats were left to cook, the orgy ensued.

Wreccans were taken aside, ordered to perform for the whims of each wifhand. The wifford, sated and bespattered, stood aside to watch. Moans rose palpably into the cirice. The floor became a carpet of moving flesh in firelight. Sweating backs, legs spreading, buttocks plunging. One wreccan was ordered to fornicate with the helot. Meanwhile the cokkers stirred the chettle as the blood began to boil.

. . . perfection could be the only word—the perfect being in perfect light. The wifmunuc stared up, faced by the radiant, perfect flesh.

"Ure give wynn!" the little wifmunuc rejoiced. "Wi give lof bi soo ure folclagu!"

"Joindre mi in me wudu fo nisfan," the figure whispered back, flesh glowing in the pinkened moonlight. "Give lof, give wīhan, ond joindre mi on doefolmon."

"Modor!" cried the wifmunuc, reaching out.

The Ardat-Lil gazed down. "Soon my time will come again," she said. "Until then, fēdde me."

Suddenly, she was back before the nihtmir, in her old body, her old world. Behind her, the hustig rose to revelry. But it took the wifmunuc a moment to get her breath back, to readjust herself. Her flesh shined with sweat in the excitement now, and in the grace of what she'd just witnessed. The wifford came into the nave and kissed her. They rejoiced.

They all ate heartily of the hot meat pulled from the chettle. They filled their bellies. The wifmunuc, enlivened now, chose the newest wreccan and raped him on the dirt floor as the others watched, their eyes full of joy, their mouths smeared red.

Before the hustig was ended, they passed the engraved cuppe. They each took a sip of the blood and sighed.

The wifmunuc gustily swallowed the rest.

Erik hoped his white hair didn't give him away. He'd left the van covered by brush miles back in the woods. Skirting town was the only way. He felt certain they were expecting him.

He wore dark clothes. He brought a flashlight and carried the shotgun across his back. The pinkened moon followed him; it seemed to harass him as he wended through the dense woods.

Providence, he thought. It was almost funny now. Was it providence that he die here, in *their* hands? *Why am I even doing this?* he asked himself. *And what am I really doing?*

He wasn't sure how to answer himself, for it was true. He really *didn't* know what he was doing, did he? If all his suspicions were real? What would he do? What *could* he do?

It was well past midnight now. Eventually, the woods broke at a quiet residential street. The street was dark, but several windows were lit. Erik followed close to the shadows.

Headlights flashed around the bend. Erik dove for cover. A car seemed to be slowing. He unshouldered the shotgun and lay still. A spotlight roved the top of the hedges he hid behind. *Cops,* he realized. The spot moved along the trees, head-level. He could hear a radio squawking. Had they seen him? Was providence so cruel to let him come all this way only to die by the same police who'd sent him away years ago? *No, no,* he thought. The shotgun grew slick in his hands. *I'm going to die right here.*

The car idled past. Erik noted the crest and letters on the door: Lockwood Police. The moonlight unveiled the driver's face. It was Byron, the kid who'd arrested him.

Soon the headlights disappeared around the next bend.

He resumed his advance through the town. He struggled to recall exactly where everything was. Here was Meade Street, and here was Lockhaven. He would have to approach from behind the town square, to avoid the police station. In jest, he pictured himself strolling openly down Pickman Avenue, whistling, waving to Chief Bard.

A block down, through high trees, the white steeple spired. *Home again,* Erik thought.

The moonlight painted the church's white walls pink. He crept around very slowly, eyes peeled. And there it was: the little stone steps which led to the access beneath the church. At the end of the steps, he could see the door.

Erik stood still a moment. Memory flashed in and out of his head like a grueling nightmare. Was this really providence? Or his own horror? It was more than just a door that stood waiting for him. It was his past.

And it was waiting, he knew, with open arms.

Martin awoke in bed, dizzy, nauseous. The darkness was like mud in his face. He'd been dreaming, but all he could recall were streams of repugnant blurs and streaks like images of vivid muck. He felt gritty and he stank. He reached over for

Ann, but her side of the bed lay empty, unruffled. Where could she be at this hour? The clock read 1:30 A.M.

Jesus, the thought muttered. He lay back, straining against the force of memory. Where had he been all day? He remembered stopping in at the Crossroads, having a few beers with Andre and some of the other guys. Then . . .

What?

He couldn't remember. He couldn't even remember coming home. All that remained were wisps of what could only be nightmare. He remembered odd tastes and smells. Heat. Sweat. Waves of moans and—

Jesus, he thought again. One of the dream's images surfaced to completion: being straddled, a hot body pinning him to the ground. Sweat dripped onto his face and chest, breasts were joggling as bizarre words seemed to ooze like sooty smoke around his head. And then he remembered the face that looked down at him, between the breasts. Not Maedeen.

It was Ann's mother's face.

What the hell is wrong with me? he asked himself in disgust. Not only was he dreaming of infidelities . . . *I dreamed I was fucking Ann's mother, for God's sake.*

The realization made him feel even dirtier. Part of it he could figure now. He'd come home late, drunk. Ann was pissed, so that's why she wasn't here. She was probably downstairs sleeping on the couch.

Can't say I don't deserve it. He'd had a problem with alcohol in the past, but he was sure he'd defeated it. He'd never be anything if he let his life's old demons come back to him. He was a poet, an artist, and he had responsibilities now, to Ann and Melanie. *I better get my shit together,* he told himself.

He turned on the night-light and got up, grabbed his robe. He couldn't stand the smell of himself. He padded down the hall but stopped before the bathroom door. He heard water running. Jesus, who could be taking a shower at this hour? He peeked into Melanie's room and found it empty, the bed unslept in.

She must've been out late too. Of course, Martin could not justifiably scold her, given his own state. He sat on the bed to wait for her to finish. The room was plush, full of antiques. He looked around, waiting, but felt distracted. Next, he found himself standing at the window.

Low in twilight, the moon looked back at him. It was nearly

full. Its odd, bright-pink light seeped into his eyes, lulling him. The light seemed to show him things—indeterminate, yet absolutely *awful* things—beyond its fixed glow.

Blood. Flesh. Evil faces.

Words.

Hūsl, hūsl, hūsl.

Give lof!

And: *You are wreccan now.*

Martin felt lost, staring into the light. His consciousness felt wavering. *What am I doing?* he heard himself. He heard a distant hissing. The shower? Yes. Something was luring him away, yet the light remained like a ghost in his eyes.

Inexplicably, he turned away from the window and walked into Melanie's closet. But why? The closet was dark, but toward the back he detected a point of light.

A hole in the wall. A hole of light.

He put his eye to the hole.

Melanie, standing in a suit of white lather. Eyes closed, she turned her face up to the torrent of cool water. Martin's eye remained open over the hole. Something forced him to watch. Now Melanie was washing the suds off her body, the water sluicing. She shut the water off and stepped òut.

What am I . . .

She towel-dried her fine, light brown hair. Martin stared at her perfectly formed rump as she bent to dry her legs. Then she straightened, patting the towel around her breasts and under her arms. She hadn't shaved her armpits in several days; Martin found the sparse covering of hair, like fine fur, to be densely erotic. Even more erotic was the contrast of her large, dark brown nipples against the flawless whiteness of her breasts.

What . . . am . . . I—

Martin was masturbating as he continued to spy on his lover's young daughter. It felt obscene, like incest, but he couldn't refrain. Melanie's skin was so bright in the bathroom light, so lustrous. Somehow, looking at it was like being on some drug. Her face, too, was beautiful, and her dark brown eyes, the mussed wet hair. Martin felt helpless against the urge to continue to stroke himself. It was vision that spurred him, the sharp white clarity of Melanie's beauty, of her flesh. Beads of water nestled in her pubic hair glittered like jewels. Martin considered what his lust had reduced him to at that moment: *I'm a pervert, a peeper. I'm a thirty-eight-year-old published author mastur-bating in a closet.* Yet he couldn't help it. He could only look on as Melanie continued to tend to herself, oblivious to the voyeur's eye on the other side of the wall.

Oblivious? came the strange question.

Melanie stood with her front toward the wall. She was looking down, drying the muff of hair and the insides of her thighs. Then, very slowly, she looked up, right at the wall. She grinned directly into Martin's gaze.

Martin felt locked in rigor. The grin struck him like a fisticuff. He nearly shrieked. The tiny pendant lay between her breasts, and in her eyes—her stark beautiful chocolate-colored eyes—he saw madness, ataxia. He saw death.

"You are wreccan now, Martin," she said through her grin.

Erik could smell it even before he entered. He could feel it. *Hustig,* he thought automatically. *Hūslfek.*

The door to the church basement was unlocked. He stepped into blackness and waited, listening. No one was here, he felt sure of that. He felt sure of something else: people had been murdered in this place very recently.

The hustigs always ended at the high moon. There were no windows, so he felt safe turning on the lights.

Here was the brygorwreccan's chamber. This was where Erik used to live. He wondered about who had replaced him. There was the bed, the old dresser, the same bare, whitewashed cement walls. In the back was a large stereo system, but that was all.

The trunk.

The trunk had been moved to the side. He opened it and was not surprised to find several shovels and a box of heavy-duty plastic garbage bags, an æsc, and a few knives. Erik had kept his money hidden in the trunk's vinyl lining, but it wasn't there. There were also a few flashlights and a few pairs of work gloves. *Tools of the trade,* he thought.

He went to the back of the chamber. The large wooden door faced him like an old nemesis. From under its crack, he could feel the giveaway draft of warm air. Erik didn't need to open the massive door for the evidence; he could see it in his mind. He could see the fire pit and stoke rods, the blood-crusted dolmen, the chettles and the iron hooks high on the cement walls.

And he could see the nihtmir propped up in the nave.

But the door was locked.

He set down the shotgun and got the small hand-æsc out of the trunk. He began to dig around the bolt. He actually giggled as he worked. *I'm gonna trash the entire cirice. See how they like that. Let the fuckers know Erik Tharp is back in town.*

The hard wood around the bolt plate was tough. The sharp æscpoint dug out a splinter at a time. Soon he exposed the edge of the bolt plate. Once he got that out—

"Brygorwreccan," announced a voice behind him.

Erik turned. A guy in leather and black hair hanging in his face stood before him. He smiled wanly, holding a double-tipped pickax at port arms.

"Welcome home," Zack said. He lunged, heaving the pickax. Erik yelled and threw his hands up.

The pickax sank into Erik's left palm, then slammed into the door, nailing him to the wood. He reached for the shotgun, felt a bone break in his hand. *Not gonna make it,* he thought, grimly frantic. He stretched, but the shotgun remained inches from his grasp.

Meanwhile, Zack came at him with a knife . . .

CHAPTER TWENTY-TWO

"Dooer, dooer," oozed the voice in the dream.

Ann strained against the turmoil of sleep. The nightmare replayed through her mind. Melanie's birth seventeen years ago in the fruit cellar while the storm raged outside. The feminine chorus, firelight dancing on naked flesh. Soft hands caressed her, roving the gravid belly, tracing the sweat-slick thighs. Ann twitched in sleep. The emblem hovered, the queer double circle; it seemed to give off the faintest glow, and she thought she could see something in its shape, but what? Mouths sucked warm milk from her swollen breasts. Tongues licked fervidly up and down over her clitoris. Her sex began to spasm as her womb began to contract . . .

"Dooer, dooer . . ."

The nightmare's eye showed it all, never faces, just the naked figures bowed in attendance. A cup was being passed around, engraved with the same emblem on the wall. Then came more words, issuing in liquid softness:

"Dother fo Dother, Dother fo Dother . . ."

And the final vertiginous image: the bright-bladed knife plunging down—

slup-slup-slup

—time after time to the hilt, into soft flesh . . .

Ann's eyes snapped open in the dark. A slice of faint pink light canted in through the window. The clock glowed 4:12 A.M.

She lay on her side in a fetal shape. She watched several minutes pass on the clock, and soon the nightmare began to fade from her mind. She began to feel better. She could hear Martin breathing lightly behind her, and then she felt his hand slide over her breasts. At first she wanted to rebel, slap the hand away. She was still mad at him, she remembered, but his hand on her breasts felt so good, so soothing. The sensation pushed the dream out of her head completely, leaving desire in its place. She moaned as the fingers tended the nipple, gorging it. Next, his hands were pushing her nightgown up over her rump. Ann kept her eyes closed. Suddenly, she felt . . . lewd. She opened her legs at once, inviting him. His hands lay her out on her back; his penis nudged her once as he moved down in the dark. The glans felt hard as a knob of polished wood. He pushed her knees up to her chin and began to go down on her.

She whined at the initial contact of his tongue, then moaned steadily. Gently, and slowly at first, his tongue traced up and down the groove of her sex. Ann felt a flood of moisture and desire collide; she hugged her knees to her chest as the tongue delved harder and more precisely. Martin was going down on her more deftly than she could remember. He made her feel so good so fast that she forgave him instantly of his drunkenness and his coming home so late. The synchronicity of his mouth and tongue against the rhythmic tremors of her hips drew her horniness out like a tension rod being twisted and twisted. Soon it would have to snap . . .

She was going to come, but she didn't want to, not yet. She wanted to come with him inside of her. "Fuck me now," she panted. She never talked dirty in bed, but tonight she couldn't restrain herself. She'd never felt like this, so wound up, so primitively *horny*. "Put your cock in me."

Martin's soft poet's hands turned her over on her belly, then hauled her hips up. The roughness with which he positioned her was almost brutal, but she liked it—the promptness, the *immediacy* of his desire. He knelt behind her splayed rump; she felt like a bitch in heat waiting to be mounted. One hand came around her hip, the fingers opening her. Ann tensed as the gorged glans nudged into her sex. All she could feel right now was her need, like electricity humming from the swollen points of her nipples to the warm pocket of her sex. It made his penis feel huge and surreally hard. She almost shrieked when he thrust it all into her at once.

He was so deep in her. One hand braced her thigh, the other came around and plied her clitoris as his thrusts drew in and out. The pleasure was excruciating. The potentiality of her orgasm ticked in her loins like a bomb about to go off. She buried her face in the pillow, to increase the angle and depth of the penetration. It was too much, too many sensations waiting to break at once. Her hands twisted the sheets into knots, her teeth bit into the pillow.

"I love you, Martin," she panted. She couldn't believe what she said next. "You fuck me so good, I love it when you fuck me like this. Do it harder, honey. Fuck me harder."

Her request was obliged. His penis pushed into her so deep she thought she'd scream. He grabbed her hand and made her touch herself as he doubled the pace of his thrusts. His hips slapped the back of her thighs. He was pounding her, his penis plunging steadily in and out as she massaged the tip of her sex with her own fingers. Her breath hissed out of her throat, the pillowcase tore against her teeth. Her orgasm exploded.

The first was an abrupt, flexing burst, followed by strings of smaller pulses that didn't want to end. His penis continued to reel orgasms out of her loins like strings of large pearls. It felt so good, so delicious, that tears squeezed out of her eyes.

Soon she was so sore and sensitive she could bear no more. Martin's thrusts ebbed, then he stopped fully, his penis still buried in her. She eased forward, felt it slip out. "I want you to come now," she whispered. Martin remained upright on his knees. She turned around in the dark. She unhesitantly grasped his penis at its base and took the gorged glans into her mouth. She could taste the wet salt of her own musk. But something was strange, something she noticed at once.

"You sure as shit aren't going to make me come like that," her bed companion remarked.

My . . . God, Ann thought. Her movements froze. Her eyes peeled open as she moved her mouth off.

It was not Martin who had made the remark. It was Milly.

The bed lamp flicked on. Ann looked up, aghast. Milly knelt before her on the bed, naked, the set of her mouth part grin, part sneer. *But . . . but . . .* was all Ann could think until she lowered her gaze. Jutting from betwixt Milly's legs was a heinous parody of the male sex organ, attached to the nurse's hips with straps. Ann was disgusted. No wonder it felt so huge—it *was* huge. It looked like a miniature table leg, polished smooth with a rounded knob. It was black, shining. Even veins had been fashioned along the rubber shaft.

"Don't look so surprised," Milly said. "You came, didn't you?"

"How did—what—" Ann stammered. A brief glance showed her Milly's room, not her and Martin's. Ann immediately pulled her nightgown down and crawled back. What was she doing *here*?

"Come on, Ann," Milly said. "Don't pretend. You liked it."

"I thought you were *Martin*!"

"Don't hand me that shit. You started it. *You* came to *me*."

Had she? *I must have,* Ann realized. "I was confused, from earlier, I mean. I must've been disoriented."

"Bullshit. You wanted it, and you got it."

Milly's grin terrified her as much as the sight of the heinous black phallus, which the nurse then gave a mocking stroke. Next, she touched her sex beneath the thing's base. Ann saw, with further outrage, that the rubber penis even came complete with molded testicles. Milly's breasts were smaller than Ann's, and somewhat flat, with large oblong brown nipples. The nipple ends stood out like round wall studs.

"Okay, lover," Milly said. "My turn now."

"No! I . . . It was a mistake!"

Milly wouldn't hear of it. She pushed Ann roughly onto her back, then straddled over her and unstrapped the penis. "Lie back," she ordered. She actually put her hand to Ann's throat as she crawled over her. Between her breasts, there was an odd pendant of some kind, a pale stone on a white string. Milly poised her sex over Ann's face, one knee at Ann's armpit, and her other foot planted on the pillow.

"Milly . . . No . . ."

Milly chuckled. Her pubis was a great, light brown bush. "You can lick my pussy for a while," she said, "then you're gonna put that rubber cock on and fuck the daylights out of me. You hear me, sweetheart?"

Ann could no longer speak; Milly's sex plopped onto her mouth. A hand grasped the front of her hair. Ann's lips sealed shut. *I'm being raped by a woman,* she thought, but she could not explain how she felt. She could scream or even bite . . . but . . .

"Go on," Milly said. "Lick it."

The light flicked off. The slant of pink moonlight was all that lit the room, falling across Ann's eyes.

"Lick it."

Ann gulped.

"I said lick it. Don't pretend you don't want to."

What it was exactly that Ann could not explain to herself was that she *did* want to.

She hesitated. The pink moonlight oozed into her eyes. Milly lowered herself some more, sitting directly on Ann's face.

"Go on. Do it."

Ann felt something release in herself, something in her conscience or her spirit. Her hands drifted up and stroked Milly's buttocks. She sighed. In another moment she was doing exactly as Milly had ordered.

"Holy shit," Chief Bard slowly muttered.

Zack's body lay like a broken doll across the floor. A single Remington 12-gauge casing shined at the baseboard. Zack had a rough, meaty hole in his chest the size of an adult fist. A halo of blood encircled the body.

Tharp, Bard realized.

He noted that the door past the gravedigger's room stood open. Someone had torn the wood out around the bolt seat. Bard, with a knowing reluctance, stepped past the dark threshold.

Aw, shit, goddamn it, shit. His MagLite played across the cirice. *Desecrated,* he thought. That's how they would see this. The dolmen had been tipped over, several of the iron chettles had been cracked. The earthen chalice lay smashed. Tharp had even tried to pry the nihtmir off the wall. Thank God he'd failed.

Bard dragged Zack's body out to the cruiser. The town lay asleep in darkness. The high hedgerow hid him and his efforts. Zack was what police called "skell": a low-life deadbeat punk, a criminal. Bard could've cared less that the boy was dead—that's not what distressed him now to the point that he felt tremors in his gut. To them, it wasn't a street punk who had been murdered, it was a brygorwreccan. This fact, and the desecration of their temple, was notice to them. They had been attacked. They had an enemy in the know.

Bard knew well that they would not like this. No, they wouldn't like this at all.

Next morning, Martin sheepishly entered the kitchen. Ann didn't look up from her orange juice and muffin.

"I'm sorry about last night," he offered.

"What do you mean?" she feigned, still not looking at him.

"Coming home late, coming home drunk," he said. "I met some of the guys at the Crossroads. We were drinking, running our mouths, and next thing I know it's closing time. You know how it is."

"No, Martin, I don't know how it is. So why don't you tell me?"

"Come on, Ann. Give me a break."

At last Ann looked up. "That's not what any of this is about and you know it."

Martin looked confused. "Why are you so pissed off? It's not the crime of the century when a guy has a few too many beers and loses track of time."

Ann huffed. "I know that, Martin, and *you* know that's not the reason I'm pissed off. Don't treat me like a fool."

"Ann, what are you—"

"Who were you with yesterday!" she snapped.

He looked at her funny. "I told you, the guys from the 'Roads."

"Right, Martin, right."

"It's true," he countered. "I was with Andre, the guy who runs the place, and Dave Kromer, Bill Eberhart, and some other guys who work in town."

"Bullshit, Martin. I *saw* you. Yesterday afternoon, I saw you driving *my car* away from that silly little general store, and there was a woman sitting next to you."

"Wha—oh, you mean Melanie."

"No, Martin, it wasn't Melanie—"

"Yes, it was, Mom," Melanie said, coming into the kitchen. She was wearing a sundress Ann didn't recognize. Casually, she opened the refrigerator and poured some orange juice. "I went into the store to get some sodas to take to Wendlyn's. Martin saw me coming out so he picked me up and gave me a ride."

Ann's brow runneled. "A ride to where?"

"I told you, Mom. To Wendlyn's. She wanted to show me her dresses. In fact, she gave this one to me. Wasn't that nice of her?"

"Uh," Ann stalled. "Yes, it was." She felt an instant fool, looking at Martin. "I'm sorry, Martin. I thought—"

Martin laughed. He came around and rubbed her shoulders at

the table. "What, you thought I was running off with Maedeen the ice cream lady?" He laughed again.

"I guess I'm overreacting to everything these days," Ann said, as if that were an excuse. "I'm sorry," she repeated.

"Actually, I can't blame you for jumping to conclusions," Martin joked. "As good-looking as I am, what woman wouldn't be constantly jealous? My expertise as a lover is world-renowned. Before I met you, women had to put themselves on a waiting list to go out with me."

"Oh, God!" Melanie laughed and left the kitchen. But Ann still felt like a shitheel. She touched Martin's hand as he continued to massage her shoulder. How long could he remain so forgiving of her quick temper and lack of forethought? She'd practically accused him of cheating on her, which was the laugh of all time, considering what she'd done last night with . . .

Milly, she remembered.

She felt horrible keeping the truth from him. If it were with another man, he'd be justified to end the relationship right now. But with another *woman*? What would he do if he knew? What would any man do?

She wanted to tell him, but what on earth could she say?

"I'm going out back for a while," he said, and picked up his pad and pen. She didn't have time to say anything. "I'm working on a great poem, my magnum opus," he went on with his mysterious poet's enthusiasm. "So far it's a hundred stanzas."

"Happy writing," she offered.

Alone now she felt even more of a shitheel. She'd never expressed any active interest in his writing because she didn't know how to. That, and what she'd almost wrongly accused him of, made her feel very low, and lower still considering her lewd foray with Milly.

Milly, she thought again. What would she say next time she saw her? She dreaded their next meeting. But she'd have to see her soon, to check on her father. This morning, Dr. Heyd had told her that her father seemed to have stabilized from last night's blunder, but that could change any minute. Shivering, she remembered the nightmare, the vertigo, and the new words the dream had whispered in her mind. *Dother fo Dother.* But what could that mean? The words made no sense. Then she remembered where they'd come from: they'd been some of the words her father had written last night when he'd come conscious. The dream had merely transplanted the words into its own scape.

That made her feel a little better. But there was still Milly. Total recollection evaded her. In pieces, she remembered what they'd done together, and she even remembered how much she'd liked it. But what had happened afterward? Ann had wakened on the couch, downstairs, not in Milly's bed.

In dread, she went up the stairs, down the hall. She could hear the awful heart monitor. She stepped in and stopped. Milly was taking her father's blood pressure. Innocuously, she looked up. "Oh, hi, Ann."

Hi, Ann? Ann thought. Ruffled, she gazed at the nurse.

"What's wrong?"

Ann cleared her throat. "Milly, I want to talk to you about last night."

"Oh, don't worry about that," Milly perkily replied. She looked fresh, rested, bereft of taint. "Your father's fully stabilized."

"That's not what I'm referring to," Ann proceeded. "I mean, you know . . . last night."

"What about last night?" Milly casually removed the cuff from Ann's father's thin arm. She wore her typical nurse's outfit, the white dress, white stockings, and white shoes. She acted as though nothing were amiss.

"Are you all right?" She came right up to Ann, put her hand on her forehead. "You look pale."

"I'm fine, Milly, I just—shit! I'm really bothered about what we did last night."

Milly laughed softly. "I don't know what you're talking about. I went right back to bed after we stabilized your dad. I slept till three A.M., then Dr. Heyd woke me up so he could go home." Her concerned look deepened. "Oh, you must've had a fight with Martin last night."

"What? What makes you say that?"

"I came downstairs a couple of times to get a Coke, and I saw you sleeping on the couch. You were tossing and turning. Bad dreams?"

Ann didn't get it. "Milly, wait a minute. I slept on the couch last night? *All* night?"

"Of course, don't you remember? I just assumed you had a

fight with Martin, so that's why you weren't sleeping with him."

Ann gauged her next question. "Milly, did I come into your room last night?"

Milly gave her a canted look. "My room? No. Why?"

Ann stared, fully confused. Then Milly said, "You poor thing. You mustn't have slept well at all. Do you feel okay? You don't seem to have a fever. Do you want me to get you something?"

But Ann felt better at once, much better. *A dream,* she realized. She shuddered at the imagery: Milly's pubis in her face, her dirty talk, and the hideous black phallus. *I dreamed the whole thing.* "No, no," she answered at last. "I'm fine, just a little mixed-up. I had the strangest dream last night."

"It must have been a humdinger," Milly responded. "The way you were tossing and turning on the couch. I was a little worried."

"I'm fine," Ann repeated. "I'll talk to you later, I've got some errands to run."

"Okay. Bye."

Ann nearly skipped out of the room. The dream had been so intense she'd actually thought it was real. Knowing now that it wasn't made her jubilant. *What do you say about that, Dr. Harold? I'm not a latent lesbian after all.*

Back downstairs, she stopped on the landing. She looked down. More steps descended to the fruit cellar, which she'd seen her mother locking yesterday. Ann felt piqued. Her recurring nightmare of Melanie's birth originated at the bottom of those stairs, where she'd given birth to Melanie for real seventeen years ago. Suddenly, she wanted to go down—she felt she needed to, if for any reason to confront the landscape of the nightmare. Perhaps if she saw it again, after all this time, she might realize what it was that distressed her subconscious to this extreme. What harm could there be?

She went down the stairs, feeling suddenly ill. Each step down showed her another detail of the nightmare. The hands straying over the pregnant belly. The hovering double-orbed emblem. The cloaked figure standing between her legs waiting for her to deliver the newborn Melanie. And the arcane words: "Dooer, dooer." Ann quickly decided she didn't want to go back into this room, yet she felt she must. She felt it contained some secret she needed to know. She could not explain the compulsion.

She turned the knob and swore. The door was still locked. It infuriated her. Why on earth did her mother insist on keeping this door locked? It was just a fruit cellar.

Now she felt driven. She raced back up the stairs. "Mother!" she called out. She checked everywhere, every room on every floor. She asked Milly, but Milly hadn't seen her. Ann's mother was not in the house.

Goddamn it, she thought. *Where the hell is she?*

The wifmunuc scowled. Chief Bard was scared; that look on her face filled him with the basest kind of dread. He'd parked the cruiser behind the fire hall. She took a final glance at Zack's shotgunned body, then slammed the trunk closed.

"This cannot be tolerated," she said.

"I know," Chief Bard admitted. His rotund stomach squirmed. Sweat broke out on his high brow.

"We've been violated, blasphemed." The wifmunuc's eyes were somewhere else, in the sky, past the trees. Bard felt grateful. They'd inspected the cirice together; Bard noted details that had escaped his earlier inspection. Amid the vandalism, they'd discovered a gas can. It was full. Clearly, Tharp had intended to set fire to their holy place. But he hadn't, as though he'd been interrupted. Something had stopped him, but what?

"He's out there somewhere, Chief Bard. He could ruin everything. Find him, stop him at all costs."

Bard's collar dug deep into his fat neck. "There's only me and Byron. I need help. The only way I can guarantee Tharp's apprehension is to call the state police."

The wifmunuc glared at the suggestion. "You will find him yourself, Chief Bard. Bringing in an outside agency is far too great a risk. They might find something we don't want them to find. You will find that miserable wretch yourself. Is that clear?"

Bard dared not look into her eyes. Like a furnace they were, like pits of hatred, terror. "I understand," he said.

"He has offended us. He has tainted us in our holy grace. You will catch him and put an end to his heresy."

Bard gulped, nodded.

Suddenly, she was gazing up into the sky. "Just two more nights," she whispered, smiling. "Such glory awaits us all."

Bard knew what she was talking about. He also knew what would happen to him if he didn't nail Tharp. "What about Zack?" he asked, more to change the subject.

She glanced with distaste to the cruiser's trunk. "Must I tell you everything? Bury the wreccan scum and get on with your job. You're wasting time. *Her* time."

"Yes," Bard said.

The wifmunuc gazed at him now, her awful eyes boring into his own. She gingerly touched the pendant at her bosom. "Give ælmesse to me. Give lof."

Aw, God, no, he thought.

"Kneel," she commanded.

Bard knelt in the dirt. He could either kneel of his own before the evil bitch, or she could make him. He had long ago learned the futility of resisting them. Beads of sweat twitched down his bald pate. Sickened, he could taste it even before it happened.

"Now," she said, "drink of me." She raised her dress to her waist. The thick thatch of her pubis shined in the sun. Chief Bard dutifully propped open his mouth as the wifmunuc began to piss into his face. She grinned down at her fat little peow, guiding the hot stream directly into his mouth. Wincing, he gulped down each caustic mouthful, felt the awful heat spread in his belly. When she'd finished, he knelt before her, dripping piss in the sun.

"You will find our little brygorwreccan, Chief Bard, and you will bring him to me in pieces. Otherwise, the next wreccan pig we bury will be you."

CHAPTER TWENTY-THREE

Dr. Harold barely heard his patients. All afternoon, his mind kept straying, reexamining thoughts and images, and homing back to the disturbed psych ward artwork of Erik Tharp.

It ate at him. After his last private patient had left, Dr. Harold went right back into the bag of Tharp's hospital records. The accounts, the bizarre drawings and words, were all he had to go on. Invented languages were nothing new to psychiatry; they accompanied many acknowledged psych profiles: tripolar schizophrenics, referential neurotics, autistics, etc. But Tharp fell into none of those categories. Dr. Harold looked more closely at the sketches. He found a clear coherence in theme, something ritualistic, which paralleled Tharp's transcripted accounts when interviewed by Dr. Greene. Tharp had also very coherently applied the cryptic vocabulary to each drawing. *Demons,* Dr. Harold mused. Tharp said they worshipped a demon. He thumbed back through the pads, to attempt a correlation between the most often repeated words and what their corresponding sketches depicted. *Peow* and *wreccan* seemed to relate to the male caricatures, while *loc* and *liloc* obviously denoted the women. *Brygorwreccan* was the word Tharp had consistently applied to himself, the self-portrait with the shovel. Then came *wīhan* and *hūsl*, which were always written around a scene depicting a clear ritual act, violence, murder.

The demon was the keystone. *Doefolmon, hustig, Fulluht-Loc.* These words implied an *event* in the sketches, a *repeated* event. But why was the latter capitalized? *Fulluht-Loc,* he pondered. *An event more significant than the others?*

I'm a psychiatrist, not a demonologist, he reminded himself. Perhaps he was attempting to decrypt Tharp's delusions from the wrong angle. Tharp possessed a delusional sexual phobia.

Most phobias and hallucinotic fugue-themes had some basis in truth, something the patient had heard or read, seen on TV. *Objectify,* Dr. Harold thought now, staring at the pads. *Rituals. Sacrifices. Cults.* He wondered. The sketches seemed almost mythological; they possessed a *tone,* a hint of something ancient, clandestine. Semicircles of figures in the woods, beneath the moon, naked, bowing. *Worshipping something,* he finished. Like the Druids or the Aztecs.

It wasn't much to go on, but he could think of no other avenue by which to proceed. He flipped through the phone book, to the department listings at the university.

I don't know anything about this kind of stuff, Dr. Harold reckoned. *So I'll find someone who does.*

By midafternoon, Ann was bored. She felt useless, uninvolved. Melanie was with her friends, Martin was off writing. Everyone but Ann was busy with something. She lingered about the house and yard. She still hadn't seen her mother around—another involvement—but that probably worked out for the best. Ann wished she had something useful to do, like help out with her father or something, pull weeds, paint the shutters—anything. She called her associate at the firm to find out how everything was going, and she was disappointed when he said, "Fine, Ann. Everything's fine. Depositions are out, we're firing back 'rogs a mile a minute, and JAX Avionics wants to settle before trial. Don't worry about a thing." She hung up, depressed.

She went for a walk through town. Maybe she'd run into Melanie and meet some of these friends of hers. But the streets stood idle as usual. A lot of cars were parked around the town hall; Ann's mother, no doubt, was conducting another of her endless council meetings. It infuriated Ann how easily her mother went on with the moving parts of her life while Ann's father lay dying. Perhaps that was just part of being realistic. Around the corner she saw several little girls playing near the woods. It reminded her how few children there seemed to be in Lockwood. She caught herself staring, and the little girls stared back. Then they broke and ran away, giggling. Next thing she knew, Ann was walking into the general store.

"Hi, Ann," Maedeen looked up from behind the counter and smiled. "How are you today?"

"Fine," Ann said. But why had she come in here? To begin with, Maedeen was not exactly her favorite person. "I'm just sort of wandering around. Where is everyone?"

"Town Hall. Today's the monthly advisory council meeting. How's your dad?"

"The same." Saying that was a more refined way of saying the truth. *He's still dying.* She browsed around the knickknacks and sundries: quilts, handmade candles, porcelain dolls. Did people buy enough of this stuff to support the store? Behind the counter, Maedeen was typing. Further back, Ann noticed a room full of tall file cabinets. "I'll be with you in a minute," Maedeen said, concentrating on her task. Then she zipped the page out of the old manual machine. "I'm also the town clerk," she informed Ann. "Whenever there's a meeting I have to prepare the minutes from the previous month, and I'm late."

"Town clerk?" Ann queried.

"Yeah, aside from running the store, I keep all the town records on file." She pointed to the little room full of cabinets. "In there."

Now it made more sense. The store was just a local formality. Maedeen supported herself as a clerk.

"I have to run these over to your mother. Would you like to come?"

"Oh, no thanks."

"Could you keep an eye on things for me? I'll only be a few minutes."

"Sure," Ann said. Maedeen left with the sheaf of papers, the cowbell jangling after her. Alone now, Ann's faint jealousy resurfaced. What could Martin see in her anyway, if he saw anything at all? *I'm better looking than her,* Ann childishly affirmed to herself. Maedeen was short and rather tomboyish, or tomwomanish, in this case. She always wore faded jeans and plain blouses, flip-flops. Melanie had told her that Maedeen's husband had died. Ann wondered when, and why. She casually scanned the big glass bowls of candy along the counter, when she noticed the small framed picture amid Maedeen's typewriter clutter. She knew she shouldn't but she did anyway. She walked around the counter. She glanced out the front window; Maedeen was still heading briskly for the town square. Ann then went to the typewriter desk and picked up the picture. The snapshot showed Maedeen, a decade younger, sitting on a

couch with a little girl—Wendlyn, her daughter. But in her
arms, Maedeen held a naked baby. The baby was a boy.

Just like Milly. A baby boy.

This was weird. Like Milly, Maedeen had only mentioned a
daughter when they'd met. She'd said nothing about having a
boy too. Why?

Don't, she thought. *It's none of your business.* Yet the lawyer
in her couldn't resist. She'd said she kept the town records here,
hadn't she? Ann glanced again out the window, to make sure it
was safe. Then she went into the file room.

It didn't take her long. BIRTH RECORDS, one drawer was
clearly marked. She opened the drawer and began to rummage.
What if someone comes in and sees me? But she ignored the
suggestion. Her curiosity burned her. The files were alphabeti-
cal. FOST, MAEDEEN. Ann opened it and found a certificate
of birth. But just one. FOST, WENDLYN. It was dated seventeen years ago. The signature of the delivering doctor was
Ashby Heyd. There was no record of a boy being born. When
Ann dug out Milly's file, she found the same thing. Only Rena's
birth certificate.

So who were the baby boys? Were they relatives' children?

Before Ann closed the drawer, she noticed a different-
colored folder in the very back. It possessed no heading. Ann
picked it up, opened it.

Stared.

Several sheets of old paper. A typed list. MALE BIRTHS, the
top of the sheet read.

She thumbed down the list of chronological dates.

FOST, MAEDEEN, *MC 1-12-80, relinquished for adoption
1-23-80.*

MC? Ann thought. *Male child?* It had to be.

She put the boy up for adoption, she realized. *Why?*

But that was not all. She found Milly's name. GODWIN,
MILLICENT, *MC 6-15-82, relinquished for adoption 6-22-82.*

My God, Ann thought.

The list went back fifteen years, women she'd never known
or heard of. Each had an MC typed behind the name, a date of
birth, and a date of adoption.

No wonder I haven't seen any boys in town, Ann came to the
bizarre conclusion. *Their mothers put them all up for adoption.*

CHAPTER TWENTY-FOUR

Scierors tied the figures down, laying open abdomens in single swipes. The helots still twitched as their organs were systematically removed. Heads were lopped off with great machetelike blades which whirred in the firelight. Genitals were sliced off groins. Some were thrown onto the fire whole, others were filleted first, the choice meats added to the boiling chettles of blood. Females, fattened for weeks on corn mash, were hauled screaming from the pens. Wreccans expertly flensed them alive as they thrashed, peeling off sheets of skin . . .

Erik shivered in the dark. These weren't just visions, they were memories. They were the feks he'd watched in his past. And he'd seen it all again, in his mind, the instant he'd stepped back into the cirice.

He'd been lucky. Zack's pickax had nailed his hand to the door. He'd reached the shotgun in time; fortunately, there'd been a round in the chamber. Zack's knife had flashed. Just as it would've sunk hilt-deep into his solar plexus, Erik had squeezed the trigger. The 12-gauge blast knocked a hole into Zack's chest, blowing him six feet across the room.

Gunsmoke rose, and a static silence. Erik dislodged the pick from his hand, bandaged himself, and entered the cirice.

Its darkness greeted him like an old friend, and its smell. The smell was always the same, like pork roast. The heat lingered in the air; embers still glowed from the great cooking pit.

The memories held him in numb stasis. He panned the flashlight through the nave, more pieces of his grim past. The chettles, the æsces, irons, carving knives, stokers, and the stone dolmen. Blood streaked the cinder-block wall, where they'd decapitated countless hūsls, and there were the iron hooks, from which they'd been hung upside down. Erik stared at all this for a length of time he could not determine. Last, he found himself gazing upon the back wall of the nave, at the uneven double-orbed sheet of gray stone, the—

"Night-mirror," he muttered.

Leave, he thought. *Leave this evil place and never come back.* But he couldn't do that, he knew he couldn't. Who else would stop them? *There's only me,* he realized.

Suddenly, he felt engulfed in rage. He broke, throwing things. He cleared the racks of utensils, kicked over the candelabra. The smaller chettles he picked up and threw, cracking them. The larger ones he could only tip over. Next, he grabbed a sledgehammer—which they used for cracking open heads—and attacked the dolmen with it. He banged and banged, but the thick granite wouldn't break. With two-by-fours, then, he managed to lever the slab itself off its seat and slide it off the twin plinths. His rage roiled, carried him, and next he was slamming the sledgehammer against the face of the nihtmir. He slammed at it for minutes, almost mindlessly. When he stopped and looked at the slight damage he'd done, he thought: *No, no, not good enough. But—*

Of course. The maintenance shed, outside. Lawn equipment and . . . *Gas,* he thought.

He dashed back outside, around the side of the church. He was giddy with excitement. What a perfect way to announce his homecoming: burning the entire church to the ground. The studs in the basement would carry to the ceiling, then everything would go. He rummaged through the shed, where they kept the mowers, and there it was, shiny red. A five-gallon gas can. It was almost full.

The pinkened moon followed him back to the stairs. It made him feel watched. *Protect me, God, protect me,* he thought, or prayed. When he was back in the cirice, he looked for the best way. *Yeah, perfect,* he thought. A full cord of wood lay neatly stacked against one wall. It would catch the studs, leading the flame to the wood rafters above. By the time the fire truck got here, the whole church would be in flames.

He unscrewed the cap, was about to douse the pile of wood with gas, when he stopped. Had he heard something? No, he *felt* something. He felt . . .

He set the can down, turned. *Erik, Erik,* he heard, but not in his ears, in his head. He stepped forward. Now a faint glow seemed to rise in the cirice, from the nave. Light like mist, like luminous fog. The fog seemed pink . . .

Erik. Brygorwreccan. Come.

"No," he croaked in his ruined voice.

He was standing before the nihtmir. Its dead gray stone seemed to glow. Yes, he could see it, could see *into it*.

Something moved there, in the pinkened depths.

A face. A—

Her face, he thought, staring.

He couldn't take his eyes away.

Protect me, God. Protect me.

The face smiled at him, a great maw jammed with teeth.

Hello, Erik, it said.

The smile lengthened, drawing up.

Erik screamed. He ran out of the cirice, up the stairs, and into the woods, his fear propelling him like a missile, away, away from that hideous unholy visage.

He lay awake now in the front seat of the van. He was staring up through the trees at the moon. The moon was pink.

"Protect me, God," he whispered. "Protect me."

But in his desperate prayer, he didn't see God. All he saw was the perverse pinkish moon, and suffused in its sphere, the memory of her horrid face remained.

Grinning at him.

CHAPTER TWENTY-FIVE

It was a dream. Of course it was.

It *had* to be.

Milly was unwrapping her legs from Ann's face. Ann had no breath. "That wasn't bad," Milly said. "You're learning."

Milly's naked body shined pale white in the lamplight. Excitement filled her nipples. Ann sat up, wiped her mouth off on her wrist. *Where am I?* she thought. She was sitting on a carpet. When she looked up, she gasped. She saw a bed, but why was she on the floor? Then she heard grim, steady beeping. This wasn't Milly's room at all. It was her father's.

"Let's see if I can find it," Milly said. She was bending over one of the dresser drawers, looking for something.

But Ann was aghast. Her father's pallid form lay still in the bed, his face sunken. Needles jammed in his arm led up to inverted IV bottles on wheeled stands. Suddenly, his old mouth popped open, and he groaned.

"You seemed to like the black one a lot last night," Milly was commenting. Was that a bottle of milk on the dresser? "Ah, here it is. I think you'll like this one even more."

Ann wanted to scream when she saw what Milly was talking about. From the drawer, the nude nurse had extracted another strap-on phallus. But this one was flesh-colored, longer, and much thicker. Milly was on her knees now, calm as she strapped the grotesque apparatus onto her hips. She turned, still kneeling. The rubber prong pointed at Ann. "Suck it awhile," Milly said. "Pretend it's a real cock, and suck it."

Ann felt shrinking. Her will tore like frayed fabric. She was repulsed, but she could not disobey.

As instructed, she commenced. Milly tittered. She leaned her groin forward, hands on hips, grinning. "That's it, that's a good little cocksucker."

Ann, eyes squeezed shut, could barely get it in her mouth. She could feel the hideous molded veins. Against her tongue she could feel the hole centered in the bulblike glans.

"This one's got balls too," Milly said.

Ann remembered the molded rubber testicles of last night's phallus. This one, though, was different. She brought her hand beneath it and felt a rubber bag of some kind, filled with some warm fluid. Then she saw the rest, a tube leading out, attached to a rubber squeezeball, a pump.

"Keep sucking," Milly ordered. "Suck me like you do Martin." She was sighing now, as though she really felt something. Ann was mortified, at Milly, and at herself for doing this. Why couldn't she stop, get up, leave?

"Yeah, I wish I had a real cock," Milly was saying, "just for tonight. A great big long *real* cock to fuck you with, to come all over your face with . . ."

Ann tried to perform her task more intently, for she knew when Milly tired of this, she'd want to put the monstrous thing somewhere else.

"Almost real, huh?" Milly was grinning. Then she pushed Ann's mouth off. "Hold still," she said. She began to stroke the rubber penis in front of Ann's face.

"I—" Ann queried. "What are you—"

"Lean up." The odd pale pendant lay between Milly's breasts. "I'm going to come in your face." Her other hand began to squeeze the rubber ball.

Ann flinched, closed her eyes. With each squeeze, the phallus squirted a jet of warm milk into Ann's face.

"There. You like that?"

Ann could not respond. More milk jetted from the artificial glans. One spurt went right into Ann's mouth. The rest ran down her breasts and legs.

Why is she doing this? Ann wondered in turmoil. Milk dribbled from her lips. *Why can't I leave?*

That was certain. The more she wanted to flee from this perverse masquerade, the more she knew she couldn't.

It's a dream, she assured herself. *Just a dream.*

"Hands and knees," Milly ordered.

"Milly, please. Don't—"

Milly slapped her face. "Just do it."

Milk dripped off Ann's nipples. She shut her eyes, humiliated. Milly knelt right up behind her and inserted the rubberized phallus into Ann's sex.

She nearly yelped. The thing was huge, it bulged her. She almost fainted when she felt how deeply the prosthetic probed her. Her mind seemed like a jigsaw, throwing pieces. Part of her thought, *Thank God Dad's unconscious, thank God he can't see this,* while another part continued to reassure, *Don't worry, it's just a dream. It's not real.*

She gritted her teeth as the thing slid hugely in and out. Each thrust nudged the bulb of her cervix. "You like it, right?" Milly asked.

"Please, Milly, I—"

She slapped Ann's right buttock hard as she could, like wet leather snapping. "Right?" she demanded.

"Yes, yes," Ann replied. The slap print buzzed on her rump. But a forbidden inkling drifted up. Part of her *did* like it.

"Close your eyes and look," Milly ordered next.

Ann didn't understand. "Wha—"

Milly grabbed the back of her hair, pushed Ann's face into the carpet.

"Look!"

Ann squeezed shut her eyes. Most of her mouth was pressed to the floor.

"Do you see?"

"See *what*?" Ann muffled.

"Her! Do you see *her*!"

Ann didn't see anything but her own disgrace. Her hands and knees felt bolted to the floor.

"What have we here?" a voice asked from above. Maedeen walked in. She began taking off her clothes. "You're breaking her in well, sweoster. Mind if I join in?"

Milly chuckled, pumping steadily. Maedeen sat down right in front of Ann, spreading her legs. She too had one of the little pale pendants about her neck. It looked shapeless, a little stone. She pulled Ann's face to her crotch. "Eat it, yeah, that's right." Ann felt helpless; she lapped frantically at the musky flesh. She was crying, gasping for breath. "I fucked your precious Martin the other night," Maedeen remarked. "Five or six times. I'll fuck him anytime I want. He's a good little peow. I'm already pregnant."

"Oh, Maedeen," Milly congratulated, grasping Ann's hips. "That's wonderful."

"And you know what he's doing now? Your precious Martin?" Milly laughed along with Maedeen. "He's watching your daughter take a shower through a hole in the wall. He's jerking off. But don't worry, he wouldn't dare touch her, he knows never to do that."

"Melanie's quite a beautiful girl, Ann," Milly added. "And she's a virgin."

"She's just what we need for the doefolmon."

Ann could make nothing of this madness. She brought her face up long enough to plead, "Why are you doing this to me?"

"We're initiating you," Milly said, thrusting deeper.

Maedeen fingered the pendant between her smallish, big-nippled breasts. "We're making you holy. For the doefolmon."

"Ready, Annie?" Milly asked. She pulled Ann's hips back, to effect maximum penetration. Ann squirmed; she felt skewered. "Come in her now," Maedeen said, and pushed Ann's face back down, and Milly was squeezing the rubber ball again, pumping. Ann felt the warm spurts of milk launch into her sex. She whined in anguish. Her disgust tremored in time with her orgasm.

Suddenly, a groan sounded from above. In panic, Ann looked up. Her father, conscious now, was leaning out of the convalescent bed, his jaundiced eyes huge on the scene below. Ann shrieked. Her father's face looked like a bad wax mask. His withered finger shook, pointing down at her.

"That's right, peow," Milly said. "We're fucking your daughter."

Ann's father was shaking, murmuring in bursts. Eventually, his twisted mouth formed words. "Guo the wifhands," he croaked. An IV line tore from his arm. "Guo the Fulluht-Loc . . ."

"Listen to him." Maedeen chuckled. "He can't even talk right anymore, the stupid helot."

"Uor mut go!"

Ann tried to get up, to go to him, but she couldn't move.

"He didn't really have a stroke, Ann," Milly said, still pumping the ball. "Dr. Heyd gave him something to fuck up his brain."

"Doefolmon!" the old man shouted best he could. "Uor mut—"

Maedeen got up. Milly withdrew the phallus. Milk flooded out of Ann's sex and ran down the inside of her thighs. "Help him!" Ann pleaded. "Help him!"

"Oh, we'll help him, all right," Milly assured. She was standing by the night table now. Maedeen leaned over the bed.

"Es unwi! Es dwola!"

"Shut up, you old fuck," Maedeen said. "Or we might decide to kill you right now."

"I don't know why we don't," Milly commented. She was preparing an injection. Ann screamed at her but still couldn't budge against whatever power kept her on the floor.

"The wifmunuc wants him alive for a while longer," Maedeen said. "To keep Ann here."

What were they talking about? What were they doing?

"Huro liloc!" Ann's father grated. "Huro succubi!"

Maedeen climbed on the bed. Her pendant swayed as she squatted over the old man's face. "Peow, thane," she said. She began to urinate. "Wīhan," she said, glaring down.

"What are you doing!" Ann wailed. "He's a sick old man!"

"He's a peow," Milly corrected. "And we piss on peows."

Now the old man was gagging, coughing urine as Maedeen pissed in his mouth. "That should quiet him down a little."

Milly jammed a needle into his arm. "Dother fo Dother," he gurgled. Then he fell limp in the sheets.

Ann continued to scream at them, but they only laughed at her outrage. Milly unstrapped the phallus and refilled its receptacle with milk. "My turn," Maedeen said. The two naked women exchanged grins. Then Maedeen strapped on the device.

Ann looked up in horror. "Wha—what are you going to do?"

Milly laughed. Now Maedeen was smearing Vaseline over the shining, veined phallus.

"Guess," she answered.

Ann awoke screaming. She jerked up in the dark, glanced frantically about, then screamed once more. Martin was not in bed with her. Her sex felt sore. Pinkish moonlight eddied through the gap in the curtains. Her nightgown billowed as she

flew out of the room and down the hall. Her father lay unconscious in the bed, the heart monitor beeping steadily. Milly was
not here. Ann leaned over her father's sunken face. The face
was dry, the pillow clean. Then she scampered to the other end
of the house. Her mother's room was empty, the bed unslept in.
Nor did she find Melanie in her own room. Confusion infuriated
her. She checked the house top to bottom.

No one was here.

Where is everybody! she demanded. *It's past midnight, and
everybody's gone!*

In the kitchen, she tried to calm herself down. She drank
some juice, wishing it were scotch. This was inexcusable. Martin must be at the bar, getting drunk. And Melanie must be with
these new weird friends of hers. And her mother, and Milly,
where could they be this late?

Images of the dream felt like splinters in her brain. She felt so
disgusted she wanted to throw up. She'd been raped by women,
by a hideous milk-spurting phallus. She'd watched Maedeen
urinate into her father's face. Where did Ann's mind resource
such obscene, pornographic imagery? What would Dr. Harold
say? What did it *mean*?

Worse was that it seemed so real. Her sex and rectum ached
dully. Harold would claim the dream meant she didn't trust anyone, that she subconsciously feared those who seemed the most
innocuous. And as for the dull ache, "conative sensory dream-
supplantation," he would say, or something similar. "It's common for tactile stimuli to linger after night terrors," he'd told
her once.

Her mind felt like a meld of ground meat. She could scarcely
distinguish between dream and reality these days. What had
happened today? The store, Maedeen's files. Had that been a
dream too? *No, no!* she felt certain. It couldn't have been! She'd
seen the birth records. In the last fifteen years over a dozen male
babies had been born, and they'd all been put up for adoption.
Why? Why were the only men in Lockwood transients? Why
were the only children girls?

Simmer down, she thought. She went back upstairs, to her
room. She hated it here. She wanted to be back in the city, back
at the firm. Everything was going wrong. Martin and Melanie
had never been more distant. Her mother's disapproval of her
had only intensified. *Nothing* was right.

Spikes of the dream returned. The mocking, naked women. The bizarre pendants between their breasts, and the even more bizarre words. They'd implied they wanted Melanie for something.

. . . she's a virgin . . . she's just what we need for . . .

Dr. Harold would claim this was only her subconscious symbolizing her fear of Melanie's vulnerability as she approached adulthood. Why did Ann sense something phony about it all?

Through the curtains, she peered at the moon. The moon peered back. Something about the dream pendants bothered her. The pink moonlight seemed to jar something loose. The pendants, like little stones. *Of course,* she realized. They seemed to bear the same cryptic symbol in her recurring nightmare of Melanie's birth. Rough, misshapen double circles.

Ann, Ann, a voice seemed to drift in her head. She was suddenly exhausted. Was she dreaming standing up?

The moon shimmered.

Go back to bed, Ann.

Ann yawned, vigorously shook her head.

Go back to sleep . . .

She climbed back into bed and buried herself beneath the covers.

Go back to sleep and dream . . .

CHAPTER TWENTY-SIX

"It's English," the old man said without pause.

Dr. Harold didn't understand. "English? But how—"

"*Old* English, Doctor. Or I should say it's more of an amalgamation, a rough mix of specific linguistic influences. Old English, Old Saxon, Old Frisian, and . . . something else I can't identify. Something that looks older."

Dr. Harold was at this moment sitting in the faculty office of one Professor Franklin M. Fredrick, who had been referred to him through the campus information desk. Fredrick was the head of the archaeology department, and also an expert on mythology and ancient religion. Various degrees decorated the cramped office, as well as many relics. Dr. Harold had brought Erik Tharp's entire hospital file in hopes that Fredrick might shed some light on the technical aspects of Tharp's delusion.

"I use the term Old English as a generalization," Fredrick was saying, scanning the transcripts of Tharp's narcoanalysis and psychotherapy sessions. "What I mean is the language of the island of England, or *Angle-land*, before it became influenced by the Germanic invasion of about 450 A.D. The scant Latin derivations are obvious, from the Roman Occupation of 55 B.C. Old English is a coalescence of tongues, and unique in its incorporation. But this . . ." He tapped one of the sheafs. "This is unusual."

"How much of it do you think is invented?" Dr. Harold asked.

"Invented?" The old man looked at him, puzzled. "None of this is invented, Doctor. All of these words are real."

But that was impossible; he must not understand. "Tharp is an escaped mental patient. We've determined that he escaped for a reason specific to his delusion."

Professor Fredrick looked the part: keen-eyed in his weathered face. Countless digs and years in hostile sun had toughened his skin to the consistency of tanned leather. He was probably sixty but he looked a hundred. On his cragged hand a gold ring glittered, whose mount centered a pebble from Golgotha.

"Is Tharp a professor or language expert?"

"Oh, no," Dr. Harold replied. "He's a drug burnout. He never graduated high school."

Fredrick seemed to smile cynically, if the toughness of his face would permit a smile at all. "That's difficult for me to believe, Doctor. This mental patient of yours—this drug burnout—is using terms, syntactical structures, and even particularized inflections that are twenty-five hundred years old. And he's doing it perfectly."

Dr. Harold looked at him. The old man must be overreacting. Tharp had done well on the standard IQ batteries, but he was essentially uneducated.

"Let me give you some background," Fredrick offered. His voice, like his face, seemed frayed by the impairment of years. "The island of England is linguistically unique simply because of its geography. The basis of the English language is a direct reflection of the major invasions of the island. The Celts, in 600 B.C.; the Romans, in 55 B.C.; and the Saxons, in 500 A.D. But before the initial Brythonic, or Celtic, invasion, there was *another* society that we know very little about. They were called the Chilterns, and they had a language all their own. So it is actually the Chiltern language that provides the first root of English."

"What's that got to do with Tharp's vocabulary in those transcripts?"

"It's not just the vocabulary, Doctor, it's the syntax too, and the conjugations. Tharp seems better versed in the Chiltern language than the entirety of the archaeological community."

That's ridiculous, Harold thought. "Can you translate any of the words?" he asked.

"I can probably translate all of them." Fredrick pointed to a random page. "This word here, *hūsl*—it means to sacrifice. An interesting thing about the Chiltern-influenced forms of Old English is that there was little distinction between common nouns and transitive verbs. *Hūsl* is a good example. It also means *sacrifice victim.*"

"What about *wreccan*?"

"Slave. The *a* is, strangely, masculine, and *o*'s are feminine. Hence: male slave."

"And *brygor*wreccan?"

"A male slave who digs graves."

Dr. Harold felt numbly stunned. "Five years ago Tharp was apprehended by police for burying bodies. Some of the bodies were children and infants. We assumed his vocabulary was invented."

"You assumed wrong," Professor Fredrick asserted. "All these words are real. *Scieror*, one who cuts with a knife. *Hustig*, a general ritual. *Fek*, festival. *Cnif*, knife. This is fascinating, and clearly religious."

Religious? "How so?"

"These words here, oft repeated, *loc* and *liloc*. They're general references to a demon, a *female* demon. Many pre-Druidic settlements worshipped female demons via ritual sacrifice. The sacrifices frequently involved children, infants."

This was maddening. How did Tharp, an amotivate and dropout, become this learned in not only an ancient language but in an ancient religious custom? "Look at the rest, here," he insisted, and dug into his briefcase. "These are Tharp's sketchpads from the ward. Tell me what you make of them."

Professor Fredrick opened the first pad, then fell into a concerned silence. For the next twenty minutes he examined one page after another. He seemed to be transfixed.

"What? What's wrong?" Dr. Harold finally asked.

Professor Fredrick glanced up quizzically. "Ur-locs," he said.

"What?"

"Several thousand years ago there was an offshoot of the Chiltern race. They were called the Ur-locs. It was an occult society, and one, I might add, that we know very little about. There can be no mistake here. Tharp knows more about the Ur-locs than most archaeology departments."

Ur-locs, Dr. Harold thought.

"They were one of the most unique societies in history, and the only settlement in England to successfully resist every invasion of the island—the Celts, the Romans, the Saxons, Jutes, and Frisians, even the Normans. We only know about them from the registries left by each invader. Every army that was ever dispatched against the Ur-locs never returned, and the Ur-locs, mind you, were an entirely *female-dominated* culture."

That at least explained something. Tharp's delusion was based on a premise of female superiority. All of the men in the sketches were clearly *subservient* to a *female* hierarchy.

"The Ur-locs themselves," the old man continued, "were small in number, yet somehow they maintained a great power over large male populations. They were served entirely by men enslaved from invading camps or conquered settlements. Men did everything for them: fought their wars, cultivated their foods, built their towns. The Ur-locs reigned over a body of men dozens of times their own size."

"But . . . how?"

"Probably just a very clever management of power and fear, like any successful monarchy. And then, of course, there are the legends . . ."

"What legends?"

Fredrick again attempted a smile. "The registries claim that the Ur-locs were witches and that they used witchcraft to enslave their attackers. That's where the religious part comes in. The Ur-locs were savagely ritualistic. Their existence revolved around a single religious belief. They sacrificed thousands in appeasement to their god. These people made the Aztecs look like the Girl Scouts."

So Tharp's delusion *was* based on an actual ancient religious system, and that religious system was based on a specific—

"Tell me about their god," Dr. Harold inquired next.

"Here, right here," Fredrick said. He pointed to the most memorable sketch, the beautiful buxom woman in moonlight whose face was just a maw of needlelike teeth. "They called it the Ardat-Lil. Tharp's rendition is nearly perfect."

Dr. Harold looked at the sketch again, and shivered in its obscene impact of perversion and beauty. The flawless hourglass figure and flawless breasts. The taloned feet. The three-fingered claws for hands. And the face, the face . . . he could only glance at it a moment before having to turn away.

Ur-locs, he thought again in a strange, slow pulse. *Ardat-Lil . . .*

Professor Fredrick was getting up. Was it the chair that creaked, or his old joints? A small statue of the incubus Baalzephon stared down from a high bookshelf, along with the multi-limbed Bengalian Kali and the squat Babylonian Pazuzu. Fredrick removed a thick, dusty text: *Pre-Druidism: A Study of the Mythologies of Angle-Land.* "This should enlighten you," he proposed, and lay the book down at a specific chapter. "Here's a field summary from an Oxford University dig near Ripon, in the summer of 1983. Quite by accident, the dig uncovered the original Ur-loc ruins." One photo showed several big iron pots. "Fek cauldrons," he explained. "The Ur-locs were cannibals, and these cauldrons, which they called chettles, were what they cooked their festival meats in." The next photo showed a great stone slab on plinths. "A ceremonial dolmen, part altar, part sacrifice platform. The Ur-locs iconized dolmens; after a thousand sacrifices, it's said, they cut the dolmens up and made things out of the pieces: jewelry, tools, religious regalia such as fonts and tribal pendants. The very first dolmen, according to the myth, served as the central icon. They called it the nihtmir, or night-mirror. High priestesses were said to actually be able to see the Ardat-Lil in it. All sacrificial communities used dolmens, and many similarly retired the older ones for a higher use in their ceremonies."

"At this dig," Dr. Harold asked, "did they find the original Ur-loc dolmen?"

"The nihtmir? No, and that's a bit strange. All the archaeological evidence suggests that the Ur-locs willingly dispersed themselves—disbanded, I should say—between 995 and 1000 A.D., and they apparently took their nihtmir with them, which must've weighed, mind you, close to a thousand pounds. It was probably about the size of a desktop."

Nihtmir, Dr. Harold reflected now. *Night-mirror.* Hadn't Tharp mentioned something similar during his narcoanalysis? And he'd mentioned chettles too, hadn't he? "What's this?" came the next query. A photo showed a pile of scrolls or something, as a field technician gingerly dusted them with a camel-hair brush.

"It's a manuscript," Professor Fredrick informed him. "The only direct written record of the Ur-loc race. It had been buried in a cairn, in some very peaty high-sulfur/low-oxygen soil. The excavators were able to photograph most of it before it disintegrated. And this," he said, "you should find *very* interesting."

The next photo showed a drawing on a manuscript page. Dr. Harold recognized the sleek body and long flowing mane of hair, the talons and tiny slits for eyes above the stretched maw for a face, and the stubby protuberances, like little horns.

"The Ardat-Lil," he muttered. "It's almost identical to Tharp's sketch."

"Indeed it is," Professor Fredrick replied. "No doubt Tharp researched the Ur-locs at a college library, and based his delusion on the information."

Of course, Dr. Harold tried to agree. What other answer could there be? Still, the proposition pricked at him, like briars. "Do you think it's even remotely possible, though, that some very distant remnant of the Ur-loc culture still exists, some cult or something?"

Professor Fredrick's eyes fixed on him. Then the old, cragged face broke, and he began to laugh.

"I suppose now is a suitable time."

"Yes," Dr. Heyd agreed.

Milly and the wifmunuc peered down from the foot of the bed, the breasts bare, the faces intent in glee. Dr. Heyd opened his black medical bag.

"Nis hoefonrice gelic tham lige," said the wifmunuc, "pæt wit waldenes, sprece forbræcon . . ."

"Fo hir doefolcyniges," Milly finished.

Dr. Heyd filled the 10cc syringe, watching a few droplets sparkle.

"I want his death to be relishing," the wifmunuc ordered him.

"Nice and slow," Milly added, her nipples erecting at the thought. "Nice and slow, for her."

Dr. Heyd nodded. The pale figure on the bed seemed to tense a little, jaundiced eyes staring up, mouth propped open.

"He's served well, in his own way."

Goodbye, Josh. Dr. Heyd inserted the needle into one of the pulsing veins of Joshua Slavik's upper arm. Then he slowly depressed the plunger.

"Wīhan!" whispered the wifmunuc.

CHAPTER TWENTY-SEVEN

§§§

"You two! Hey!" Sergeant Tom Byron shouted.

The figures scampered away into the woods.

"Come back here! This is the police!"

Giggling fluttered up. They'd looked like kids, hadn't they? Several tree trunks seemed pasty with some dark shine. Byron touched a trunk and his finger came away red.

Blood, he thought.

Chief Bard had dispatched him to search the woods around the edge of town, which made little sense to Byron. A lot of things didn't make much sense lately. Bard wasn't telling him much. Had he gotten a tip? It infuriated Byron that his own boss didn't trust him with confidential information. What made Bard so sure Tharp would be hiding out in the woods?

And now this . . . these kids. Who were they? What were they doing?

Byron delved into the thicket. Fallen brush crunched underfoot. He tried to follow the giggling, and their sounds, but the brush grew so thick in places that he could barely pass without a machete. The late-afternoon sun drew mist up from the forest's moist ground. He felt pricked, perspiry, and pissed off.

But then the thicket subsided. A trail seemed to etch a line through the woods. Byron followed it. He noticed more wet trees lining the way. Someone had painted them with something, something like blood.

Byron then stepped between a pair of gnarled oaks.

He stared down. *What in God's name . . .*

He'd stepped into a small dell, a clearing. Three girls stood there, as if they'd been waiting for him. They were grinning.

They were also buck naked.

"Who the hell . . ." But then he recognized them. Wendlyn

Fost, Maedeen's daughter. Rena Godwin. And the third, Josh Slavik's grandkid. What was her name? Melanie?

Byron looked around for guys. A bunch of naked girls usually meant that a bunch of naked guys were close at hand. But there were none, he saw. There was only him.

"What the hell are you girls doing?"

They only grinned in response. They were passing something around, smoking. *Pot smokers,* he concluded. But this stuff didn't smell like pot at all. It smelled light, cinnamony.

"We're waiting for you," one of them, Rena, said.

Byron stared at them. They didn't seem the least bit concerned that they were standing naked in front of a police officer. He gulped, though; he couldn't help it. They were just teenagers but—*Christ,* he thought. Three pairs of breasts stared back at him, three pubes. Rena, the youngest, barely had any hair at all. The other two looked fuller, more shapely. But what were those pails on the ground? And brushes?

"Peow," Melanie Slavik said. Her eyes looked bright but . . . funny.

Then Wendlyn added, "Let's give lof."

Rena giggled.

Give lof, Byron thought. It was a slow thought, slow like blood oozing from a wound. Something was happening.

The three faces—the three grins—seemed to reach into him, drag him down like drugs. *They're kids,* he kept thinking. *They're just kids . . . I can't . . .*

They converged, laying him out. His vision seemed detached; he saw only in fragments, diced glimpses. Faces hovered over him, bodies, breasts. The little stone pendants swayed like pendulums as they eagerly clustered about him, unbuttoning his shirt and pants. Their giggling made him sick; soon it didn't even sound human. It sounded wet, clicking, like voracious eating.

"The Fulluht-Loc is coming . . ."

"The doefolmon . . ."

"Give lof! To the Modor!"

"Wīhan!"

"Dother fo Dother!"

They had his penis out, which was already erect, pulsing. Melanie ran her hands up over his chest. Wendlyn was stroking his face, suspending a big nipple over his mouth. And Rena, whose own giggles sounded muffled, was fellating him.

This was all wrong, part of him knew. It didn't matter that they'd come on to him. They were kids. He could lose his job for this, even go to jail. But that part of him faded. He lay there as if staked to the ground. He *couldn't move*.

"Lots of muscles," Melanie cooed, rubbing. "He'd make a great wreccan."

"Shit on him," Wendlyn said.

"He's big," Rena stopped long enough to say. "Look!"

They giggled, appraising it.

Now Rena had his service piece out, a Colt Python. She cocked its gridded hammer, prodded his testicles with the barrel.

Byron was shivering, terrorized. He felt the cold end of the barrel poke into his scrotum, trace his shaft.

"Don't worry, little baby," Melanie said.

"We won't shoot it off," Wendlyn promised.

She and Rena traded places. Wendlyn mounted him. "Ooo, you're right. He's real big," she commented, and inserted him into herself. Rena straddled his head, pushing the nearly hairless furrow against his lips. "Lick it, lick it," she commanded in glee, then began urinating.

Byron felt pinned down, buried in madness. Hot urine streamed against his face, into his mouth. He couldn't breathe. Wendlyn rode him ferociously, slamming her hips down against him. Both Byron's heart and his genitals felt like they would explode at the same time.

Rena climbed off. Melanie was getting something out from under a log. Wendlyn rode him faster, harder, eyes turned up.

She shuddered, then shrieked—

Byron exploded into her sex—

As Melanie slid the sharpened cnif against his throat, cutting immediately and right to the bone.

"Wīhan!" Rena celebrated.

Byron's blood spurted out of his neck precisely in time with his orgasm. He died a minute or two later, when they began to slice his belly open.

Erik scouted the woods. The sun was going down. He had pretty good bearings now. He could even see the Slavik house from here. He'd need to go in soon, but he didn't dare yet. A big Fleetwood had pulled up as he watched. He didn't want to go into the house when a lot of people were there. They'd have plenty of preliminary rituals before the actual rite. That should give him enough time.

He knew the cops were onto him; no doubt Bard had found the brygorwreccan's body—they knew he was close. He went back deeper into the woods, to conceal himself until it was time.

But what was that he heard? Erik stopped, poised himself to listen. Voices, it sounded like. Quiet voices.

He followed, moving as lightly as he could. Soon he thought he detected movement, pale shapes in the darkening light.

He looked past some trees, into a dell. A girl, naked, was walking away. Two more stooped over something. It didn't take Erik long to realize that what they were stooping over was a corpse.

A cop, he thought. They were eviscerating him, putting certain organs into a plastic bag. The thinner girl seemed to be sawing something. This, too, did not surprise Erik. He'd seen it all before. The slender girl sawed off the cop's head and put it in the bag.

Wifhands. Younger ones. He thought he recognized them.

Then they rose. They turned slowly, grinning. Their pendants dangled. Their white flesh was smeared with blood.

"We know you're there, Erik," the older one said.

Rena Godwin giggled. "We can feel you."

The other one was the wifford's kid, Wendlyn. "Come here."

"No," Erik said. He raised the shotgun. "You don't have me anymore."

The two girls laughed.

"We have you. You've been blessed."

"You'll always be ours."

No . . . I . . . won't, he determined. He could feel it already, their pull on his brain, like the moon.

"Come to us, Erik," Rena said.

"The little brygorwreccan."

Their young faces beamed, the stare of their eyes sinking into his head like daggers, like cnifs.

"Come to us."

Erik stepped forward. The shotgun was charged, but he scarcely even felt it now. It felt like something he was holding in a dream.

"Let us give you fulluht. Let us make you holy again."

Kill them, he commanded himself. He tried to aim the gun, but his arms barely moved.

"The doefolmon is coming."

"The Fulluht-Loc."

"You've come back to be with us. We welcome you, Erik. We will take you back into the cirice."

No, pounded the thought like hammer to stone. *I'll kill myself first.*

He would, he knew he would. Anything to be free of them. They were so strong against his will, much stronger than before.

They began to come forward. Wendlyn outstretched her hand, smiling softly. Rena came up behind her.

Kill them, he demanded of himself. *Kill them before they—*

"Little peow. Kneel—"

—change, he thought.

Erik squeezed his eyes shut. His mind felt released from a fetter. His forearms shot up, brought the shotgun to bear.

"No!" Rena shrieked.

His finger contracted. The shotgun jumped behind a great flash and concussion: *ba-BAM!*

The round socked a hole into Wendlyn's throat. Blood flew out of her like thin, flailing tentacles. Rena, screaming, flew at him with a small glinting æsc.

He racked another round and fired. The hand holding the spike flew off the end of her arm. He cycled the shotgun once more, raised it to her face.

Her face . . .

His teeth clacked shut.

The third round of 12-gauge exploded in her face. Her head blew apart in wheeling, wet chunks.

Gunsmoke shifted up like a ghost. It tinged in his nostrils. *Before they change,* his thoughts continued to tick. His face felt like a flat plate of stone when he looked down at the two naked forms. Their dark blood pumped slowly into the soil.

The part of his mind that still belonged to this world told him, *You just killed two kids.*

"No, I didn't," he answered himself in voice. "I just killed two monsters."

He racked another round into the chamber and stalked off back into the darkening forest.

CHAPTER TWENTY-EIGHT

Dooer, dooer, the dark voice groped. The black words seemed to drag her down, deeper, deeper into the strange, chanting labyrinth of the dream.

Ann awoke in the terrible crimson vertigo, the knife—

slup-slup-slup

—sinking to its guard into her abdomen.

Slup-slup-slup, she heard, wincing. She brought a hand to her flat, sweat-moistened belly. She was naked in bed, drenched. The room was empty. She gasped when she saw the clock: 8:12 P.M. She'd slept the entire day away, and well into evening.

She showered in a cold torrent, hoping the spray of water would revive her. She felt terrible, as if hung over or drugged. She shivered as she washed herself; her hand guiding the bar of soap felt like someone else's hand, like the fluttering hands of the nightmare, roving her, stroking her stretched belly.

God, was all she could think. She felt haunted; she didn't even feel real. Each movement as she dressed prodded the worst headache of her life. What was wrong with her? Something was terribly wrong; she could feel it. Something wrong with . . . everything.

She must be sick—that was it. She must be coming down with flu; that's why she'd slept so late. She went downstairs for some juice and heard car doors closing.

Ann peeked out the sidelight sash of the front door. Her mother's Fleetwood was backing out the drive. It looked like there were several people in it.

She frowned. The car drove off. Dusk was settling. A bright, pinkened moon peered over the horizon. It was full.

Something shattered. Upstairs.

Ann spun around. She raced up the staircase. Something else shattered. It sounded like glass breaking.

The heart monitor's beep down the hall sounded slow, irregular. Ann's breath lodged in her chest when she spun into her father's room. Saline bottles lay shattered around the outer rim of the throw rug. The wheeled stands lay toppled over. Ann's vision rooted to the bed.

Her father lay sprawled, half over the convalescent rail. Blood dripped out of his arm from where the IV needles had torn out. He was convulsing, his mouth locked open. His eyes bulged as if lidless. Ann could only stare. His right arm, tremoring, began to lift. The crabbed hand unfurled.

His mouth jittered but no sound came out. He was pointing at her.

"Oh, Jesus . . . Dad . . ."

His hand fell to the bed. The slow *beep-beep-beep* of the Lifepak monitor stopped—

—then flat-lined.

He'd been leaning over for something. Ann's wide gaze slowly lowered. The nightstand, she saw. The antique, enameled nightstand seemed to have something on the side facing the bed.

Writing? she thought. It looked like . . . writing.

She cast it aside. She dragged him over, leaned down. She attempted CPR as she best knew how. Each downward push against his frail chest pumped a little more blood from the torn IV hole at the inside of his elbow. She craned his head back, pinched shut his nostrils, and blew.

Nothing.

The flat line droned on.

He's dead, she realized.

Her downward stare seemed drawn by something. She stared at the side of the drawered nightstand.

Her father had written something on it. He'd used his own blood:

DOEFOLMON

LEAVE MELANIE, MARTIN,

EVERYTHING. GET OUT WHILE

YOU STILL CAN.

"The Ardat-Lil was a succubus," Professor Fredrick explained. "Or I should say, the supreme succubus, the first lady of hell."

"Succubus," Dr. Harold repeated the word.

"A female sex-demon. Many variations exist throughout world mythology, and it's interesting how many ancient religious modes reflect a reverence to identical gods and antigods. The Ardat-Lil is no exception. The Scottish Bheur, the German Brechta, the Scandinavian Agaberte, the Teutonic Alrune, the Egyptian Aldinoch—they're all names for the same thing. They're all the Ardat-Lil."

Succubus, Dr. Harold thought. The word even sounded evil. It seemed to walk across his groin like a tarantula.

Professor Fredrick lit a pipe with a face on it, puffing sweet smoke into the air. "The Ardat-Lil has a very racy history. The Ur-locs believed that when the earth was made, half of heaven's angels were banished. Sound familiar? On the first day of his banishment, Lucifer decided to take a stroll around the earth, which he found, to his complete dissatisfaction, to be inhabited by peace-loving humans who were completely bereft of sin. They all rejected him immediately, and Lucifer, mind you, doesn't take kindly to rejection. Therefore, he decided to corrupt the human race, by tricking them into turning away from God. This may sound familiar too. Anyway, Lucifer searched for the most beautiful virgin in the world and after six days he found her—a young woman named Ardat. Lucifer promised to make her his queen if she turned away from God, and Ardat, as you've probably already guessed, agreed. They sealed the agreement by having intercourse. Ardat became pregnant, and after only six days, gave birth to a beautiful baby girl. This baby eventually bloomed into a woman even more beautiful than her mother, so beautiful that Lucifer deemed any name unworthy of her beauty. She was known simply as the Daughter."

"Or the Ardat-Lil," Dr. Harold supposed.

"No, not quite. The Daughter was so beautiful that Lucifer, notorious for his hormones, couldn't resist. She was beautiful, but she wasn't evil, and Lucifer wanted an *evil* little girl. So he changed himself into an anonymous man, whom the Daughter fell in love with. It was all a ploy. The Daughter married the man, had intercourse with him, and then *she* became pregnant. In other words—"

"Lucifer seduced his own daughter."

"Exactly," Professor Fredrick said. "The *Daughter* then gave birth to an even more beautiful baby girl, and she turned out to be heinously evil. She was known as the Daughter of the Daughter, or the Ardat-Lil. That's what this repeated term in Tharp's sketches refers to." Professor Fredrick pointed to one.

Dr. Harold read, beneath a drawing of a woman giving birth on a dolmen, the words *Dother fo Dother*.

"The dohtor, or in the Chilternese form, the Dother fo Dother, was half human, half devil, the worst of both parts, and she was therefore condemned by God to eternity in hell. However, like many demons, she was born with the power of incarnation, and it is the bounden duty of all demons to perpetuate evil. Through time, the Ardat-Lil gained followers on earth, human followers, who were granted *sub*carnate powers in return for their worship. A coven formed—"

"The Ur-locs," Dr. Harold conjectured.

"Right, whose existence revolved solely around the worship of the Ardat-Lil. They served her in many ways, by ritual, by sacrifice and cannibalism, and by eliminating all men from the bloodline, or bludcynn—another word which Tharp refers to quite frequently. The Ur-locs, according to legend, turned men into slaves via something called the sexespelle; it has always been thought that intercourse with a succubus functioned as a pact with the devil. All coven members—

wifhands—had the power to become succubi for short periods, during which they seduced men and hence enslaved them. They'd trick men into thinking they were dreaming, have intercourse with them, and that was that. Any man who had sex with a wifhand in the succubi state was lost forever to the coven's will."

"What are these words here?" Dr. Harold asked, pointing to further sketch pages. "Are they *all* relative to this system of worship?"

"Oh, yes," Professor Fredrick answered. "*Ælmesse*, alms; *lof*, praise in ceremony; *cirice*, church. *Thane*, *helot*, and *peow* all mean the same as *wreccan*: male slave—one who has fallen to the succubi. *Wīhan* means to make holy. The Ur-locs believed that the only way to make a man holy was to kill him—and often *eat him*—in homage to the Dother fo Dother."

"And these? Wifford? Wifmunuc?"

"A wifford to the Ur-locs was their version of a verger or a seminarian, a religious hierarch. The wifford was second-in-command of the coven, and in constant training to replace the coven leader upon her death. The leader was called the wifmunuc, the one closest to the deity."

Dr. Harold grimly stroked his white mustache. He considered this, and what the old professor had said earlier. What a ghastly vision . . .

"Not a pretty topic, I assure you. Despite their obscurity, the Ur-locs proved one of the most savage societies to ever exist." Professor Fredrick then emptied the smoking guts of his pipe, *tap-tap-tapping* them into an obsidian ashtray that once served as an Assyrian blood tap. "There's a summation, though, in an ultimate respect, I mean."

"I'm sorry?" Dr. Harold said.

"There's a point to all of this. I don't believe for a minute that an Ur-loc cult could actually have survived all this time, nor do I believe in the occult. However, I do have an observation to make, which you should find exceedingly uncanny." Fredrick released a roughened chuckle. "Would you like to hear it?"

The dying pipe smoke sifted up. From the bookshelves, and

from odd perches all about the office, the stone likenesses of demons persisted in their frozen stares. And splayed across the
desk lay Tharp's drawing of the Ardat-Lil, shimmering in its
obscene beauty . . .

"Yes," Dr. Harold said. "I'd like to hear it very much."

CHAPTER TWENTY-NINE

{ornamental flourish}

Ann fled down the hall, then slowed. Then she stopped. What was she thinking? Her father was dead. With his own blood he'd written a warning. But what did that really mean? Ann stood still in the paneled hall, blinking.

He'd suffered a massive stroke. He was delirious. He didn't know what he was doing.

There.

She let reality catch up to her. As usual, no one was in the house. *What do I do now?* It was a good question. What do you do when someone dies? Call an ambulance? A funeral home? Mustn't a doctor declare him dead first? Ann felt disconnected. It was her father who lay dead in the next room, not some stranger. Oddly, even guiltily, she felt relief.

His torment's over, she realized. This was a good thing. What must it have been like for him, immobile and brain-damaged? In death, her father had found the peace that his illness had robbed him of. Now Ann understood why people always said "It's a blessing" at funerals. Her father's death *was* a blessing.

The acknowledgment made her feel better. She went downstairs and sat on the bottom step, chin in hand. The total lack of sound made the house seem even more empty. How would Melanie take her grandfather's death? And what would her mother say? But in a moment Ann realized she was reaching for distractions. Above all, what continued to gnaw at her was the same thing that had been gnawing at her for months.

The nightmare.

Pieces of the nightmare kept sifting in her head, and that terrible scarlet vertigo. How could anything be so obsessive? Her own father had just died, yet the preoccupation with the dream remained. *Slup-slup-slup,* she could still hear the sound, and the voice of the sinister birth attendant: "Dooer, dooer."

Ann struggled to escape the awful imagery. There were things that needed to be done. *Get off it!* she screamed to herself. She must call Dr. Heyd at once, tell him that her father had finally passed away. But—

Slup-slup-slup, she could still hear in her mind.

Dooer, dooer.

Rising, she winced. But when she went to the phone, something caused her to glance down the stairwell which led to the basement. Even in the dim light, she could plainly see that the door, which her mother kept locked, stood open.

What am I doing? Call Dr. Heyd! she ordered herself. Next thing she knew, however, she was descending the stairs.

Then she knew, or she thought she did. The basement was where Melanie had been born; it was the setting of the nightmare. That was the lure—the grim curiosity which urged her down the steps. Suddenly, the room seemed forbidden; it enticed her. Ann hadn't seen the basement in seventeen years.

But she was determined to see it now.

The old wood of the steps creaked as she continued down. The door opened in dead silence. Ann still couldn't imagine why her mother always kept it locked. It was just a fruit cellar, a basement.

It seemed warmer the instant she stepped in. A single nude light bulb hung from the ceiling. There was an old washing bin, some old furniture, and an ironing board. Shelves of jarred fruit and pickled vegetables lined one entire wall.

She looked blankly ahead. Something wasn't right. A few more seconds ticked by when she realized her disappointment.

She'd hoped that seeing the basement might shake loose a memory that would solve the nightmare and free her of it. The nightmare was of Melanie's birth. Melanie was born here. Therefore—

The misconception bloomed.

This isn't the room in the nightmare.

It was all wrong. The room in the nightmare was longer, the ceiling higher. The entire shape of this room was different.

Yes, Ann felt disappointed. The room showed her nothing that her subconscious might be hanging on to. Why had the dream placed Melanie's birth elsewhere?

Time. Memory, she considered. She'd misconstrued it all. The past seventeen years had obscured her memory totally. Her dream had therefore built its own room.

But why?

It scarcely mattered. She turned to go back up and noticed several file cabinets. One thing she *never* noticed, though, was the reason the door had been open. It hadn't been left open, it had been *broken* open, the bolt prized out of the frame.

The file cabinets looked rooted through. One was filled with old newspapers and books, its drawer tilting out. Ann closed it and looked through the second drawer: some manila folders apparently out of order. And a spiral pad. *Looks like Martin's pad.*

She picked it up and stared. It *was* Martin's pad. The cramped hastened scrawl left no doubt.

Why would Martin keep his poetry drafts down here?

She flipped through some random pages.

"Wreccan," one poem was called, but what on earth did that mean? It was dated several days ago. Ann squinted, reading.

Flawed worlds die quickly as the dreams of men:
a pointless parody.
Yet nightly we arise, her song in our heads,
wreccans of the descending herald.
We are her birds of prey.
We'll come to see you *someday.*

What an odd poem. Ann didn't understand it all, and it didn't seem like Martin's style one bit. He usually wrote in meter and a Keatsian rhyme pattern. She turned to the next poem: "Doefolmon."

O wondrous moon,
of your truth I drink.
Upon the herald's caress,
in wondrous pink!

This one bothered her. Like the first she didn't know what it meant, and it didn't seem like the kind of thing Martin would write.

Moon. Pink, she thought. Did he mean the equinox she'd been hearing about on the news? A special lunar position which caused the moon's light to appear pink at certain times during the night. She looked out the small ground-level window. Beyond the forest, the full moon hung low.

It was pink.

But something else nagged at her. *What?* she thought. Then her eyes thinned. The poem's title, "Doefolmon." *Doefolmon,* she repeated. A word that made no sense. But—

Doefolmon. Before her father had died, in his delirium, hadn't that been one of the words he'd written?

This cruxed her. Perhaps she was wrong—yes, she must be. Dr. Heyd had said that massive-stroke victims frequently wrote things with no memory of alphabet sequence. How could Martin possibly have used the word days before her father had written it?

Impossible, she agreed.

Most of the rest of the pad seemed filled with one long poem. She remembered Martin mentioning it the other day, a magnum opus of over a hundred stanzas. This must be it. "Millennium," it was entitled.

She didn't read the whole thing, just bits and pieces. Throughout she noticed more strange words. *Wifmunuc, Fulluht-Loc, wīhan, cirice.* What did these words mean? The metered poem seemed to deal with some kind of reverence, of worship, but it was alien to her.

She turned to the last stanza, the end.

In her holy blood now we are blessed.
Sweet deity of eons in darkness dressed.
Through fallen heaven, so swiftly she soars.
"Dooer," enchants the wifmunuc.
"Come into our world from yours."

Ann felt turned to granite as she stared at the bizarre verse. Again, she thought, *Impossible,* but for another reason. *Dooer,* Martin had written, the same word spoken by the figure in her nightmare.

Dooer, she thought.

There could be no explanation. She'd never repeated any of the nightmare's details to Martin. Had she spoken the word aloud in her sleep? But if so, why would Martin use it in a poem?

Now her confusion ganged up on her. She shivered as she replaced the notebook, a sense beneath her skin like dread. Then
she noticed the albums. Photo albums.

Ann had seen her mother and her friends looking through
them several times. She picked one up, opened it—

What the . . . She couldn't believe it.

It was pornography.

Lurid snapshots glared up at her. Ann could not imagine anything so explicit, and so absolutely *obscene*. Each picture depicted a different sex act. Oral sex. Group sex. Lesbianism.
Sodomy. Women grinned in raw light as blank-faced men penetrated them in every plausible way, and some implausible. *This
is crazy,* Ann thought. Why would her mother have this . . .
smut?

She was too shocked to contemplate the issue more deeply.
Each page showed her a new, greater obscenity. But as she
flipped further through the wretched album, that cold tingling,
like dread, came back to her. Some of the figures in the photos
looked awfully familiar.

By the fifth page she was picking faces out of the orgies.

Here was Milly on her hands and knees, fellating one man
while another penetrated her from behind. Next, Mrs. Gargan
squatting atop someone's hips. The Trotters swapping marriage
companions. And Milly's daughter, Rena, with her knees
pushed back to her face as some young man mounted her. And
next—

My God.

The next showed Ann's own mother having intercourse with
Dr. Heyd. And next her own father . . . sodomizing a man as her
mother and several other women looked on, grinning.

Ann was shaking. She thought she'd be sick. Then she turned
the page and stared.

A pretty teenage girl was sitting on another girl's face. The
girl on top was Melanie.

A vacant-eyed man was sodomizing a woman with her buttocks propped up. The woman was Maedeen.

The man was Martin.

Ann felt dead standing up.

The second album beggared description.

Naked figures seemed smeared with something dark. It
looked like blood. More figures drank from a cup, all nude, all

with weird pale pendants suspended between their breasts. Ann
felt all the breath go out of her when she turned the page.

A female corpse hung upside down against a bare-wood wall,
headless. Blood poured into a big pot. Next, a male corpse was
being gutted by a man with a thin, sharp knife. The man was
Ann's father. Dr. Heyd was trimming fat away from what appeared to be a liver. Martin was stuffing offal into a big plastic
bag. Still more photos showed more men stoking an enclosed
pit fire, tossing things in. A black cauldron bubbled. Large
roundish objects lay deeper in the embers. Ann knew they were
human heads.

I must be dreaming again, Ann sickly tried to convince herself. None of this could be real.

Then she turned the next page and saw:

Milly lying upon the slab, naked, drenched in sweat. Her legs
were propped up and widely parted. She was pregnant.

Naked women stood about her, gazing down in reverence.
But betwixt Milly's spread legs stood a cloaked figure, with
hands out as if to accept something. And next:

The hands holding up a glistening newborn child.

And next:

Ann screamed.

It was the same. Everything. Milly giving birth was identical
to the scenario of Ann's nightmare. And then the final photo,
the symbol. The odd double circle looked like a flat slab of
stone hanging against a dark wall, but its shape was—

The same, she realized.

It was exactly the same.

"Does it all seem familiar?" queried a cragged voice.

Ann screamed again and dropped the album. She stepped
back and stumbled, glaring up in terror.

A figure stepped out of the back of the basement. He'd been
there the entire time, watching her from the dark.

The figure took another step: a young man with bizarre short
white hair, in jeans, sneakers, and jeans jacket. His face looked

extant, lean in some crushed prevalence. He was holding a shot-gun.

"Ann Slavik," he said. He looked at her, as if curious. "My name is Erik Tharp. Though the people around here call me brygorwreccan."

The shredded voice left no doubt. The same voice that had called her, had warned her on the phone not to come here.

"They're subcarnates," he told her. "They're monsters, all of them. And your mother is their leader."

Ann tried to speak but her terror damped her voice.

"They enslave men with her power, they sacrifice to pay her homage. They've existed for thousands of years, Ann, solely to worship her."

"H-her? Who?"

Erik Tharp gave her a broken smile. "Of course, you don't know about it. You weren't supposed to. You're part of a blood-line that worships a devil."

Ann's head reeled . . .

"Does it sound impossible?" Erik Tharp continued. "What do you think all that stuff is in those albums? Do you dream, Ann? What do you think those dreams are about? They're not really dreams, they're visions—visions of the past to reflect the future."

Visions of the past, she thought. But what could Melanie's birth have to do with the future?

"Have you seen any male children in this town? Have you?"

"No," she said, still staring up. "I looked at the town birth records. It said that all the male children ever born here were put up for adoption."

"Of course that's what it said. Heyd has to cover himself."

"What?"

"The records are falsified, by Heyd. Those kids weren't put up for adoption. They were sacrificed."

The word seemed to eddy in her head and grow like a blood-stain.

"Males are not allowed in their bloodline. Any sect member who gives birth to a male must hand it over for immediate sacri-fice, to appease *her.* I ought to know, Ann. I'm the one who used to bury the bodies."

Ann still couldn't think right. How could she believe this madness? Erik Tharp was an escaped mental patient. He was

certifiably insane. But then she remembered the photo albums . . .

"I came back to stop this, Ann. I came back to get you and
your daughter away from here. That's the only way."

"What are you talking about!" Ann finally screamed.

He looked down at her. It seemed painful for him just to talk.
"For the last millennium they've been breeding themselves for
this event, Ann. You and your daughter are part of that event."

"What event?"

"The Fulluht-Loc," he answered. "The doefolmon."

CHAPTER THIRTY

"Doefolmon," Professor Fredrick said.

Dr. Harold squinted back. "Yes, another of the words that Tharp makes frequent reference to in his sketches. What does it mean?"

Fredrick relit the big pipe. Its carven face depicted vacant agony. "It means, roughly, 'moon of the devil,' and it's another terminology that proves how thoroughly Tharp researched the Ur-locs before his delusion overtook him. The doefolmon was considered a portent, like a biblical sign, and a precursor to their holiest rite—the Fulluht-Loc."

Harold's nose crinkled against the cloying fetor of the tobacco. That, and the queer face on the pipe, harassed his attention.

"It was their incarnation rite," Professor Fredrick said.

Incarnation. Harold considered the word, and its implications. *To make flesh.*

"*Fulluht* is another weird meld of Old Saxon, Old Frisian, and some older Chilternese constituents; it means essentially 'baptism' or 'baptismal,' and *loc*, as I've said, is a reference to—"

"A female demon," Harold recalled. "A succubus."

"Yes. Hence, *Fulluht-Loc* can be translated as 'baptism of the succubus.' It's the ritual that their entire system of belief revolved around. It's what they lived for."

The window framed full dark now; Dr. Harold had been here all day scarcely without realizing it. He could glimpse the moon through the high trees of the campus quadrangle. It seemed pink.

"The basis of their entire religion was offertory," the old professor went on. "The zeal with which they sacrificed inno-

cents was intensively devout. Everything they did was an offering. Sex. Murder. Cannibalism. They'd even anoint initiates
with the blood of sacrifice victims. They'd paint trees with the
blood, to mark the territory of the succubus, to make it blessed.
The Druids did the same thing centuries later, which might
cause you to wonder about the nature of religious influence."

But Dr. Harold was wondering about a lot more than that. So
many questions itched at him now, like stitches healing. "But
what you mentioned earlier," he said. "The ultimate point?"

Fredrick's ancient face looked grimly amused. "The Fulluht-
Loc. The incarnation. According to the legend, this can only
occur during the doefolmon, and supposedly the Ur-locs
succeeded at it once."

"The incarnation, you mean?"

"Correct. From what could be translated from their manu-
scripts, the Ur-locs claimed that a successful incarnation occurred a thousand years ago, just before their race disappeared."

Dr. Harold contemplated the supposition. No, like Fredrick,
he didn't believe in demons, but . . . what was he thinking? "I
don't quite follow you. How did this incarnation supposedly
come about?"

"Remember what I said before," Fredrick replied. "Everything the Ur-locs did was an offering. They were devoted to the
notion of the bludcynn, or the sanctity of their bloodline. What
they offered to the Ardat-Lil, ultimately, was themselves."

"I still don't quite—"

"The element of *offering*, Doctor. Sacrifice. Blood. Faith.
Everything. The Fulluht-Loc was an *offering* of one of their
own, a physical gift of substitution. What I'm saying is that, on
the doefolmon, one of the Ur-locs' own bludcynn would *become* the Ardat-Lil. This was foreseen, mind you, years before-
hand, upon the birth of the substituted body."

"Foreseen by who?"

"By the wifmunuc, the leader. They were supposedly clair-
voyant. The doefolmon was considered the holiest time, much
like Christians would consider the Second Coming. This was
essentially the same thing, the return of their god onto the
earth." Professor Fredrick's time-worn hand tapped out the pipe
again. Behind him, in the office window, the moon was rising.
"But what you should find most curious of all," he amusedly
went on, "is the timing."

"The timing?" Dr. Harold queried.

"The doefolmon. Astronomers have recently identified it—a peculiar astronomical configuration. You've probably been hearing about it on the news lately."

Had he? *The equinox,* he thought. "I've heard something on the weather channels about the equinox."

"Yes. That's what the doefolmon really is. Of course, astronomers don't call it the doefolmon"—Fredrick cragged another chuckle—"they call it a tangental lunar apogee. You've probably noticed over the past week or so that the moon appears pink. It's what's known as a straticulate refraction, the moonlight shining through the upper atmosphere at an anomalous angle. It's very, very rare, and quite precise—a vernal equinox that occurs at the exact same moment as the moon becomes full."

Dr. Harold's eyes narrowed.

"And that's the curious part," Fredrick went on. "Even an old, skeptical atheist such as myself must admit. The last time this happened was exactly a thousand years ago, and exactly a thousand years ago was when the Ur-locs supposedly succeeded in incarnating the Ardat-Lil."

CHAPTER THIRTY-ONE

"It's happening now, right now," Erik Tharp told her in the dark confines of the basement.

He'd been talking, and she'd been listening, staring at each of his raddled words as though they were deformed faces. *Incarnation,* she thought. *Fulluht-Loc. Ardat-Lil.* It was insanity, and this was supposed to be an insane person. Yet the things he'd told her rang of a spectral memory, inklings dripping like a wound in the back of her mind. Ann's confusion amassed. It was the confluence of it all—what Tharp had disclosed, plus the dream and what she'd seen in the albums—that left her unable to reckon anything.

"The Ardat-Lil is already here," he was saying through the haze of her quandary. "But certain things have to take place before she can be incarnated through the host." He paused, looked right at her. "That's why I escaped. To make sure those things don't happen."

Ann felt slick in the sweat of her own dread. *Melanie,* her mind tolled again and again. That's what the dream meant: Melanie's birth was the birth of the host. *They want my daughter to serve as the physical body for this . . . thing.*

"Your daughter's a virgin, isn't she?"

Ann nodded.

"She wasn't born in a hospital, was she? She was born here, in Lockwood. Wasn't she?"

"Yes!" Ann shrieked.

Tharp loaded several rounds into the shotgun. "We have to find her and get the two of you away from here. We have to do it now. The doefolmon is tonight."

Martin, Ann thought. "What about—my fiancé?"

"Forget him. He's one of them now. Forever."

235

Tharp roughly grabbed her arm, yanked her toward the steps.
"They're all at the cirice now—"

"The what?"

"The church. They're getting ready." Tharp paused on the
stairs, as if pricked by the palest vision. He was staring at nothing for a moment, or perhaps at the ghost of what he used to be.
"Come on," he said next. He was thumping up the stairs, with
Ann in tow. "If we can prevent the incarnation rite itself, or
even the kin sacrifice, then they'll be ruined. They won't be
able to do this again for a thousand years."

Ann huffed up the dusty wood steps. *What did he say?* "The
kin sacrifice? What's that?"

"It's like a trigger for the whole ritual," Tharp's ragged voice
grated on. "The final offering to the Ardat-Lil. Proof of faith."

Kin sacrifice, Ann was still thinking. Suddenly on the stairs
her joints locked up. Her mind blanked, and—

Slup-slup-slup . . .

The vermilion vertigo embraced her again, like a desperate
lover. The vision of the great blade plunging down again and
again into the squirming naked abdomen . . .

"Come on, come on!" Tharp was commanding. He slapped
Ann hard in the face. She blinked at him, numb. Then he was
leading her up again.

Now Ann understood it, the vertiginous visions and how they
related to the nightmare. *Kin sacrifice,* she realized more fully.
She tried to assimilate. *They want Melanie to be the host. For
the host to become the Ardat-Lil, she must first sacrifice her
own kin. Me.*

That's what the vertigo was trying to show her.

Melanie must murder me before she can become the demon.

Again, Ann's thoughts cloaked her. They were on the landing
now; Tharp was leading her to the kitchen. "We'll go out the
back. We'll follow the woods to where I got the van parked.
You'll wait there while I go look for Melanie."

But at the end of the paneled hall, Tharp stopped, oddly turning to her. "Did you hear that?"

"Hear what?" Ann said, diffused.

His eyes twitched. His shredded voice croaked on, "I
could've sworn I heard—"

Ba-BAM!

Ann screamed. A chunk of the entrance molding exploded

into splinters. Tharp was pushing her backward as a dark cackle issued from the kitchen. Then came another loud *ba-BAM!* as they dove across the foyer. A hole the size of a fist blew into the wall.

A figure stepped into the hall, holding a huge revolver.

"Surprise! I'm back!" Duke Belluxi announced to them.

As Fredrick put away the books he'd gotten down, Dr. Harold was remembering, for no real reason, the odd coincidence. Erik Tharp was from a town called Lockwood. Yes, that was odd. One of his private patients, Ann Slavik, the lawyer suffering night terrors, was from the same town.

Coincidence, he thought. *How could it be anything else?*

"I'm afraid that's all I have for you," Professor Fredrick said, and sat back down. "The Ur-locs were a very obscure society; there's simply not that much information available about them."

"But enough for Tharp to discover."

Fredrick shrugged. "I've spent my entire life pursuing the remnants of civilizations whose beliefs were rooted in superstition. I've been from Nineveh to Knossos. From Jericho to Troy to Rhodes. And do you know what I've discovered? In all those places, over all those years?"

"What?"

"There are no superstitions. No credence to any subjective belief that has ever been asserted. They're just stories, fables, people making fables in order to explain themselves."

"Of course," Dr. Harold said. "But it is interesting: Tharp's escape in conjunction with an equinox that occurs only every thousand years."

"He's no doubt a very good researcher, that's all. Do you suppose you'll catch him?"

"We informed the state police that Tharp would most likely return to the geography of his delusion, but they didn't put much stock in it. The most recent murders indicate that he's actually moving *away* from the seat of his original crimes."

"That could be a ploy, couldn't it? Tharp's intelligence quotient is quite higher than average."

"I know. That's what bothers me."

"Where exactly do you think Tharp is returning to?"

"A little town up on the northern edge of the county," Dr. Harold answered. "It's called Lockwood."

Professor Fredrick subtly laughed, fingering a tiny stone statue of Xipe, the Aztec god of the harvest. "You're kidding me, right? He's from a town called *Lockwood*?"

"Yes. What's so funny?"

Fredrick's eyes suddenly appeared huge in their amusement. "It's almost a joke—the name, I mean."

"I don't under—"

"Lockwood," Fredrick said. "Break it down. Lock for *loc*. Lockwood, 'wood of the loc.' Wood of the—"

"Succubus," Dr. Harold realized. *More coincidence?* "That is strange. And you're sure there's no way an actual Ur-loc cult could be in existence today?"

"I don't see how. Unless the bloodline really did remain intact, as the legend indicates. The Ur-locs dispersed themselves a millennium ago, after the last supposed incarnation. They disappeared without a trace, quite like Christ's disciples after his death. The demon incarnate supposedly blessed them all, then sent them out into the world to spread her influence for the next thousand years." Fredrick again chuckled, a sound like creaking wood. "But of course to believe that, you'd have to believe the original myth."

This latest abstraction didn't set well with Harold. Actually, none of them did. *I do not believe in demons,* he reaverred. He began putting Tharp's transcripts and sketchpads back into the big leather bag. One pad slipped from his hand and fell open. When he picked it up, a page slid off the other. They'd been stuck together somehow; he'd never noticed it.

His eyes fixed down. It was a sketch he'd never seen.

"What is it?" Professor Fredrick asked.

"I . . ." Harold replied. He paused. "Impossible."

Fredrick leaned over and looked. The pointillistic sketch showed a cloaked figure standing between a pregnant woman's legs. The figure's hands formed a cradle, as if to receive the newborn. Beneath, Tharp had written the single word:

DOOER!

And behind the figure, the symbol seemed to hover:

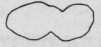

Ann Slavik's nightmare, Harold realized. *To the last detail.*

"It's just more of the same thing," Fredrick said, not realizing Harold's shock. "The symbol is the nihtmir, the night-mirror, and the word, *dooer*, is part of the incarnation litany. It's the final acknowledgment of the birth of the host."

"What's it mean?" Harold croaked more than asked.

"Denotatively it's a concrete noun, meaning, essentially, *door*. But the religious *con*notation goes quite a bit further, not a noun but an elliptical statement of welcome. The mother of the host was considered the door through which the host of the Ardat-Lil would come among them."

The revelation seemed to collapse, like a bombed building. Dr. Harold's eyelids felt peeled open.

"I've got to go," he said. He got his coat, his keys, and made quickly for the door.

"But it's almost midnight," Professor Fredrick pointed out. "Where do you have to go at this hour?"

"To Lockwood," Dr. Harold replied.

CHAPTER THIRTY-TWO

"Upstairs! Quick!" Erik shouted as three more bullets punched holes along the wall of the drawing room. Ann screamed after each heavy, concussive shot; her senses dispersed like confetti. Laughter black as char rattled from the hall as Erik and Ann pounded up the stairs. The shadow turned below. A sixth bullet exploded the mirror at the top of the landing, raining glass.

Impulse had caused him to flee upward; a high vantage point was easier to defend. *He's reloading,* Erik thought. He dragged Ann to the floor around the corner and brought up the shotgun.

Sweat and hysteria glazed Ann's face. "Who is . . . *that!*"

"My former traveling companion," Erik replied, understanding none of it yet. "Stay behind me, stay down."

Duke, Erik thought. His hands shriveled against the shotgun. *The fucker followed me here.* But how?

"Hey, buddy-bro!" erupted the familiar voice from downstairs. "Thought I'd come back for some of that dandy head! Ain't ya pleased to see me?"

Erik replied with a stray shot down the stairwell. Even the 12-gauge report sounded feeble against the Webley's mammoth .455 concussion. "I killed you, you sick fuck!" Erik grated to yell.

"Must be that dandy head you give," Duke Belluxi replied. "Brings a fella back from the dead, ya know?"

Did I miss all those times? Erik wondered in spite of his prickling, bare-eyed terror. The fact smashed into his consciousness: Duke was back. Duke was here, now, just downstairs. And he'd definitely be wanting some revenge. Plus he still had that giant revolver, which didn't lighten the matter. But Erik was sure he'd put several shotgun rounds into Duke's chest back at that second Qwik-Stop . . .

240

This is not going to be one of my better days, Erik realized.

He fired two more stray shots down the stairs. "Just get out of here, Duke!" he attempted to bargain. "If you don't get out of here right now, I'll have to kill you!"

Duke belted out a good, hard laugh. "You already tried that, didn't ya, faggot? But just to show you I'm a fair guy, I'll give you another chance. How about that?"

What the fuck? Erik still couldn't see his enemy, but in a moment, he could hear him.

He could hear him coming up the stairs.

He must be crazy, Erik thought, and then frowned. Considering where Duke had spent the last decade, his state of mind was not even debatable. But the guy was coming up the stairs, knowing full well that Erik was armed . . .

Wait, wait, he told himself. Ann quivered, clinging to Erik's shirt. *Not . . . yet . . .* The footfalls continued to ascend, each fat *thump!* inducing a different image of atrocity. *If this guy gets me, I'm . . .* but Erik didn't even bother to contemplate the rest of the conjecture. What Duke would do to him was bad enough to ponder. But what he would do to Ann was significantly worse by comparison.

Erik paused another second, then rolled out on the landing. He had two rounds left in the shotgun. He raised the bead, touched the trigger . . . then paused. Memory drew his stare out like elastic.

Duke stared back, halfway up the steps. His plump, sociopathic face grinned almost childlike, all big teeth and chubby cheeks.

"Hey, fairy. Long time no see, huh?"

Erik's finger depressed. The gun bucked behind a spew of sparks as the spread of 12-gauge rammed into Duke's chest.

Duke tumbled like a bag of stones down the steps.

That was too easy. Erik, bewildered, stared down at the Remington's bead, then raised his head. Shooting Duke had been no more complicated than spearing a fish in a bathtub. It seemed almost as if he'd *let* himself be gunned down . . .

Gunsmoke drifted. Duke's bulk shape lay limp at the bottom of the steps, sprawled across the fine slate foyer.

Ann crawled forward, her hair in strings. "Did you—"

"I got him this time. Christ . . ."

Erik, regrettably, did not weigh the incongruities. Who

would? The task ahead summoned him: getting Ann away, finding her daughter, breaking the maleficent thousand-year-old chain of the Ardat-Lil. He helped Ann up, brushed her hair out of her face, and tried to calm her down. She shivered in his embrace. *Probably half in shock,* he concluded, not that he could blame her. How could she possibly deal with all that had happened and all that she'd learned in the last handful of minutes? Erik did not expect her to.

"Come on, come on." He led her back down the stairs, keeping the Remington tipped toward Duke's motionless bulk. The wifmunuc, no doubt, was already starting the preliminaries to the rite. But they still didn't have Ann, a fact which only thickened the grimness of the circumstances. They needed Ann, and that could only mean—

That the wifhands are out looking for her, Erik concluded.

"We still have time," he tried to console.

"Time?" Her voice sounded cracked, hoarse. "You said the doefolmon is tonight."

"Yeah, but not till four in the morning or something like that. I've been dreaming about it for months, and you have too, haven't you?"

"Yes," Ann replied.

"And haven't most of the dreams occurred around then?"

Ann's terror-drained face tightened in reflection. "Yes," she repeated. "Almost every time, I'd wake up, and the clock read 4:12."

"That's why. The dreams were really portents."

They stepped over Duke's body and made for the kitchen. "Same plan," Erik informed her. "We'll go out the back. I'll take you to the van, then I'll go look for your daughter. She'll be at the cirice—the church—now. Getting her out shouldn't be too risky. Most of the wifhands won't be there."

"Why?"

"They're looking for you, and so are the wreccans. Giving them the slip is the hard part. The rest'll be easy."

Ann didn't look convinced.

Erik stopped at the kitchen entrance.

"What?" Ann asked. "Let's get out of—"

Bullets, Erik thought. None of it would be easy if he didn't arm himself more effectively. He only had one round left for the shotgun.

Duke's revolver, he reminded himself.

"Wait here. I'll need Duke's gun too." He went back to the dim foyer and peered down. The giant revolver still lay in Duke's grubby, squab hand. Erik knelt, fished around in his adversary's jacket for bullets, then—

Holy sh—

What he noticed in that fraction of a second was all that his destiny would ever amount to. Duke's plaid flannel shirt lay in tatters, but there was no blood. Through the holes he could see smudged, pocked white and several balls of buckshot that clearly had not penetrated Duke's torso.

Bulletproof v—

In one split-second motion, Duke's left hand grabbed the shotgun barrel, and his right hand snapped forward. Erik froze.

The revolver was aimed directly at his face.

Duke leaned up, grinning proudly as ever. "Fooled you again, huh, fairy?" he remarked.

Ann stood in the entry, letting the pulse of her thoughts slow down in time with her heart. The sweat of her fear sucked her clothes to her skin. Then the thought replayed:

Kin sacrifice. Melanie must murder me before she can become the demon . . .

Time seemed to congeal before her face; all motion, even the world's, seemed to freeze. Ann sensed something but didn't know what. She stepped down the short hall to the foyer. Erik Tharp knelt at the body, rummaging for bullets. Suddenly, he seemed poised, his joints locked up. Then—

—his skull divided into three segments.

She never even seemed to hear the sound of the shot. She felt concussion, and heat, then Tharp's head simply . . . burst. Wet hanks of brain slapped her in the chest. It all happened so fast she couldn't even react. Tharp's body collapsed before a fine gray cloud of smoke . . .

And through that smoke, the figure rose: Duke Belluxi grinning behind the giant revolver pointed at Ann's face.

CHAPTER THIRTY-THREE

"So you're the one," the madman observed. The end of the gun barrel looked big enough to admit a thumb. "You're the one he came back for."

Ann stood taprooted in her terror. The chunks of Tharp's brains fell off her blouse, leaving glistening stains. A piece of scalp, tufted with white hair, stuck to her forearm. Duke's hair was the same strange color. He took a step forward, his grinning face broad as a carved pumpkin. Behind the closely set eyes, Ann saw sheer, raging madness.

"The cocksucking little fairy set me up," Duke informed her. Old bloodstains streaked his pants. "He used me to help him bust out, thought he was smarter than me." He veered the mad grin down and laughed. "How smart are you now, fucker?"

Ann's mind swam. If she tried to run, he would kill her. But somehow she also knew that if she didn't run—if she tried to placate him, bargain with him—he'd also kill her. She could see that fact. She could see it in his eyes.

"Tharp kept talking about destiny, like he was put on earth to do something special. He wasn't shit. But me, I got a *real* destiny. Know what it is?"

Ann couldn't reply, couldn't even move.

Duke was all over her at once, wielding his massive body with a nearly eloquent finesse. Ann screamed as he dragged her to the floor by a handful of hair. As his weight sidled onto her, so did the meaty, fetid stench of him. He straddled her chest; she could only squirm within herself. His mad eyes focused down. Chuckling, he tore open her blouse, snapped off her bra. Then the chuckle shrank into a demented stare. Ann gagged when he drooled into her mouth. His breath grew short as he traced her nipples with the revolver.

"You're gonna be my best nut yet," he promised her. "Oh, yeah, you sure as shit are. I can tell just by lookin' at ya."

He opened his trousers and withdrew himself. Suddenly, his stench stupefied her. Dried blood matted his pubic hair.

Then he plugged the revolver into her navel.

"That faggot Tharp, he used to blow me for quarters. Always makin' phone calls. He was calling you, wasn't he?"

Look at the moon tonight. Ann remembered the words. She nodded tensely.

"Why?" Duke Belluxi asked, and pinched a nipple.

Doefolmon, she thought. *Fulluht-Loc.*

Duke laughed. "Doesn't matter none to me. Now, don't take this personal, honeybunch, but it's best if you're dyin' slow while I'm boppin' ya. Gives me a better nut—know what I mean?"

Ann tremored in her paresis. Duke cocked the big, clunky revolver, growing erect in time with his pulse. Through the front bay window, the moon shimmered pinkly.

Ann prepared to die. She closed her eyes—

Then the awful weight was gone.

Ann turned where she lay, looking ahead. Duke Belluxi was being dragged across the carpet by . . . something. Ann caught glimpses of faces, flesh. Duke thrashed as he was pinned to the floor by quick, snatching hands. Abruptly, he was screaming in hoarse bursts. *What's happening?* Ann dumbly wondered. She felt in shock. Duke's heels and palms pummeled the floor, his body arching up. Two fingers sharp as masonry nails sank promptly into his eyes. Two more clawlike hands ripped his trousers off. Ann could only stare frozen at the dreamlike sequence of horror . . .

Two shapely, concupiscent bodies knelt over Duke with grins like shards of glass. A long taloned finger raised a skewered eyeball to a needle-toothed mouth. The eyeball was eaten whole, like a grape. Humor was licked off the elegant finger. Lust-swollen breasts shined over the atrocity. Ann could only continue to catch glimpses at first. Pale pendants swayed as Duke's body twitched with vigor. The figures persisted in their delighted butchery—Duke's abdomen was laid open, exposing glistening organs. Blood flew like spaghetti and sauce. The closest figure grinned down at Duke's genitals. A mouth like a knifecut in fresh meat opened heinously wide; rows of glassine teeth sparkled. A moment later, the mouth lowered, gritting down. Duke's penis and testicles were quickly eaten out of the apex of his groin. A river of blood gushed onto the carpet.

Then the first figure's mouth spread likewise. The top of Duke's skull was bitten off. Orbs of brain glimmered. Duke Belluxi died in flinching convulsions, atop a blanket of his own blood and offal.

Holy Mother of G—

The two figures looked at Ann. They seemed amused. Ann's mind crumpled at the impact of recognition. One figure straightened up on her knees, her nipple ends erect as coat pegs; she chortled, smearing Duke Belluxi's blood over her breasts and abdomen like some luxurious lotion. The other figure was sloppily eating gobbets of Duke's brains out of the cranial vault.

Milly. Maedeen, Ann realized. *But . . .*

It was something she apprehended rather than saw, a recognition that somehow reared *beneath* the tainted features: pronglike taloned hands and feet, elongated heads, bottomless, primeval eyes.

Not women, Ann's thoughts verified. *Things.*

Maedeen rummaged for plump morsels amid Duke's plundered gut, while Milly rather greedily slurped blood and spinal fluid out of the emptied skull. They paused only briefly to grin at Ann.

By now her incomprehension turned her limp. Laughter followed her as she was dragged away suddenly from behind. She was being helped up, urged out the back door into darkness. She was insensible.

"Come on!" a voice bellowed at her. Rough hands shook her at her shoulders. "Snap out of it!"

Ann's eyes roved up, focused on the plump face in moonlight. It was Chief Bard.

"It's tonight, Ann! We've got to get you out of here!"

Her awareness returned in pieces, in slabs. "What . . ."

"They're succubi, Ann. They're part of a cult that's as old as civilization," Bard told her, dragging her now toward the woods behind the house.

"Then it's all true," Ann muttered. "Everything Tharp said—"

"Yes!"

"They want Melanie to be the physical body of—"

"Come on!" he yelled again.

But the voice stopped them in their tracks. They turned, staring. In the sliding glass door, Maedeen stood looking after them. She was holding what appeared to be one of Duke Belluxi's lungs. Even at this distance, Ann could see the chaotic features of her transformed face, and the teeth glittering like chisel blades.

"Bring her back, Bard!" croaked the inhuman voice. "You can't get away from us! You can never get away!"

Bard yanked her on through the brambles. The moon followed them like a distended, pink face. "I'm one of their helots," he panted to explain, "but they never fully initiated me because they needed someone on the outside. I'll be goddamned if I'm going to watch any more innocent people die for their devil. It's your mother, Ann—she's the wifmunuc. They've been waiting for this day for the last—"

Thousand years, Ann finished in thought. Tharp had said the same thing. But—

"Melanie," she said. "We have to get Melanie."

"Melanie's lost! She's part of the bludcynn now. She's not your daughter anymore, she's *hers*!"

Ann pulled against him. "I'm not leaving Melanie!"

"I might be able to get her later," Bard said. "But the most important thing right now is to get you as far away from the cirice as possible. If they don't have you when the moon goes into complete apogee, then the Fulluht-Loc can't take place."

Could he really get Melanie back, or was he just placating her? Ann couldn't think of a way to resist him; he was saving her life, after all. She supposed all she could do was hope and pray.

He'd parked his police cruiser at the end of Senlac Street, in the dark. He was sweating, harried. He rushed her into the passenger side, jumped in himself, and gunned the engine.

He paused on the shift. "It's all true, Ann."

"I . . . I know."

"And I'm sorry."

Ann tilted her head. He'd saved her life. What did he have to be sorry about?

His chubby face turned to her. "I'm very, very sorry."

"But I'm not," rose the voice from the darkness of the backseat.

Ann flailed, screaming. Bard's fat hands grappled at her. He clamped her head in the crook of his elbow. She shrieked at the sharp deep prick of pain.

"Well done, Chief." Dr. Ashby Heyd's face emerged into the pink light. "There, fine." He gingerly withdrew the hypodermic needle from her neck. "That's a good girl," he said.

CHAPTER THIRTY-FOUR

Dr. Harold didn't know what he was thinking. He'd stopped only briefly at his house—for his gun. Clinical psychiatrists easily received state gun permits. *But what do I need a gun for?* he queried himself.

What did he expect?

The highway seemed to thwart him, its abandonment, its wide, open darkness—or something. His high beams stretched out ahead of the car only to be sucked up by interminable black.

He did not try to calculate the coincidences, and the facts, that had been revealed to him tonight. *What am I thinking?* the question returned. It seemed fat, like a dull, protracted headache. *What do I think I'm going to do?* He felt certain that Tharp had already returned to Lockwood, that he was there now.

But where does that leave me?

He could call the police, but what would he tell them? That Tharp had gone back to the locale of his crimes to prevent the incarnation of a female demon? *They'd be committing me,* he considered. Besides, the authorities had ignored his and Greene's early recommendations. Why should they listen now?

Maybe I should listen to myself.

The moon seemed to pace him, its odd pink light flittering through lone stands of trees. The light and the constant drone of the tires threatened to lull him at the wheel, or hypnotize him. Yes, he felt thwarted, he felt pushing upward against some bizarre mental gravity that was bent on repelling him. *Paranoia,* he dismissed, or tried to. He felt he was racing against something, but he couldn't imagine what. Time, perhaps, or unprecedented fears.

Or impossibilities, he thought.

The moon was so full now it looked pregnant in its raw light;

it looked heavy enough to drag itself out of the sky and fall to earth. *Doefolmon,* the strange word came to his head. *Moon of the devil.*

And another word, a name: *Ardat-Lil.*

He could not erase the image from his memory. It seemed indelible—the sheer beauty wed into the features of sheer repugnance, sheer evil. Most religions were born out of reaction to other religions; their roots were obvious. But the Ur-locs? Pre-Christian? Even pre-*Druidic*? What bizarre sociology could've created such an idea?

Dr. Harold did not attempt to contemplate an answer.

He felt sick in increments, waning as the car droned on into the inclement dark. The pinkened moonlight on his face felt warm, humid. He could see it still, Tharp's harrowing psych ward sketch transposing into a vision of stunning clarity: the perfect hourglass physique, the large and perfect breasts, and then the bestial three-fingered hands with talons like meat hooks, and—

The face, he remembered.

—a black, thinly stretched maw full of stalactitic teeth.

How long had he been driving now? It seemed like all night, or a week of nights. Perhaps he'd been driving in circles, his sense of direction perverted by Tharp's perverted imagery.

Perhaps I've died and gone to hell, and this is how I am to spend eternity, driving forever in darkness.

Then the big green road sign flashed in the headlights, a beacon to his relief.

Lockwood, 15 miles.

The moon shimmered beyond the sign, beyond the night.

Beyond the world.

And beyond the eye of Dr. Harold's mind, the sketch of the creature seemed to turn to flesh and smile.

CHAPTER THIRTY-FIVE

The dream is vivid, hot—it always is.

"Dooer, dooer."

"It's always the same: the back arching up, and waves of moans. The tense legs spread ever wide, the swollen belly stretched pinprick tight and pushing . . . pushing . . . pushing forth . . .

Then the image of the cup, like a chalice, and the emblem on its bowl like a squashed double circle:

She senses flame behind her, a fireplace perhaps. She senses warmth. Firelight flickers on the pocked rock walls as shadows hover. A larger version of the emblem seems suspended in the background, much larger. And again she hears the bizarre words:

"Dooer, dooer."

She's dreaming of her daughter's birth. Birth is painful, yet she feels no pain. All she feels is the wonder of creation, for it is a wonder, isn't it? Her own warm belly displacing new life into the world? It's a joyous thing.

Joyous, yes. So why does the dream always revert to nightmare?

The figures surround her, they seem cloaked or enshadowed. Soft hands stroke the tense sweating skin. For a time, they are all Ann's eyes can focus on. The hands. They caress her not just in comfort but also—somehow—in adoration. Here is where the

*dream loses its wonder. Soon the hands grow too ardent. They
are fondling her. They stroke the enflamed breasts, the quivering belly. They run up and down the parted, shining thighs.
The belly continues to quiver and push. No faces can be seen,
only the hands, but soon heads lower. Tongues begin to lap up
the hot sweat which runs in rivulets. Soft lips kiss her eyes, her
forehead, her throat. Tongues churn over her clitoris, and voracious mouths suck milk from her breasts.*

*The images wrench her; they're revolting, obscene. Wake up!
she commands herself. Wake up, wake up! She cannot move.
She cannot speak.*

*Her orgasm is obvious, a lewd and clenching irony in time
with the very contractions of birth. Behind her she senses frenzied motion. She hears grunts, moans—*

—then screams.

Screams?

But they aren't her screams, are they?

*She glimpses dim figures tossing bundles onto a crackling
fire. Still more figures seem to wield knives or hatchets. The figures seem palsied, numb. She hears chopping sounds.*

*The dream's eye rises to a high vantage point; the circle
moves away. Naked backs cluster about the childbirth table.
Now only a lone, hooded shape stands between the spread legs.
It looks down, as if in reverence, at the wet, bloated belly. The
belly is pink.*

*Moans drift up, and excited squeals. The firelight dances.
The chopping sounds thunk on and on, on and on . . .*

"Dooer, dooer," bids the hooded shape.

The belly shivers, collapsing.

A baby begins to cry.

"Ann, Ann?" queried the familiar voice.

Ann's eyes opened, but at first she saw nothing. Soft murmurs seemed to hover about her like vapor. Color shifted—
orange—and she sensed a pleasant pulse of heat. Again she'd
had the nightmare of Melanie's birth . . . but where was she?
She knew she couldn't be in bed. Beneath her felt cold, hard,
like stone. Then, as suddenly as her realizations—

Slup-slup-slup . . .

Her vision blanked again, bringing the image of crimson
vertigo—

The wide knife plunging down—

Slup-slup-slup . . .

"Ann. Wake up."

The face formed, a reverse dissolve. It was Dr. Heyd.

Her eyes at last came into focus. Cloaked and hooded figures surrounded her, looking serenely down. Ann's gaze panned. One by one she recognized the ovaled faces: all of Lockwood's elderwomen. Around each of their necks hung a pale pendant, like a piece of stone on a white cord. At Ann's feet stood Maedeen and Milly, and standing between them, in a cloak not of sackcloth but of black silk, was Ann's mother.

Ann couldn't move from where she lay, though she felt no lashings of any kind. She was completely naked before them all. It felt as though ghosts squirmed over her, holding her down.

In the background, more figures busied themselves. Shadows bent to stoke the flames within a great brick furnace. They were all men, she could see, and they seemed faltering, devoid of all will. Another man poured some dark fluid from a vessel into a large earthen cup. A chalice.

The women lowered their hoods, their eyes wide in some deep intent. The man passed the cup to Ann's mother. The man was Martin.

He did not look at her at all.

"Blud fo cuppe," the wifmunuc intoned. "Nis heofonrice, bute nisfan."

The coven responded: "Us macain wīhan, o Modor. Us macain fulluht with ēower blud."

The chalice was passed around, each woman mouthing a silent prayer, then sipping. When the chalice had made the entire circle, the wifmunuc, Ann's mother, consumed the rest of its contents.

Engraved along the cup's rim, the glyph could be seen—the weird double circle. And when Ann's mother bent to set the chalice down, Ann saw the glyph again, a much larger version, behind the circle. It was not a carving, she noticed, but a large slab of flat stone hanging from the rear wall. Ann's eyes could only remain fixed ahead. The wifmunuc turned around, her hands splayed. Then she leaned forward and kissed the great rectangular slab of stone.

"O Mother, Holy Sister, Holy Daughter—"

"Bless us on this holy night."

Now the heat swelled to a prickling intensity. Ann felt sweat gather liberally between her breasts and trickle down her sides. Her sex felt tingling, but from what? Her breasts felt enflamed with desire.

"Receive this offering . . ."

But there was no desire in her heart, only a misshapen terror. *Receive this offering . . .* She shivered in the heat as she realized what it was she lay upon: a stone altar.

Receive this offering—

A stone altar, a sacrificial slab. *The kin sacrifice,* she remembered Tharp's words just before he'd died. This rock slab was what Ann was to be sacrificed upon, by her own daughter.

It's like a trigger to the whole ritual, Tharp had said. *The final offering to the Ardat-Lil.*

The coven grinned down at her. From either side, Milly and Maedeen touched her daintily, as though her naked flesh were iconic. Her mother remained at the foot of the altar. Her silken mentel was so fine as to be partly transparent. The woman's body showed through the sheer material. Though close to sixty now, her large dark-nippled breasts scarcely sagged at all. Her body had remained firm, robust.

"You've been dreaming, haven't you?" the wifmunuc inquired.

Now the recurring nightmare came together: Melanie's birth as a foreshadow to this night. Through her mother's malefic ploy, Ann had given birth to a child destined to become a monster.

"Yes," the woman said. "You've been shown all along. Do you understand now? You are a keystone to history. Do you understand how important you are?"

Ann still felt rooted to the slab, but she could lean up to look her mother back square in the face. "You want Melanie for this madness!" she screamed.

"Dother fo Dother," Milly said.

"Daughter of the Daughter," Maedeen translated.

"Our savior," Ann's mother added. "Our deliverer."

"This is crazy!" Ann spat. "You're all crazy!"

"Through this holiest night, our god will come among us in the flesh, Ann. To bless us for the next thousand years."

Behind her, Dr. Heyd opened a long thin box. From the box,

Martin and Chief Bard lifted a gossamerlike gown of the purest, sheerest white.

"Rise," Ann's mother said.

Ann's paralysis loosened. She felt like a puppet being risen by wires. The elderwomen guided her off the altar, urged her forward. Her arms raised by no volition of her own. Then the stunning paralysis returned. She stood upright but could move no further.

"Bring the mentel."

Martin trudged forward. He slipped the lambent gown over Ann's head. It slid against her flesh like mist. Martin stood to look at her; his eyes shone dull, flattened. No recognition was exchanged.

Then he walked away.

"Melanie has served well," her mother said. "We all have."

The white gown must be some symbolic raiment, a ritual garment in which to be sacrificed. "Where is she?" Ann croaked.

"You've been dreaming of it all along," her mother replied.

Maedeen added, "But it wasn't *Melanie's* birth you were dreaming of."

"It was your own," her mother finished.

Ann felt lost in this information. In her confusion she could only stare back at her mother's gaze.

"*You* are the Daughter of the Daughter, Ann. *You* are the new Ardat-Lil."

Ann tremored with the words. Her eyes felt skinned open. In the high ground window, the pink moon bloated to fullness. Only then did she note that the edges of her gown were wet. In panic, she glanced down. Her arms were slick to the elbows with blood.

The circle parted for her to see.

On the earthen floor a naked figure lay: a corpse in a great spread of blood. The heart had been cut out of the bosom and laid aside next to a long, wide knife.

Ann gasped through vision like a chasm, or like staring down from the highest place of the earth. The butchered corpse was Melanie. It was her blood that now dripped fresh from Ann's hands.

The wifmunuc pointed to the rear wall of the church. "Look into the nihtmir, Ann. Look into the face of our queen."

The great slab of stone seemed charged now with some spiriferous energy. Its flat pocked surface changed before her eyes, to a perfect silver plane.

Ann gazed into the reflection of her own face.

Crimson spheres gazed back at her. The mouth opened in horrid astonishment, a colossal black orifice full of shardlike cuspids and incisors. Shining silken hair hung adrift in the night-mirror's radiant static energy.

She raised a hand to touch her cheek, but it was not a finger that appeared in the mirror's veins. It was a long, sleek talon, sharp as an awl.

High atop her forehead, two diminutive nubs protruded.

She turned to reface the coven. All members then fell at once to their knees, voicing prayers of praise and homage to their deliverer in the flesh.

The Ardat-Lil smiled down upon its new flock.

EPILOGUE

◊◊◊

The night had indeed thwarted him, the night in all its loss of
reason, its queer moonlight, and its inexplicability. He'd taken
three wrong turns, and twice he'd found himself driving unlit
back roads in circles. Then the driver's-side front tire had
blown. Half an hour later, the spare had blown. He'd driven on
the rim awhile, and next the oil pump had seized up. It had only
taken a few minutes before most moving parts of the engine had
fused.

He'd had no choice then but to walk the rest of the way. Not
one vehicle had passed him, not one potential ride. By the time
he'd actually made it to the small secluded municipality of
Lockwood, dawn was less than an hour away.

Dr. Harold felt lost even when he'd found it. The town lay in
total darkness. The police station and fire hall were empty. He
walked several residential streets, and found doors wide open,
no persons within. More walking and he realized that he had yet
to see a single car anywhere in the township's perimeter.

Piqued, he made his way back to the main drag. He stood in
the middle of the desolate street and looked up. Just above the
high steeple of the church, the moon shone down. It looked
bloated to hugeness, gravid. Its weird pink light seemed hideous
now. It tinted his face, blurred in his eyes.

Moon of the devil, he thought. *Moon of the succubus.*

The pink light made him feel enslimed in some portent, or
some chasmal acknowledgment.

What? he asked himself on the dark street. *An acknowledgment of what, for God's sake?*

It was in the church that he found it, or actually the basement
of the church. Another church of sorts, a chancel of evils which
refused to allow description. The air was warm in these

257

cramped confines. Behind a small room which looked like living quarters, he discovered the lair of their black reverence. Much blood was seen soaked into the dirt floor. The stench of cooked flesh wafted before his face like ghosts. Perhaps they were ghosts, the remnants of spirits freed through heinous acts. Blood had dried to shellacked blackness atop a great stone altar; charred bones and skulls lay scattered about, amid indescribable scraps of fleshy sinew.

This church was as empty as the entire town. Its population had fled, but to where, and for what? *Where did they all go?* he wondered.

Dr. Harold then walked to the back of the unholy nave.

Twin metal hooks stuck out from the rearmost wall, mounting hooks as if to hang something from. Nothing hung there now—there was just an outline of dust and age against the old wood. Whatever had been there had been quickly removed, taken away.

Dr. Harold's eyes remained fixed upon the spot.

The outline was clearly visible, that of a great squashed double circle.